WAKE THE DEVIL

ALSO BY ROBERT DANIELS:

Once Shadows Fall

WAKE THE DEVIL

A THRILLER

ROBERT DANIELS

CROOKED
LANE

NEW YORK

Copyright © 2016 by Robert M. Daniels Corporation

Published in the United States by Crooked Lane Books, an imprint of The Quick Brown Fox & Company LLC.

Crooked Lane Books and its logo are trademarks of The Quick Brown Fox & Company LLC.

Library of Congress Catalog-in-Publication data available upon request.

ISBN (hardcover): 978-1-62953-771-9
ISBN (paperback): 978-1-62953-798-6
ISBN (ePub): 978-1-62953-799-3
ISBN (Kindle): 978-1-62953-800-6
ISBN (ePDF): 978-1-62953-801-3

Cover design by Andy Ruggirello
Book design by Jennifer Canzone

Printed in the United States.

www.crookedlanebooks.com

Crooked Lane Books
34 West 27th St., 10th Floor
New York, NY 10001

First Edition: September 2016

10 9 8 7 6 5 4 3 2 1

In memory of my father. The best man I ever knew.

Prologue

Dr. George Lawrence stood in line with six other people at Georgia's Stone Mountain Park, waiting to board the aerial tram. With him was his wife, Rachel. Four teenagers cutting school that day and a Japanese couple made up the rest of the passengers. Far above them, suspended from a thick metal cable, was a red-and-white boxcar slowly making its way to the loading platform. Everyone in the group watched its descent.

It was November, and in the dense forest surrounding the mountain's base, the leaves were just beginning to change. Over a three-week period, the area would turn into an impressionist painting with reds, yellows, golds, and oranges on display. From an airplane, the colors were so vibrant they seemed to be the work of man rather than nature. The park now boasted a golf course, nature trails, a restaurant, a petting zoo, and a scenic railroad that toured the grounds. The bucolic environment was a welcome change from the 6.5 million people living in metro Atlanta.

By and large, the countryside looked much as it had a hundred fifty years ago, when the original acreage was sold for a shotgun and barrel of whiskey. At the time, there were two schools of thought about which party had come out ahead.

Rachel had organized their trip two days earlier. Like her husband, she was also a doctor, and both were on the edge of exhaustion, having just completed three operations in a row. The final one lasted twenty-three hours and involved separating the two hemispheres of a nine-year-old girl's brain in an effort to free her from a series of epileptic seizures that were racking her frail body daily. Neither George nor Rachel would have traded the smile on the child's face when she woke, or her parents' look of gratitude, for all the tea in China.

The following day they allowed themselves the luxury of sleeping in. They were in the middle of breakfast when Rachel informed George they were taking Friday off. No emergencies loomed and no procedures were scheduled. In preparation for the trip, Rachel had instructed their staff to refer anything that came up to their partners and not to call them unless the office was on fire. Maybe not even then.

Balding, lanky, thirty-five-year-old George was a little uneasy about their impromptu vacation, but he'd been married long enough to know arguing with his wife was not a preferable alternative. The couple had been together since their third year of medical school at Johns Hopkins.

"Oh, damn," Rachel said, drawing George from his thoughts.

"What?"

"I left my phone in the car."

George put an arm around Rachel's shoulders and gave her a squeeze.

"We're on vacation today. Remember?"

"Maybe I should get it."

"Relax, I've got mine with me. If anyone has a problem, they'll call."

"You mean they'll call me," his wife said. "You never answer your phone."

"Well . . . I'll make an exception this time," George said.

Rachel didn't appear convinced. For all her talk about relaxing, he knew she'd worry about being out of contact with the office. As pediatric surgeons, emergencies involving children often sprung at them out of the blue. It came with the territory.

The cable car had reached the halfway point in its gradual descent but was still a couple hundred feet above them. On the opposite side of the mountain, carved into a sheer granite face, was a memorial to three of the South's heroes, each mounted majestically atop a horse: Robert E. Lee, Stonewall Jackson, and Jefferson Davis, the Confederacy's only president. Native Georgians tended to refer to that distant unpleasantness as the War of Northern Aggression rather than the Civil War.

A crease formed between Rachel's eyes. "Maybe I should run back and get it . . . just in case."

George was familiar with that expression. Inevitably she would obsess about the phone until it ruined their outing. Such was the extent of her dedication to their profession and the children they cared for.

"I'll go, honey," he said.

"No, you head on and get us a table. I'll catch the next car up," Rachel said, handing George a wicker basket. She kissed him on the cheek, stepped out of line, and began walking rapidly toward the parking lot.

George watched her for a moment and shook his head. When he turned back to the mountain, he made eye contact with the Japanese man in front of him and nodded to be polite. The man returned the greeting with a nod of his own. George checked his watch. In a few minutes, it would be eleven thirty. The day was clear with no rain in sight. The air smelled heavily of pine. Overhead, a few white clouds drifted lazily across a robin's-egg sky. Conscious of the weight of the picnic basket, George hefted it a couple times and frowned.

What the heck did she put in here?

"Big," the Japanese man said.

"Yeah, she always overpacks," George told him.

The man smiled, nodded again, and pointed to the mountain. "Very big."

"What? Oh, I see. Yeah, definitely big. Like Mount Fuji."

"Ah," the man said, with a slight bow. He seemed pleased at the reference.

The tram finally arrived and eased into the loading dock, coming to a halt with a thump. The name "Stone Mountain" was written on its side in white letters. Oblivious to George and the Japanese couple, the four teenagers boarded first and moved to the front of the car, talking animatedly amongst themselves. Thirty seconds later the door rolled back along its track.

George looked out the rear observation window hoping to catch a glimpse of Rachel, but the Visitors Center was in the way. The mountain loomed above him. Shaped like a great gray whale or an upside-down soup bowl, it was the largest mass of exposed granite in the world. After a slight pause, the car lurched forward and drew away from the dock, rising into the air.

As they continued to climb, the parking lot came into view. Because it was a weekday, the lot was only lightly crowded. With the added height, he had no trouble picking out his white SUV and the shape of his wife hurrying back to the loading platform. He took in a breath and let it out. A day off wasn't such a bad idea after all. As soon as they could put two weeks together without the world coming to an end, he resolved to surprise Rachel with a real vacation. It had been four years since their last one, and even on that trip, it had rained every day. Maybe a cruise, or that trip to Europe they'd been talking about since college. George smiled and whispered "Rachel" to himself.

*

When Rachel saw the tram appear above the Visitors Center, she slowed to a walk. According to the brochure she had picked up when they arrived, the trip would take nine minutes. The return was only eight.

Why was that? Gravity, she decided.

Rachel checked her phone. No messages. Excellent. A break, even a small one, was just what they needed. Surgeons were human, and tired doctors made mistakes, and mistakes cost lives.

She was nearly back at the platform when a loud bang from the control room at the end of the loading dock startled her. Instinctively, she looked up at the cable car. It had stopped moving and was hanging suspended above the valley.

Several seconds passed and nothing happened. The car simply stayed where it was.

"Aw, nuts," Rachel said under her breath. "Just our—"

A flash of light from a second explosion directly above the tram reached her before the sound did. Rachel gasped as a hand of ice closed around her stomach. Time seemed to slow. Unbelievably, the metal cable separated and the car, now held aloft by nothing, began a free fall back to earth.

Chapter 1

Emory University's Carlos Museum is smaller and more intimate than its cousin in Atlanta, located some ten miles away. It was currently hosting a traveling exhibit on primitive art, specifically cave paintings. Jack Kale was there. It wasn't that cave paintings interested him. His presence had been requested by the museum's director. Earlier that week, Michael Goodell had asked Jack to solve a mystery. Everyone loves a mystery—except cops and anthropologists.

The stars of the exhibit were three skeletons recovered from a glacial cave in the Austrian Alps. Forensic anthropologists had dated the bones at fifty thousand years old. After the Vienna exhibit concluded, it was Atlanta's turn. While arranging for transport to the States, curators noticed a number of marks and nicks on two of the three skeletons. Thus far, no one had been able to explain them. The popular consensus was the marks were as old as the skeletons. Goodell, a scientist himself, contacted Jack hoping he could shed some light on their origin.

For the past two days, Jack, a forensic psychology professor and former FBI agent, had been studying the bodies and taking measurements in what was perhaps the oddest venue he had ever worked in.

The museum had gone to considerable lengths in recreating the Austrian cave where the bodies had been discovered. Jack now found himself standing on a dirt floor examining the remains of three people who had died fifty millennia ago. The Viennese curators had provided photographs so the bones could be placed in their original positions. Around him, the cave walls were decorated with ancient paintings of hunting scenes. The exhibit was scheduled to open later that week.

When the double doors at the far end of the gallery opened, admitting a blade of light into the room, Jack glanced up from his work. He'd been using a magnifying glass to examine the smallest of the bodies. Remnants of a tanned leather dress the girl wore had managed to survive the passage of time thanks to an avalanche sealing off the cave. Year after year, century after century, snow fell and ice formed, growing ever deeper, until a landslide tore part of the hill away to reveal the entrance. A father and son on a weekend trek noticed the opening and decided to investigate. Their discovery sent ripples throughout the archaeological world.

Detective Beth Sturgis and her partner, Dan Pappas, entered the gallery accompanied by two people. One Jack knew; the other he didn't. Janet Newton had been his boss for a number of years when he was still with the FBI. She smiled at him and wiggled her fingers slightly in a greeting. Pappas and the man beside him nodded. Beth Sturgis winked but kept her expression neutral. The four remained just inside the door, waiting for him to finish. He was already certain their visit wasn't social.

The cave was dimly lit with small incandescent lights recessed into the ceiling and cleverly hidden behind rocks. Director Goodell stood off to one side observing, arms folded across his chest. He noticed the new arrivals but made no move toward them.

Without focusing on anything in particular, Jack lifted his head and asked, "Are you still there, Bernhard?"

"I am," a German-accented voice replied from a speakerphone sitting on a table outside the cave.

"Two detectives have just entered the room accompanied by a third gentleman who I suspect is also a member of their profession. With them is Ms. Janet Newton, a deputy director with the FBI. Shall I continue?"

"Police officers *and* the FBI, you say?"

"That's correct."

"Given what you've told me about our three ancient friends, that seems about right. Any objections, Michael?"

6

"None," Goodell replied. "Welcome, ladies and gentlemen. Dr. Kale was about to explain what happened. Come closer if you wish."

Beth and Pappas exchanged glances, then looked at their companions. Janet Newton nodded and they moved to where Goodell stood, taking up positions behind him. Goodell was in his late fifties, medium height, and dressed in a dark-blue suit with a pale-yellow shirt and a maroon tie. His hair was a salt-and-pepper mixture.

He explained to the new arrivals, "On the phone with us is Dr. Bernhard Streck, director of the Vienna Museum."

Polite greetings were exchanged. Goodell supplemented his comment with some details about the discovery and what they were looking at.

As he was talking, Beth's attention turned to the skeletons. They were spread out about five feet apart and looked as though they had fallen involuntarily as opposed to having lain down to sleep. The largest was resting on its face. From the size, she concluded the bones were that of a man. Slightly smaller and a short distance from him was a female, lying at an angle. The smallest, clearly a child, was curled up next to the woman, her knees drawn in. Without being told, she knew she was looking at a mother and daughter. For no reason she could identify, an ineffable sense of sadness descended upon her. A moment later, Jack put her feeling into words. "We're looking at three people who were murdered."

"Dear God, Jack," Streck said. "How can you tell?"

Jack continued. "I don't think anyone can say for certain, but I suspect this is the case. The nick on the man's spinal column and lower rib cage indicates he was stabbed from behind. The wound becomes progressively wider the deeper in it goes, angling upward toward the heart. It's also triangular in shape, which is consistent with the head of a flint spear Michael tells me was in use at the time. The museum has several good examples available."

Goodell indicated his agreement with a slight inclination of his head and said nothing.

In the subdued light, Jack paused and glanced around the cave pensively. Whatever he was thinking, he kept it to himself. For a moment, he had the impression of a mild subterranean wind passing across his skin. He continued his narrative.

"The injury to the woman's left hand is what we call a defensive wound. This occurs when someone throws up their arm to deflect a downward blow. From the crush-type mark on the side of her skull, I'd say she was rushing to help her mate when the killer or killers turned on her."

The man with Beth and Pappas shook his head and kept watching. From the manner in which his eyes moved, taking in the cave's details, Jack was certain he had guessed correctly. Law enforcement. No doubt about it.

Streck inquired, "What about the little girl? You said there were no wounds on her."

"Murdered nonetheless," Jack said. "According to the medical examiner who was here yesterday, she was about four years old at the time she died. Certainly no more than five. The human skull closes at a predictable rate and allows us to pinpoint age with some accuracy."

"Yah, but if there were no wounds . . ."

"What I believe happened is this . . . seeing her parents struck down, and now left alone in a hostile and frightening world, the child crawled to her mother and lay down beside her, where she eventually died of thirst or hunger or both. Her bones show the type of brittleness that results from dehydration."

"Jesus," Pappas said, turning his head away.

"From the crude cooking utensils and remnants of a fire ring, they must have been eating or about to eat when it happened."

He stood, brushed the dirt from his trousers, then placed the magnifying glass on the table next to the phone. The only sound in the room came from air passing through the return vents. Jack studied them for a moment and decided they were the source of his subterranean wind.

For several seconds, no one spoke. Beth looked at the tiny skeleton, its hand resting on the mother's shoulder, and felt her throat constrict. It was so small. So fragile. She wondered if this woman had sung to her child and held her hand when they went for a walk. Whether she told her daughter what the birds and animals dreamed of as her grandmother had done for her when she was a child.

Streck's voice returned to the speaker. Even though he was five thousand miles away, the director of Vienna's museum was not immune to the sense of loss and tragedy in the gallery.

"Thank you, Jack. I see it's nearly closing time," Streck said. "I believe I'll walk across the street and have a glass of schnapps . . . perhaps two. Then I will drop by my daughter's home for a few minutes. Good day to you all."

Chapter 2

After they disconnected, Beth came back to the present and introduced FBI Special Agent Todd Milner to Jack. From his earlier comment, it was obvious he already knew Janet Newton. Nevertheless, the other woman surprised her by saying, "Jack and I are old friends."

Beth's expression prompted a further explanation.

"I should have mentioned it earlier," the deputy director said. "We worked together for several years." Her smile broadened and she extended a hand. "It's good to see you again, Jack. You look well."

"So do you, Janet."

Milner commented, "Interesting story you put together, Professor." He then turned to Michael Goodell and inquired, "Would you mind if we borrow Dr. Kale for a few minutes?"

"Not at all," Goodell said. "Jack, thank you for coming in. A stiff drink doesn't seem like a bad idea right now. Pull up a rock and make yourselves comfortable, people. My office is available if you need it."

"We'll be fine," Milner told him. "Please excuse the interruption."

Goodell returned a tight-lipped smile and took his leave.

Milner was in his early thirties with sandy-blond hair he combed straight back. He appeared reasonably fit, possessed intelligent features, and like most FBI agents, was dressed in an understated gray suit. He was around six feet tall, which put him about an inch or two shorter than Jack.

Milner said, "Director Newton and I went to the North Precinct looking for you and were told you were back teaching at Georgia Tech."

"My position with the department was temporary," Jack said. "How can I help you?"

Before proceeding, Milner looked to the deputy director. She nodded for him to continue.

"Two days ago a cable car at Stone Mountain fell, killing seven people."

"I saw that on the news."

"Unfortunately, it wasn't an accident," Milner said.

"Oh?"

"Both Interpol and the Bureau have been tracking an individual known as the Sandman for some time now. He appeared on the scene after you left us, so you've probably never heard of him. He's thought to be responsible for as many as twelve assassinations in eight different countries over the past few years. The Israelis gave him his name because of some situation in the desert."

Jack glanced at Beth and Pappas and read nothing in their faces. He folded his arms across his chest and leaned back against a boulder waiting for Milner to continue.

"We received information from an informant that the Sandman was hired to make a hit on one of the cable car's passengers."

"Hired by who?" Jack asked.

"A man named Sergei Borov. I'll get to him in a minute."

Janet Newton said, "One of the people killed Friday was a doctor named George Lawrence. He and his wife, Rachel, are, or were, scheduled to testify next week before a grand jury along with their partner, Willis Landry. In light of what happened, I'll have to check on where that is now. Rachel Lawrence and Landry are also doctors. It was simply a stroke of luck she wasn't on the tram when it went down."

"What about Landry?"

"He was at his office seeing patients."

"Good. So what makes them important?"

"Approximately four weeks ago, strictly by chance, all three observed Borov meeting with a bank official in an underground parking lot. Borov was seen passing a briefcase to the man. We think this will tie into the U.S. Attorney's money laundering case. We're talking about a lot of money."

"But you don't know what's in the briefcase," Jack said.

"Not yet," Milner said. "We expect to develop that shortly. A federal judge just issued a search warrant for the banker's home and computer this morning. He works with National Guarantee & Trust, Borov's bank."

"Doesn't seem like a lot to go on," Jack said.

"You've had less," Janet Newton pointed out.

A look passed between them that Beth picked up on. Obviously, there was some meaning behind the comment, which only irritated her further. The deputy director had mentioned she knew Jack but never said anything about them working together. But it was neither the time nor the place to make an issue of it.

Dan Pappas added, "White Collar Crimes and Vice have been after Borov for some time now, but they've never been able to make anything stick. He owns a chemical plant in Duluth that manufactures lawn and garden products. You've probably seen his stuff in stores.

"One of Todd's men, an agent named Gabe Alonso, was assigned to follow Borov regarding the feds' investigation. Unfortunately, Alonso's suddenly dropped off the face of the earth. The Bureau called Captain Baxter and asked if we would stop by his house to check on him. Beth and I went out. Everything looked fine, except there's no sign of the guy. His car's still in the garage and from the food in the microwave, it looked like he was just sitting down to eat."

Milner added unnecessarily, "Agents on duty are supposed to check in regularly."

Jack nodded and asked if anything unusual was recovered at the home.

"Beth collected a number of samples and brought them to the lab. Furman's been doing the work-up. As of an hour ago, there was nothing significant."

It was still early in the day, but the big detective looked like he'd been wearing his suit for a week.

"And your source indicated this Borov hired the Sandman to eliminate the witnesses," Jack said.

Pappas nodded. "Borov's bad news. Dave Childers was running a snitch who's on the inside of his operation. He heard a rumor about a hit that took place in New York involving a senator's aide on the congressional foreign affairs committee. The aide was killed by a hit and run in the Bronx last week. Three days later, the snitch's house burned down with him in it. We're assisting New York's homicide investigation in cooperation with Todd's people."

Milner said, "Some of the chemical products Detective Pappas mentioned have made their way into the hands of the Syrian government who've been using them to gas their own people. On top of that, Borov's also branched out into weapons and electronics."

"Is there anything that ties him to the crimes?" Jack asked.

"Nobody testifies against him," Milner said, shaking his head. "The FAA confirmed he was in New York City at the time the aide was killed, but that's as close as we can get. There are also a series of phone calls we picked up from the pen registers on the aide's phone that make references to someone called 'The Russian.'"

"So what does this have to do with me?" Jack asked.

"You've been on the job before, so you know this kind of killer. It doesn't take much to imagine the problems we're facing. Now that the Sandman's entered the picture, things have gotten immensely more complicated. The witnesses need to be protected and he needs to be stopped."

Several seconds passed. Jack waited for Milner to continue, thinking he was going to ask him to analyze a piece of evidence. Nothing happened. He looked from one person to another for an explanation. No one spoke. The answer dawned on him a moment later.

"By me?"

"You, Professor."

"You're crazy. I've been out of the game for almost eight years."

"That's not quite accurate. Detectives Sturgis and Pappas said you were instrumental in stopping that serial killer—the Scarecrow's apprentice—several months ago."

Jack turned to Beth Sturgis who merely raised her eyebrows. Her face was the picture of innocence.

"That's because she kidnapped me," Jack said, pointing at Beth.

Milner smiled. "I heard about Ms. Sturgis's technique. Chief Ritson told us you performed admirably during the investigation."

That probably wasn't what Ritson said. On at least two occasions, he had accused Jack of being a loose cannon and threatened to fire him.

"This isn't a good idea," Jack said. "You have hundreds of qualified people—"

"Professor, the clock's ticking. We can't afford to lose these witnesses," said Milner.

"Look, I'm flattered," Jack said. "I just don't think you've thought this through."

He turned to Janet Newton for support. She responded by motioning with her head toward the door, indicating she wanted to speak in private. Jack looked at Beth, but her face remained neutral as they moved off.

Chapter 3

When they were out of earshot, Jack asked, "What's really going on here, Janet?"

"It's pretty simple. We want your help."

From prior experience, things were never *pretty simple* with Janet Newton. She was self-directed, confident, and like an arctic ice-breaker, prepared to plow through any obstacles to achieve a result. She was also a damn good cop.

She said, "The past is the past. From my standpoint, you've more than wiped the slate clean. It's time to rejoin the living, Jack."

He knew she was right but chose to ignore the reference to his final case with the Bureau. After that madman Howard Pell had killed his young partner, Jack's evisceration of the killer during their fight at Cloudland Canyon had gotten the Bureau sued. "Why me?"

"Because nobody thinks the way you do. I speak from personal experience."

Jack started to respond, but the deputy director held up her hand for him to wait.

"Let me put my cards on the table. We're stumped by the Sand-man and fresh out of ideas. An investigation lasting six years has almost nothing to show for it. The man's an enigma our best profilers can't get a handle on. What little we do know indicates he's brilliant and adept at changing his appearance. He gains weight, loses weight. Has a scar one day, it's gone the next. His hair is blond on Monday and black on Tuesday. He's also a genius at getting inside no matter

15

how many precautions are taken. To put it bluntly, if he wants you dead, you're dead. Frankly, he scares the hell out of me."

The unspoken part of her message was beginning to dawn on him. "You're getting pressure from upstairs," Jack said.

"Like you wouldn't believe, and it extends all the way to Pennsylvania Avenue. The grand jury convenes in six days and the U.S. Attorney is all over us to know what we're doing. We're dealing with the most ruthless and efficient killer we've ever been up against. I'm not saying this lightly. He'll use anybody or do anything to achieve his goal. My counterparts in MI5, France, Israel, and Russia all share this view. Bad doesn't begin to describe this man."

Jack looked down at his feet for several seconds, then said, "Janet, it's not that I don't want to help. It's just—"

"I meant what I said. The past is the past. You're not responsible for what happened to Connie Belasco. No one ever thought you were except you."

"It's a little more complicated than that," he said quietly.

Janet Newton ignored the comment. "Milner was telling you the truth. Noah Ritson did have some good things to say about you. He was also candid and mentioned you were enrolled in NA for a prescription medication problem. How's that going?"

"Day by day, as with any addiction."

"Good. Is it under control?"

"As much as it can be," Jack said.

"Understood. What else do I need to know?"

This was typical of her. Charge straight ahead and manage any problem on the fly. Still hoping to step away gracefully from the situation, Jack decided to tell her about his panic attacks. She listened thoughtfully while he spoke.

"But you say they've tapered off over the last few months," Janet said.

"I thought we had a handle on what was causing them, but apparently that's not the case. They could show up at any time and put people at risk."

"Or they might continue to abate as you get better."

"Yes, but—"

*

It was a little-known fact that the FBI vetted their own profilers and had been doing so for years. Janet Newton knew a great deal about what made Jack Kale tick. Perhaps more than he did about himself. She surprised him by asking, "Does your job interest you, Jack?"

"What kind of question is that?"

"A simple and straightforward one. Does your job interest you? Your life? A few months ago, you helped catch a serial killer and promptly went back to teaching. Maybe that's what you wanted. Now I find you here in a cave examining the remains of three people who died when the world was young. What happens next? Back to the classroom again to mark time until the next mystery pops up? I'm really curious."

"I don't know," Jack said.

"I do."

"Really?"

"It's here now, standing in front of you. I'm offering you a second chance. Trust me, they don't come around that often. Take it. You have a choice. I just don't think letting your mind fade away by degrees is what you were meant for. Do you?"

Her words struck home as she knew they would. Jack Kale had been given three gifts that made him a great profiler: meticulous attention to detail, an incredible instinct to see how seemingly unrelated facts about a person's psychological makeup came together, and an almost obsessive desire to take things apart and see how they worked. A problem without a solution was something incomplete and unacceptable to him. His dishes were never left in the sink, and his books were always put away.

Janet had known this man for a long time, and one trait always stood out: a desire to test himself almost to the point of compulsion. She doubted that had changed over the years.

The deputy director reached out and took Jack's forearm. "Some time ago I offered to bring you back into the Bureau. Frankly, it's where you belong. That offer is still on the table. If you want a way in, this is it. I'd also consider it a personal favor."

*

17

Marvelous, he thought.

Janet was right about one point. Ever since the serial murders several months ago, he'd settled back into his role of teaching sophomores at Georgia Tech introductory criminology. It was safe, secure, without conflict, and frankly, boring. Against his own inclinations, like a race horse responding to the sound of a starting trumpet, he felt a tick of excitement about matching wits with an opponent like the Sandman. He heard Janet's words and understood the threat this man posed, but they were just that . . . words. Whoever he was, Jack had no feel for him. At the moment, he was merely an abstract concept.

Jack glanced across the room at Beth, wanting to know what she was thinking. The events of several months ago, along with their romantic involvement, had set his feet on a road he wasn't sure he should go down anymore. Still . . .

"How do you see my role?" he asked.

"Most of what I've been doing with the Bureau has been regional, so this position is a little new to me. I've been at it less than a month. This is Milner's case, which means you'll be working together. My impression is he's smart and resourceful. He's also going off the wall because Gabe Alonso was one of his men. Todd knows we're in trouble and is willing to step aside and let you take over. Right now, there are too many agencies involved, the ATF, DEA, us, the Atlanta cops, not to mention Homeland. If you say yes, I'll make it happen. You'll be classified as a returning agent, on a six month trial. I'll postpone the medical, physical fitness, and weapons exams until sometime down the road. Right now, we need a profiler to understand what makes the Sandman tick."

Jack shook his head and informed her, "Profiling is only part of the picture. It sounds like magic when it works as long as you tally the successes. But it's only part of the whole. By itself, it's one of three legs on a stool. Put it together with solid forensic analysis and sound investigative technique and you've got something workable."

Jack broke off what he was saying. He was preaching to the choir. Janet Newton had a string of successes to her credit and was one of the best investigators he'd ever worked with. She was smiling, already confident his decision had been made.

"What else?" she asked.

"I'd like Sturgis and Pappas to work with me. We make a good team."

"Done," Janet said, extending her hand.

Jack accepted it, conscious he was allowing himself to be swept up by the tide. But the deputy director didn't release his hand immediately.

"You'll report directly to me, rather than going through a lead agent or the SAC. If push comes to shove and Milner won't go along with your decisions, let me know and I'll pave the way."

That made sense on at least one level. Janet Newton was not the type to relinquish control, particularly where it might involve her future.

"Not a problem," Jack said.

"Fine. Let's not keep the others waiting."

When they returned, she informed them, "Jack's agreed to head up the investigation. He'll be working with Special Agent Milner. Assuming your department agrees," she said, turning to Beth and Pappas, "we'd like both of you assigned to the task force. Whatever backup or support is needed, if your department can't furnish it, we will."

"We'll have to clear that with the bosses," Pappas told her.

"Leave that to me," Janet said.

Jack looked at Beth and Pappas trying to gauge their reaction. Beth shrugged. Pappas raised his thumb indicating the decision was fine with him.

The deputy director went on. "After the arrest is made, and an arrest will be made, APD and the Bureau can share credit. We don't need any turf battles. The important thing is to keep those people alive, and nail Borov and his assassin."

Now that the words were out, Jack felt a strange sense of relief. For the past several months, if not the past several years, it seemed like he'd been treading water. He wasn't sure returning to the FBI was the answer. Police work had its highs, but there was also a downside, at least for him. Much of the time he and Beth had been chasing the Scarecrow's apprentice, he'd been sick to his stomach. Nevertheless, there was no denying he also felt alive again while the hunt was on. Strange. It might be worth discussing this with his doctor.

"Where are the witnesses now?" Jack asked.

Pappas told him, "Dr. Lawrence is at home making funeral arrangements for her husband. I assigned a uniform to stay with her."

"Good. As long as she's secure, I'd like to look at the evidence Beth recovered at Alonso's home." He then turned to Milner: "If your people have recovered any of the bomb parts, I'd like to see them, as well."

"There won't be much left," Milner said. "What little we have has been turned over to APD's crime lab. It's been difficult because the area under the lift is dense forest."

"I'm familiar with it," Jack said. "If we need more help, bring in as many cops as necessary. I don't care if we have to draft a troop of Boy Scouts. I want that bomb."

Milner nodded. "Anything else?"

"Not at the moment," Jack said. "Let's get to work."

Chapter 4

When they exited the museum, Jack was surprised to see the sky had grown considerably darker than when he went in. It now looked like rain was on the way. Beth had ridden with Pappas, so they took his car to the crime lab. On the ride, she casually brought up the question of his relationship with Janet.

"Janet was my boss before being promoted to ASAC. Obviously, she's moved up the ladder since then."

"She didn't mention you both worked together when we met."

"That's odd."

"That's what I thought," Beth said, then after a pause added, "She's very tan."

"Excuse me?"

"Tan."

"I'm not following."

"It's November in Atlanta, Jack. I suspect technology. Don't men notice anything?"

Apparently not. Jack turned his palms up in an I-don't-know gesture.

"So you only knew each other through work?" Beth said.

"Basically."

"Basically?"

There was quicksand ahead. Jack decided the best way to handle the matter was with the truth.

"There might have been some tension between us, but nothing came of it. She was married at the time. So was I."

"Well, she's not married now. At least she's not wearing a ring."

Jack thought about this for a moment and told her he hadn't noticed.

"Um," Beth said, not sounding convinced, "were you glad to see her?"

"Not glad, not sad," he said, switching lanes. "I have mixed feelings about being drawn into another case."

"You could have said no."

"I could. But more people might die unless this Sandman's caught. Besides, aren't you the one who's been wanting me to get back into police work?"

"And you start listening to me now?"

Jack smiled and said, "I always listen to you, dear."

They weren't married yet, but were sounding more and more like a married couple every day. Beth smiled and squeezed his hand.

"Would you like me to back away?" Jack asked.

"No. That's one reason I love you. You always do the right thing."

"Only one?"

"There may be others. Try me later."

Her voice trailed away as she became absorbed in the file on her lap. A few minutes later, she looked up when Jack pulled into a shopping center and parked in front of a bagel shop.

"What are you doing?"

"Wait here," Jack said, exiting the car.

He was back ten minutes later carrying two large paper bags.

"You didn't have to buy lunch. Dan and I ate before the museum."

"Secrets of the trade, my child."

Beth shook her head. Once they returned to the road, her thoughts turned to the man next to her. He had a dry, if bizarre, sense of humor and could always make her laugh. She'd entered their relationship wholeheartedly, making the commitment to sell her house and move in with him several months earlier. Neither had been disappointed. Jack was solid, reliable, and a wonderful lover. There was a lot to be said for those qualities. So far, their life together had been everything she'd dreamed about. She couldn't remember being as happy. Working together, she thought, would only cement things further. Lost in her thoughts, it took a moment to realize they were at the police complex.

They parked under a sign that said "Official Vehicles Only" and went into the lab. Jack carried the food.

Atlanta's crime lab was state of the art, run by Ben Furman and two assistants. They handled evidence gathered by three thousand cops across the metro area as well as a number of surrounding counties. Though his training was in clinical psychology, after joining the FBI Jack had become fascinated with forensic evidence and had acquired an extensive knowledge that was the envy of experts throughout the profession. Then to the puzzlement of all and at the height of his career, he'd dropped out of sight, left the Bureau, and become a recluse. This hiatus lasted for approximately eight years, until Beth Sturgis entered his life asking for help to catch a murderer.

*

Nelda Latham, wearing a white lab coat, was frowning at a glass slide she was holding up to the light when they came through the door. Officially she was a lieutenant with the Atlanta Police Department, but she hadn't been in uniform or carried a gun in ten years. Nelda was of average height, was slightly overweight, and had short brown hair, which she had recently begun to color. Her eyes drifted away from the slide and immediately locked on the bags Jack was carrying.

"Bagels," she said, sniffing the air.

"Naturally," Jack said.

"And cream cheese?"

Jack held up the second bag.

"With chives?"

"Only a barbarian would show up without them. I also have a walnut and lox spread."

Nelda pulled her lab coat open and lay down across a long white table, throwing her arms wide. "Take me," she said. Then, raising her head, she asked Beth, "You don't mind, do you?"

Beth made a dismissive gesture with her right hand. "He's yours," she said, and headed toward a cabinet against the wall where she retrieved several plates, knives, and a handful of paper napkins.

"You think I'm that easy?" Jack said.

23

"Yes," both women answered at the same time.

Feigning indignation, Jack turned to Ben Furman for support. Furman looked up from the microscope he'd been peering into and nodded helpfully.

"Hmph," Jack said, plunking himself onto a high-top stool.

"It's illegal to bribe the police, you know," Nelda said, snatching a cinnamon-raisin bagel from the bag Jack was carrying.

"Absolutely," Beth said.

"You think this will buy you some influence around here?" Ben Furman asked, shoving himself back from the table. He then rolled his chair down the length of the room until he reached them.

"Of course not," Beth said, handing him a plate.

"Actually we were expecting you," Nelda said. "Chief Ritson called to let us know you were on the way. I understand we've got the Sandman again."

"You're familiar with him?" Jack asked.

"Six years ago, he took out a gas station with a bomb trying to kill an informant in the witness protection program. The bomb was set off from the pawn broker next door and configured to blow outward. It left the shop intact."

"Did he get the informant?" Beth asked.

"No, but the car he was working on did when the lift collapsed. The man's clever as hell and ruthless beyond belief. I've been dying for another crack at him. We busted our butts on that case and came up with nothing."

"Tell me about the ruthless part," Beth said.

"The gentleman who owned the pawn shop had this fancy security system you activate with a thumbprint. After the explosion, Teddy Larson went next door to see if maybe he had seen or heard anything. He found the guy unconscious in a closet, minus his thumb."

A shudder went up Beth's spine. She put her bagel back down.

*

Rachel Lawrence stared out the window at the rain. She was sitting in her living room drinking straight gin. Will Landry was next to her, feeling awkward and ill at ease as the tears rolled down her face. Normally the most resolute of people, unshakable Rachel was coming

24

apart. She knew it. The bottle was about half full. He watched her take another swallow. Will didn't think getting drunk was a half bad idea. He only wished he could find a way to comfort her. It was Will, not Rachel, who had called George's parents to break the news of his death.

Thirty-four-year-old Rachel was tall and slender. Her features were pleasant but unremarkable with a nose that was a little too pointed, and a mouth that was not full enough. Her brown hair came just to her shoulders. As a rule, she wore only a little makeup. According to her mother, her eyes were her best feature, blue and shining with intelligence. At the moment, they were swollen and puffy from all the crying.

A former army doctor with shrapnel in both legs, Willis Landry still walked with a limp from an RPG that had hit his vehicle during Desert Storm II. He was forty-five now, tall, gaunt, gray-haired, and thought he had witnessed all the misery one human being had a right to see years earlier. He also took it on himself to notify the staff and their remaining partner, Stuart Patterson, of the tragedy. Everyone was devastated. Patterson, the practice's manager, said he'd cover for them as long as necessary.

A uniformed cop was there when Will had arrived. He stepped into the kitchen to give them some space. Will assumed his presence was related to what they'd seen in the parking lot several weeks earlier. Periodically, the cop would get up and go through the house checking the doors and windows.

Rachel took another drink.

"Maybe you should go easy on that stuff," Will said, putting an arm around her shoulders.

Rachel looked at him through bloodshot eyes, then leaned back and put her head on his shoulder. More tears rolled down her face.

"What am I gonna do?" she asked.

The words were not directed to him, but up at the ceiling.

Will held her tighter. Everything he could think of sounded like a Hallmark card. He finally just spoke from his heart.

"Live, survive, heal. Go on. That's what George would want. I'm here. We all are."

Rachel put her glass back down and turned her head, first one way and then the other. She felt like she was getting thinner, disappearing. Not in her wildest dreams did she think anything could hurt this badly.

Rachel buried her face in Will's shoulder.

*

Wesley Simms was surprised to see how much Atlanta had grown in the last six years. According to the electronic population sign across from Piedmont Hospital, the city was now well over two million people with another four million in the surrounding countries. The streets, however, weren't teeming with pedestrians like New York or Chicago. In fact, only he and a few others were out that afternoon. The rain had passed, but it looked like more was on the way. People were probably at the malls, which seemed to stay perpetually busy from the time they opened to when security started throwing shoppers out late into the night. As a city, Atlanta was beautiful and clean, but definitely not a walking town. Twice, people had stopped to ask if he needed a ride. They appeared mildly surprised when he told them he was just getting some exercise.

Wesley, a solid man of about five foot eleven, was in his late thirties and had taken care to dress casually in good quality clothes. Nothing fancy, just upper-class items designed to fit the neighborhood he was wandering through. His charcoal gray pants and plum V-neck sweater were understated. Beneath the sweater was a knit long-sleeve white shirt.

Three days earlier, he had dropped by the ASPCA and adopted the dog who was now walking beside him. Nothing special about it. Just a small, reddish-brown mutt of indeterminate parentage. The ASPCA people had even given him a leash and box of dog biscuits. The dog seemed pleased to be outside. No one gave them a second glance, which was exactly what he wanted. Deep in conversation on his cellphone, Wesley turned onto the next street.

Have you examined the house yet?

I'm just about to.

Keep your eyes alert for cops, son. They might have the place staked out already.

I know that. I'll be careful.

Two minutes later, Wesley and his four-legged companion came abreast of a two-story brick home with a neatly maintained lawn. He was in no particular hurry and described it to his mentor in some detail down to the dormant Bermuda grass, trees, and foundation plantings.

Is there anything you can use, boy-o?

Yes, sir. The front has a large bay window. I can see two people inside sitting on a couch, and, uh oh—

Uh oh, what?

There's a cop with them. He just came to the front door and lit a cigarette. You were right.

Give him a friendly wave and continue walking. Not fast, not slow. Same steady pace.

Not a problem.

What about the surroundings? Any opportunities there?

Across the street is a small buffer of trees. Beyond that is a church which should work just fine. It's high enough so the trees won't be a factor when I take the shots.

Excellent, I'm proud of you, my boy.

Wesley smiled, disconnected, and continued up the street. He turned at the next corner and headed for the church. His sniper rifle was in a case in the trunk of his car on the next block. He spared a quick glance at the cop who was still on the front steps smoking. Filthy habit. The idea of putting smoke in his lungs made him cringe. As soon as they were out of sight, he unclipped the dog's leash, removed his collar, then took two biscuits from the box and placed them on the ground. The dog began eating.

"The best of luck to you, my friend," he said, patting the dog's side.

The dog didn't look up as he walked away.

Chapter 5

Beth borrowed Nelda's desk and continued studying the Sand-man files. What she was reading about the killer and the various techniques he employed to take out his victims concerned her. She was anxious for Jack to see it. The Sandman was unquestionably intelligent, as Nelda had said, and planned his jobs down to the last detail. That was obvious immediately. Police forces on three continents hadn't come close to nabbing him. In each instance, he'd outwitted them. Not a small feat considering the talent arrayed against him. He seemed to be a phantom who could vanish at will, leaving no trace of himself. Even the most stringent precautions taken by the German police a few months earlier had come to nothing. Posing as a carpet layer working in the captain's office, the Sandman had simply waltzed through their security and killed two men in their own police station. A video camera showed him on the way out, only this time he was dressed as a cop. Astounding.

Across the room, Jack was looking over Ben Furman's shoulder as he examined the evidence Beth had brought back from the missing FBI agent's house. No one had heard from Gabe Alonso in more than fifty hours. That didn't bode well. Shortly after they arrived, Dan Pappas and Todd Milner entered the lab. Everyone was praying Furman could work some magic with what Beth had found.

It was obvious Milner was upset about Alonso. Very upset. Beth felt for him.

As a rule, cops and the FBI didn't get along. Now that Jack was back with the Bureau again, she'd be sleeping with one of them.

Wonderful. Jack could just as well have gone to work with the APD as she'd been suggesting for the past few months.

"A house divided," she muttered to herself.

Milner started to pace. Out of nervousness, she thought. Earlier, he told them he'd worked with Gabe Alonso for three years. To make matters worse, the man was married and his wife was four months pregnant.

Jack said, "You mentioned something about a congressional aide being killed earlier. Is there anything concrete connecting the Sandman to that?"

"Not definitively," Milner said. "Homeland Security went over their facial recognition software at all three airports in the New York area. They even checked the Westchester airport. Three possible candidates emerged, but no solid matches. Not a surprise where the Sandman is concerned. The Germans and Israelis believe he uses plastic surgery to alter his appearance, even to the extent of adding and removing implants."

"I've got a couple of gray fibers here," Furman announced, "some dirt, and . . . three red hairs."

"Human?" Jack asked.

"Can't say yet."

"Can you put them on the screen?"

A moment later, a high-definition image appeared on the overhead computer monitor.

Pappas asked, "Do we know what color the Sandman's hair is?"

"Depends on the day and his victim," Milner said.

"Any residue on them?" Jack said.

"Nothing," Furman answered. "Best guess . . . they're animal. Not sure if I can pin down the type without more."

"Did Alonso own a pet?" Jack asked Milner.

"I'd have to check with his wife and I've been holding off on doing that."

"Let's not wait," Jack said.

Milner shook his head and moved off to a corner of the room to make the call.

Jack turned to Pappas. "Where are the witnesses now?"

"At Rachel Lawrence's house. You want me to check on them?"

Jack nodded and continued to stare at the computer screen.

*

The officer guarding Rachel and Will answered before the first ring had died away. He put the call on speaker phone.

"Dixon, this is Pappas. How are things there?"

"Everything's good, Sergeant. Quiet as a tomb."

Pappas wished he'd picked another phrase. "What are the witnesses up to?"

"Not much. They're in the living room." Dixon lowered his voice. "The wife's been drinking pretty heavily. Can't blame her. Dr. Landry's sitting with her. He seems like a decent sort to me."

"Any visitors? Deliveries? People stopping by?"

"Nothing. Like I said, everything's cool."

"Good," Pappas said. "Keep on your toes."

"The only person who's been by was some guy out walking his dog a little while ago."

Without turning around, Jack asked, "What kind of dog?"

Pappas checked to see if Dixon heard the question.

"I don't know, Sarge. Some kind of mixed breed, I guess. They kept going."

"Color?" Jack asked.

There was a pause on the line as the officer thought about this. "Kind of red, I think. Didn't seem like a big deal."

"Tell me what's across the street from the house," Jack said.

"A tree buffer," Dixon said. "About seventy-five to a hundred feet deep. I can see right through it. There's no one there."

"Great," Pappas said. "Make sure the curtains stay closed and keep them away from the windows."

"And what's on the other side of the buffer?" Jack asked.

"Bunch of houses and a church," Dixon said.

Beth's head came up. "A church?"

"Right."

"In London, the Sandman fired from a church roof to make a hit on a Serbian mobster. It was a twelve hundred yard shot."

Jack stared at her for a second, then told Pappas to scramble the SWAT team.

*

Through the Leica scope on his rifle, Wesley watched the cop speaking on his cellphone. The rifle's front stock was resting on a bean bag he'd purchased at a toy store that morning. Most churches were empty at that time of the day. Some had day care, community, or school programs, assuming the congregation was large enough and wealthy enough to support them, but the sanctuaries were generally deserted.

He felt rather bad about killing the priest. Poor timing on the old man's part, walking in on him. But unexpected problems periodically came up. The key was to be flexible and adapt. Sunday services were two days away and he doubted anyone would discover the body hidden in a side chapel before then. By that time, he'd be gone. South America was a long plane ride away, and he'd always wanted to see Rio de Janeiro. The scenic photos of the city fascinated him.

His thoughts turned to the last time he'd been in church as a participant. It had to have been at least twenty-five years ago, and that was back in his native Ireland. Maybe more. For a moment, Wesley wondered if it was bad luck to kill a priest, then shrugged it off and resumed his vigil.

The rain had started again, just a light mist, but it meant he would have to factor it along with the wind, angle of deflection, and amount of drop on the bullets. His beloved spotting scope read the distance at 992 yards. Difficult, but doable.

After the phone conversation, the cop went back inside to shoo the wife and friend away from the window. It was probably his supervisor calling. Also not unexpected. Sitting alongside the rifle was Wesley's cellphone.

Do we have a problem, boy-o?

Not really. The cop closed the drapes and moved them out of the room. They're in the kitchen now.

Abort the mission?

No, sir. I can still see inside. The wife and friend are having coffee. And here comes our erstwhile officer. The other two will freeze when I take him out.

Body armor?

Definitely. But that won't stop a .50-caliber round. I don't need to kill the man, just drop him.

Good thinking. Go to it, boy.

Wesley would have preferred being in a prone position. Unfortunately, the belfry's retaining wall prevented that. Didn't matter. He could make the shot just as well standing and using the wall for support. The rifle was a .50-caliber Barrett that fired three-and-a-half-inch bullets. It weighed thirty pounds and was accurate to two thousand yards. Checking the branches below and the direction the clouds were moving, he estimated the wind at no more than ten miles per hour. He began to slow his breathing, willing his heart rhythm to follow. Three shots. One for the cop. Two for the witnesses. Tap, tap, tap. No more. Finger resting lightly on the trigger, he waited. The cop was moving in and out of the scope's field of view. Breathing slower still, he pressed his cheek against the rifle stock so much it became a part of him. He could feel the wonderful cold seeping into his skin.

Ahh, here's our cop again. Wesley's finger slowly tightened on the trigger.

A flash of blue lights caught the corner of his nonsighting eye, pulling him away from the targets. Moving along Peachtree Road at high speed were three black SUVs. He listened. No sirens. They were on a silent approach. Very odd. He nudged the cellphone closer.

Problem here, Father. Law enforcement is closing in from the south. Estimate two minutes to arrival.

The Mentor let out a long sigh.

Safety first, son. There'll be other chances. We still have a little over six days.

I can still take one out.

A complete mission or nothing. That's our money-back guarantee. Let's get you out of there.

*

Later, the two cops who knocked on the rectory door would remember the priest as an elderly, medium-sized gentleman. Obligingly, he opened the sanctuary and let them take a look around, then showed them the door leading up to the belfry stairs. The men were thorough and professional and apologized for disturbing him.

"Is there a problem, officers? We don't have many crimes here at St. Bernadette."

The taller of the two laughed and said, "Nothing to do with you, Father. We're looking for a sniper."

"Dear God," the priest said, struggling to keep the shock off his face. "Are you serious?"

"Unfortunately, yes. He's not getting away with it, Father. Remember to keep your doors locked and call us if you see any strangers in the neighborhood."

"Rest assured, I will. You good men stay safe."

How could they have known so quickly? Let's get you out of here.

Chapter 6

Wesley Simms was wrong about when the body of Father David Beckley would be found. Late that afternoon, a member of the church's cleaning crew dusting the side chapel noticed a dark-red stain slowly seeping out from under the altar. When he recovered from the shock of what was behind it, the man went outside, threw up, and promptly called the police.

Todd Milner reached Maria Alonso at her parents' home in Richmond, Virginia and broke the news that her husband was officially missing, not just incommunicado due to an assignment. As additional protection, Dan Pappas was dispatched to Rachel Lawrence's house with two more cops. Jack and Beth elected to go the church and examine the scene where the priest had been killed.

The church's bell tower stood in stark contrast to the darkening sky. Evening was coming on quickly. Rumbles of thunder accompanied by flashes of electricity could be seen in the distance. As the sun set, the temperature continued to drop. The rain had increased in intensity and was blowing sideways, one sheet following another. It knocked leaves off the trees and sent them spiraling to the ground. The first cops to respond had set up barricades and stretched yellow crime scene tape across the church entrance.

Inside the sanctuary, people spoke in hushed tones. One look was sufficient to confirm Father Beckley was dead. At Jack's request, the medical examiner waited for Beth to finish her examination. Over the last eight months, she'd applied herself to learning his forensic techniques with a fervor that surprised him. She could now locate and analyze evidence on par with any technician. The woman definitely had a competitive streak. Confident in her abilities, Jack watched her work as she covered the area in and around the side chapel meticulously. She ran a sticky roller from her evidence kit across the floor, then over the alter itself. After that, she used a Polilight to search for prints. Several friction ridges were revealed. Jack doubted they'd be of any value. The killer had almost certainly worn gloves. In under an hour, she managed to fill six separate plastic bags with what Jack called trace: little bits of material that might or might not prove useful later. It wasn't the items that were supposed to be there that interested him. It was what he dubbed "outliers": things you wouldn't expect to find. Early on in his career, he'd become a believer in Locard's Principle, which argued that in every murder a transfer takes place between the victim and the killer. That transfer might be minute, but it was always there.

While she was occupied, Jack donned a pair of blue Tyvek shoe covers and wandered around the church. According to the maintenance man, the front door was always locked, except when services were being held. The side door and the door to the priests' residence, however, were both left open. A few questions revealed there were actually two priests who tended the parish of St. Bernadette. One was now behind the altar. The other was in Houston visiting his sick mother.

It now seemed obvious the SWAT officers had spoken with the Sandman. Their description of him as "an elderly gentleman" was confusing, but understandable in light of what the files said about his ability to change his appearance.

Significantly, the Sandman hasn't succeeded in killing the witnesses, which meant he'd been forced to improvise. That might work to their advantage. There was a special corner in hell, he decided, for someone who murders a priest. He looked at the figure on the cross at the front of the church and closed his eyes.

Jack's wandering had a point. He was trying to determine the assassin's way in and out of the church. Ultimately, he came to a halt at the back of the sanctuary. His vision grew unfocused as he attempted to place himself in the killer's head. Given the Sandman's penchant for meticulous planning, it was clear his intention had been to use the building as a staging area. Nevertheless, Jack doubted the killer had gone there *intending* to murder a priest or don a priest's habiliments. The murder was an unnecessary complication, as was his meeting with the police. Both were risks that gave rise to the possibility of mistakes. And mistakes led to evidence.

Jack made his way into the rectory and found Father Beckley's quarters. They consisted of a simply furnished sitting room, a bedroom, and a bathroom. The bedroom contained a four-poster bed and a comfortable-looking armchair. The sitting room had a desk and a freestanding set of shelves with books, a few photos, and an autographed baseball from the Atlanta Braves. Jack smiled, remembering that priests were human. Nothing significant jumped out at him until he got to the closet. There he found an empty clothes hanger lying on the floor as if it had been pulled off in haste. Next to it was a black suit.

How many suits did a priest own? He had no idea. Three seemed like a reasonable number, but it could easily been five or even ten. One was still hanging up and one was on the dead priest.

Out of curiosity, Jack looked in the clothes hamper. Crumpled beneath some towels were a black jacket, pants, and a vest with the traditional cleric's collar. The jacket and trousers were good quality wool that a dry cleaner would generally handle, not something that would go in the wash. Gradually, a picture of what happened formed in his mind. SWAT's arrival had either interrupted the Sandman or delayed his departure. Father Beckley, it seemed, was in the wrong place at the wrong time.

If a rifle was being used, as it had been in London according to Beth, the killer needed a vantage point for a clear shot. He looked up at the ceiling . . . the bell tower. Like most people, criminals were creatures of habit. They tended to reuse what worked for them in the past. He left the clothes where they were and returned to the sanctuary.

Beth was just finishing her examination when Milner arrived with his own technician. Unnecessary, but they weren't familiar with her skills yet. Milner introduced Alan Komanski to them.

"Al's been with us for twenty years," Milner said. "He's about as senior as they come. If anyone can find a needle in a haystack, he can. No offense, Detective."

"None taken," Beth said, backing her way out of the cramped chapel. "Another pair of eyes is always welcome."

Milner informed Jack, "You fellows have something in common. Al was Marine CID, too."

Jack shook his hand and asked where Komanski had served.

"Wherever the job required," Komanski said. "You know how it is."

"Sure."

Komanski was a little under six feet, with a prominent nose and intense blue eyes. Jack placed him in his midfifties. Despite his age, he looked like the kind of man who ran triathlons as a hobby. He'd kept his military crew cut, something Jack didn't see much of anymore. Komanski glanced at the shoe covers on Jack and Beth's feet and gave a brisk nod of approval.

"Can't be too careful about contaminating a scene," he said. "Believe it or not, cops are among the biggest polluters."

"I'll remember that," Jack said.

Beth recalled Jack mentioning the same thing to his class the first time they met, but chose not to comment.

"If your girl's done, I'll give the place a thorough going over and see if I can work some magic," Komanski said.

Jack winced inwardly. Beth was in the process of pulling off her latex gloves. She paused for a second, said nothing, and continued.

"I noticed you walking around when I came in," Milner said. "Spot anything significant?"

He explained, "I checked Father Beckley's residence and found a priest's jacket, pants, vest, and a clerical collar stuffed at the bottom of his clothes hamper. I think the Sandman put them on when he met with our SWAT officers to pass himself off as a priest. Beth should—"

"You touch anything?" Komanski asked.

"Just the top of the hamper. I was wearing gloves."

"What about the clothes themselves?"

37

"I used a hanger to move the towels and other items aside. Everything is still in the same position."

Komanski shook his head. "You should have waited for me."

"Since I didn't know you were coming, that would have been a little difficult. I was very careful."

Milner quickly added, "Dr. Kale used to be one of us, Al. He knows his way around."

"Psych profiler, right?" Komanski said. "I remember hearing about you."

"Correct."

"Nothing personal, but that psych stuff sounds like a lot of mumbo jumbo to me. No one knows what goes on inside these guys' heads."

"You may have a point," Jack said.

"Well, no help for it now. I'll check out the clothes when I'm done here. You and the gal try to avoid getting hands-on, okay? If you see something of interest, holler. With a little luck, we'll nail this bastard."

"Sure thing," Jack said. "The gal and I'll be up in the bell tower. Want to accompany us, Todd?"

"I'll be along in a bit. Right now I need to identify the Sandman's points of ingress and egress."

"Excellent idea," Jack said. "C'mon, gal."

As soon as the door to the stairway closed, Beth shoved him. Jack had to struggle to keep a straight face.

"Gal?"

"As a psychologist, I sense some hostility here," Jack said.

"Yeah? Well I'm finding there are more horse's asses in the world than horses," Beth said.

Jack began to chuckle and kissed her on the forehead. "You sure about me getting back into police work?"

Beth pushed him away. "I'll let you know later. Watch where you're walking. I can see some footprints."

"You're very observant for a girl."

Beth gave him a sour look, then opened her evidence kit and took an electrostat image of the clearest prints.

"Think this is our man?" she asked.

"It's possible. They could be from a janitor, or Quasimodo for that matter. One side looks like it's been wiped."

They found the same situation at the roof. The Sandman had erased whatever evidence of himself he might have left behind. The rain had taken care of the rest. The same wipe marks appeared directly under the tower's southeast opening. It was on a direct line to the Lawrence home.

"He set up here but didn't take the shot," Beth said, talking to herself.

"Might not have had a chance," Jack said, squinting through the blowing rain. "Great view of the surrounding area. Our guys told me they were on a silent approach."

"Silent or not," Beth said, "he could see them coming five miles off."

Jack nodded. The Sandman's adaptability was impressive. He and Beth spent twenty minutes examining the area and found nothing. He was just starting to get a sense of what they were up against.

They met Milner and Komanski at the bottom of the steps and told them what they'd seen.

Komanski surprised Beth by apologizing if he came on a little strong. Probably as a result of Milner talking to him, she thought.

"I didn't mean any disrespect. Too much time in the service is all. We're all on the same team as far as I'm concerned."

Beth smiled. "Apology accepted."

"You wouldn't know it to look at me. But I have a sensitive side."

"Really?"

"Yep. I watch *Dancing with the Stars* with my wife."

She wasn't sure that equated with sensitivity. Nevertheless, she nodded enthusiastically.

"Some of those gals . . . I mean, women, are amazing," Komanski said.

"They are," Beth agreed.

"The other night they showed this clip from an old black and white movie with Fred Astaire and Ginger something."

"Rogers," Jack said.

"Yeah, Rogers. That's the one. Let me tell you, she matched every step Astaire made. Pretty damn impressive, you ask me."

"Except she did it in high heels going backward," Beth said.

The FBI tech's eyes slid sideways, and he frowned as he thought about that.

Without another word, Beth gathered her evidence kit and headed for the door.

Chapter 7

On the way home, Jack placed a call to Dan Pappas. He was at the Lawrence house waiting for Dwayne Stafford to relieve him. If there was any question about the Sandman being in town, the priest's murder had dispelled it.

"How are the witnesses?" Jack asked.

"Antsy and angry as hell that no one has spoken to Borov yet. I told them it probably wouldn't do much good."

"Agreed. Do they understand what we're dealing with?"

Pappas lowered his voice. "Between you and me, I'd say no. The good news is they're cooperating. Doc Lawrence is a trooper. It's a damn shame what she went through, but she's trying to pull herself together. She's been making calls to her office for the last hour scheduling patient tests. No question she's really involved with those kids."

"Better she's staying busy," Jack said. "What about the other witness?"

"Landry's a solid citizen. He's former army and loyal as hell. He's staying in the guest room tonight. They both asked to meet with you tomorrow."

"Me?"

"Yeah, I told 'em you were heading things up."

"I don't see what I could say—"

"Jack, the woman just lost her husband. Now some nut wants to kill her and Landry because they happened to see this Borov pass off a suitcase. They've both had it pretty rough. Her more than him, obviously."

41

"Understood," Jack said. "Beth and I will be out to speak with them in the morning." He looked at Beth, who nodded her agreement.

"Get some rest, Dan."

*

Marta greeted them at the door when they came in. Each had to endure a series of lapping kisses from the big German shepherd. Beth asked Jack to feed her and take her for a walk while she took a bath.

"How come that's my job?" he asked.

"She's your dog."

"What happened to share and share alike? Equal partners? Women's lib?"

"It's a flexible concept," Beth said.

Jack looked at Marta for support. She raised her eyebrows.

"I'm surrounded," he muttered and headed into the kitchen.

As he was getting Marta's food ready, he heard the water go on upstairs. Traditionally, Beth's bath lasted anywhere from forty-five minutes to an hour depending on how much she needed to unwind. Generally a book or play by Shakespeare went in there with her. Early on in their relationship, he'd been surprised to find she could quote entire passages from *As You Like It* and *A Midsummer Night's Dream* by heart. Impressive. Once a month, she and several friends in her all-women reading club got together over lunch to discuss books. The group included a lawyer, a doctor, and a Superior Court judge. He once walked in on a meeting and had the distinct feeling he was intruding. He left as quickly as possible.

He had just started reviewing the first Sandman file when Marta nudged him with her nose indicating she was finished eating. He looked down at her. Her tail thumped against the nearest cabinet.

"It's still raining out, you know."

Marta stayed where she was, watching him.

"You don't like the rain, remember?"

No reaction except a tail thumping against a kitchen chair.

"Right. I'll get an umbrella."

They walked through the quiet Brookhaven neighborhood past house windows spilling warm incandescent light onto the lawns. Inside, people were preparing dinner; kids were doing homework and texting each other, probably both at the same time; seductions were under way; people were worried about their children, paying bills, or what to do for the weekend.

Marta kept her nose low to the ground, checking for scents. The rain had let up and was now a steady drizzle rather than the downpour that had drenched everything earlier that afternoon.

Jack reflected on how the day had turned out. He'd begun it reconstructing the murder of three people fifty thousand years ago and had finished the day doing virtually the same thing. Not much in the way of advancement for the human species. If he allowed those facts to depress him, they would. He was good at compartmentalizing and shoved the comparison away.

As it always did when he was feeling morbid, his mind turned to his former partner, Connie Belasco. She'd been dead now almost nine years. It hardly seemed that long. Great kid, solid cop. So eager to please and show she was one of the guys. Not unlike Beth, really. He owed Connie a visit.

The cemetery was twenty minutes away and it had been a while since their last talk. Mostly it was him talking and her listening, but every once in a while he thought he could hear a whisper. Perhaps, as his friend said, the dead find a way to communicate with the living. Morris Shottner, the psychologist he saw, would probably think he was nuts if he ever verbalized that. As always, he cautiously approached the subject of Connie in his mind, because thinking about her often brought on one of his panic attacks. What he told Janet was true. Since hitting on the trigger that precipitated them during his case with Beth, the attacks had certainly levelled out, but it was frustrating that they hadn't disappeared entirely. The last one had come three months earlier. Maybe they would disappear altogether one day. It would be nice to have a life without them.

Jack felt the leash tighten behind him as Marta slowed, her way of saying she was ready to go back. They turned and started for home. It was just cool enough out and there was enough dry wood in the garage to start a fire. Beth would enjoy that after her bath.

Thoughts came and went, particularly about how his life had changed since Elizabeth Sturgis had entered it. She was five foot nine with brown hair and the largest green eyes. Add to that, she was funny, quick witted, and intelligent as hell. At thirty-three, she was six years younger than he was. He'd never met anyone like her and didn't expect to. An added bonus was that she and his thirteen-year-old daughter, Morgan, got along really well. They'd become Twitter and Facebook friends and spoke regularly, sending each other pictures and inane messages about what they were doing at any given moment.

The last time Morgan had come to visit, she had broached the subject of living with them. Apparently, Jack's ex-wife's new boyfriend had become a source of friction. Morgan made him promise not to say anything until she thought the matter out further, which was typical of her. She was a serious and contemplative child. He told her not to make any snap decisions and to give her mother a chance to work things out.

To his pleasant surprise, Beth was in favor of Morgan relocating. She was close to her own family and saw it as a good decision for all involved.

That discussion had started him thinking about the subject of marriage. He knew Beth was the one and that it was time to make their relationship permanent. For some reason, taking that step still scared him. Over the last eight years, he'd basically given up the idea of finding someone to love again. Beth had changed this. They'd been together what? Eight months? She knew the worst things about him—his frailties—and to his everlasting astonishment they were still all right with her.

"What do you think about marriage?" Jack asked Marta.

Marta had no opinion, but he was certain she approved.

A few weeks earlier, he'd asked Dan Pappas if he knew any reliable jewelers in town. Pappas told him he had a friend in the diamond business. Jack hadn't mentioned marriage, but he supposed their loosely kept secret had managed to spread its way around the police department. As it turned out, everyone had a friend in the diamond business. Dwayne had one. Dwayne's partner, Ed Mundas, had one. Even Beth's secretary knew somebody who could give him a great deal.

While Beth was trying on clothes a month earlier, he took the opportunity to speak with a saleslady at Neiman Marcus's jewelry department. He hadn't purchased a diamond in a long time and was surprised by how much they had gone up in price. She told him the more colorless and clearer a stone, the higher its price. Made sense. When Beth returned carrying her purchases, he was positive the lady winked at her as they were leaving the store. Privately, he was convinced some mystical form of communication existed between women where engagement rings were concerned. Though Beth said nothing about it, she seemed unusually affectionate that evening.

Definitely time, he decided. Just as soon as they caught a killer that police on three continents hadn't come close to in six years.

Chapter 8

After reaching the house, Jack dried Marta off and got the fire going. Beth was still upstairs soaking. He then started some water boiling for the pasta he planned to make and took two chicken breasts out of the fridge, coating them with olive oil and flattening them with his knife. He had no doubt she'd be hungry when she came down. The amount of food that woman could eat and still stay in shape amazed him. Of course, going to the gym four days a week helped. If there was an ounce of fat on her, it was a well-kept secret.

By the time the water was starting to boil, he heard Beth stirring and placed the chicken breasts in a frying pan. Having just been fed, Marta lost interest in watching him and wandered into the family room. In under a minute, she was asleep on their love seat by the fire. He added a few shallots to the pan then tossed the pasta into the boiling water.

Beth came padding down the steps wearing a white terrycloth robe and a pair of his slippers she'd appropriated after moving in. Jack had given up any hope of getting them back and purchased another pair for himself.

"Oh, you made us a fire," she said.

"Dinner'll be ready in a minute," Jack said. "In there or here?"

Beth came up behind him and slipped her arms around his waist and rested her head on his back. "How 'bout here? Then we'll go inside and relax. Marta's unconscious."

"Rough walk."

By unspoken agreement, neither discussed the case. Instead, they talked about everything else under the sun, from visiting her folks over the upcoming holidays to shopping for new lawn furniture and a grill when the weather was warmer. Ultimately, Beth informed him his daughter wanted to go skiing with her class over the winter break.

"I didn't know that," Jack said, surprised.

"If it's all right with you, of course."

There was no reason to object . . . apart from the cost. He'd been skiing before and knew trips like that came with a hefty price tag. You could bribe an Atlanta politician for less.

"I gather Morgan asked you to pave the way?"

"Not in so many words. It'll be a lot of fun. Her whole class is going and Lake Tahoe is gorgeous."

"You've been there?"

"A guy I was dating took me a few years ago," Beth said.

For some reason, that annoyed him, but he kept it to himself. "Are you in favor of the trip?"

"Of course."

"Did she tell you what her mother said?"

"To ask you."

"Which means she doesn't want to pay for it."

"Probably," Beth said.

A thought occurred to him. "What if we surprise her and join her out there?"

"Jack, she'd die of embarrassment."

"How come?"

"Trust me. I was a thirteen-year-old girl."

He didn't have much to say about that.

"Is there anything else I need to know?"

"Well, there's a really cute boy in her class she likes named Josh, who's going too."

Jack put down his fork. "Thirteen is way too young to date."

"I agree," Beth said. "But they don't exactly date these days. They hang out in packs, like wolves."

It was depressing how much he didn't know about his daughter and how quickly she was growing up and how much of it he was missing. He really did want to see her, but was willing to defer to Beth.

As to the growing up part, there wasn't much he could do about that, either. Morgan had been five when he and Katherine split.

Every time he saw her after being apart, he was shocked to see the changes. The last time he took her shopping for a new pair of jeans, she went into the dressing room Hannah Montana and came out Miley Cyrus.

After dinner, they adjourned to the family room, sat on the couch, and watched an old movie. The fire, expertly built in his opinion, insinuated its heat into the room. Marta continued her slumber. Every so often, her front paws twitched. He wondered what she was dreaming about. Beth snuggled her way under his arm and placed her head on his chest.

The movie was an old Jimmy Stewart film about a six-foot-tall invisible rabbit named Harvey. Six feet four inches, to be precise. Jack had seen it a dozen times but was content to watch it again. Beth giggled at the jokes and found it charming.

For reasons beyond his understanding, the film's sponsor that evening was Viagra.

"Hm," Beth said when the third commercial aired.

"What?"

"Nothing."

"You can't just say hm, and leave it like that."

"Well, I was wondering. Have you ever tried it?"

"No," Jack said indignantly, looking at her.

"Just asking."

"Why?"

"Maggie Tannenbaum says that fifty percent of men over forty have some degree of dysfunction."

"I'm thirty-nine."

"Still . . ."

"Still, what?"

"She's a doctor, Jack."

"She's a *podiatrist.*"

"They're doctors, too. Maggie told me her husband tried it."

"For God's sake, Max is sixty-five. He's lucky if he can walk across the room." He paused and thought for a moment. "Have you been, uh . . . dissatisfied?"

"Oh, no," she said quickly. "Of course the last time—"

"That was just once," Jack said. "I was thinking about those stupid skeletons at the museum."

"Don't get upset," Beth said, rolling over on top of him.

That was when he noticed the front of her robe was undone. He pulled her down to him and kissed her. She responded by pressing her hips into his.

"Oh," she said, shifting her hips slightly. "It doesn't seem like you need those pills after all."

Afterward, Beth stood and languidly stretched in the firelight totally without inhibition. She picked up her robe, but didn't put it on, draping it over one shoulder instead. Jack lay there waiting for his heart rate to return to normal as she walked to the steps.

"Care to join me upstairs?" she asked.

"Right now? I'm still trying to get my breath back."

"That was round one, honey. You know how us gals are."

Chapter 9

Five Days to the Grand Jury

The Lawrences lived in an upscale subdivision in the middle of Atlanta. Jack and Beth, running a little late that morning, pulled up to the front of the house and parked. Azalea and Camilla bushes, dormant with the approaching winter, lined the home's foundation. Several hanging flower baskets filled with purple and yellow pansies were suspended from black angle brackets at the corners. The house was a reasonable size, though not ostentatious, and consistent with others in the neighborhood. It appeared to be a pleasant, comfortable home with a lot of nice touches. What it did not have were any police cars in the driveway.

"Damn," Beth said.

As soon as they exited their vehicle, she moved her suit jacket to the side to allow easier access to the 9 mm semiautomatic Beretta on her right hip.

"Are you carrying?" she asked Jack.

"Actually . . . no."

"My backup's in the glove compartment. Doesn't the FBI have rules about carrying a weapon?"

"They must," Jack said. "It's been a while."

Beth shook her head and waited while he retrieved the gun. As they approached the front door, each moved to opposite sides. Beth knocked. Several seconds passed without an answer.

"Where the hell are they?" she said.

"Call Dwayne Stafford," Jack said. "He took over for Pappas this morning."

Beth removed her cellphone and called her secretary for Stafford's number. She asked if Nolvia knew where the detective was.

It wasn't possible to hear Nolvia's answer, but Jack was familiar with the look on Beth's face. Before he could ask the obvious question, she disconnected and was placing a second call. Her voice remained calm when Stafford answered.

"Dwayne, listen carefully," Beth said. "You're in a highly dangerous situation. I'm not exaggerating. More important, the witnesses are in danger. Didn't Pappas explain what's going on?" She listened to his reply and then continued.

"I understand you couldn't stop them from leaving the house, and it's great the Bureau's sending marshals. Right now they're our responsibility. I want you to secure Doctors Lawrence and Landry and keep them away from any windows. You heard the man we're after killed a priest yesterday?"

More conversation followed.

Beth acknowledged the comments and went on. "I don't give a damn if they have patients. Arrest them for littering, or looking at you cross-eyed. Just get them someplace safe. We're on the way."

*

The medical practice's office manager, Elaine Reynolds, finally pulled herself together and managed to stop crying. Known to her friends as Lanie, she had been with them for the last five years. Rachel Lawrence sat across from her in Lanie's office on the eighth floor trying to comfort and assure her that everything would be all right. She wished someone would comfort her.

With George gone, covering his rounds at the hospital was now a priority. Just because Rachel was hurting didn't mean the patients weren't. Her partner, Stuart Patterson, had canceled his vacation to Las Vegas and was doing his best to pitch in. Rachel knew he couldn't manage everything on his own.

As she left Lanie's office, all she wanted was to go home and crawl into bed, but two of the young children she'd operated on were still in critical condition. She needed to be there. End of argument. Like Stu Patterson, she was a senior partner now, except she didn't feel much like a senior anything. Her life had been ripped apart by an event that even now she could hardly believe had happened. She kept seeing the tram fall, like a movie playing in an endless loop. That morning, after a fitful hour or two of sleep, she awoke thinking George was in bed with her. Except there was no George anymore. Brilliant, sweet George. God, how she missed him.

Rachel had gone through her morning rounds on autopilot, until she came to little Wendy Montero. For the first time since the girl was three, no more seizures racked her body. With all her heart, she wished George could have been there to receive Wendy's hugs. They had partnered in the operation. The child's mother actually kissed her hands when she entered the girl's room. The joy that act of gratitude gave her was indescribable. Little did the family know, it had taken every ounce of strength she possessed to get dressed that morning, put on a little makeup, and find her way to the hospital. Rachel continued to go through the motions praying that some sense of normalcy would find her. The routine was familiar, and ultimately satisfying, but it would have been far easier to remain in the dark with an arm across her eyes.

*

A lone female officer stationed at the garage entrance was checking cars as they came in. Two others were on duty at the building's front and rear entrances. The officer was a heavy-set black woman. The nameplate on her chest read "C. Chambers." Beth exited the car and identified herself.

"We don't have enough people," Chambers said. "In addition to this door and the rear entrance, there's a bridge that connects the building to the hospital. Anybody and his brother can get in. The building manager told me they have deliveries coming all day in addition to the regular mail. Ain't no way you can secure this place without shutting it down."

Jack took a couple of steps back onto the sidewalk and examined the red granite structure. He was inclined to agree. After thirty seconds, he concluded the building was indefensible. When he was through, he turned and studied the office buildings on either side, as well as those across the street. This was a nightmare waiting to happen. They were on Peachtree Street just south of Tower Place, a popular Atlanta business complex. Traffic was congested, though moving freely.

Beth gave voice to his thoughts. "We have to get them out of here."

He inquired where the medical office was.

"Detective Stafford's with them up on eight. When you speak to Dr. Lawrence, tell her I was real sorry to hear about her husband. What a thing to happen."

"It wasn't an accident," Beth said.

"Say again?"

"Someone set off two explosives: one at the bottom of the mountain and one that took out the cable."

"Jesus," Chambers said. "Why? They're doctors. They help people."

"We're not sure ourselves at this point. Would you call Stafford and let him know we're on the way up?"

"Sure thing," Chambers said, reaching for the hand mic on her shoulder. "Anything special I need to know?"

"Just stay alert. Anyone coming in here better have a good reason. I wish I could give you a description of the man we're after, but we don't know what he looks like. I can tell you this; he is an assassin and a cop killer."

*

"Well, well, what do we have here?" Wesley whispered to himself. "Not one, but two plainclothes detectives briefing the cop."

He studied the pair for several seconds through his scope. The man was tall and solidly built. Possibly an athlete of some sort. Pleasant face. Good features. Not particularly handsome. The brunette was also tall and quite pretty. No, wrong word. Beautiful was more accurate. Something about her face sparked a long buried memory, but he pushed it away. From the conversation with the cop, it was hard to tell which of them was in charge. That might be important. Kill the head, the body dies. The details are what got you. The woman was wearing a black blazer over a blue blouse and a pair of tight jeans with high heels. Fashion conscious, but those heels would make running difficult.

Wesley's thoughts came in like strobe bursts. Call the Mentor and let him know? Handle the situation himself? More information was needed. Superior knowledge and planning were everything.

He scratched the back of his hand and shifted his attention to the man's eyes. The scope's optics were clear enough to see they were hazel, alert, and moving methodically across the building he was in. Sensing the intelligence behind them, he inched backward deeper into the shadows.

Yesterday, the cops had shown up unexpectedly. Of course, discovery was always a possibility, and he planned for it. He wondered if this man could be the reason. If so, having him for an opponent would mean having to raise his game. Not a bad thing, because certain people helped define him.

Wesley's fingers trailed across the rifle's stock. Take him out now, or wait and see what develops? A shiver coursed through his body. No one had mounted a serious challenge for him in a long time. Shooting fish in a barrel was no fun. None at all.

Cops or FBI? Didn't matter. Still, their presence might explain why the witnesses hadn't come to the window yet. You plan not for what your enemy can do, but for what he was capable of.

Did the man's eyes just stop at his window?

Not possible. He had to block out his thoughts. Slow his heart rate. Concentrate on the task at hand.

Tap. Tap. That's all it would take.

Sooner or later, the witnesses would leave the building or come to the window. Either way, they were his. Wednesday was only five days away. Then Brazil. Copacabana Beach, Ipanema, the falls at Iguassu, and so many other things he'd read about. He couldn't remember if the seasons were reversed there. Definitely have to check that out.

*

They found Rachel Lawrence in her office reviewing a patient's chart. Dr. Will Landry was across the hall in an examining room evaluating a ten-year-old boy with a web hand. There was still no sign of the U.S. Marshals Todd Milner had promised. After his conversation with Beth, Dwayne Stafford appeared somewhat sheepish. He introduced Jack and Beth to Rachel.

"Dr. Lawrence, I'm Jack Kale and this is Elizabeth Sturgis with the Atlanta Police. Please accept our condolences on your loss. I understand you asked to see me. How can I help you?"

Rachel's first question was if they had any leads in the case yet.

He was about to respond, but stopped when Will Landry came in. She introduced them.

"We're confident what happened at Stone Mountain had something to do with the meeting you observed several weeks ago," Jack said.

"All George, Rachel, and I saw was one man passing another a briefcase," Will Landry said. "We didn't even know who they were."

"But you identified Sergei Borov," Jack said.

"After the prosecutor showed us his picture," Landry said. "Why hasn't anyone spoken with him?"

"I don't know," Jack said. "Detective Pappas mentioned it to me last night. That will happen, I assure you. To be honest, I don't think the odds are good Borov will break down and confess. Our job is to keep you both safe and catch the man who planted those bombs."

"And after that we're on our own?" Rachel said.

Jack smiled. "It's not quite so venial. What I meant to say was, we intend to take the killer out of the picture, permanently. I promise the government won't use you and throw you to the wolves."

"Your faith is encouraging," Rachel said.

Jack raised his eyebrows. It was something he did when he didn't know what to say. Beth took up the slack.

"Given the circumstances, we thought you might be at home for the next few days."

"Ordinarily, I would," Rachel said. "Right now I have kids who need my attention. So does Will. I also have a husband to bury. I don't have the luxury of hiding out and forgetting about them."

"You understand your being here creates all kinds of problems. We evaluated the building on our way in and it can't be defended. Not only are you at risk, so is your staff and those children you care about. Believe me when I say this killer will stop at nothing to achieve his goal, which unfortunately means killing you both."

Rachel started to reply, but Beth held her hand up and cut her off.

"Hear me out. You don't know this, but there was an aborted attempt on your life yesterday. It resulted in the death of a priest across the street from where you live. I need you to understand, this is not a joke. It's something you both need to take seriously."

"Who was it?"

"Father David Beckley."

Rachel's mouth opened in shock. She and Will exchanged glances. Several seconds passed as they processed the information. As much as Beth hated giving out this sort of news, it was necessary to get their attention.

Rachel finally said, "I know David Beckley. I can't speak for Will, but I can't put my life on hold. I have rounds to do and children who require careful follow-up."

"Actually, she did speak for me," Will Landry said. "I'm needed here now more than ever."

*

Jack listened to the exchange and considered the woman in front of him. It was clear that whatever decision was to be made or whatever compromise they reached would come from her. She was casually dressed in navy-blue slacks and a white cashmere sweater that she wore under her lab coat. There was a class and determination about her that he liked. What stood out was a force of personality that was almost palpable. When Rachel concluded what she had to say, her jaw became set and determined. She folded her arms across her chest as though she was protecting herself from further hurt. She had already suffered an unspeakable loss and was clinging to her profession and the needs of her patients just as a drowning man might cling to a piece of wood. Jack understood that. In the parlance of psychologists, it was called deflection. He had no desire to add to her burden, so he decided to try a different approach.

"Your presence here also places Dr. Landry at risk. To be perfectly blunt, you're both in a great deal of danger."

"Forget it," Will said. "I'm not leaving."

Jack looked from one to the other. Will Landry placed his arm protectively around Rachel's shoulders.

"Would you be willing to use a safe house for the next few days as a compromise?"

Rachel started to respond, but he continued before she could do so.

"Think about this before you answer, and when you do, you'll both need to agree. If you don't, I'll be forced to make some hard decisions I'd rather not have to."

They were intelligent people and understood what he was saying. Protective custody could be forced on them if they didn't cooperate.

"That might work," Rachel said slowly. "Will?"

"I guess I could do that," Will said.

"We'll have an officer with you at all times and you'll have to follow their directions. This isn't a situation any of us can take lightly."

Rachel informed him, "I'll do it provided I can still come to the office and make my rounds. If a surgery is necessary, Stu Patterson can cover for us, unless it's a problem he can't handle. If that happens, I guess we'll deal with it at the time."

"Good," Jack said. "If everyone works together, we'll come through this all right."

Rachel's laugh was rueful, "I said the same thing to our staff just before you arrived."

"Have you noticed anything out of the ordinary this morning?" Beth asked.

"Like what?"

"People showing up you don't know, phone calls, odd packages being delivered, anything."

"We know all our patients," Landry said. "Every one of them has to check in with the secretary. The only person who's been here today who's not a patient was a fire marshal to inspect the wiring."

"A fire marshal?" Beth said.

"We're expanding to next door. The group who was there moved out and we took over their lease. We have all kinds of wiring that needs to be done first before we can move in."

"I assume there were no problems," Jack said.

Landry shook his head. "Nothing he mentioned. The man only stayed a few minutes. He didn't even look at the junction box."

Beth turned to Dwayne Stafford and asked, "Is that right?"

"I was here the entire time," Stafford said. "He just looked around and left."

Dwayne Stafford was a tall gangly young man with sandy brown hair who generally worked with Ed Mundas, another detective with Robbery-Homicide. Together they made up the team of Frick and Frack, as the cops had dubbed them. Both were solid officers and relentless at tracking down witnesses and leads.

"You check his ID?" Beth asked.

"The guy was in uniform, Beth."

"A priest was in uniform yesterday," Jack said.

He and Beth exchanged another glance.

"I'll call Fire to confirm it," Beth said. She turned back to Stafford and said, "Show me where he looked."

Chapter 10

While Jack was speaking with the witnesses, Beth reached the fire department and asked for the watch commander. He wasn't in, so she left a message. After retrieving her evidence kit from the cruiser, she began a systematic search of the area where the fire marshal had been. It was possible she was wasting her time, but better safe than sorry. It took the better part of an hour to collect a variety of samples. These included two black threads, which were promising because they might have come from one of Father Beckley's suits. She also recovered several grains of a reddish substance with the coarseness of sand. She had no idea what they were or if they would be significant. Jack was better at that stuff and had an uncanny way of linking isolated bits of what seemed to be useless items into evidence.

They had yet to hear from Milner or the U.S. Marshals, which meant Dwayne Stafford needed to remain on the job until relieved. He was agreeable though obviously bored. Early that morning, Jack had gone part way through the Sandman files and the more he read about the killer, the worse it got. He decided there was no alternative other than to provide the doctors round-the-clock protection. He placed a call to Captain Koster who confirmed two uniform officers would be there in thirty minutes. The Atlanta PD seemed happy to help as long as the investigation remained under one roof—theirs.

They said good-bye to everyone and left to meet Dan Pappas. Beth's secretary had relayed a message saying he wanted to get together for lunch at Linden's, a cop hangout at the Peachtree Battle Center a short distance from where they were.

*

Linden's was essentially a glorified diner that had been at the same location for sixty years. Jack had been there once or twice and liked the place. They took a table near the back. As far as he could see, the menu hadn't changed, nor had the décor, which was something out of the fifties. He wouldn't have been surprised to see Frankie Avalon walk in singing "Beauty School Dropout." The booths were large enough to seat six people and the tables were Formica. The seats and their backs were vinyl. Each one had a paper napkin dispenser and a small jukebox where you could select what song you wanted to hear by flipping through some pages on the inside. There were a lot of Frank Sinatra and Elvis selections. The most recent rock groups appeared to be either the Beatles, the Rolling Stones, the Monkees, or the Dave Clark Five.

The Monkees? SerÑusly? Jack shook his head.

A low whistle from Beth caused him to look up. Dan Pappas had just entered the restaurant with Janet Newton and a man he didn't know.

"This place is great," the deputy director said, sliding into the booth next to Jack. "I've never been here before."

Dan Pappas got in next to Beth and introduced Carmine Donofrio with the U.S. Attorney's office. Donofrio was dressed in a business suit and had prematurely white hair. It looked like he went to a good stylist. Jack guessed he was about forty.

Donofrio said, "I'm glad we could get together, Kale. I've heard some good things about you from Director Newton."

"It's Dr. Kale," Beth said.

"Excuse me?" the attorney said.

"I'm here because my office needs to be kept in the loop about any developments. We've invested a lot of time putting together a case against Sergei Borov. I'll be leading the prosecution team."

"Shouldn't be a problem," Jack said.

"So, what can you tell me?"

"Not much at the moment. We're fairly sure there was an aborted attempt on the witnesses yesterday. Unfortunately, it resulted in the death of a priest. That would seem to confirm the Sandman's already in town. Detective Sturgis and Al Komanski, an FBI technician, each collected evidence samples at the scene that have been turned over to Atlanta's Crime Lab for analysis."

"That's it?"

"Considering we got the case less than twenty-four hours ago, yes. Since then we interviewed the witnesses and determined they can be better protected in a safe house. Actually, we just came from their office. They were agreeable, provided they can continue with their hospital rounds."

"I'm not sure I like that," Donofrio said. "I was considering placing them in federal protective custody."

"I already made the deal with them," Jack said. "Let's see how it works out."

"Your deals don't bind the U.S. Attorney's office, Dr. Kale."

Janet Newton placed a hand on Donofrio's arm and said, "If Jack made an agreement with them, he has the support of our office."

"They have sick kids to attend to," Jack added.

"There are plenty of doctors in Atlanta," Donofrio said.

"I gave my word, Mr. Donofrio," Jack said quietly.

The attorney let out a breath and said, "Maybe you don't understand what's at stake here. Sergei Borov is priority one."

Jack said, "My impression was keeping Rachel Lawrence and Will Landry alive was priority one."

"You know what I mean."

Jack didn't reply.

Donofrio's finger beat a rhythm on the tabletop for several seconds. He took a sip of the iced tea the waitress had brought, maintaining eye contact with Jack over the rim of his glass. Jack returned the look and waited. He'd met people of Donofrio's type before and as a rule didn't care for them. His father, an air force colonel, had been that way. "All right," Donofrio said. "I'm outvoted. I'll go along with your plan . . . for now. Janet thinks a great deal of your abilities." He took a business card out of his wallet and slid it across the table. "My home number is at the bottom along with my private e-mail. I want daily progress reports."

"You'll be updated as the matter evolves."

Everybody has an agenda, Jack decided. Janet wanted the killer stopped. The attorney wanted to make his case. Borov probably wanted to continue selling his chemicals, arms, and electronics to whoever was interested in buying them. And the Sandman wanted two witnesses dead.

Donofrio's attention was momentarily distracted by a waitress walking by in a short skirt. He tracked her progress for a moment, then asked Jack what his next move was.

"Detective Sturgis collected some samples at Rachel Lawrence's office that we'll be taking a look at later. We're also waiting for a call from the fire department."

"I don't follow."

"Double checking. Apparently one of their people came out earlier to inspect the wiring. Given what happened at the church yesterday, we just want to make sure it was legitimate. Then I need to finish reviewing the Sandman files. Everything was pretty hectic yesterday."

"I can be of some help there," Janet said. "We received more information from German police this morning."

"Do that when I leave," Donofrio said. "What about this evidence you found?"

"Well . . . we're not sure it is evidence yet," Jack said.

"You're confusing me, Dr. Kale."

"It all depends on whether a real fire marshal was there or not. Hopefully one was. The general rule is at the beginning of a case you gather a lot of data and samples. Usually you don't know what will fit and what won't until somewhere down the road. Examining everything takes time, but I don't think we can be too cautious here."

Donofrio still didn't get what Jack was talking about and turned to Beth for clarification. Jack noticed his eyes had strayed to the top button of her blouse, which was undone. Clearly, the man was a pig.

Beth informed him, "Assuming we're not jumping at shadows, most of what I found are what we call trace items. There was also a shoeprint, which we might be able to match against the one I found at the church yesterday, along with a couple of threads that could have come from the priest's clothing. What I'm interested in are some red grains I picked up. According to Ben Furman—that's the crime lab technician who worked the Stone Mountain scene—similar grains were taken into evidence from the tram's control room on the loading dock. I saw them at the church, and again at Dr. Lawrence's office. That makes three times. No way it can be an accident."

Donofrio nodded.

Beth continued. "I agree with Jack. It's way too early to reach any conclusions." She added for Janet Newton's benefit, "We'll be sending them to your people for further analysis. If the fire marshal really was the Sandman, those grains might give us some clue as to where he's hiding. By the way, any idea where Todd Milner is? We haven't seen him today."

"I'll check," the deputy director said, taking out her phone. Her thumbs moved rapidly over the keypad as she sent him a message.

"I suppose what I'm really asking," Donofrio said, "is whether you have a plan for nailing this bastard. It's obvious traditional methods haven't worked in the past . . . no offense, Janet."

She glanced up from her typing, gave him a frozen smile, and continued.

"You're correct," Jack said. "This man is extremely smart and apparently quite resourceful. He's been a general pain in the ass to a number of law enforcement agencies for a while now, which makes him unique. I see no reason why that will change. My thinking is if the mountain won't come to Muhammad, Muhammad will have to go to it."

"A trap?" Donofrio asked.

"At this point, it's just a preliminary thought. We know what his goal is, and we know he's operating under a short time frame because the grand jury is scheduled to meet soon. I believe this gives us an advantage. What we don't know is *how* he'll strike. Fortunately we can control where, and possibly lure him out into the open."

Beth glanced at Janet Newton, who was listening to the exchange, sat back in her seat with a satisfied smile. Beth was used to Jack developing strategy on the fly. Pappas had once compared him to a fighter coming off the ropes. It was mystifying and occasionally satisfying to observe, but at the moment it annoyed her though she wasn't sure why.

"I like it," Donofrio said.

Janet Newton told them, "I just texted Todd. He should get back to me quickly."

"Ask him about the marshals he was supposed to have at the docs' offices," Pappas said.

"I will."

Jack had placed his phone on the table when he sat down. He glanced at it and returned his attention to the U.S. Attorney.

"All right," Donofrio said, pushing himself away from the table. "I'll leave you people to your work and look forward to reading those reports."

They watched him walk out. Dan Pappas also slid out of the booth saying he needed to order lunch for Dwayne Stafford. Jack checked his phone once again, then excused himself to use the restroom.

Chapter 11

When they were alone, Janet asked how Jack was. Beth wasn't sure if there was more than one meaning behind her question or how much she knew about his panic attacks, so she chose a neutral answer.

"Fine," Beth said. "He's brilliant. If anyone can catch this Sandman, it's him."

"Did you enjoy working with him a few months ago?"

"I did. You have to stay on your toes," Beth said. "He tends to jump from one thing to another, but there's usually a reason for it because his mind works so quickly."

"I remember," Janet said with a wry smile. "I understand he's divorced now."

"That's right."

"And if I recall correctly, he had a young daughter. Did she stay with him or go with her mother?"

"They're living in California now. Jack flies out to see her on holidays and she came to visit for a few weeks last summer."

Janet Newton was quiet for a moment. "When he and I were speaking earlier, he mentioned having a problem with taking too much medication. I guess that's what I was referring to when I asked how he was doing."

"He seems to be okay," Beth said.

"Would that be something you'd know?"

"I think so."

The deputy director nodded to herself and turned her glass first one way and then the other, eventually centering it on a paper coaster.

"A lot of people were surprised when Jack resigned from the Bureau. I don't know if you know, but they actually made a TV movie about him. Changed the names, of course. He was considered a rising star . . . a big one. Then out of the blue, there was an incident. I can't get into the details. What I need to know is if he'll be able to see this case through to the end."

"I'm sure he will," Beth said. She was becoming increasingly uncomfortable with the direction the conversation was taking. "Maybe you should speak with him."

"I have," Janet said. "He says he's fine. I hope that's true because there's a lot riding on this case. Between you and me, I think Jack is wasting his time teaching. It's like he's been hiding out from the world. I offered him a chance to come back to the Bureau. We're in desperate need for people with his talents. To say the least, they're prodigious. Your boss, Noah Ritson, feels the same way. Of course, Ritson wants him with the APD, which would be a mistake. In the long run, we can do a lot more for him. How do you see it?"

This wasn't something Beth wanted to talk about. If Jack went with the FBI, they could literally ship him anywhere. Discussing private matters went against her grain. She'd seen his panic attacks first hand. They were frightening and scared the hell out of her. She also knew about Connie Belasco because Jack had told her. The first time she'd witnessed one of his attacks, she thought he was dying. The decision he'd been faced with was unbelievable. Psychologists might not be able to pinpoint the source scientifically, but to her it seemed fairly obvious. More puzzling was why they hadn't gone away. Diminished, yes, but they were still there. She was torn between wanting what was best for him, even if that meant rejoining the FBI and going wherever they sent him, and wanting to build a life together as a couple. Was it wrong to want a life with the man you loved? She'd been raised to believe partners supported each other and helped the other grow.

On the ride to the restaurant, Jack had told her Janet usually found a way to get what she wanted. Looking at the deputy director, a shiver went up her spine because of the carrot she was holding out. It had the potential to turn their lives upside down.

"I really don't have an opinion," Beth said. "Jack needs to do what's right for himself and his daughter. I have no experience with your organization, so it's hard to say. To be honest, I was surprised when you mentioned you and Jack had worked together."

"Oh, we go way back," Janet said. "So what's your story? It must be good because he specifically asked for you."

"There's not much to tell. My dad's a cop up in Charlotte and I've been with the department a little over six years."

"Married?"

"Divorced."

Janet nodded as if that was expected. "Things didn't work out?" she asked.

"You could say that," Beth said. "He wanted an open marriage."

The deputy director blinked. "What the hell does that mean?"

"William was a professor at Boston College. He figured sleeping with his students was one of the job perks."

"Sick. I can see why you divorced him. I take it you didn't share that view."

"Not quite. He saw himself alive; I saw him dead."

Janet laughed.

"How about you?" Beth asked.

"My ex was decent enough. But it's tough being married to the Bureau and keeping a relationship going at the same time. So when did you and Jack meet?"

"About eight months ago. I went to him for advice on my partner's recommendation because he was the one who caught Howard Pell. From where we stood, it looked like we had a copycat on our hands."

"I remember reading about that in the papers," Janet said. "I wasn't involved in the original Scarecrow case, but I recall we committed a lot of resources to finding that madman. Of course, it was Jack who put it all together. That was the beginning of his problems. He wound up leaving the Bureau as a result. If he hadn't, he'd probably be deputy director today."

"Was that his last case?" Beth asked.

"Yes."

Janet Newton took a small compact mirror from her purse and examined her makeup for a moment, then reapplied her lipstick. She was an attractive woman with honey-blonde hair that came just to her shoulders and eyes that were more violet than blue.

"So, in your opinion, Jack's in a good place to handle this situation?"

"I think so," Beth said.

"When I say a good place, I mean mentally and emotionally. I know there's nothing wrong with him physically. He hasn't changed much in the last ten years. A little more mature in the face maybe."

Beth frowned at the last remark. The frown deepened when Janet laughed to herself at some private memory.

The deputy director noted Beth's expression and explained. "One of the cases we worked together required us to pose as a married couple. We wound up sharing a room."

One of Beth's eyebrows rose. "Oh?"

"Everything was on the up and up. Jack's very proper in that regard. When I say there's nothing wrong with him physically, it's because I walked in on him coming out of the shower. He blushed like a school boy."

"I see."

Beth wasn't nearly as amused. Her reaction fell somewhere between annoyance and being offended. On the other hand, Janet had no idea she and Jack were lovers or that they lived together. At least she hoped not. That didn't mean she wasn't probing a little. You don't get to be a deputy director of one of the world's elite law enforcement agencies by being a fool. Was there a point behind these comments? Beth's instincts told her yes, which was a problem. If she disclosed her relationship with Jack, that would be all Janet needed to remove her from the case.

Saw him coming out of the shower! What was the penalty for slugging an FBI agent? Beth resolved not to respond. Let her make of that what she would.

Janet surprised her by reaching across the table and covering Beth's hand with her own. "He seems to think a lot of you. Would you consider giving him a gentle nudge in the right direction? I only want what's best for him. I also believe what's best for Jack is also what's best for the Bureau."

"I, uh—"

"We're living in troubled times. There are people out there who hate us. If this turns out well, there's every chance Jack could start handling the type of cases that could make a big difference to our country."

Shit, Beth thought. Shit, shit, shit. Nothing like hitting below the belt. How do you argue against your country, particularly when you know she's right?

"Sure, I'll talk to him, Janet."

The words came tumbling out before she had a chance to stop them. An image of someone rolling a hearse up to the door on their relationship popped into her mind.

To make matters worse, her secretary had let it slip Jack was looking at engagement rings. No one in her damn department could keep their mouth shut. Of course, she was elated to hear it. So much so, she'd surreptitiously been looking at wedding bands in the mall and practicing a surprised expression in the mirror when he finally popped the question. If things went the way the deputy director wanted, they'd probably station him in Abu Dhabi, or worse, Washington, DC, where she lived. Beth felt the color in her face rise.

She glanced up to see Jack coming down the hallway.

"Shush," Janet said. "He's coming back."

The deputy director winked and withdrew her hand.

Wonderful.

Chapter 12

Wesley Simms was still in the office across the street waiting for his chance. A polite knock on his door caused him to look up from the desk he was sitting at.

"It's open, Mr. Schulman. Come on in."

An Atlanta SWAT officer holding an AK-47 assault rifle pushed the door open but didn't enter.

"Oh," Wesley said. "You're not Abe Schulman."

"No, sir. Sorry to interrupt. We're just checking offices."

"For what?" Wesley asked, looking over the top of his glasses.

"Nothing to be alarmed about, Mr. Walker," the cop said, glancing at the name on the door. "A man was shot yesterday and we had a report the shooter might be in this building."

"Are you serious? Who was shot?"

"A priest, unfortunately."

"Holy crap," Wesley said, putting down his pen. "Come in—look around if you want."

"That won't be necessary," the cop said, seeing the rooms were empty. "Just these two offices, right?"

"Right. Just these two. Who the hell kills a priest? That's sick."

"No argument from me, sir. Sorry to disturb you. Have a good day," the officer said and began to close the door.

"You, too."

Wesley shook his head and went back to the notes he was pretending to write. He listened for the sound of the lock clicking shut and kept his face neutral. He was still shaken by the appearance of the police at the building he had chosen. From his window, he watched the cops converge on the entrance from both directions. There was no longer any doubt they knew he was in Atlanta. Their showing up at the church settled that. Of course, he'd prepared himself for the possibility, but it was still annoying. Move—countermove. Sometimes, that's the way these things went.

A few seconds passed and there was still no lock click, which meant the cop was still there. The Mentor whispered in his ear to keep writing.

"Sir," said the cop, opening the door again. "What are those two doors at the back of your office?"

Startled, Wesley looked up. "Cripes, I thought you were gone. What did you say?"

"The doors. Where do they go?"

"One's to a supply closet; the other's to my bathroom."

"I'd better give them a quick look."

Head scanning from side to side, the officer came into the room, alert for any signs of danger. Cautious.

"Not a problem," Wesley said, lapsing momentarily into his Irish accent.

He tossed his pen down and pushed himself away from the desk, nearly stepping on the body of Leland Walker, attorney at law, stuffed into the foot well. He waited until the cop was satisfied.

"Sorry. The fellow we're after is awfully dangerous. We were told to be extra cautious."

"Hey, I appreciate it," Wesley said. "Thanks for coming."

"Fan of Coke?" the cop asked, motioning with his chin to an empty half-liter bottle Wesley was holding.

"Not really."

"What's the bottle for?"

"It makes a cheap but effective silencer."

"Wha . . ."

The killer drew his gun and fixed the bottle over the muzzle so quickly the cop had no time to raise his weapon. One shot was all it took. The young man's head snapped backward, with a startled expression on his face. Wesley dragged his body into the supply closet, picked up the file he'd been looking at, along with a law book, and left the office.

*

Janet Newton was telling Jack and Beth, "In Tel Aviv three years ago, a man slipped into a synagogue during a Saturday prayer service and used an ice pick to kill a retired colonel in the Israeli army when he went to the men's room. One thrust at the base of the skull into the brain. Later that morning when their emergency people responded, a bomb went off, killing six others and injuring twenty more. Among the dead were the colonel's wife and son."

"So he's a terrorist?" Beth asked.

"An opportunist," Janet Newton said. "The bomb had no purpose except to create confusion and give the Sandman a chance to get away."

For the third time, Jack checked his cellphone then asked, "What did forensics say about the bomb's construction?"

"It's in the file," Janet said. "The Mossad looked at the pieces they recovered, but no prints or DNA on anything."

"Which may be significant," Jack said. "His caution indicates his prints or DNA are on file somewhere."

He glanced at the phone again and began tapping his fingers on the table.

*

Wesley examined his reflection in the glass sign by the elevator doors listing businesses and their suite numbers. Still shaken by what happened, he made a deliberate effort to calm himself and smoothed his hair into place. His suit was a blue pinstripe. Just another lawyer heading to court. Under his arm was a thick manila folder bulging with papers and secured at the top with a thin metal clasp. Along with the file was a black book with red lettering on the spine indicating it was Title Nine of the Official Code of Georgia on Civil Practice.

It took some effort to keep the agitation off his face. Warning bells were going off inside his head. This was the second time they'd shown up. Once, luck. But twice . . .

Steady on, son, the Mentor said. Keep looking at that deposition.

I know, Father. It'll be tough getting out of here. They're all over the place.

They're checking offices for a sniper, not people leaving. There's a cafe on the first floor. Let's grab a bite to eat. Have to keep our strength up.

Wesley shook his head and got on the elevator.

In the cafe, he selected a table at the side, put down his file, and calmly went to the refrigerator case and took out a chef salad and a bottle of peach-flavored Snapple. People complained about the price of gas, which was selling at close to $3.50 a gallon. But a gallon of Snapple was going for around $37.00. Crazy.

It took him fifteen minutes to finish eating. During this time, he browsed the deposition. Boring. He finally opened his cellphone and began to speak in a low voice.

Better now? the Mentor asked.

I'm fine.

Anything here we can use, son?

There's always something if you look carefully.

That's my boy. What are the cops doing?

Going in and out of the lobby. If they follow standard procedure, they'll do a personnel check in three to five minutes.

Guess it's time to leave, then.

*

Head down and still pretending to read intently, Wesley nearly collided with a female SWAT officer on his way to the elevator. He apologized and kept moving. Once he reached the underground garage, he pressed a button on the lawyer's car entry fob. It took two tries before a pair of headlights flashed and a polite chirp identified the Audi's location. Very cool. He liked Audis. Those Germans really knew how to make cars. Minutes later, Wesley found himself driving north on Peachtree Road to the address in the file.

*

Janet Newton's briefing continued. "The Sandman's employed a variety of ways to take out his victims. Bombs and a .50-caliber rifle are among his favorite weapons, but he's also used knives and poison. The only commonality we can see is his penchant for disguises."

"I'd like to know more about them," Jack said.

"In Madrid, a member of their Parliament was murdered. Their police checked the street cameras and did a head count of the security personnel on duty at the time. Turned out there was one more head than they bargained for."

"Any physical description?" Beth said.

"A woman."

"You told us we're looking for a man, as in Sandman."

"We are," Janet said. "He may have been working with a partner at the time, which is contrary to what we know about him. All the cameras showed was the back of the phony cop's head."

The deputy director was about to continue when Jack's cellphone buzzed. He held up a hand for her to wait.

"Hi, Ben. What do you have?"

Jack listened to the response, nodding.

"You sure they're street shoes?"

Another pause. Beth and Janet exchanged glances.

"Fine," Jack said. "Did you notify Pappas and Sheeley? Good. We're on our way."

As soon as he disconnected, he informed them, "There's about to be another attempt on the witnesses."

"How do you know?" Beth asked.

"From the evidence you collected," Jack said, getting up.

She and Janet both stood and followed him to the door.

"You were correct about verifying a fire marshal was at Rachel Lawrence's office. A little while ago, I sent the electrostat image of the footprint you found to Ben Furman. He identified the shoe as a Braxton Strider, street model, men's size ten . . . leather sole."

"So?"

"The fire department wears shoes with thick rubber soles and rein-forced steel toes for safety. I told Ben if the electrostat didn't match to call Glen Sheeley and scramble SWAT. They should be at the building now."

Their trip took ten minutes. As Jack predicted, the area was teem-ing with police. The SWAT commander met them in the lobby with more bad news.

"Dispatch reported a man's body was found in a dumpster not far from here. Most of the clothing had been removed along with his identification."

"What about finger prints?" Beth asked.

"Great idea, if the guy had any fingers."

Her mouth opened in shock. Not something you hear every day.

"Whoever killed him took the fingers for a souvenir," Sheeley said.

"It's the Sandman," Jack said. "He was ID-proofing the body. I imagine that will be our fire marshal."

Sheeley made a face. He was a huge man, close to two hundred fifty pounds. From the size of his chest and arms, Sheeley looked as if he could step into the ring at any pro wrestling match. His head was completely shaved. Despite his size, Beth heard he relaxed by building ships in bottles.

"What are your people doing?" Jack asked.

"Going door to door in both buildings across the street like you suggested. We've eliminated everything below the seventh floor because the angle's too steep for a shot."

"What about another bomb?" Janet Newton asked.

"Not enough time," Jack said. "Dwayne Stafford with Robbery-Homicide was there with the witnesses and had the man under observation the whole time except when he went into an empty office next door. Beth double checked it and saw nothing suspicious."

"Maybe we'll get a description," Janet said.

That prospect didn't excite anyone.

The SWAT commander took the hand microphone off his shoulder and called for a com-check, just as Wesley predicted.

One after another, the team members responded, with a lone exception. "McNamara, com check. Report," Sheeley repeated.

He was met by static.

Sheeley turned to the nearest cop and asked what building and floor McNamara had been assigned to.

"That one on the right, boss. Mac and Harry Chu are going from fourteen and working their way down."

"Chu, come in," Sheeley said.

"Chu, here."

"What's your status?"

"I'm finishing twelve now, Captain."

"Where's Mac?"

"He's taking eleven down through eight. So far everything's quiet."

The sergeant Sheeley had just spoken to was also trying to raise McNamara on his walkie-talkie. He shook his head indicating it was a no-go.

Sheeley keyed his mic again. "Mac, what's your twenty?"

"How about getting a GPS location on his cellphone?" Beth asked.

"Great idea."

*

Less than five minutes later four SWAT officers emerged from the eighth floor at opposite ends of the hall. Using triangulation from cell towers, dispatch was quickly able to identify Leland Walker's office as the location of McNamara's cellphone. Jack, Beth, and Janet waited by the elevator until the scene was declared safe. Both Janet and Beth had their weapons out, as did Jack. It was unnecessary because there was enough firepower in that hallway to kill Stone Mountain. If anyone came out of the door showing a gun, their chance of living more than one second was nonexistent.

Harry Chu, another officer, crouched in front of the attorney's door and carefully examined the lock. When Chu flashed the SWAT commander a thumbs up, Sheeley responded by motioning him to try the handle. It was open. With weapons at the ready, Chu and his companions entered the office.

Seconds passed.

Finally Chu called out, "Clear."

Jack let out the breath he'd been holding. Almost immediately that was followed by a curse, prompting Glen Sheeley to draw his weapon and follow them in. After what seemed like an inordinate amount of time, but was probably less than a minute, Harry Chu stepped out and jogged down the hall to where Jack and the others were. His eyes were red-rimmed and it was obvious he was struggling to hold himself together.

"Sir, Commander Sheeley would like you and the ladies to join him."

76

Jack set off down the hallway. He found Glen Sheeley staring at something in the storage closet. The lunch he'd just eaten felt like a rock in Jack's stomach.

Danny McNamara, known to his friends and fellow officers as Mac, was lying on his side staring at the wall.

Whatever they say in the movies and books about cops stoically viewing the bodies of their dead companions is pure bullshit. Unless you're made of granite, the sight hits you like a body blow. Tears were rolling freely down Sheeley's face.

"Kid must have surprised the subject," Sheeley said, his voice thick and hoarse.

Jack nodded slowly and without any conscious thought, he pulled a pair of black elastic gloves out of his pocket and began putting them on. The smell of blood in the room was now apparent. He had the impression of stepping into a nightmare. He'd met McNamara once or twice and liked him. They had even shared a beer together one night when Beth was working late. Mac had told him he was enrolled at Georgia State University studying psychology. He looked at the boy's body and felt his stomach clench. What a waste. What a miserable waste.

"Look at the back of that Coke bottle," Beth said, pointing. "The back's blown open."

"Poor man's silencer," Jack said. "Is this office supposed to be empty?"

Looks were exchanged before Sheeley told one of his men to find the building manager.

*

They were standing in the second of two offices. The first was a waiting area containing modest furnishings and a desk for a secretary. Leland Walker's office was appointed slightly better. Wooden floors, oriental area rug, bookshelves lining one wall, and an old-fashioned roll-top desk. Behind that was a credenza with a computer and a flat screen monitor. Above the credenza was an open window that offered an unobstructed view of Rachel Lawrence's building. Jack noted that all the papers on the credenza had been pushed to one side. Its flat top made a good base to rest a rifle on.

77

Glen Sheeley asked, "Anybody familiar with Walker or know what he looks like?"

"About sixty, gray hair . . . big fellow," Janet Newton said.

Everyone turned to the FBI director, who was staring at the back of the desk, or more precisely, at the foot well.

After moving the desk chair aside, Janet squatted down and checked the body for a pulse. A moment later, she stood, smoothed her skirt and shook her head.

"Everyone out please," Jack said. "Except you, Detective Sturgis."

*

His voice seemed to be coming from a tunnel. A little while ago, Beth had been thinking of marriage and wedding bands. Now she was thinking of Danny McNamara and whoever was under that desk. Just after she transferred to Homicide, Mac had asked her on a date. He'd been so awkward and so much at a loss for words she wanted to hug him.

Jack's touch on her elbow seemed to steady her. She pulled herself together and asked Glen Sheeley to send an officer for her evidence kit. Jack went behind the desk to confirm the body was that of Leland Walker. One by one, he checked the man's pockets and retrieved a wallet and cellphone. After that, he stood and seemed to go inert. The only thing moving were his eyes taking in the room's details. Months later, if asked, he'd be able to describe everything there down to the last paperclip. Several minutes later, satisfied with his inspection, he turned his attention back to the dead attorney. In the meantime, the officer had returned with Beth's evidence kit.

Because rigor mortis had set in, it took some effort to move Leland Walker out from under the desk. While Jack managed that, Beth photographed the entire scene and handed her video camera to one of the SWAT officers, who recorded what she and Jack were doing.

Unlike the attorney, rigor had not set in on McNamara yet. No great insight was required to understand what had happened. The Sandman had come in, killed the lawyer, then surprised McNamara before he had a chance to react. Jack said there was a small chance the killer might still be in the building. Sheeley ordered that the search continue and advised all officers to shoot first and ask questions later.

"This place is a disaster," Beth muttered.

She wasn't referring to the murders, but the number of people who had tromped through the crime scene. Outside the window, the rain-heavy clouds appeared to be moving off to the east as the sky continued to brighten. Inside the room, the atmosphere was maudlin.

*

While Beth worked the front office and gathered samples, Jack examined the attorney more closely. Leland Walker looked disappointed. Not angry, not in pain, just sad, as if he realized in those last moments that his life was being stolen from him.

At the same time, the image of his late partner, Connie Belasco, came into his mind as she lay dying. His pulse began to quicken and his heart started to pound in his chest.

Not now. Please not now.

As it always did, his mouth went dry when those memories emerged from the recesses of his mind. Using the techniques his doctor, Morris Shottner, had shown him, it took nearly a minute to get himself under control. Self-conscious, he spared a covert glance at the officers in the doorway and at Janet in particular to see if anyone had noticed. They were in conversation with each other and no one seemed to be paying him much attention.

He looked again at Leland Walker and another thought came to mind. Despite the mutilation and horrific pain Connie had been in, her expression in the end was not all that dissimilar to the lawyer's. Anger began to replace the pressure in his chest.

"Sooner or later," Morris Shottner had told him, "we all have to give up the dead."

"Not this time," Jack whispered to himself and continued his examination of the victim.

There were no signs of a struggle, which he thought was unusual. The lawyer was a large man. Perhaps not in the best condition, but by no means a lightweight. Most attorneys were combative by nature, so why hadn't he put up a fight?

From the general shape of the wound, he concluded the Sandman had come up behind Walker, pulled his head back, and slashed his throat from right to left, which meant there was a good chance the Sandman was left-handed.

Beth told him she'd found a number of footprints and was making images but needed to obtain comparisons from everybody who had been inside. Jack nodded absently. Little by little, he was beginning to see the room through the killer's eyes. The conclusion that came to him was surprising. Selecting this office was no random act. It was the result of careful planning, which scared him even more than the panic attack.

*

Building manager Samantha Pershing, accompanied by a SWAT team member, arrived carrying a file under her arm. She was a brunette in her midtwenties. Jack made the introductions and asked if anyone had explained the situation to her.

"The officer just told me you were looking for a man and asked me to bring Mr. Walker's file."

He had the unpleasant task of informing her that the attorney and an Atlanta police officer had just been murdered twenty feet from where she was standing. Some of the color left her face and she took a step back as if to distance herself from the room.

Jack continued, "Miss Pershing, I understand what a shock this is, but we need your help. Did you know Mr. Walker well?"

"Only enough to say hello."

"I understand. What sort of security does this building have?"

"All our tenants have keys to the front and rear entrances and their own office. We lock the doors at six PM. The tenants are also issued a card for after hour access. They can use it to enter the garage, as well."

"Which is underground."

"Correct. Is this related to the break-in we had a few weeks ago?"

"I don't know," Jack said. "What happened?"

"Nothing much, really. Several offices along this line were broken into. Whoever did it moved some things around and went through the file cabinets, looking for drugs or maybe money. We reported it to the police. They thought it was probably a drug addict."

Jack filed the information away, unsure if it meant anything, then asked whether the building had security cameras.

"There's one at each entrance and two for the parking decks," Samantha said.

While checking Leland Walker's pockets, Jack had noted there were no car or home keys. He then asked if she knew what kind of car the lawyer drove. The manager consulted her file and told him it was a late model white Audi. She further informed him the only other person authorized to enter the office was his secretary, who was at home ill. Jack thought he already knew the answer, but sent an officer to the garage to check if the Audi was in Leland Walker's assigned parking space.

At one point, he glanced at Janet Newton. She was in the process of sending another text message, he assumed to Milner, who had still not made an appearance. The deputy director had already lost one case agent. From her expression, it wasn't hard to guess what was going through her mind. Like her, he was beginning to worry over Milner.

His thoughts were interrupted by the returning officer, who informed him that Leland Walker's parking space was empty. The Sandman had waltzed right past them and driven off in the lawyer's car.

Chapter 13

Thankfully unaware of what had happened across the street, Rachel Lawrence was in the office of her partner, Stuart Patterson, a talented orthopedic surgeon. He had just handed her a Dr Pepper and told her he had sent Elaine Reynolds, still unable to stop crying, home.

Having a plain-clothes detective roaming the office, even one as pleasant as Dwayne Stafford, only made matters worse. When the staff asked why a police detective was there, typically forthright Rachel told them the truth.

Patterson also learned their nurse, Lucinda Anglin, after leaving for lunch, hadn't returned. They found a note on her desk saying she had resigned. Rats deserting a sinking ship.

With no one to cover for him yesterday, he had worked late into the night seeing not only his patients, but those of George, Rachel, and Will Landry. The sixty-five-year-old felt like he was back in Viet Nam doing triage. Despite the fact that it was the middle of the day, the drapes in Patterson's office were closed, per Detective Stafford's request. It was the same in the other offices. The result was a dark and heavy atmosphere. To the blunt Patterson, a defensive end at Auburn almost forty-five years earlier, it felt like they were hunkered down in a foxhole, which was more or less true. He had known George and Rachel for a long time and had attended their wedding. Looking at his partner now, he could see the signs of strain. Amazing she was there and able to function at all. Definitely a gamer, he decided. A gamer who loved children and who'd fight like a wildcat to protect them, even at the cost of her own life.

Patterson plunked down on the couch next to her.

"How you doin', kiddo?"

Rachel looked at him with a wan smile. "If things got any better, I couldn't stand it."

"How are you doing?" he asked again.

It took several seconds for the tears to form in Rachel's eyes. She hid her face behind her hands. "I'm a mess, Stu. I can't stop crying."

Patterson didn't know what to say, so he gently rubbed her back. "I know."

Rachel lifted her head and frowned. "Why is it so quiet outside?"

Patterson let out a breath and informed her that Lucinda had quit.

"Shit," Rachel said. "We can't continue like this. We'll go out of business."

"No, we won't," Patterson reassured her.

"I'm sorry this ruined your vacation," she said.

"You didn't ruin anything. Las Vegas'll be there next month. I only go to visit my money anyway."

The attempt at humor fell flat. She informed him, "They want to put Will and me in a safehouse."

"That might not be a bad idea."

"I need to be here. You can't continue working sixteen-hour days."

"I can and we'll manage."

"How?"

Patterson didn't have an answer to that. If the cops didn't catch the killer, there was a good chance they'd have to start referring their patients to other doctors. He was willing to tough it out, but it wasn't a good situation. Rather than share these thoughts with her, he said, "I don't know, kid. But we'll work it out." The words didn't sound convincing even to him.

Chapter 14

Wesley liked the way the Audi drove. It was very smooth with responsive steering and neat leather seats. He settled back and continued passing through Brookhaven, formerly an Atlanta suburb but now its own city. He maintained a steady speed at the posted limit. No sense being pulled over. He glanced down at the file, found the number he wanted, and placed a call.

"Hi, this is Nick Harris. Is Miss Quinn at home?"

"This is she. Can I help you?"

"Miss Quinn, I'm Lee Walker's associate. He asked me to touch base with you so we could go over your deposition. I'm lending a hand on the case."

"I didn't know Lee worked with anyone."

"We have a number of cases together. Lee's on trial in Savannah for the next two days."

"I see."

"I was wondering if I might stop by and get your signature on your deposition. It needs to be filed with the clerk's office this week," Wesley said, reading the attorney's note.

"Lee thought the insurance company would settle out of court."

"He's probably right. Unfortunately, with these guys, you have to let them know you're serious."

"Of course."

According to the file, Ms. Quinn was a dental hygienist, thirty-nine years old, and lived alone with her parrot. Charming. Also convenient.

"By any chance," Wesley said, "would you know Jason or Cathy Gibbons?"

"No, why do you ask?"

"I noticed you fell outside Saint Anne's. Jason and Cathy are congregation members there and old friends of mine."

"The names are familiar," Mary Margaret said. "I just switched to St. Anne's after I moved, so I don't know that many people. The ones I've met have been very nice."

"I used to belong there, but I'm at Holy Innocents now," Wesley told her.

Adaptability was the key. Quinn was an Irish-Catholic name. So was the one he had just made up. What better way to put someone at ease than talking to a member of their own congregation?

"My girlfriend Suzanne attends Holy Innocents," Mary Margaret told him.

"Suzanne?"

"Suzanne Beamis. She's about thirty-five with brown hair. Very pretty. She's always asking me to go to services with her."

"Hm, I don't think we've met," Wesley said. "You should definitely come visit us. We're a friendly group."

"Well, maybe I will."

"Listen, I've just finished my last errand. Would it be convenient for me to stop by now?"

"If you give me fifteen minutes to tidy up. The place is a mess."

"Don't go to any trouble, ma'am. Lawyers are tougher than Sunday penance."

Mary Margaret Quinn giggled and disconnected. Pleased with himself, Wesley smiled and continued driving.

*

When he pulled into the driveway of her home, Mary Margaret was waiting in the doorway to greet him. Her ash-blonde hair was tied in the back with a blue ribbon, and she was dressed in jeans and a plaid shirt that looked like it had been washed about two hundred times. There was a smudge of dirt on her cheek. Wesley waved to show what a regular guy he was as he exited the car.

"Come in," Mary Margaret said, shaking hands. "I was cleaning out the garage when you called."

Wesley rolled his eyes. "I promise this won't take long."

The home was tidy and pleasant with early American style furniture. As expected, there was a grandfather clock in the hallway and overstuffed sofas covered with white floral patterns in the den. Photographs of Mary Margaret and her family lined the walls.

Growing up, he'd had pictures in his home too, but he couldn't remember much about them. Every year the memories seemed to fade a little more. He'd only been eight when his parents were killed by a drunk driver. After that, Wesley spent several years in a church-run orphanage with Father Michael. Their motto etched in stone above the entrance read, "With love and the Holy Word, we mentor all God's children."

On the bookshelves was a picture of Jesus, eyes cast upward toward heaven. On the shelf directly above that was a sculpture of a pair of praying hands. As Wesley stared at the hands, memories of Saint Ignatius seeped back into his consciousness.

Over the years, he tried to recall if any of those memories were pleasant or if anything good had come from his stay there. It always ended the same way—he thought about something else. Strange how his mind worked, compressing several years into a few images that pushed their way into his dreams at night or hovered on the edges of his consciousness.

For a while, he had managed to avoid Father Michael and the hands that seemed to linger on his shoulder a beat too long. It was the same with the good-natured pats on the butt boys received at the end of their rugby or soccer games. As their coach, Michael always had an excuse for being in the locker room and around the showers. The priest explained to the new boys that it was his job to make sure nothing dirty happened there.

Wesley was observant and a quick learner. He noticed the looks that passed between the older boys when Father Michael would fix his attention on a newcomer.

Arthur Nilson, a friend whose locker was next to his, whispered one day, "Get dressed quick, mate. The cyclops has his eye on you."

Glancing in the mirror, Wesley saw that Arthur was right. Michael Hardy, with his thick glasses, was watching them from the doorway. Arthur kept his towel around his waist and finished pulling his underwear and pants on. He gave Wesley a meaningful look and hurried out the door.

Did you scrub up good, boy-o?

Yes, Father.

Excellent. Cleanliness is next to godliness.

The priest glanced around to make sure they were alone, then said, Maybe I'd better check.

Five years was a long time to spend in an orphanage. Twice a year when the government sent inspectors from Youth Services, no one complained. At least not often. Father Mike considered gossip malignant and a sign of resistance to the wisdom he was trying to impart. Worse, it was evil. When the priest became agitated, there was a price to pay. He'd appear in the dormitory with a wooden pointer taken from one of the classrooms and tell the offender to follow him. "Spare the rod and spoil the child."

Eventually, Arthur Nilson, a shy, introverted boy, reached his limit and ran away. Two days later, the police brought him back to the home. Concerned about such behavior, the priests decided the young man was simply confused and in need of guidance. To reflect on his sins, they placed Arthur in their quiet room, where he was visited every day by Father Michael.

It came as a shock to everyone there when they found the young man hanging from a pipe in the ceiling. He had tied his sheets together and looped them around his neck.

When Father Donovan, Saint Ignatius's head priest, broke the news of Arthur's death to the boys, he noticed Wesley displayed no reaction at all. Odd, because they were best friends. "Shock. The boy's in shock," he had concluded.

The following night, someone set fire to the rectory, killing Father Donovan and two clergy members. Of fourteen-year-old Wesley Simms, who went by a different name at the time, nothing was ever heard again. Ultimately, a prayer service was held for him, as well.

"Hello," a shrill voice said, pulling Wesley from his thoughts.

Startled, he turned to see who had spoken and found himself looking at a green and yellow parrot, perched on a slender branch in a cage.

"This is Sweetie Pie," Mary Margaret said, introducing them. "He comes from Venezuela."

Marvelous, Wesley thought, *another* 2*legal alien*. He'd forgotten about the parrot.

"Hello, Sweetie Pie," Wesley said.

The parrot responded with a wolf-whistle and began negotiating its way along the branch. When it got to the bars, it cocked its head sideways, looking at him with a black eye like a tiny marble.

"He's very friendly," Mary Margaret said. "If you want a buddy for life, scratch his head. He absolutely loves it."

"Well, I . . ."

"He won't bite," Mary Margaret assured him. "Parrots are very intelligent."

What the hell does intelligence have to do with biting?

The thought of coming into contact with whatever germs the bird was carrying made his stomach churn. Nevertheless, he stuck his fingers through the bars. Sweetie Pie obligingly lowered his head and exposed the back of his neck. He was surprised at how little substance there was. Just feather stalks and paper thin skin. He desperately wanted to wash his hands.

"Pretty bird," Sweetie Pie said when he was finished.

Mary Margaret beamed like a proud parent. Wesley felt like throwing up. He managed to force a smile to his face and said, "Quite a talker, isn't he?"

"A regular chatterbox. If I don't cover his cage, he'll keep me up all night. May I get you something to drink, Mr. Harris?"

"Call me Nick. I'm fine," Wesley said. "Thank you anyway." Instinctively, he glanced around the room, taking an inventory of its contents. When he was finished, he turned his attention to the outside. A sliding glass door led to a patio with a small round wooden table and four chairs. In one corner was a black-and-tan lounge chair with thick cushions. At the opposite end of Mary Margaret's little patio was a barbecue grill. The backyard was enclosed with a six-foot-tall pine fence stained to make it look like redwood.

Good privacy. No direct view of the house.

"Aren't you forgetting something?"

Wesley stared at her.

"The deposition?" she prompted.

"Oh, yes. Sorry."

"Did you leave it in the car?"

"Actually, no."

Chapter 15

Rachel Lawrence was at home on the telephone with a radiologist from Scottish Rite Children's Hospital going through a report he had just e-mailed her. The MRI on young Richard Steincamp had been positive for a cerebral bleed where Wernicke's area, the part of the brain concerned with the comprehension of language, was located. This was the reason the eight-year-old had become confused and disoriented. Words had suddenly stopped making sense to him. Everything now sounded like a complete mish-mash, or word salad, as one of her colleagues put it.

"Probably why the kid's pitching a fit," the radiologist said. "He's frustrated and can't express what's wrong."

"I agree," Rachel said. "We'll have to release the pressure. Is Tom Bannerman available?"

"He's still in Atlantic City at a conference. I left a message."

"How much has the bleed increased since the last scan?"

"Three to five percent. We have him on blood thinners to see if they'll make a difference."

Rachel glanced at Will Landry, who was listening on speaker. He was a general surgeon and couldn't handle problems in the brain. Stu Patterson was a bone specialist, so he was out.

"Get the boy prepped. I'll be in at seven AM. We can't wait any longer."

The radiologist asked, "Rachel, are you sure you're up to this? I mean, with George and all? We can always fly Ezra Cohen in from

Houston. I spoke with his office a little while ago. He can be here in twenty-four hours."

"That's twelve hours more than I think this kid has," Rachel said. "I'll be fine."

"You're sure?"

She wished people would stop asking that.

"I'd better be," Rachel said.

Once the call ended, Will Landry fixed a gin and tonic and brought it to her. Back on duty again, Dwayne Stafford was in the next room reading a book. He also heard the conversation, but said nothing. By rights, they should have been at the safehouse by now. But Rachel had insisted on stopping at her home to pack a suitcase, which wasn't unreasonable. Unfortunately, the calls started as soon as she walked in. They were followed by faxes and e-mails as the situation with the boy worsened. He considered calling Jack Kale to update him but shelved the idea. As long as they made it there by evening, he figured that would be good enough. After that, he'd accompany her to the hospital in the morning since the operation now appeared inevitable.

Rachel started to take a sip of the drink and put it down. "I think I'll lay off this stuff for a while."

"Good decision," Will said. "What's the word on your sister?"

"She's flying in tonight from San Antonio to help with the funeral arrangements. Right now everything just seems so overwhelming."

"You're doing a great job," Will said.

"Looks can be deceiving," Rachel said. "Did you know our anniversary's next month?"

Will wanted to steer clear of that maudlin subject. He didn't think dwelling on George's death was healthy, but there was no help for it. Will smiled and shook his head in the negative.

"Did I ever tell you how we got engaged?"

Will Landry shook his head again. It didn't make a difference if he was there or not. His instincts told him it was better to let her talk. This was her way of grieving.

Rachel continued, "We'd just graduated college and decided to go to New York to celebrate. Neither of us had any money. For three days, we did every dumb touristy thing you can imagine . . . the Circle

Line around Manhattan, the United Nations tour, museums—I can't remember how many of those we saw—Broadway, even the Forty-Second-Street library. Have you ever been there? It's huge."

Will Landry started to reply, but Rachel went on before he could.

"On the second day, after visiting the Stock Exchange and Chinatown, we just started walking and found ourselves in front of the Empire State Building. George wanted to go up. I thought it was silly, but I gave in.

"When you get to the top, they have an observation deck with binoculars mounted on stands. You can see New Jersey from up there."

"Who'd want to?" Will asked.

"Eventually we got around to talking about our future. I said it seemed a little scary. I mean, suddenly we weren't in school anymore and there was this great big world out there waiting for us. All that craziness you see on TV makes you realize how dangerous it is.

"George brushed the hair off my forehead and told me if I wanted to see our future I should look through the binoculars. He made this big show of positioning it, then stepped away. When I finally looked, something was blocking my view. I pulled my head back to see what it was. George was standing there holding an engagement ring. Like a big idiot, I started crying."

"Sweet story," Will said.

There was a long pause as Rachel took a breath, "It was the best day of my life."

Without another word, she got up and went to her bedroom to finish packing. Will and Dwayne, who was also listening, made eye contact with each other.

"This sucks," the doctor said.

"It does."

*

Jack and Beth were in the crime lab examining the evidence collected at Leland Walker's office. They had spent nearly an hour going over the building's security tapes before Jack spotted a white Audi sedan pulling out of the garage. Beth had spoken to each of the officers who were working there to see if they had noticed anything unusual or suspicious. One by one, they came up empty before stumbling across a female SWAT officer who recalled nearly bumping into a man coming out of the garage earlier. She told them she thought it was a lawyer.

"What gave you that impression?" Beth asked.

"Well, he was dressed like one. You know, the blue pinstripe suit and all. On top of that, he was reading a deposition and carrying a big file under one arm, along with a law book. I figured he was on his way to court."

"Do you recall what time that was?" Jack asked.

"About a quarter to one."

"Pretty close to when that Audi left the garage," Beth commented.

"What hand was he carrying the file in?" Jack asked.

The officer thought for a moment, then said, "His right one."

"And the deposition was in his left?"

"Correct."

Jack nodded. "What about a physical description?"

"A little shorter than you. Gray hair, glasses . . . black frames, medium build, and clean shaven. Was that the guy we're looking for?"

"Probably," Jack said. He turned to Beth. "Can you get a BOLO out on that car?"

"Done," Beth said. "I'm also having the street cameras checked to see if we can track him."

"That's why I love this woman," he said.

Beth's mouth opened slightly. Now that he was with the FBI, apparently Jack decided their relationship didn't need to be a secret any longer. She looked at the officer to see if there was any reaction from her. Other than a wink on the way out, there wasn't one.

Take that, Janet Newton, she said to herself.

"They're a match," Ben Furman said, pulling Beth from her thoughts.

"What is?" Jack asked.

"Those threads match the priest's suit. It's definitely our man."

"Anything else?"

"More of those reddish particles," Furman said, checking his microscope again. "My guess is they're terra-cotta with some marble dust mixed in."

"That's an odd combination," Beth said. "Where would you find them together?"

Furman shrugged. "A stone and tile place, or maybe a home improvement center."

Beth turned to Jack for his opinion. He might have been following the conversation, but it was hard to tell. He was staring out the window, not at anything in particular. Just staring, deep in thought, posture straight in his chair. The expression was one she knew well. His mind was someplace else. Ben Furman also noticed and rolled his eyes. A moment later, Jack emerged from wherever he had gone and said, "I want to know more about the file he was carrying."

"Why?" Furman asked.

"Because I think it might be significant."

"I'm not following," Beth said. "He probably grabbed a random one out of Walker's cabinet for looks."

"Possibly. But everything we know about this man indicates he leaves very little to chance. I suspect that includes a bailout plan. Do you recall the manager telling us there was a break-in several weeks ago? Nothing appeared to have been taken, but the file cabinets were rifled."

"Jack, if a file was taken he probably ditched it in the first trash can he came to. It was just a prop."

"Maybe you're right. Let's call some uniforms and have them check the receptacles in the parking deck. I'd be interested to know if he took it with him."

"He could just have easily have dumped it someplace else," Ben Furman said. "I agree with Beth. I think it's a waste of time."

Jack nodded slowly. "We're in agreement that he was using the deposition for appearances, which the SWAT officer said was in his left hand. The wound on Walker's throat indicates the murderer was left hand dominant. Let's think for a moment. We're dealing with a stone-cold killer. If there was trouble, he'd want that hand free to go for a weapon. But it wasn't. So why carry three props: a deposition, a file, and a law book? That's overkill. No, something about that file was important enough to take with him. Like the office selection, I don't think it was random at all. In fact, I'm willing to bet the earlier break-in was a reconnoitering session. He also came to the building wearing a blue pinstripe suit, which means he planned the hit well in advance."

Beth stared at him for a moment, then said, "Damn."

"Exactly," Jack said. "It's just a shot, but sometimes these things pay off. Do you still have the information sheet Samantha Pershing copied for you?"

"Right here."

"Let's see if we can track down Mr. Walker's secretary. Maybe she can tell us which file the Sandman took."

Beth stared at him for a second.

"Did I leave something out?" Jack said.

"No . . . it's just sometimes you scare me."

Before Beth could say anything further, the lab door opened and Janet Newton came in followed by Todd Milner.

"Glad to see you're in one piece," Jack said. "We were getting worried."

"Sorry," Milner said. "I was tied up. The cops in New York found Gabe Alonso floating in the East River. They needed his dental records to confirm identification."

"Was he supposed to be in New York?" Jack asked.

"Yeah. He flew up to interview the senator and look over the aide's computer. I was hoping they might give us a line on the killer. Just another dead end in this damn case."

"I'm sorry, Todd. Was the MO the same as the fire marshal?"

Milner's mouth tightened and he nodded. It was clear he was upset. "I had to break the news to Maria."

"I'm really sorry," he said again.

Beth and Furman echoed the sentiments.

"Bring me up to speed, would you?" Milner asked.

Jack spent a few minutes doing so. Milner and the FBI director listened without comment. At one point while Jack was explaining his conclusions, Janet smiled and a look passed between them. Beth didn't know what that signified, which only served to resurrect her earlier annoyance. It was like being at a party where people were telling inside jokes.

If it's so damn good, let the rest of us in on it.

"Lot of speculation here," Milner commented.

"That's basically what you do in the absence of hard evidence or clues," Jack said.

"All right, let's say I buy your theory," Milner said. "How do we find what's in the mystery file if the attorney's dead?"

"His secretary's not," Beth pointed out.

"You have her name and contact information?"

"Right here."

"Let me handle that," Milner said. "I haven't been much help so far. If there's a cell number listed for her, we can track her down."

"Great idea," Jack said.

Beth got up and went to the copy machine. When she returned, she saw Janet put her hand on Jack's shoulder and lean forward. She whispered something in his ear. They both laughed. Beth practically tossed the file at Milner, then stalked out of the office, saying she'd see them later.

Jack watched her go, wondering what was wrong with her today.

Chapter 16

Todd Milner looked through the file, found what he wanted, and left, taking the deputy director with him. Jack and Ben returned to analyzing the evidence. Approximately twenty minutes passed before the door opened and an Atlanta cop stuck his head in, "Is there a Professor Kale here?"

Jack raised his hand. "That's me."

"My sergeant said to tell you the Boy Scouts were a good idea." The cop held up two large paper bags.

"The bomb parts!" Jack said.

"Jeremy Sparks and Geoff Lewis from Troop 1322 found these about an hour ago."

"Where?"

"Scattered all over the base of the mountain. The kids have been working like demons out there."

"I love it. Did the boys touch anything?"

"Not that I know of. As soon as they located a piece, they called Sergeant Hicks. We took photographs then used gloves to bag everything."

"Excellent," Jack said. "Let's see what you brought us."

The cop was a compact black man with a shaved head who looked to be somewhere in his early forties. A tag on his chest indicated his name was, "L. Dixon."

"What's the 'L' stand for?" Jack asked.

"LaDante."

Jack's eyebrows lifted. "Is that what they call you?"

"Not to my face. I go by LD."

"I'm Jack, LD. This is Ben Furman who runs the place. Grab a seat."

The cop nodded a greeting and pulled a stool up to the long table where they were working. Ben Furman removed the contents and divided them onto two metal trays.

"Amazing these things survived," LD said.

"Not really," Jack said. "Everyone believes when a bomb goes off it destroys itself. Usually that's not the case. Often, more than ninety percent of it survives, but pieces are scattered in a million directions and are therefore hard to find." Jack picked up a piece and examined it. "This looks like part of a timing circuit board. Am I correct, Ben?"

Furman was in the process of adjusting the focus on a digital camera. A series of flashes followed. He glanced at what Jack was holding and lifted his thumb in reply. "As soon as I download these images, I'll fire off a priority request to a tech I know at the FBI's Explosive Reference Collection. They might be able to help."

"How?" LD asked.

Jack said, "Apart from the obvious, like finding a finger print, the way a bomb's constructed can provide a clue as to who its maker is. The rule of thumb is we need about eight matches."

"Good news and bad news," Furman announced. "There are bits of paper here, which leads me to think we're dealing with a military-grade explosive. I'd say C-5 as opposed to C-4."

"Where would the bomber get that?" the cop asked. "It ain't like you can run down to Home Depot and ask for this stuff."

"No, but a fellow like Sergei Borov who sells military weapons might come in handy," Jack said. "Can you tell anything about the circuit board, Ben?"

"The FBI will probably have the manufacturer. Three numbers are visible and a part of the fourth."

"You said good news and bad news. Which was that?"

"The good."

"And the bad?"

"Totally commonplace. It's sold in about a bazillion stores and online."

Jack shook his head. "You technical types really have a language all your own, don't you?"

Furman smiled and said, "One thing I don't see is a shunt."

"What's a shunt?" LD asked.

"An electrical wire that sets the bomb off automatically when it's cut," Furman explained. "There's also no evidence of a mercury switch, which means it wasn't triggered by altitude."

"Meaning it would blow when the tram reached a certain height," the cop said.

"Exactly," Jack said. "That's because there was no need for one. The killer knew they were there."

"How?"

"I'm not sure how, but he knew."

"You're saying he was watching," Furman said.

"Had to be," Jack said. "Think it through. What are the odds the Sandman set two bombs up at Stone Mountain on the off chance the Lawrences might stop by for a visit?"

Furman and Officer Dixon looked at Jack, who raised his eyebrows twice in reply.

Chapter 17

Beth Sturgis had already reached the same conclusion. Early on in the case, it occurred to her that the killer needed advance knowledge to plan for the Lawrences' presence at the park.

Everything had been coming at them so quickly that she hadn't had time to discuss her theory with Jack. As she drove, she wondered if he had told her everything about his relationship with Janet Newton. The woman was clearly attractive and well put together. If you threw in successful and intelligent, it only made matters worse. The directions these thoughts were taking made her uncomfortable. She'd been in relationships where the other party had been less than candid. Cheating was the word. But trust was at the core of what she and Jack had together. Without it, no relationship could survive. She felt guilty for doubting him and angry at herself for being jealous.

It had taken several months to get over being kidnapped and nearly mummified by the killer in the serial case and she was still not completely free of that trauma. Those cold, gray eyes and their last conversation still haunted her dreams. The department shrink helped, but it was mostly Jack who'd been there for her at every turn. Having a shoulder to lean on wasn't a bad thing at all. A year earlier, it would have been her father, a man she admired greatly. Now it was Jack.

After a few minutes, she began to analyze why she was reacting the way she had to Janet. She was not jealous by nature, at least not overly so, and Jack had certainly given her no reason to be now. She conceded that having been married in college to a professor who went after anything in a skirt might be coloring her perception. Being a cop only added to the problem, or maybe it was her basic insecurity. The bottom line was she trusted Jack. But how well could you know a person after only seven months? Since they'd been together, she had learned there were a number of sides to him, sides she hadn't seen before. Not that she was complaining, because most of them were good.

The other day she'd been discussing this very subject with her friend Celeste at their morning workout. They'd met as undergraduates at Boston College and had remained close over the years. Somehow both had wound up in Atlanta. Celeste was now a published author with a number of magazine articles to her credit and a book she was presently working on. She liked Jack and approved of him, but had been openly skeptical of Beth giving up her home to move into his. To her surprise, Jack agreed and suggested she rent hers out—just in case.

For her part, she never harbored any doubts, at least none she was willing to verbalize. Just too stubborn, he had guessed. She was also aware of her impulsive nature but remained convinced the decision had been correct. There would be bumps along the way. Of course there would. That was normal. They'd deal with them as they came up. She wasn't sure if the appearance of Janet Newton on the scene constituted one. Time would tell, and obsessing over it wouldn't do any good. Still . . .

*

The granite monolith rose out of the ground in the distance, growing ever larger as Beth approached. On a clear day, Stone Mountain could be seen from twenty-five miles away. Even the astronauts onboard the International Space Station had reported seeing it on their orbital passes.

As she pulled into the visitors' lot, she caught glimpses of several Boy Scouts and cops searching the trees for more bomb parts. Jack had texted her that the first batch had arrived and they were in the process of analyzing it.

She was grateful there were no reporters or news trucks present. Handling the media was Jack's job, something he did pretty well.

When working with reporters in the past, he was always candid, to the point, and never ducked a tough question. The deputy chief had asked her to do one press release in their last case and she had. But all the time she was talking it felt like she was about to put her foot in her mouth.

Better Jack than me.

This was her second trip to the mountain. The first had been after the explosions, but that was mostly as an observer while Ben Furman worked the scene. After retrieving her evidence kit from the trunk, she proceeded to the passenger-loading platform. An area surrounding the control room had been cordoned off with yellow crime scene tape. Unconsciously, Beth adopted the same folded arms posture Jack did when he studied a scene as she began her observations. Ben was an excellent technician but there was nothing like getting a hands-on feel. Clearly, the control room and the tram were primary sites, but they weren't the only game in town. Now that she had a better idea of the person they were dealing with, there was more she hoped to learn.

She spoke to herself out loud, brainstorming different possibilities. "All right, ingress and egress are obvious. The park only has two gates, so you came in the same way I did. Now where did you watch George and Rachel from? Not the loading platform, because you'd stand out like a sore thumb. And not the Visitors Center, because there's no clear view of the tram. The trees are possible, but you'd have a tough time explaining why you were there if a park ranger happened along. That leaves the summit. With a pair of binoculars, you'd fit right in. Just another tourist out for the day."

She was certain Jack already knew this. But she was here now and he was back at the lab playing with his evidence. Coming in second had never appealed to her. She squinted up at the mountain for several seconds then turned her attention to the control room and ducked under the tape.

According to Furman, the killer had picked the lock to gain entry. When Furman examined it, he noted scratches, machine oil residue, and bits of graphite. The lock, however, was made by a company that advertised their stuff was pickproof. The cops she spoke with in Burglary confirmed that, so something didn't fit.

Beth continued her self-talk, a habit she'd acquired since joining Robbery-Homicide. Jack seemed to think it was funny, but never said so aloud.

"Okay, Sandman, you're good, maybe even brilliant. But are you *that* good?"

Out of curiosity, she walked around the little building. It was nothing more than a concrete box designed to house the computer that controlled the cable car. Ever since the system had been automated years ago, there had been no need for an operator. The blast had irreparably damaged the controls, freezing the car in midair, but otherwise the building was intact. It had one window at the front and one in the back. Thirty yards away, amidst various granite outcrops, the mountain's tree-line began. A foot-wide gravel border ran around three sides of the control room on the mountain side. The fourth was the cement platform.

Nothing looked promising until Beth noticed one of the glass panes had no putty around the edges. Using a fingernail, she carefully touched it and found it was loose.

She returned for her evidence kit and went inside. An area directly under the window had been swept. She concluded the Sandman had used it to enter when he set the first bomb in the control room, then cleaned up after himself to eliminate any evidence. Remembering what he had done at the church and in Tel Aviv, according to what Janet Newton had told them, it also meant the scratches around the lock and the oil residue Ben noticed had been staged.

"Maybe you're not so smart after all," she muttered.

Using a penknife, she carefully pried the glass free and dusted for prints. Two smudges appeared, which had likely been made by a cotton glove. Next, she fixed her attention on the floor and along the wall. She found several fibers and another substance she couldn't identify by looking at it. She was now seeing the room with fresh eyes. After twenty minutes, confident it had revealed all its secrets, Beth went back out to the platform. Her goal was to find the Sandman's vantage point.

With the tram out of commission, the only way to the top would be by foot. She took a breath and started walking. A serpentine path wound in and out of the trees for about a hundred yards and then gave way to bare granite. It was steep, but not overly so. Despite the cool air, she soon found herself sweating. Other women glistened. She sweated.

The mountain's shape was roughly oblong with sides that extended outward. This meant there was no easy way to view the loading platform from up top. If you looked down, all you'd see was rock directly below until you reached the apex where it bulged outward. It took her nearly an hour to make the assent. There she found a restaurant and a few picnic tables. She was the only visitor that day. Beth began scanning the area.

The closest spot with an unobstructed view of the base appeared to be about a hundred feet below her on the mountain's south side. Unfortunately, a four-foot chain link fence stood in the way. On the other side of the fence was a small group of boulders with a cluster of trees growing between them that looked promising. With a growing sense of anticipation, she made her way toward the boulders and wound up sacrificing a good pair of shoes when she climbed the fence. The reason for the fence became obvious after several feet. The slope was now precarious, something she hadn't realized when looking at it from the top. Simply negotiating her way across the rock was a challenge. Countless years of exposure had worn the granite smooth. The farther she went, the worse her footing became. It was like being on the side of a roof. Instinctively, she pressed herself back into the mountain for safety.

She realized her mouth had gone dry and her heart was thumping in her chest. This was an entirely different kind of fear from being confined to enclosed places. It was something she could see and control, and to be honest, it was slightly exhilarating. The boulders were now twenty yards below her.

After reaching them, she began a methodical search. It quickly became obvious someone had been there. Bits of leaves and accumulated debris had been pushed to the side, probably when his shoe slipped on the rock. The patches were barely visible but stood out against the granite. Using a roller from her evidence kit, she picked up more of those reddish particles she'd seen at Rachel Lawrence's office and at the church. Conclusion: the Sandman had visited all three places. Four, if you counted the law office. Now they had to find out where these grains came from. In that regard, Jack was spooky. She'd seen him pull rabbits out of hats enough times to know it was no accident.

But wouldn't it be delicious to beat him at his own game?

Beth bagged the evidence and filled out the chain-of-custody cards. Excited by her discoveries, she placed a call to him.

"Guess what I found?"

"A shoe sale at Nordstrom."

"Watch it, Kale. This is better."

"Hard to imagine," Jack said.

"I'm at Stone Mountain. The Sandman didn't pick the control room lock. He set it up to look that way."

"How so?"

"The graphite, scratches, and machine oil Ben found were staged. He came in through the window, set the first bomb, and then swept up after himself, like he did at the church. I collected two bags of evidence and more of that red dust *outside* the building under the window. One of the glass panes had been removed and replaced. He was clearly covering up. Any luck on where it comes from?"

"I was just discussing that."

"With Ms. Newton?"

Beth rolled her eyes. *I can't believe I just said that.* She shut her eyes and resisted the impulse to bang her head against one of the boulders.

"Janet left a little while ago," Jack said. "I wish we knew more about this man."

"Like his DNA or who he is?"

"That would be helpful."

"Wouldn't it?"

There was a pause before he realized she was waiting for his next question.

"Is there something you'd like to say, Detective?"

"What's it worth to you?"

Jack looked up at the ceiling and shook his head. "Dinner and a massage."

"Deal. I located the Sandman's observation point near the mountain top and collected three more bags of evidence. This is where he set the bomb off from, Jack. No other place makes sense."

"Excellent. But I don't know that that merits—"

"And I found two hairs. Human by the look of them." Beth wished she could see Jack's face.

He took a second to process that, then said, "See you at home. You want the massage before or after dinner?"

"After. The last time you gave me a massage, I got screwed out of the meal—literally."

Jack was still laughing when he disconnected.

*

She was in the process of wrapping up when a rumble of thunder in the distance stopped her. In the west, over Atlanta's skyline, a dark line of clouds had formed. She'd been so absorbed in what she was doing she hadn't noticed the weather changing. The wind had also picked up.

Time to go.

As she stood, something caught her eye. Something she hadn't seen a moment ago. Eight feet below her at the base of the last boulder was what looked like a cigarette butt. At first she thought she might be mistaken and stared at it harder. This was too good to pass up.

Because the slope was particularly steep, she would have to crab walk forward on her rear end to reach it. If she was lucky, really lucky, it might contain DNA. A small chance, but you never knew.

Having moved well out onto the mountain's exposed surface, Beth found herself being buffeted by increasingly stronger wind gusts. Worried, she checked the skyline again.

Not good. An old boyfriend who raced catamarans in New York once explained if a section of the sky is clear and another is hazy, there's a good chance the latter contains rain. She could see the hazy part coming toward her like a curtain.

Damn. Just what I need.

The cigarette butt was still too far to reach. Easing herself down the final few feet, she failed to account for gravity, overbalanced, and picked up speed. Using her legs as a brake, Beth came to a precarious stop just in front of the boulder.

"Gotcha," she said, placing it in another plastic bag. Her efforts were further rewarded by locating two more hairs. Her joy, however, was short lived. The wind was getting worse, whipping her hair sideways across her face.

Any thoughts of filling out another evidence card were quickly abandoned. The only way to reach the base meant climbing back to the top and locating the trail again. Another glance over her shoulder confirmed the rain was definitely coming. And it was coming fast.

Thirty seconds later, the first drops began to fall—not much at first, but enough to wet the rock's surface and make traction extremely difficult. After several exhausting minutes, she had gained perhaps twenty-five feet from the mountain's edge. Beyond that was a sheer drop.

We're in trouble.

The prospect of shuffling back to the group of boulders occurred to her. At least there she'd have a few trees to protect her and could use her cellphone to call for help. Embarrassing, but better than the alternative.

A clap of thunder shattered the heavens, followed by two brilliant flashes of electricity that lit the clouds. Beth flinched. The drops were hitting the rock more quickly now.

"Aw, c'mon," she muttered. "Seriously?"

There was no one to answer as the sky let loose.

Move, move, move.

The trees were almost directly below her. In good conditions, it would have been difficult using two hands, but with one clutching the evidence kit and her precious samples, progress was horrendous.

Just when she thought she might reach safety, her foot slipped. She screamed and began grasping for a handhold. Found nothing but smooth rock. She was sliding and there was no way to stop herself.

The evidence kit went flying, clattering noisily end over end and disappearing over the edge. To Beth's horror, she was following it. In desperation, she tried to dig her heels into the granite. It was no use.

Chapter 18

Out of nowhere, a hand grabbed the back of her jacket. Gasping, Beth twisted around to see who had saved her. She found herself looking into the face of a park ranger.

"Ohmigod, thank you. I was going over the edge."

The man didn't reply. He simply stared at her from behind a pair of dark glasses. All she could make out was his silhouette. His hand maintained its grip. One of his legs was braced in a small fissure in the rock.

"Dangerous up here," he said quietly.

"Thank you again," Beth said. "You saved my life. Would you pull me up, please?"

Again the man didn't respond.

"Pull me up, please."

"You're an interesting woman. May I ask your name?"

What the hell was this? "It's Elizabeth Sturgis. I'm a—"

"Detective with the Atlanta police. Yes, I know that."

A cold trickle of fear began to form in the pit of her stomach. Beth glanced down. She was about ten feet from the mountain's edge, maybe less. After that—oblivion. Her heels were unable to find any purchase.

"I asked you to pull me up."

"I feel like we're old friends, Elizabeth. You and the gentleman with you the other day, the one with the hazel eyes. It was difficult to tell who was in charge. What is his name?"

"Cut the games and pull me up," Beth said.

"May I point out you're in no position to give orders, girl. So I'll ask again. What was the name of the man with you?"

"Who are you?"

"Oh, I think you know that. A shadow in the night. Shakespeare's Puck. A breeze passing by your window. His name, please."

"Go to hell."

"Probably," Wesley said.

He opened his hand and Beth screamed as she began to slide. Before she'd gone a foot, he grabbed her again.

"This is beginning to bore me. I doubt I'll be able to catch you the next time. A name please."

She was hyperventilating. Thoughts of tumbling through the air seized her. Despite the rain, her face had broken out in a cold sweat.

"Oh, well," he said. "I tried."

"Jack Kale!" she screamed. "His name is Jack Kale!"

"A detective like you?"

"He's with the FBI."

"Ah."

"Are you going to pull me up?"

"In good time."

The rain was coming down with some force now. Another clap of thunder boomed, this time over their heads.

"Gets the blood going, doesn't it?" the man said. "You seem like a pleasant person. Unfortunately, I have a job to do, and you and your friend have been getting in the way. That's not a good thing. Not a good thing at all. I have no interest in terminating your life, but if your interference doesn't cease, you'll leave me no choice. Frankly, there's nothing you or Mr. Kale can do to save those people. They're dead already."

Little by little, Beth's hand had been moving toward her gun.

"If your right hand moves another inch, I'll release my grip. Do you really think you're fast enough? I mean it would be like that fellow in *Die Hard* who went out the window. Hans something. Great movie, by the way. He didn't have time to shoot and neither will you. So let's make a deal. I'll do what I have to do, and you and Mr. Kale can continue to live nice, long lives. Yes?"

Beth glared at him as the rain struck her face, plastering the hair against her forehead. She was furious with herself for giving him Jack's name. Furious and ashamed.

She said nothing.

"Well, you didn't say no. I'm feeling generous today. Elizabeth, Elizabeth, let's hope we don't meet again."

She saw his free hand move and felt the Taser charge surge through her body. The last thing she remembered as she lost consciousness was a bolt of lightning exploding directly behind the killer. It outlined his shape, like something from the darkest part of her dreams.

Chapter 19

Later the world began to take form. Beth looked around and found the Sandman had dragged her back to the outcrop, wedging her body between two boulders. There was no sign of him. The rain felt like ice as it ran down her neck and the back of her shirt. Her shoulder was tender from where the Taser shock had hit her. She began to shiver. Going back up was out of the question. Traction had been bad before; it would be impossible now. Thank God her cellphone was still with her. She pulled it out and dialed 9-1-1.

"Officer needs assistance. This is Detective Beth Sturgis. I'm trapped on Stone Mountain about a hundred feet below the restaurant."

There was a good chance the radio operator had never fielded a call like this. Nevertheless, he reacted in a professional manner and told her he was sending Fire and Rescue and would stay on the line with her until they arrived.

It was an hour before two figures appeared out of the gloom. They found Beth huddled in a fetal position, nearly unconscious. A stretcher was lowered on a rope and slowly, gradually, the responding officers pulled her back to the safety fence, where two more of their battalion were waiting.

"No offense, ma'am, but how the hell did you get down there?"

Somewhere along the line, Beth had lost her shoes. Teeth chattering, she said, "Inch by inch. Maybe not the best idea."

The sergeant nodded and introduced himself as Lou Davila. "Let's get you into the restaurant and get some hot coffee in you."

It took thirty minutes before she stopped shivering.

The rescue team was great. They put a couple of blankets around her and never once cracked any jokes at her expense.

"Bet this doesn't happen often," Beth said.

"Couple times a year," the sergeant said from the door.

"You're kidding?"

"Wish I were, ma'am."

"Knock off that ma'am stuff, would you?"

"Sure thing. You up here looking for evidence?"

Beth nodded and took a sip of her coffee. "Did a helluva job, didn't I?"

"Good of you to try though."

Beth debated whether to tell him she'd been rescued by the killer and decided against it. They already thought she was half demented venturing out on the rock under those conditions. Worse, everything she'd collected had gone over the edge along with her kit. At the moment, all she wanted was to go home. What she'd done was unforgivable. The unspeakable act of a coward. She was disgusted with herself. She wouldn't blame Jack if he walked out on her. Then again, it was his house. She'd have to leave. There was no way he could ever look her in the eye, or worse, trust her. Partners didn't betray partners, much less a man one wanted to marry. What a mess. An acid feeling was building in her stomach and it wasn't from the coffee.

"You feeling well enough to get out of here?" Lou asked.

Beth stood, steadied herself, then looked down at her feet. "Think I can make it down barefoot?"

"Hm, maybe we can fix that. What size do you wear?"

"Ten."

Davila seemed surprised.

"I'm a big girl," Beth said.

The fireman smiled and grabbed his walkie-talkie. "Joey, call the station house and have someone pick up a pair of sneakers at Walmart, women's size ten. Socks, too. Send them up top ASAP." He turned back to Beth. "Full service organization."

Beth put her arms around him and hugged him.

*

The ride home was bad. Unable to get her mind off what happened and what she viewed as her own cowardice, she pulled off the road twice to wait until she calmed down. Her breaths had been coming rapidly and she was gripping the wheel so hard her hands hurt. Images of plunging off the mountain kept playing and replaying in her mind. At one point, she could have sworn she saw the Sandman's silhouette standing at the side of the road watching her as she drove by.

"This is nuts."

She thought of calling Dr. Berman, the department shrink, but shelved it. Her face was burning with embarrassment. She should have protected Jack. Instead, she gave him up to the killer. What a wife she'd be. The first sign of danger and she folded like a lawn chair. Contempt for her own weakness continued to grow. Homicide was not the place for her. Better to go back to writing environment citations. Beth pounded the steering wheel in frustration.

*

Calmer by some degree when she finally reached home, she found Jack in the backyard cooking hamburgers and grilling corn on the cob. Nothing fancy, but one of her favorite meals. Marta sat close by supervising as usual.

"Hey," Jack said, kissing her. "I heard you had a rough day."

"Good news sure travels fast."

"Dan called me when the officer needs assistance went out. He was pretty worried."

"I'll call and let him know I'm okay later."

Jack's attention sharpened. He looked at her more closely. Not touching base with your partner after a situation like that was unusual. Almost as unusual as not letting your lover know you were unharmed.

"New shoes?" Jack said, glancing at her feet.

"I lost mine trying to get back up. The Sandman's spot was almost a hundred feet below the summit. I also lost the evidence when I slipped."

"It's all right. Maybe some of it survived the fall. I'll have the uniforms start looking."

Beth nodded. Didn't reply.

Warning bells were starting to go off. He already had a shorthand version of what happened from the Fire and Rescue people. Her lack of communication was not only puzzling; it was uncharacteristic. He waited for her to expand on her comments. Instead, she stared at the backyard absently rubbing Marta behind her ears. He broke off a tiny piece of burger and offered her a sample.

"I'm not hungry right now. Would you mind if I take a bath?"

"Sure, go ahead."

Beth nodded and went into the house.

Jack watched her go and said, "Something's not right."

Marta let out a low whine and leaned into him with her shoulder. He shook his head and turned the grill's flame down.

After an hour passed with no sign of Beth, he was now certain something was very wrong. He went back outside, shut the grill, placed everything on plates, and brought them back inside. In the kitchen, he covered the food with plastic wrap and listened for some sound or movement upstairs. Maybe she'd fallen asleep in the bath. He was about to investigate when his cellphone buzzed.

"Where the hell is she?" Dan Pappas said.

"Upstairs in a bath, I think," Jack said, keeping his voice low.

"You're kidding me. I'm having a freakin' heart attack here."

"I'm serious. She came home a little earlier, didn't want to eat, and went straight for the bath. I haven't heard a peep since."

"Jesus Christ. Now I know something's wrong. When was the last time Beth Sturgis turned down a meal? Is she all right?"

"Apart from a scrape on her forehead there were no injuries I could see, except she lost her shoes."

"Her shoes?"

"She was wearing sneakers when she came in."

Pappas processed this for a moment. "I spoke to a guy named Davila a while ago. He and his partner were the ones who found her. She was curled up in a ball between two boulders. It was raining like hell so it took them a while to get to her."

"Damn," Jack said. "Maybe I'd better go check on her."

114

"You want me to come over?"

"Let me see how she's doing and I'll call you."

After they disconnected, Jack crept quietly up the stairs and into the master bedroom. There was no light under the bathroom door. Beth was lying on her side fast asleep. The time on the digital clock on his nightstand read 7:05.

Chapter 20

Four Days to the Grand Jury

The following morning Jack rose early, fed Marta, and started breakfast. He'd called Dan Pappas back before going to bed and told him what happened. Both thought something was definitely off, but neither knew what to do. They decided maybe a night's rest would put things right. Jack promised to have Beth call him when she woke.

Having passed on dinner he was certain she would be famished now. He had lain awake most of the night thinking she might get up at some point. Generally, they slept in the nude, except when she was cold. Then she appropriated one of his T-shirts. Last night she'd fallen asleep in her bathrobe.

By habit, Beth was usually the first up in their house. She liked getting into the office by eight AM and beating the traffic. It was seven thirty and he hadn't heard her stir. She'd been asleep for twelve hours.

"Want to wake Beth up?" he asked Marta.

The German shepherd's tail began to wag. Having four legs, she easily beat him up the steps and bounded onto their bed. Marta took over his spot and placed her nose inches from Beth's face. When Beth failed to respond, a pink tongue darted out and licked her cheek. Beth pulled the covers over her head.

Jack went around to her side and sat on the edge of the bed, found the back of her neck, and very gently began to run his fingers over her skin.

"Hey, sleepy head, want some breakfast? It's almost seven forty."

"Um," came a voice from under the covers.

"Don't make me come in there," Jack said.

"Honey, leave me alone. I just want to rest."

If she had ever slept for more than six hours, he couldn't remember it. Marta pawed the covers.

"Stop," Beth said.

Marta cocked her head to one side, decided no one wanted to play, and jumped off the bed. Jack sat there not knowing what to do.

"Want me to call and tell them you're running late?"

"I'll do it later."

That seemed to be the end of the conversation. From experience, he knew better than to try to force her to talk.

*

After Jack left the room, Beth picked up the telephone and called her partner.

"Why the hell didn't you call me last night?" Pappas asked. "I've been worried sick."

"I'm sorry, Dan."

"Something the matter, kid?"

"Yeah, I'd say so."

"Wanna talk about it?"

"I've done something terrible."

"Like what?"

The words came out in a rush. Pappas listened and didn't comment. When she was done, there were tears rolling down her face.

"I'm a coward, Dan. Jack's going to hate me."

"Jack won't hate you."

"He will. He'll never trust me again. It's the worst thing I could have done."

Pappas wasn't so sure about that and he didn't see what was so horrible. But everything he said to make her feel better was going in one ear and out the other.

"You want me to come over and talk to him?"

"That'd make me an even bigger coward. I think I should resign from the force."

"Oh, come on. Listen, Jack's an okay guy. Just tell him the truth. He'll understand. And don't make any decisions about turning in your badge. That's just depression talking."

"I'm a coward, Dan. You should get another partner."

"Look, I'm no psychologist. Promise me you won't do anything stupid until you at least speak with him."

"Would you ever trust me again?"

"I do trust you, Beth. I want your promise."

It took several seconds but she finally said yes.

"Just take some time and think it through. A lot of times things look better when you step back, you know?"

Beth finally said okay and promptly lay back down again. It was ten AM by the time she came down the stairs. Jack was at his desk reading one of the reports Todd Milner had furnished. If anything, it looked like she hadn't slept at all. She was dressed in jeans, a white T-shirt, and running shoes, her own.

"Interested in something to eat?" he asked.

She shook her head in the negative and sat on the couch holding her elbows. Over the past two hours, Jack had obsessed about what the problem was to the point he was convinced she wanted to break up. Obsessing was more or less normal for him, but it was the same feeling he had when Katherine had approached him about a divorce. For some reason, going down the second hill of a roller coaster came to mind. You already knew what the first one was like and prepared yourself for the next plunge. He waited.

"We need to talk," Beth said.

Here it comes. She's found someone else and wants to break it to me easy. Wonderful. Just wonderful.

Jack said nothing.

"I've betrayed you."

"Betrayed me." He took a breath and let it out, then said quietly, "All right. Care to tell me with who?"

"The Sandman."

Jack blinked. "You're having an affair with the Sandman?"

"*What? No.* What are you talking about?"

"What are you talking about?"

"You're going to hate me," Beth said.

"I could never hate you," Jack said. "How in the world could you betray me with the Sandman?"

As a psychologist, he'd heard every manner of crazy story. This had to top the list. Beth started slowly and gradually picked up speed, not unlike a roller coaster, until the words were coming out in a rush. He sat there staring at her.

"Let me get this straight. The Sandman had you by the collar and was threatening to let you fall off the mountain if you didn't tell him my name."

"Yes."

"So you did."

"Yes."

"And that's how you betrayed me."

"I did, Jack. I'm horrible. A complete coward."

Still hugging her elbows, she leaned forward from the waist. Marta rose from the rug and went to sit by her, putting a paw on her knee. Jack had never seen anyone look quite so miserable. He decided to try a different approach.

"Faced with certain death, in a moment of panic, you blurted out my name to save your life?"

"Yes," Beth said, burying her face in her hands.

Jack went to the couch and put his arms around her. "Did he leave you a phone number?"

"What are you talking about?"

"I'd like to give him a call and thank him. If it wasn't for him, you'd have gone off that cliff. Am I correct?"

Beth nodded.

Jack took her by the shoulders. "I could care less whether he knows my name. In fact, I'm glad he does."

"He said he'd kill us if we didn't stop the investigation."

"All right. What do you say we take a vacation? A cruise maybe."

"You're making fun of me."

"Never. Well, maybe a little. You're the bravest, most wonderful woman I've ever met. I wouldn't trade you for anyone in the world . . . except maybe Jennifer Lopez."

"Jack Kale, don't you dare make fun of me. This was the worst thing I could have done."

Several seconds passed. She was in pain and trying to treat it lightly wasn't working. His face grew serious.

"No, the worst thing you could have done would have been to let me spend the rest of my life alone."

Marta finally had enough of being ignored and jumped onto the couch where she promptly pushed her way between Jack and Beth. She lay half across Beth's lap, resting her head on Beth's chest. Tears began to roll down Beth's face.

"You don't understand," she said.

"Actually, I do. You had a normal human reaction in an abnormal situation. I'm fine with it."

"How could you ever trust me again?"

Jack nearly laughed but caught himself in time. "Which of us has a Ph.D. from the University of Georgia?"

"You," she answered in a small voice.

"In my professional opinion, I think the only cure for your problems are my banana pancakes."

The specter of her failure, at least as she perceived it, retreated slightly. She was still not completely convinced. Nevertheless, she put her arms around Jack's neck.

"With chocolate chips?" she asked.

This time Jack did laugh. He kissed her on the lips, then on each cheek and finally her forehead. "Coming up."

"What are we going to do about the Sandman?"

Jack stopped in the doorway and turned around, the smile fading from his face. It was replaced by a look she hadn't seen before.

"Something massive," he said, and went into the kitchen.

Chapter 21

Wesley Simms sat at Mary Margaret Quinn's desk wondering if he was losing his touch. It would have been so easy to drop the pretty detective off that mountain, but she reminded him of another Elizabeth. He realized that now. Silly, because she'd been dead for more than twenty-five years. He shook his head. The mind is a funny thing.

Killing Elizabeth Sturgis wouldn't have accomplished anything. He'd still have to deal with the FBI agent who was probably in charge of the case. It wasn't unusual for the cops to call them in. Their resources were extensive.

Somehow they had figured out his plans—again. Well, third time was the charm, as they say. That hadn't happened since he got into the business. He knew the possibility existed and it was something you plan for. Sooner or later the police would identify Mary Margaret's file as missing and they'd come around to check on her. If he was lucky, they would think she'd been a random selection like the priest. The truth was he was counting on them showing up. The thought brought a smile to his face.

Wesley glanced across the room at Mary Quinn sitting quietly and erect at her dining room table, almost as if she were alive. In front of her, Sweetie Pie the parrot lay on a plate. He'd set the table for three. Not random either. Three was an odd number and the cops would stop to wonder what it signified. Absolutely nothing, of course.

On the computer screen in front of him was a photo of Jack Kale. The hazel eyes were filled with intelligence and . . . something else he couldn't identify. He didn't like looking at them.

Wonderful tool, the Internet. Nothing ever really goes away. New information might push the older stuff back into a remote corner, but look hard enough and it was still there waiting for you.

He continued reading the article he had found. It seemed at one time, Mr. Kale had been a celebrity of sorts and the subject of a made-for-TV movie. Impressive. One of the earlier stories had dubbed him an "FBI Superstar." The man who brought down serial killer Howard Lincoln Pell and solved an impossible kidnapping in California that had every law enforcement official stumped. After his triumph with Pell, nothing. Strange. He wondered what happened to him. The articles seemed to dry up. A gap of eight years ensued before he found the next one, a small piece noting "former" Federal Bureau of Investigation Agent Jack Kale had joined the Georgia Tech faculty to teach forensic psychology. The writer said Kale had been a profiler for the Bureau.

Continuing his search, Wesley found that after his long hiatus from fighting crime, the impressive *Dr.* Kale had come out of retirement to team up with Elizabeth Sturgis. Together they apprehended an acolyte of Howard Pell who had gone on a killing spree of his own. He liked the *Atlanta-Journal*'s headline: "Jack Is Back." Wesley felt honored, and maybe a tiny bit nervous. He was confused because Elizabeth had told him he was with the FBI. Could she have lied to him? That would be very disappointing. Either way, there was no question he was involved. The question now was what to do about it. One or the both of them had guessed his plans and that was cause for concern. The answer didn't present itself immediately as it usually did. He'd have to give the matter more thought. He weighed the possibilities for twenty minutes before he decided to err on the side of caution. The clock was ticking.

Sitting on the table next to him was his cellphone.

Scouting the competition, boy-o?

Yes, Father. It seemed the right thing to do.

Know thy enemy.

As you taught me.

And next?

I don't know when they'll get here. But we have to assume they will.

Agreed. It seems our Dr. Kale is something of a wizard. So have you made plans to receive our guests, my son?

Of course.

Chapter 22

Four Days to the Grand Jury

Rachel Lawrence winced as she read the radiologist's latest report. A second MRI conducted on the boy showed the subdural hematoma had increased in size. That meant more pressure on the brain. If not released, it would result in permanent damage or worse. There was no longer any choice. At five AM, she informed Dwayne Stafford she had an emergency on her hands and couldn't wait any longer. A little boy's life was at stake. The operation had to be moved up. The detective told her to do what she had to. Once it was over, she promised they'd go straight to the safehouse. He accompanied them to the hospital and left a message for Jack Kale informing him of the situation.

*

The procedure lasted three hours. After the boy was taken to recovery, an exhausted Rachel made her way back to her office, lay down on her couch, and finally went to sleep.

She awoke to find she wasn't alone. Sitting across from her, leafing through a book of Cartier Bresson photographs, was the tall detective she'd met earlier. He wasn't particularly handsome, though not entirely unattractive either. He was wearing dark-brown slacks, a blue oxford shirt—the kind her husband had favored—and a brown-and-black herringbone sport jacket. His shoes were solid-looking cap toes.

"Feeling better?" Jack asked.

"Not really," she said, pushing herself up.

"How'd the operation go?"

"Well, I think." Rachel squinted at him and rubbed her temples.

"Headache?"

"Um."

Jack went into the bathroom and returned with a glass of water and two Tylenols. Rachel accepted the pills and downed them.

"Most people pick the Ansel Adams book," she said, motioning to the shelves with her chin.

"Wonderful landscapes," Jack said. "Being a psychologist, I find people more interesting."

"And you became a cop. How'd that happen?"

"Long story."

The drapes in her office were partially closed except for a slender opening where they didn't quite meet. A rhomboid of sunlight stretched across the floor. From where he sat, Jack could see the wind sending leaves spiraling into the air.

Rachel asked, "Is there a reason you're sitting in my office?"

"There is," Jack said. "I thought we had an agreement. You and Dr. Landry need to be in the safehouse. When you're here, our ability to protect you is compromised. I understand emergencies happen, but I need your word you'll try to stay there as much as possible."

"Where is Will?"

"Seeing patients."

"Are you sure this is necessary? It makes me feel like I'm a prisoner."

Jack looked down at his feet for a moment. "I don't blame you. If the situation was reversed, I'd probably feel the same way. Unfortunately, the man we're dealing with is extremely determined and extremely clever. I don't think the police have seen anything like him before. Yesterday he followed Beth Sturgis to Stone Mountain and told her we need to back off the case. I'm not sure what he's expecting, because that's not an option. Forgive me for being blunt, Doctor, but until further notice, you can't go back to your home. I'm afraid that's now nonnegotiable."

"Because he knows where I live."

"Without question. And he knows where you work."

Rachel took a deep breath and let it out.

Jack waited for a moment then asked, "May I ask how your decision to visit Stone Mountain with your husband came about?"

"We'd just completed three operations in a row and were burned out. I put my foot down and told George we were taking a day off."

"Who else did you tell?"

"Our staff, of course."

"In person or by phone?"

"Phone."

"Did you e-mail any of them?"

Rachel thought for a moment. The expression on her face changed. "No, dammit. I put it on Facebook." She squeezed her eyes shut. "How stupid was that?"

"In a normal world, not very," Jack said. "But this isn't a normal world. I wouldn't beat yourself up over it. If the Sandman didn't find you there, he'd have come at you a different way."

"Sandman?"

"That's the FBI's name for him. They picked it up from the Israelis."

Rachel shook her head. She sat back and watched the patch of sunlight for several seconds, then said, "You didn't come here to yell at me about the safehouse. What is it you want?"

"Actually, I'm not sure yet. The first step is to make sure you and Dr. Landry are out of harm's way. If there's a problem with one of your patients, we'll deal with it."

"Don't be angry at Detective Stafford. I told him I needed to stop by my house to pack a few things. Once we were there, the situation with the boy came up."

"He already explained it to me and I'm not mad. To answer your question, I'm thinking of trying to draw the killer out. Doing that will require your help."

"Tell me."

"We know the Sandman was watching your office. The murdered lawyer and police officer across the street make that certain. Just because we managed to interrupt his plan doesn't mean he'll pack up and go home. If you're agreeable, I'd like to make a show of transferring you to police headquarters. But it will be just that—a show. The department maintains housing facilities there and occasionally witnesses use it. They also have two houses here in town for the same purpose. Using decoys, we'll let him think you're at the main building. We'll be waiting for him. In reality, you'll be at one of the safehouses. Not too long ago he attacked a police station directly in Germany and I'm hoping that will make him bold enough to think he can do it again."

Rachel nodded.

Jack continued. "From his standpoint, the clock is counting down, which means he'll have to act soon. I've always believed it's better to fight on your own turf and on your own terms."

"Will and I talked about this last night. He, George, and Stu were all friends. We want to help."

"Wonderful. When can you leave?"

"Let me see how my patient is doing. If there are no problems, I'm yours."

*

It took about a half-hour to run the neurological tests. Curious, Jack accompanied her to the recovery room and watched. When the boy's eyes fluttered open, the first thing he saw was the smiling face of his doctor.

"Hi, Tiger," Rachel said. "How are you?"

The second the boy answered, Rachel squeezed Jack's hand so tightly that he winced. The child had gone into surgery having lost his ability to understand speech. It was one of the brain's mysteries. With the pressure now relieved, things would return to normal.

Rachel used a penlight on the boy's eyes to see how his pupils reacted and was in the process of checking his voluntary and involuntary reflexes when Jack stepped out of the room to answer his phone.

"Kale? Milner here. Where are you?"

"With Dr. Lawrence at the hospital. We had a false start on getting her to the safehouse."

"Understood. I have some good news. I'm here at Leland Walker's office with his secretary. She says the missing file is on a lady named Mary Quinn who lives in Roswell."

"That is good."

"I just got off the phone with Pappas and Sturgis. We're on the way there now along with APD's SWAT team. Want to join us?"

"Maybe later. I need to make sure Rachel and Will are safe first. Are you aware Beth Sturgis had an encounter with the Sandman yesterday?"

"What?"

"She'll fill you in on the details. Basically, he told her to drop the case because there was nothing we, meaning you and I, could do to help the witnesses. According to him, they're already dead."

"Screw that son of a bitch."

"Todd, you have more experience with this man than I do. Frankly, I don't trust anything he says. He leads you down one alley while he's going up the next. In other words, nothing's as it seems. I think there's a reason for everything he does, which includes his encounter with Beth yesterday and his selection of Miss Quinn."

"Agreed."

"If you see *anything* out of the ordinary at this woman's house, let's run forensics on it. Is Komanski still around?"

"I sent Al back to Washington. He looked over what Beth found and had good things to say. That's high praise coming from him. Between you and me he's still pissed about that dancing backward in high heels crack."

Jack smiled. It was pretty clever. He asked about Komanski because there was no sense in him and Beth duplicating their efforts. One tech was sufficient and he could use her elsewhere.

"All right. Hopefully Miss Quinn's fine."

"Why wouldn't she be? He probably grabbed the first file he laid his hands on to get out of the building without attracting attention to himself."

Jack didn't feel like going through his explanation again. "I had some other thoughts on that that Beth can fill you in on. Right now I need to move the doctors."

"Okay," Milner said. "I'll call you with what we turn up."

"Just be careful. This could be a mistake on his part or it could be a trap."

Chapter 23

Todd Milner passed Jack's concerns on to Beth. In return, she brought him up to speed on Jack's plan. Mary Quinn's home was located at the end of a cul-de-sac in Dunwoody. After studying a map of the neighborhood, Glen Sheeley decided to divide his teams into two squads and enter the house from the front and back. Infrared images revealed no mobile hot spots inside, which meant no people were present. Nevertheless, caution was still indicated.

Todd Milner managed to locate Mary Margaret Quinn's social security number and tracked down her employer. They were told the hygienist was at work Tuesday and had left at her normal time. The office manager was concerned when she didn't show up the next day, which wasn't like her. They thanked him for his time and studied the house further. Nothing appeared out of place, but the woman's failure to report didn't bode well. Could it be something related to the case? The office manager had given them the phone number for her sister in Birmingham. They called and learned she and Mary Quinn hadn't spoken in a week. Next, they tried her cellphone.

As quickly as hopes built that she might simply be out of the house, they were erased when triangulating signals from three different cellphone towers indicated her phone was inside. Pappas called Jack and relayed that information.

"This don't look good," Pappas said, a sentiment shared by everyone there, including the SWAT commander.

Sheeley also got on the line and informed him he wanted to hit both doors simultaneously, then send Beth in to do her thing. "You good with that?"

"Let's do it," Jack said. "Carefully."

"Okay, everyone, we're hot," Sheeley announced over his com unit. "Red and Blue teams move out."

Jack instructed Dwayne Stafford to watch the witnesses and started walking down the hospital's long corridor toward a window in the hope of getting better reception. Beth and Pappas attached themselves to the Red Team, who were taking the front door. Officers carrying a weighted battering ram quickly moved into position.

"Make sure you check for booby traps," Jack said, remembering what the Sandman had done in Tel Aviv. There was no response. He glanced at the screen and saw there was only one reception bar showing. Jack repeated his warning. Still no answer.

Swearing under his breath, he started jogging for the nearest exit. He could hear them talking but the words were clouded by static.

"Red Team in. Blue Team in. Kitchen clear. Bedroom clear."

Then came the words he was dreading. "Jesus, Mary, Mother of God, will you look at this?" The note of shock in the man's voice was obvious.

Jack began to run, racing down the stairs. "Look at *what*?" he yelled into the phone.

He covered the twelve flights to the ground floor in under a minute, taking steps two at a time. At the building's entrance, he heard Beth order everyone out.

"Jack, I don't know if you can hear me. We've cleared the house. I'm about to start my walk-through. You should see this."

"I'm here!" Jack shouted. "I had to get outside. Describe what you're looking at."

"He killed her and put her at the dining room table like she's about to eat. Ohmigod, there's a dead parrot on her plate. Why would he do that?"

Even Beth, who was normally quite calm, and who had seen a number of homicides over the last eight months, sounded shaky.

"What else are you seeing?"

"Just a standard house. Nothing out of the ordinary. Except . . ."

"Except what?"

"Nothing. I'm just spooking myself. I need to run the Polilight over the dishes. The table's set for three people. What does that mean?"

"I have no idea. What were you about to say?"

"Something's not right."

Whatever Beth was feeling communicated itself to Jack. "I need to know what you're seeing," he repeated.

"Quit bugging me. I'll figure it out. I've got a partial print on one of the glasses."

"No, you don't. It's misdirection. The Sandman doesn't make those kinds of mistakes. What were your impressions when you first came in?"

In the background, Dan Pappas said something, but he missed most of the words.

"Did Pappas just say something about sour?"

"Yeah, that's it. There's a sour smell here like spoiled milk. I've almost got the print—"

"Out!" Jack screamed. "Out now! It's a time delay fuse. He's rigged a bomb!"

Three seconds ticked by followed by an explosion that was so loud it forced him to pull the phone away from his ear.

"Beth! Pappas! Jesus Christ, someone answer me. Sheeley, come in. What just happened?"

The SWAT commander's voice came on a second later. "Oh, man, this is bad. A bomb just took out the side of the house. We need EMS and Fire here."

Sheeley was shouting into his hand communicator. Jack couldn't hear the other end of the conversation, just the commander yelling, "Now! Now, goddammit, now! We've got officers down everywhere!"

It sounded like chaos. The explosion had hit Jack like an uppercut to the solar plexus. For a moment, he felt paralyzed, rooted in place. He forced himself to move. He was operating now on pure instinct. Desperate to know if Beth and Pappas were still alive, Jack ran for his car. And stopped. This was exactly what the Sandman wanted. He punched the disconnect button and called the uniform officer on Rachel's floor.

They're dead already.

Rick Swerdlin, a twelve-year veteran on the force answered.

"This is Jack Kale. We've got a code red. The Sandman just set off a bomb in Roswell. Secure the witnesses immediately. Anyone makes a move on them, you're greenlighted to shoot first. Got it?"

"Loud and clear."

"Good, relay that to Detective Stafford."

Jack's next call was to Ed Mundas, Dwayne Stafford's partner.

"Where are you?" He asked without preamble.

"At the station, waiting on you."

"Have you heard what happened?"

"Bob Baxley just came running in here and told us. We're trying to follow it on the scanner. Sounds like all hell's breaking loose."

"It is. Is there anything on Beth Sturgis or Dan Pappas?"

"Not so far."

"The second you hear something, call me. Not in an hour. *Immediately.*"

"Understood."

"From this moment on, you're to consider we're under attack. Call Dwayne and tell him we need to move those witnesses now. Childers and Spruell will make a show of transporting our decoys to the station. Once they're gone, you and Dwayne get them to the safehouse."

"Childers and Spruell are standing by," Mundas said.

"Get rolling," Jack said.

"On our way, Doc."

Chapter 24

Jack disconnected and sprinted to his own car, sick with worry over Beth. Tearing out of the parking lot, he nearly took out a light pole. En route he called dispatch, identified himself, and asked what the status was on the explosion.

"I'm sorry, sir. I don't know who you are and I can't release anything without proper authorization."

"I'm an FBI agent, goddammit."

"Yes, sir. But I have no way of verifying that. Right now, you're a voice on the phone. No disrespect."

Jack pounded his steering wheel. "Connect me with Deputy Chief Ritson."

"He's out of the building at the moment."

"Probably on the way to the explosion, where I'm trying to get. What about Nolvia Borjas? She's the RHD secretary."

"That I can do. Have a nice day."

A second later, Nolvia came on the line.

"Nolvia, Jack Kale. Have you heard anything on Beth or Dan?"

"No, it sounds horrible. We're listening to it on the scanner. The television's calling it a possible terrorist attack."

"That's because they're idiots. I need an address."

Thirty seconds later Jack had what he wanted. A minute after exiting the highway he knew which way to go. It was just a matter of following a line of fire and emergency vehicles, their lights flashing, and their sirens going at full blast. He kept redialing Pappas and Beth's phones, praying one of them would answer.

Skidding to a halt at the scene, he parked against the curb so as not to block the ambulances. Everything was a mess. At the end of the cul-de-sac people were running, a cop was trying to direct traffic, and water was being pumped onto the side of a ruined two-story home. A gray cloud hung over it like a shroud. The blast had taken out not only one side of the house, but the bushes and a red Japanese maple that was now lying on its side on the lawn.

Jack dodged emergency workers and cops and made his way to where the firemen were fighting a blaze at the garage. Inside, he caught a glimpse of what looked like a white Audi sedan, the lawyer's stolen car.

There was still no sign of Beth, Pappas, or Todd Milner. He caught a fireman by the arm and asked about the casualties.

"I'm not sure, man. EMS is treating the survivors at that house across the street," he said, pointing.

A cluster of SWAT officers were gathered around a body on a stretcher, watching the medical techs work. Jack started toward them but only got a few feet before a strong hand closed around his arm. He found himself looking into the scarred face of Dan Pappas. The detective's shirt and jacket were ripped in several places.

"Where's Beth?"

"She's okay. They've got her in the back of that ambulance on the end."

Jack was already moving.

"Yeah, I'm okay, too!" Pappas yelled to his back.

Jack waved over his shoulder.

A technician was applying a butterfly bandage to Beth's forehead. She was sitting up. Her face was streaked with dirt and one of her shoes was missing. The moment she saw him she jumped up and into his arms. When they finally separated, Jack turned his palms up in a silent question.

"I can't keep losing shoes like this," Beth said.

Jack let out his breath. He didn't know whether to be angry at her for not leaving the house sooner or relieved. He settled on relieved.

"Talk to me," he said.

"It was bad. After you started yelling to get out, I screamed for Dan to run, then dashed into the bathroom and jumped in the tub. It's cast iron and shielded me from the blast. I'm a little deaf right now."

Jack's shoulders slumped. "Who'd we lose?"

"I saw them carrying Todd Milner away on a stretcher. He may still be here. I'm not sure. Three of Glen Sheeley's people definitely didn't make it."

Jack closed his eyes. They were men and women he knew. Beth lowered her voice and said, "Uh oh, here comes the deputy chief."

Six-foot-five Noah Ritson, survivor of four mayoral administrations, moved through the crowd accompanied by his aide, stopping to check on the wounded and speak with the officers. He and Jack made eye contact. When Ritson was finished, he motioned with his head for Jack to join him.

Ritson said, "Todd Milner gave me a rundown on what happened. He has a bad gash on one arm and got pretty banged up, but I think he'll be all right. I'd like your assessment of the situation."

"Basically it's what it looks like, Chief. The Sandman rigged a delay fuse hoping to take as many of us out as he could."

"Why?"

"Hard to say. The woman whose house this is . . . was, is Mary Quinn, who has no apparent connection to the case other than that missing case file. At least none I can see. Neither did the attorney representing her."

"Wrong place, wrong time?"

Jack watched a tech wrapping a bandage around Bobby Sanchez's stomach. He'd met Sanchez before. The officer winced, saw him, and nodded a greeting. Jack had to push the anger and frustration building inside him away. At the moment, he wanted to punch someone. Oddly, he felt his face go red as a sense of humiliation settled over him. He realized the Sandman had outsmarted them. The deputy chief was still waiting for an answer.

"It's possible, but I don't think so. The Sandman doesn't leave things to chance. Not even the little details. The lawyer's office was selected because it's directly across the street from the medical practice."

"What about Ms. Quinn?"

"Two possibilities. Either he wanted us out here to create maximum damage to impede the case, or it was a ploy to leave the witnesses unattended."

"But you didn't."

"No, they're on the way to the safehouse. Our decoys left the admin building earlier and should be back at the station by now. You'd think an assault there would be out of the question, but he didn't hesitate to attack police headquarters in Munich or an army base outside of Liverpool. If he's coming at us there, hopefully the Ghosts will spot him first," he said, referring to Atlanta's elite surveillance squad.

"You really think he'd try the main building?"

"Steve McFadden texted me a few minutes ago. They've been watching a man hanging around the front entrance, who appears to be checking things out. We're taking that seriously."

Ritson shook his head in disbelief.

Jack continued. "Nothing the Sandman's done has been predictable, which is fine. We can deal with that. But there's a second problem. If the lawyer and Ms. Quinn weren't chance selections, we have to assume there's a leak someplace. It's not so much that he knew we were coming. He might have planned for that like he did in Israel and Madrid. It's that he knew *when* we'd be here. It's either us, the U.S. Attorney's office, or the Bureau."

Ritson's blue eyes went as hard as marbles. "Milner just got himself blown up and lost one of his own people. What about further up the line at the FBI?"

"Like Janet Newton?"

Ritson raised his eyebrows and said nothing.

"I've known Janet a long time. I can't imagine her talking to anyone."

"Donofrio?"

"He wants to take jurisdiction and turn the witnesses over to the U.S. Marshals. We talked him out of it. I don't see him either, but it's clear someone's talking."

Ritson considered this for several seconds. "I feel comfortable with our people, do you?"

"Completely. That's why I'm stumped."

Ritson said, "Donofrio called my office yesterday wanting to know why he wasn't receiving reports. Personally, I don't like the sonofabitch. He gives me the creeps. If there's a leak, my money is it's on his end."

"Which may be why he hasn't been receiving those reports."

The deputy chief stared at Jack and said, "You're an odd fellow, Dr. Kale."

"Aren't we all?"

"I consider myself a monument to normality," Ritson said. "Art Koster told me what happened yesterday. Tell me why the Sandman didn't kill Beth Sturgis."

"To be honest, Chief, I don't have an answer. I suspect this man doesn't kill out of emotion, at least now. That may not have been the case in the past. Maybe he didn't feel the need to just then. Either way, I'm not complaining."

Ritson paused to watch an ambulance make a three-point turn. His arms were folded across his chest, and his face was somber. He said, "People just died on my watch. I don't take that lightly. Until further notice, the green light stays on. Am I making myself clear?"

"Crystal."

"You like being a fed again?"

"I haven't had much time to think about it."

"My offer to join our department remains on the table."

"I know that."

*

Noah Ritson considered the man in front of him. Jack Kale was a hard fellow not to like. While they were speaking, his eyes were never completely at rest. They continued moving, taking in everything around him, weighing possibilities. If anyone was capable of stopping the Sandman, it was him. Few people were blessed with his analytical abilities. Other cops knew it. The deputy chief believed the FBI was the wrong place for him. That might be self-serving. Jack Kale and the beautiful detective standing a few feet away made a good team. Yes, he knew about them. It was his job to know. Beth Sturgis was smart, savvy, and a fine investigator. More important, she was a good influence on Kale, who at times seemed his own worst enemy.

"Still attending those NA meetings?" Ritson asked.

"I am."

"Good. We'll talk later."

Jack started to reply, but the deputy chief held up a hand. "Now's not the time. Tell your girlfriend she can stop pretending to watch them pump water onto the house. It's really not that interesting."

Ritson nodded to them and walked away.

*

Using the underground parking garage, Will Landry and Rachel Lawrence were bundled into an unmarked SUV driven by Dwayne Stafford. Ed Mundas was in the seat next to him holding an assault rifle.

Jack assumed the Sandman was monitoring their police frequencies, and probably watching the hospital as well. As a result, the detectives were transporting the witnesses to the safehouse using an unmarked car. He was praying that would be enough to throw the killer off.

By prior agreement, a special SWAT unit known as the Ghost Squad had already been dispersed around the main station. These officers were the best in the business and generally employed to follow organized crime figures. They were so adept, when Jack had asked if there was any chance they'd be spotted, the lieutenant in charge looked at him like he was crazy. Fair enough.

From what Noah Ritson told him when he ran the plan by him, in the ten years since the squad had been formed, they'd never once been made. On two different occasions, they proved instrumental in stopping terrorist plots. This was in spite of the cell's security people who were supposed to detect if the cops had them under surveillance.

As soon as the decoy van was under way, Dwayne sent a coded message letting the lieutenant know the game was on. It was just a question of whether the Sandman would take the bait. If so, they'd be waiting for him.

Chapter 25

The beige SUV moved quietly through Atlanta's streets. Sitting in the backseat, Rachel and Will observed the two detectives escorting them to the safehouse.

"You must be getting tired of seeing us," Will said.

"Oh, no, sir. Y'all are very pleasant people," Dwayne Stafford told them. "I was telling my partner that earlier."

They looked at Ed Mundas, a tall, brown-haired man, approximately the same age as Dwayne Stafford. Both men had heavy Southern accents and tended to complete each other's sentences. Jack Kale had assured them they were in good hands.

Mundas said, "Dwayne and I sometimes get stuck guarding downright unsavory types. Y'all are a breath of fresh air. You just sit back and relax, 'cause we're gonna take good care of you."

"Mr. Kale seems very competent," Will said.

"Boy's smarter than Bill Gates," Mundas replied. "He teaches at Georgia Tech. I never know whether to call him professor or doctor."

"He's a doctor?"

"Psychologist. Not sure if that's the same thing as y'all."

"It's in the ballpark. Can you let us in on the plan?" Will said.

"Sure. Just a little while before we left, two folks who favor you and Doc Lawrence came out of your office building. Our boys dressed them up in body armor complete with helmets so you can't make out their faces. They were driven to the main precinct. Kinda crazy to think someone's nutty enough to try us there, but what are you gonna do?"

"And you'll be waiting for him," Rachel said.

"Us, the FBI, and every cop in the tristate area. He gets outta that one, we're gonna change his name to Houdini."

"Sounds good to me," Rachel said. "If I could borrow a gun and have five minutes alone with the bastard—that would make me happy."

Mundas smiled. "We'll see what we can do, ma'am. We're here to serve. Y'all like pizza?"

*

From a rooftop sixteen blocks from the Atlanta Police Department's Administration Building, Wesley Simms watched a gasoline truck pull into the parking lot. The lot had two pumps where the cops could fill up before taking their cruisers out. By his estimate, it would take about two hours to fill the underground tanks. A few minutes earlier he observed the cops make a grand show of transferring the witnesses inside. Great performance. First-class stuff. Really. Apparently they thought he was stupid enough to buy it. If he cared, he'd have been insulted.

Ten minutes after the first van and its tail cars pulled out of the garage, his spotter reported the real transport vehicle carrying the witnesses had gone mobile.

Elvis has left the bu²ding.

Of course he knew where the safehouse was located. He'd known about both houses two days after accepting the contract. His source had also given him the details of Jack Kale's "plan." *So much for that.* He smiled. It was called basic intelligence gathering. Expensive, but necessary.

Wesley's thoughts drifted once again to Rio de Janeiro. The weather in Atlanta had turned cold over the last few days, which didn't agree with him. Warm was definitely better. Warm weather and women in microscopic bikinis with smooth skin and agreeable attitudes.

He frowned as another thought occurred to him. He needed to pick up a book on Portuguese.

Wesley turned the volume on his police scanner up a notch. The frenzy seemed to be dying down. Hopefully, Dr. Jackson Kale was there when the bombs went off. Elizabeth was another matter.

Something about her disturbed him. He knew it was probably the resemblance to his sister, but there was something else he couldn't quite put his finger on. Still, he didn't want her harmed. If they followed their own procedures, the detectives would wait to go into a scene until after the cops cleared it, and by then it would be too late.

Removing a small bottle of hand sanitizer from his pocket, he squirted some onto the palms of his hands and began rubbing vigorously. The thought of touching that disgusting bird still revolted him. When he was done, he put the bottle away and went to his car. Time to pay the witnesses a visit.

*

The safehouse wasn't a house at all but a midrise condominium located just south of Buckhead. The state had seized it from a drug dealer who was now serving the second year of his fifteen year sentence. The city in turn acquired it from the state, which had no desire to pay a seven thousand dollar a month mortgage. The current owner was a man who'd been trying to obtain a liquor license for his "Gentlemen's Club" for two years without success. He was delighted to lease the property to the city for one dollar per annum in return for the Planning Commission abandoning its objections. Deputy Chief Noah Ritson had brokered the deal.

After seeing the witnesses safely installed, Ed Mundas, connoisseur of pizza in all forms, left to pick up two pies from his favorite shop on Roswell Road. He guaranteed them it was the best in town. Dwayne Stafford rolled his eyes at his partner's enthusiasm.

The condo consisted of two floors and a balcony that overlooked a nicely landscaped courtyard and a swimming pool. The building surrounded the courtyard on all four sides, with each unit sharing more or less the same view.

"Nice place," Rachel said, looking around. "George and I used to wonder what it was like in here when we drove by."

"Must be pricey," Will observed.

Stafford informed them their unit had been on the market for two million dollars, then filled them in on how Atlanta had come to own it.

"The owner just traded this for a strip joint?" Rachel said.

"When the Platinum Club relocates, it'll probably make that back and then some," Stafford told her.

"But still . . ."

"They have some really beautiful women there," Will Landry said.

Rachel's eyebrows lifted in surprise and she turned to her partner.

"I mean, I don't know personally. That's just what I heard. In fact, Nate Moskowitz was telling me—"

"I'm going upstairs to take a nap."

Both men nodded. Said nothing.

Once they heard her bedroom door close, Dr. Landry shook his head and walked over to the sliding glass door that led to the balcony.

"Don't believe that'll work, Doc."

"Why not?"

"We made a few modifications after acquiring this place, like welding the door shut. Let me walk you through them. The glass on all the windows and doors is bulletproof. They tell me it'll stop most bullets."

"Most?"

"Well, I don't know anything that'll stop a .50-caliber armor-piercing round, which is what the Sandman used in Paris last year. So I'd ask you and Miss Rachel to keep the drapes shut and away from the windows. We've stocked up all kinds of good things to eat and drink if you're hungry."

"Except pizza."

Stafford smiled. "Except pizza. Ed's a fiend for that. Drives me nuts cause he wants to eat it five days a week."

"My partner Stu Patterson's the same way. Not quite so obsessive, but close. His thing is Chinese food."

Stafford shook his head and continued. "When you're here, there's no cellphone use. That GPS stuff can track you down pretty good, so keep 'em off if you don't mind. Should you need to make a call, the phones have two separate lines. Just press a button and dial straight out."

"Understood. I'll tell Rachel."

"Appreciate it. Now we know y'all can't just drop off the face of the earth, having patients and such, so there's a high speed computer in the den. And there's a media room across the hall if you get bored. It's got a hundred and fifty-six channels on satellite dish."

"That's a lot."

"Sure is." The detective glanced upstairs and lowered his voice. "Got some naughty ones, too. You just need to punch in a code. Six-six-six, I believe it is."

"Six-six-six? Seriously?"

"That came from Chief Ritson's wife when she found out, but don't quote me."

Will Landry laughed. "Your secret's safe."

"Now each room has a red button next to the light switch. Don't push it unless there's an emergency. If you do, all hell will break loose."

"Why?"

"That button tells Commander Sheeley to send in the cavalry. He's not real understanding about mistakes."

"I'll remember that," Will Landry said.

"I've gotta say, you and Doc Lawrence are doin' the right thing staying here. The captain gave us a briefing on this Sandman yesterday. He's no one to fool with. You follow our directions and we'll get you through everything in one piece. You have my word on it."

"Thank you, Detective."

"How's she holding up?" Dwayne asked, pointing upstairs.

"Better than I would if the situation was reversed."

"Y'all pretty good friends with the Lawrences?"

"George and I were roommates in college. That's where he met Rachel. I actually had a crush on her first, but things didn't work out. I don't care what I have to do. I want to help nail the asshole who murdered him."

"Well, sir, we're sure gonna try. Before we picked y'all up, I was reading through your file."

"I have a file?"

"Everybody's got an FBI file. Least everybody associated with this case does. I understand you saw some combat in Iraq."

"A little bit," Will agreed.

"More 'n a little, I'd say. Got you a Purple Heart and a Bronze Star."

"I forgot to duck."

Stafford laughed, but then his face grew serious. "So did my brother, Harry. Two days before he was set to ship out a roadside bomb killed him and one other feller in his squad."

"I'm sorry," Will said quietly.

"Yeah, me too."

The detective walked over to the wet bar, reached underneath and came up with a bottle of scotch and two glasses. "I'd like to buy you a drink, Doc, for your service to our country."

"I thought cops weren't supposed to drink on duty."

Dwayne Stafford poured each of them a shot and said, "I heard that, too."

Chapter 26

Beth had just stepped out of the restroom when someone called her name. She turned to see Janet Newton coming down the hall. They exchanged pleasantries. Janet noticed the scrape on her forehead and asked how she was.

"I'm fine, deputy director. I just banged my head when I dove into the tub to avoid the blast."

"Thank God you did," Janet said. "I've been hearing about it all morning. We lost some good people today. I want you to know how sorry I am. And we can drop all the deputy director stuff. Janet is just fine."

Beth smiled and asked how Todd Milner was doing.

"The EMTs released him a little while ago. He insisted on coming back here. I volunteered to be his ride."

"Todd's a good guy."

"I'm glad we ran into each other, Beth," Janet said. "You have a few minutes?"

"Sure."

"If there's a cafeteria around, I'll buy you a cup of coffee."

"It's on the second floor," Beth said.

Once they were seated, Janet told her she had just come from a meeting with Noah Ritson. "He speaks highly of you. He's also very concerned about a leak. That explosion was a set up."

"I know," Beth said.

"Any ideas who's talking?"

Beth shook her head. "Not a clue. I've been going over and over it in my mind. I trust our people."

"And I trust mine. Which leaves the U.S. Attorney's office."

"It's possible, but it doesn't make sense. Jack's been sending them reports. Donofrio wants to nail Borov and the Sandman as much as we do, maybe more."

"I take it no one told him you were on the way to Mary Quinn's home," Janet said.

"Not that I know of," Beth said, "which brings us back to the leak. Honestly, I'm drawing a blank."

The deputy director took a sip of her coffee and looked around the cafeteria for several seconds, then commented, "Sometimes I think the same person designs these places all over the country. Why didn't you tell me you and Jack were living together?"

"Why didn't you tell me you were his partner when we first met?"

"Because I didn't think it was relevant. Living together is. It can compromise his judgment."

"How?"

"Are you seriously asking me that? You're a rookie. If Jack's worrying about you, he won't be concentrating on the case. Either that, or his attention will be split. Trust me. I know this man."

"So do I," Beth said. "And I'm not a rookie. I've been with the department for nearly seven years."

"Six of which you were writing environmental cases. According to Noah Ritson, you transferred to RHD less than a year ago."

"I can handle this, Janet."

"I'm not questioning your competence, but there's no substitute for experience. You're also impulsive and that can be dangerous, not only to yourself, but to others around you. This is an FBI operation and I can't put my people at risk. You're out."

They sat looking at each other across the table.

"What's this really about?"

"Exactly what I told you."

"I don't think so. Jack's not a fool. If you tell him you're taking me off the case because of a conflict of interest or whatever you want to call it, you'll risk losing him. I know he's protective. I also know about Connie Belasco. He carries the guilt around like an anvil and it eats him up. The damn thing is, his panic attacks have been decreasing over the last six months. There's a doctor he sees who's helping him. What I'm saying is, we're a good team and we work well together."

"He told me that too."

"And he was right. He also told me there was nothing between the two of you, something I'm having trouble believing at the moment. Because I think that's what we're really talking about here."

"This isn't a subject for discussion. Moreover, it's none of your business."

Beth leaned back in her chair.

"You're kidding, right?"

"I'm not."

"C'mon, Janet. Let it go. I can do this job. I lost friends today and I want to catch this bastard as much as you do. The second I think I'm a liability, I'll take myself out of the equation. Give me a chance and you won't be sorry. Neither of us wants to make a mistake that will jeopardize the investigation."

The deputy director's fingers drummed on the table. Her eyes never left Beth's. After several seconds, the silence began to grow uncomfortable.

"All right," Beth finally said. "I'll turn my notes over to Todd. He can take it from there. I wish you wouldn't do this." Beth stood. "Thanks for the coffee."

"Sit down. I wasn't kidding about your lack of experience being a detriment. You're on the case because Jack specifically asked for you. Had I known what I know now, I never would have agreed to it. I'll give you the chance you're asking for, but the moment I feel he's having to babysit you or you're slowing things down, you won't have to worry about taking yourself out of the equation. I'll yank you without a second thought. Whatever you might think, this isn't a popularity contest. I want the Sandman and the White House wants Borov. The two are connected at the hip. Don't screw this up, Beth. There's too much at stake."

Beth wanted the last word, but she settled for simply nodding and said, "Thank you." She watched Janet Newton walk out of the cafeteria with the distinct feeling she had just dodged a bullet.

Chapter 27

Corporal James Fillet, age twenty-eight, was watching a man who'd walked past police headquarters three times for what looked like no apparent reason. Along with his partner, Charlene Handler, another member of Atlanta's Ghost Squad, they'd tracked him to Piedmont Park where he was now flying a model airplane.

Charlene spoke quietly into her hand communicator, a device that utilized a bandwidth the Ghost Squad didn't share with other cops.

"This is a waste of time, Jimmy. The guy's some kind of hobby nut."

"Then why'd he walk by the admin building three times? There's no reason for that, Charly."

"I don't have a clue."

"Lieutenant says to track his movements; that's what we do."

"I gotta pee," Charlene said.

"Go ahead. We start to move, I'll let you know."

"Back in five," Charlene said.

"I'll update Kale on the status."

*

Jack picked up the phone on the first ring. With him in the administration building were Beth and Todd Milner, who'd been treated and released from the hospital an hour earlier. The grand jury was set to meet in three days. There was a tension present in the room that everyone was conscious of. Milner's arm was in a sling and he was still wearing the clothes he'd been blown up in. Shortly after he arrived, Beth took one look at him and went to the kitchen Robbery-Homicide used for a break room, wet a cloth with warm water, and spent a minute cleaning the dirt off his face.

"Thank you, Detective."

"Beth."

"Beth," Milner smiled.

Across the room Jack said, "He's doing what?" He hit the speaker button on the phone so the others could hear.

"Flying a model airplane."

Jack looked at Milner, who raised his shoulders, then at Beth, who turned her palms up.

It was a clear day with only a few high white clouds. But as the afternoon progressed, the temperature had continued to drop as a front moved into Atlanta. From his sixth-floor window, Jack could see people clutching their coats tighter as they crossed the street. Women kept a hand on their skirts.

"How's the weather out there?" Jack asked.

"Kinda cool. Probably in the midforties."

"And this man's flying a model airplane?"

"Looks that way, Dr. Kale."

"Let's drop the doctor and leave it at Jack."

"No problemo," Fillet said. "I'm Jimmy."

"What specifically is he doing with the plane? Stunts?"

"Not really. He's just hovering and practicing takeoffs and landings."

Jack's finger beat a steady rhythm on the desk. "How long's he been at it?"

"Maybe forty-five—whoa."

"What?"

"Almost had a midair collision with a helicopter guy."

Jack sat up straighter in his chair. "What helicopter guy?"

"He just got here a while ago. He's on the other side of the lake. Now that I'm looking at it, I'm not sure you can call it a helicopter. It's more like a flying starburst."

"Describe it."

"Six arms shaped like a star with an engine at the end of each one. He had it hovering about fifty feet above the ground for a few minutes and just set it back down to refuel."

Jack shook his head and told the officer to call him if anything unusual happened. Something was bothering him, but he couldn't put his finger on it. Some fact hovering at the edge of his consciousness. They'd been led into a trap earlier and people had died. He couldn't afford to make that mistake again. Though no one had said anything outright, he was positive from the way people in the hallways had averted their eyes when he passed, they were holding him responsible for the deaths.

"Hovering," he repeated to himself. "Where's Dan?"

"He went home to change clothes. Then he's going to relieve Frick and Frack. What's wrong?" Beth asked. "I know that look."

Jack took a moment to reply. "The Sandman doesn't have a set pattern we can build off. Basically, he adjusts his tactics to fit the circumstances. Most of the time, he appears to have acted alone. But that's not to say he always does."

"What good does knowing that do us?" Todd Milner asked. "We have no clue what the man looks like. Maybe he's working with a partner. Maybe not. It's just speculation. We can pick up those model airplane clowns, but I don't see what good that will do us."

Beth didn't seem enthused by the idea either.

Jack said, "Director Newton told us after the Madrid killing the police checked their security cameras and counted one more cop than they were supposed to have."

"That's right," Milner said.

"Less than a minute following the shot an explosion went off at street level taking out a light pole."

"Also correct."

"But the bullet that killed the minister came from an elevated position on top of a library."

"Meaning he had to have a partner," Beth said, "or he planted the bomb and set it off by remote."

"Or the Spanish police screwed up," Milner said. "They're not known for their efficiency."

Jack took a breath and let it out, then asked Beth if Ben Furman had any luck with the partial print she'd risked her life to recover.

"It wasn't enough for a match," she said.

Annoyed, Jack went to the coffee pot and poured himself a cup. After a single sip, he looked at it and frowned. There was probably an unwritten rule somewhere that said coffee in police stations had to taste like gasoline. In previous situations, he'd been able to place himself in the killer's head and try to think what they were thinking. That hadn't happened with the Sandman. Try as he might, he had no feel for the man. He stared out the window again and looked down at the tanker truck.

Refuel.

Like the people in Madrid, they'd already had one explosion killing three officers Jack knew and liked. He continued to analyze the facts hoping something would come to him. An audible change had settled over the administration building. People were speaking in hushed tones and moving quietly through the hallway. Several women's makeup had streaked from crying.

Gasoline.

The man the Ghosts had under observation had passed the building not once but three times. He might just as well have held a sign up. If the Sandman was planning to hit them, what would three trips accomplish that couldn't be managed in one? And why make no effort to conceal his presence?

Refuel.

Irritated, Jack grabbed his walkie-talkie and called Jim Fillet again. "What's he doing now?"

"Still landing and taking off. After he's airborne, he'll circle the park once or twice then set it back down."

"What about the other man?"

"Basically, the same thing. Lift off, hover, touchdown. He's using a laptop to control it. There's a crowd of six or eight kids watching him."

"How big is the hovercraft?"

"Hard to say from here. Let me check with my partner. She's closer."

Jack waited.

Gasoline. Refuel.

Fillet came on the line a few seconds later. "We're guessing about four feet around."

"And the plane?"

"Big. The wingspan's got to be four feet as well. I'd guess the body's probably five feet overall."

"You ever fly model airplanes as a kid?"

"A few times. The landings always killed me."

"Me too," Jack said. "What did you use to control it?"

"A little RC unit with levers for the rudder and flaps."

"Ask your partner," Jack said.

Fillet did. "She said to tell you she's a girl."

Jack smiled. "Point taken. Either of you ever see anyone use a computer to fly those things?"

Neither had, but they conceded it had been a long time since they'd paid attention to model airplanes or how to control them.

"Move in and pick them up. Secure whatever it is they're flying, including the laptop and plane's control unit."

"Roger that. It'll take a minute or two."

Beth and Milner who'd been listening to the conversation were both looking at him like he'd lost his mind.

"Jack, what are you doing?" Beth asked. "Two people flying model airplanes? I can't see how that's relevant."

"Give the order to evacuate this building."

"What?"

"What does Borov produce?"

"Chemicals," Beth said.

"And military arms and electronics," Milner added.

"Which includes drone aircraft," Jack said.

It took a moment for the implications to dawn on him.

"Fuck. Even if he has a drone, what harm—"

"We passed a gasoline truck in the parking lot downstairs. A drone doesn't need to attack the building. If that truck goes up, it'll take out a city block. I want these people out of here right now. I don't know how much time we have."

*

Dan Pappas was pulling out of his garage when his cellphone went off. It was Beth.

"Where are you?" she asked.

"About to get on the road."

"You're on the way to Frick and Frack, right?"

Pappas could hear an alarm going off in the background and raised voices. "What the hell's happening there?"

"I'm in the stairwell at HQ. Jack's having the building evacuated."

"He's crazy. You'd need an army to—"

"He thinks the Sandman's about to hit us with drones. They're going for a gasoline tanker in the lot."

"Holy shit. Are you sure about this?"

"You want to bet against him?" Beth asked.

"Actually . . . no."

"Communications'll be down for a few minutes. All incoming calls are being rerouted through the precincts. Call me when you arrive at the safehouse."

"Will do," Pappas said. "You make sure you get your ass outta there too. Drones. I'm too old for all this Star Wars crap."

*

The fourteen hundred people who worked in Administrative Services exited the building in a surprisingly orderly fashion. No panic. No screaming. No hysterics.

Glen Sheeley and his SWAT team set up a two-block perimeter in all directions. Barricades were erected, and an emergency services plan no one thought they would ever need was set in motion. The feeling of having just stepped into a CNN news report spread from person to person.

As soon as he was outside, Sheeley made for the gasoline tanker and ordered the pumping stopped. He jumped in the cab and reached for the ignition key.

"Wait!" the driver yelled. "You can't start the engine until the hose and tank cover are in place. We'll go up in a fireball."

"Do it."

At almost the same time the driver was yelling, the SWAT commander's com unit went off.

Jim Fillet said, "I couldn't reach Dr. Kale. We picked up the men."

"Great."

"No, sir, it's not. The plane and that flying star just disappeared over the tree line. They're headed in your direction."

"How long do we have?"

"A minute. Maybe two."

A shudder went up Sheeley's spine. He disconnected and thought rapidly, then shouted to his second in command, "Get the sharpshooters in position. We've got two drones incoming from the north-northeast. Tell them to knock those fuckers out of the air."

Chapter 28

Wesley Simms heard the order to evacuate go out over his scanner. Traffic was being rerouted. Emergency Services placed on alert, along with the trauma teams at Grady, Crawford-Long, and Piedmont hospitals. Even hospitals as far away as Emory University and Northside were told to get ready. News trucks with satellite dishes sped along the streets. Similar orders to evacuate City Hall, the state capitol complex, and Fulton County government buildings were issued. Perfect. If he'd written the script, he couldn't have asked for more. All the official government buildings in Atlanta's downtown were clustered together within a few blocks of each other. Even the Richard Russell Federal Building was being emptied. It was simply beautiful.

Whistling to himself, Wesley set a small explosive charge on the junction box in the condominium's basement. During his first trip, he'd taken note of the sensors and cameras. Fortunately, they didn't work very well without electricity. Even if someone managed to activate the panic button there'd be no one to hear it for the next few minutes. His cellphone beeped.

Is everything okay, lad?

Excellent.

That's my boy. It's a fine lookin' officer you make in those SWAT clothes. Now make me proud.

*

155

Dan Pappas thought he heard a shot a second after the elevator doors closed. He drew his gun. When they opened onto the sixth floor, his worst fears were confirmed. Ed Mundas lay dead in the hallway. Two pizza boxes were lying next to him. There were three bullet holes in his chest. The detective immediately took out his cellphone and called his partner.

"Code Red! Code Red! We're under attack."

As if in confirmation, a burst of short automatic weapons fire came from inside the condo.

"We're less than a minute out!" Beth yelled.

"I don't have a minute! He's going for the witnesses. Mundas is down. There's weapon fire coming from inside. I can't wait on you."

Pappas had taken no more than two steps before an explosion followed by an enormously bright light came from the inside of the condo. Another burst from an automatic weapon followed. Smoke poured out of the door that had just been blown open. Pappas bent down, pulled Mundas's 9 mm off his hip, and charged inside.

*

Out of his peripheral vision, Wesley saw a large man enter the room holding two guns. A shiver of fear ran through his body. Jack Kale was coming for him. As he anticipated, his being dressed as a SWAT officer caused the other man to hesitate. Holding his hand up, palm out, he pointed emphatically toward the second floor. Across his face was a black balaclava. Pappas's glance was only momentary. Wesley then pointed to where Dwayne Stafford was lying and reached down to check his pulse.

He could hardly believe what he was hearing. Sirens in the distance getting louder. Impossible. How could they have figured it out again? Forcing himself not to panic, he looked up at Pappas and shook his head. The message was clear. Dwayne Stafford was dead. He then pointed to the staircase. At the top of the landing lay the body of Dr. Will Landry.

Wesley was in the process of bringing his gun around when their eyes locked. Pappas snapped off two shots, both of which went wide, then dove for cover behind the overturned dining room table. The burst from Wesley's weapon also missed when Dwayne Stafford,

156

who'd only been stunned, reached up and grabbed the gun. The killer clubbed him unconscious.

Hampered by the smoke, Dan Pappas returned fire. Wesley moved to his right and tossed a second stun grenade, covering his ears. The sirens were almost on them. How? How could Kale have known? No time for the last witness.

A short blast from his AK-47 blew the balcony's sliding glass door apart. Removing a coil of nylon rope from his belt, he looped it over the safety rail, and quickly lowered himself down to the floor below.

Chapter 29

The scene outside the apartment was worse than Jack imagined. It looked like they'd fought World War III in there. Stafford was on his knees frantically trying to administer CPR to his partner as Pappas looked on helplessly. When he saw Jack, he shook his head. After a few more seconds, he bent down and put a hand on Dwayne Stafford's shoulder. The young detective had been pounding the chest of a dead man for two minutes.

"C'mon, kid. There's nothing you can do."

Stafford shook the arm off and continued to try CPR.

"Jesus," Milner said, under his breath.

With Jack's help, Pappas finally pulled Stafford away. The look on his face was one of confusion.

"He's gone, Dwayne," Jack said.

They stared at one another before Stafford burst into tears. Jack turned to look for Beth for the first time and noticed she wasn't there.

*

As soon as she saw the rope hanging over the balcony, Beth understood what had happened. It was the Sandman's escape route. Without thinking, she bolted for the stairwell and started down, reasoning he would try to reach the basement rather than hide on the floor below. She pulled out her walkie-talkie and advised the SWAT commander she was in pursuit.

"Wait for backup, Sturgis. Don't try to take this guy . . ."

The com unit's signal died before she could make a reply. Beth continued down the stairs. The minute she came through the basement door, she registered the lights were out. If the Sandman planned ahead as well as Jack said he did, he probably knew the layout thoroughly, which would put her at a major disadvantage. Through a little light coming in from an air vent at street level, she could see the room was extensive and ran the length of the building. Sweeping her gun in both directions, she started forward listening for any sound.

After ten feet, she froze. Up ahead of her to her left a shoe scraped across the cement floor. Her fellow officers would be there in a minute. The Sandman probably knew this as well. It wasn't necessary to take him out, only delay him till they arrived.

Reaching into her pocket, she found a quarter, and pitched it well to her right. Three shots exploded in the dark. She immediately sighted on the muzzle flash, and fired off five of her own spreading the pattern out. The Sandman returned fire immediately. Moving to her left now, Beth bumped into a cinderblock pillar and used it for cover. The sound of more foot falls followed.

"C'mon guys. We're down here," she whispered.

Time seemed to stretch as they continued their cat and mouse game.

Her mouth was dry as she fought to keep the blood from rushing in her ears.

The next sound she heard came from deeper in the dark. Up ahead she saw a shadow move in the dim glow of a safety light. She fired three more times. Two bullets answered her. The resulting flash was momentary but enough to confirm they were entering a connecting tunnel between the condominium complex and the building next door.

How many shots was that? Eight. Four left in the clip.

Once again, the shadow moved. And once again Beth fired. Twice this time, trying to conserve her ammunition. The idea of entering a tunnel frightened her because there would be no cover.

Another movement. This time passing under the light. Beth dropped into a combat stance and took aim, but held off. He'd been too quick for her.

The corridor ended at a wall and turned right. Above, she could hear the faint sounds of traffic and an occasional horn blowing. They had to be crossing under Peachtree Road. She caught a glimpse of the Sandman disappearing around a corner at the end of the second tunnel. With every sense heightened, Beth started after him.

She reached the corner as the Sandman was about to enter a flight of stairs.

"Freeze!"

The killer spun around and leveled his weapon.

No choice now. Beth pulled the trigger and fired. Both shots went wide as the slide on her weapon locked open. The bullets she thought would end her life never arrived. The Sandman cocked his head to one side as if he was examining a bug and stood at the end of the corridor watching her. No one spoke.

"Are you still afraid of the dark, Elizabeth?"

Before she could respond, the killer fired a short burst at the ceiling destroying the safety light above her head, plunging the area into night. Beth ducked out of reflex. When she looked again, he was gone.

As soon as she regained her composure, she found the spare magazine in her jacket pocket. Rammed it into place. Raced for the steps. She came out in the lobby of an ornate art deco building on the other side of Peachtree Road. It was empty. Frustrated, she ran out to check the street, but the Sandman was gone.

*

Wesley Simms changed clothes in the building's storeroom and emerged from the rear entrance dressed as a jogger.

Exit strategy. He loved that phrase. No plan survives first contact with the enemy. The answer? Leave yourself a rabbit hole to disappear into. Father Mike knew everything. In the three years he trained him outside of Dublin some twenty years earlier, he'd drilled that into his head over and over. Any mission could fall apart. When that happened, it was a matter of life or death. Run away and fight another day.

*

The inside of the condo looked like a tornado had ripped through the place. Furniture was everywhere. Smoke still hung in the air. Blood from Will Landry's chest dripped steadily onto the marble floor underneath the landing, forming a dark-red pool.

At the top of the stairs, Rachel Lawrence sat with her back to the wall like a broken doll, legs extended, staring at the body of her friend. At first glance, Jack thought she was dead, but then he saw her eyes move. At the sight of Landry's body, his stomach sank.

The Sandman had been one step ahead of them from the beginning. The marksmen had just taken up positions to shoot down the drones when it had finally come to him. The parallel to what happened in Spain was unmistakable. As in Madrid, there was a crowd filling the street, the result of a bomb threat. That's when two thoughts occurred to Jack simultaneously. One, the explosion wasn't the point, the distraction was. Two, when it happened, everyone took their eye off the true targets. It was all a ruse. Misdirection. Don't watch the hand holding the coin; watch the one I'm waving in your face. The Sandman's goal had always been Rachel Lawrence and Will Landry. He had played them perfectly—played *him* perfectly.

Jack sensed Pappas and Milner beside him. All three watched as the medical technicians ran up the steps. They needed only a glance to see their services would not be required that morning. Rachel still hadn't moved. One of them checked her for injuries then helped her to her feet.

"What happened here?" Jack asked Pappas.

"I came in at the tail end. It looks like Landry went after the Sandman with a lamp. Sonofabitch shot him point blank. Dwayne was down and I was pretty sure he'd also bought it. Thank God the vest saved him."

"What about the Sandman?" Milner asked.

"He went over the balcony. We exchanged shots, but I couldn't see shit with all the smoke."

The FBI agent walked outside, examined the rope for a moment and pounded his fist against the railing, then started making calls on his hand communicator. Jack was about to ask where Beth was when she walked through the door.

"Where've you been?"

"Chasing the Sandman."

"What?" Anger flared in his chest. It was a stupid, reckless thing to do. He bit back the rest of what he was going to say and waited.

She explained what had happened and the killer's delay in taking a shot at her in the tunnel when he could easily have done so. Jack shook his head, confused.

Pappas inquired, "Did you see what he looked like?"

"He was dressed like a SWAT officer and had his face covered. I put a BOLO out on him."

"You shouldn't have tried to take him alone," Pappas said, echoing Jack's thoughts.

"I just reacted," Beth said. "I was calling for backup when I lost the signal."

Pappas was about to say something else but paused as they carried Will Landry's body down the steps. Rachel Lawrence was behind them. She appeared to be in shock. Jack approached her.

"Rachel, I—"

Her slap caught him across the face, turning his head sideways.

"We trusted you." Her voice was barely more than a whisper. Before Jack could reply, she walked out of the room.

Chapter 30

The slap caught everyone in the room by surprise, particularly Jack. Rachel's retreating back was an accusation, worse than if she'd said he had murdered Will Landry himself. Jack's face burned with shame, but it wasn't from the blow. The extent of his failure, as he perceived it now, hung in the air along with the flash grenade's smoke. He could feel their eyes on him. He knew what the others were thinking . . . and he agreed. He'd failed for the second time in one day. Without a word, he followed her through the door.

Dan Pappas was the first to recover. He turned to Beth and said, "The Sandman had his fingers on Stafford's throat. He was pretending to check for a pulse."

Surprise registered. "Was he wearing gloves?"

"Negative. He took one off to check. That's why I hesitated. I thought the little fucker was one of us. His middle two fingers were on Dwayne's carotid artery."

Beth wanted to go after Jack. No one could have figured out what the Sandman was planning as quickly as he had. They'd have needed a crystal ball. At times he could be so frustrating she wanted to scream. Instead of feeling pride at having saved Rachel, she was certain he blamed himself for Landry and Mundas's deaths, if not everyone who died at Mary Quinn's house as well. Torn between wanting to console her lover and her duty to secure what might be a vital clue, Beth chose the latter.

*

Dwayne Stafford sat quietly, staring straight ahead, and let Beth Sturgis examine his throat. He knew it was possible to recover latent fingerprints from a person's body provided you moved quickly enough.

The body armor he'd been wearing had saved his life. Ed hadn't been so lucky. If not for those stupid pizzas. The detective clenched his jaw and let the tears roll freely down his face. Beth turned her head away so as not to embarrass him. He and Ed had discussed the possibility one of them might be killed. Both were less than six years out of college and, armed with the invulnerability of youth, neither believed it would ever happen.

The young detective was dreading what came next, breaking the news to Ed's parents. They lived in Vinings, a small community north of Atlanta. Growing up, he'd spent as much time at their home as he had at his own. He and Ed had gone through grade school, middle school, and high school together. They'd played on the same baseball team. Ed was their pitcher. Their teammates had dubbed him Lurch because he was so tall. Dwayne felt numb, unable to move.

Watching the ME take his friend's body away, his mind refused to accept what his eyes were seeing. Surely this was one of Ed's stupid jokes. He was just outside waiting to walk through the door with that ridiculous horse laugh of his. "Good one, huh, Dwayne?"

Yeah, Ed. Good one.

"I'm done," Beth said, touching his arm.

"So am I," Dwayne said.

He stood and left the room. Dan Pappas looked at Beth for a moment, shook his head, and followed him out, leaving Beth alone with Todd Milner.

"I'm so sorry," the agent said.

"Me, too," she said quietly.

"We're losing people left and right. First Gabe, now your guy."

"Ed Mundas," Beth said. "His name was Ed Mundas."

Milner nodded. "You want me to run those prints?"

"I'll drop them off at the lab on the way home. I still need to finish up here."

"Sure," Milner said, and waited a beat. "You understand we have a problem, don't you? We can't let Doctor Lawrence return to her home. She'd be a sitting duck."

"That's where Dan Pappas went," Beth said.

"Oh, I thought he was going after Detective Stafford."

"Dwayne'll come out of it. He needs to notify Ed's parents. After that . . . I don't know. Losing a partner this way . . ."

She took a deep breath and rubbed her face with her hands, then mentally divided the apartment into quadrants and began the search for evidence, moving mostly by rote.

"Mind if I talk while you're working?" Milner asked, adjusting his arm sling to a more comfortable position.

"Go ahead. If I don't answer right away, I'm not being rude."

"Understood. I know Kale's still in charge, but we need to bring more people in. The Sandman's not going away."

"Neither are we," Beth said over her shoulder.

"The Bureau has a safehouse we use for federal witnesses. It's run by the Marshal Service. I say we move Dr. Lawrence there."

Beth paused to check her cellphone, then informed him, "That was Dan. He has her. They're on the way to HQ."

"Great. I'll let Director Newton know. I guess we can talk about the second safehouse later."

Privately she agreed with Milner but was not about to say anything that would undermine Jack's authority. She continued with her examination occasionally stooping down to pick up some tiny bit of material and bag it. Considering the number of people who'd been through the condo in the last hour, she wasn't hopeful.

The FBI agent watched and commented, "You're wasting your time."

"I know," Beth said. "Just gathering my thoughts."

"Any idea where Kale went or what he has in mind?"

Beth laughed to herself and said, "That would be a neat trick."

"He did a tremendous job," Milner said. "Using the drones as a diversion never occurred to me."

"That's Jack," Beth said absently, as she squinted at a black thread.

"There's another problem," Milner said.

Beth stopped walking and closed her evidence kit. "How did the Sandman know about this place?"

"Exactly. It means we have a leak. There's no other way to say it."

For a moment, she considered telling him she and Jack had discussed this earlier, then dismissed the idea.

Milner continued. "Our problem is containment. There are simply too many people in the loop. Us, your department, the U.S. Attorney's office. We have to figure out a way to stop the flow."

"I know."

"Ideas?"

Beth shook her head. "I'm tapped out right now, Todd."

Milner let his breath out. "I need to brief the boss. We're in trouble here, Detective."

*

Beth arrived home expecting to find Jack there. He wasn't. Nor did he answer his cell when she called him. She fed Marta and took her for a walk. Passing lights from cars were just beginning to impact the growing darkness. On the next street, she met a neighbor walking her collie and stopped to chat. The neighbor inquired about Jack.

"He's great," Beth said, hoping she was telling the truth.

The woman was Deena Marchado, an accountant who worked out of her home. From past conversations, she knew Deena had once been an actress but had left the profession a few years earlier. She was forty-eight with two teenage sons and had just let her boyfriend move in a few months ago. The moving in part gave her and Beth a common ground, though in reverse.

Deena inquired, "Were you involved in that craziness downtown?"

"Right in the middle of it," Beth said.

"Jack too?"

Beth said he was and filled her in on the broader details, wanting to end the conversation and get home as quickly as possible.

"Wow. I'll bet you guys just wanna put your feet up and chill."

"You got that right," Beth said.

"Is he making supper again?"

Beth smiled for an answer, which to her mind was better than telling a lie.

"Well, I won't keep you," Deena said. "I wish he would teach Jerry to cook. That man can burn water."

Shortly after she entered the house, the phone began to ring. It was a detective named Jeff Sibley, who worked computer crimes.

"Beth, sorry to bother you. I thought I'd better give you a call. I'm at Kaleidoscope. Jack's here."

"Oh?"

"He's been putting it away pretty good."

"Really?"

"Look, I don't want to get in your business. I know you're sort of together and, well . . . it's not a good idea if he drives."

Beth wondered how many people in the department knew about them. The fact that Jeff had called Jack's home instead of hers was a partial answer.

"I appreciate it, Jeff. I'm on the way."

*

Kaleidoscope was the neighborhood restaurant in Brookhaven where they had gone on their first date. Well, maybe not a date exactly, because Dan Pappas was also there, but she thought of it that way. Over the last few months, she'd been incredibly happy and was sure Jack felt the same way. She loved how his mind never stopped working and the way he looked at her. And when he touched her, it still felt like the first time. They'd managed to connect on a level she never thought possible. And now this stupid case was chipping away at it.

Beth told Marta, "I have to pick up Daddy. Be right back."

Marta's large brown eyes watched her.

"Yeah, me too."

On the drive, she thought about the situation they were in. It wasn't good. Jack's tendency to blame himself came as no surprise; she'd seen it firsthand with the guilt he carried over the death of his ex-partner. Unfortunately there was no time for that now. Both Rachel and the department needed him at full strength with all his faculties intact. They might be able to stop the Sandman, but the prospects weren't encouraging without his help. The killer had already taken out two of the three witnesses.

She entered the parking lot at the rear of the restaurant and saw Jack's BMW there. Jeff Sibley was waiting for her in the lobby. He made a small motion with his head toward the back of the restaurant. Jack was at a table with another woman. Sibley looked awkward.

"I'm sorry. I didn't know who else to call. They were talking at the bar and just sat down."

"It's not a problem, Jeff. Thanks again. I'll take it from here."

The detective seemed happy to get back to his dinner.

"Loving is trusting," Beth muttered to herself and started for the table.

Chapter 31

Rachel Lawrence saw Jack's eyes shift past her shoulder and turned to see who or what he was looking at.

"Have a seat," she told Beth. "We're celebrating my escape."

"Your escape?"

"Don't be angry with Detective Pappas. He brought me to your headquarters. I snuck out after he was gone."

Beth turned to Jack, who started to rise and didn't quite make it. He sat back down heavily, reached forward, and pushed a chair out for her.

"What a nice surprise," Jack said. "Elizabeth Sturgis . . . Doctor Rachel Lawrence. Doctor Lawrence . . . the lovely Elizabeth Sturgis."

Beth shook her head and sat down. Jack's eyes were bloodshot and his face flushed.

"It's nice of you to join us," Jack said. The "nice" came out as "nicesh."

Rachel and Beth exchanged glances.

Beth asked, "Does headquarters know you escaped?"

"Jack called them."

"What are your plans?"

"Before or after I bury my husband? The funeral's on Monday. You're invited. My sister's been taking care of the details."

"You haven't answered my question."

Jack searched for the waitress, spotted her, and held up three fingers signaling for another round. Beth reached behind his back and waved her off. If Jack noticed, he didn't say anything.

"Life goes on. That's what Jack was telling me," Rachel said.

"Fine," Beth said. "Life goes on. But yours won't if you're running around out here. Have I mentioned there's a killer stalking you?"

"That won't be a problem," Rachel said. "I have to go out of town tomorrow."

"Why?"

"For an operation."

"Where?"

"NYU's Medical Center."

"The one in Manhattan?"

"You know it?"

"I lived there for a couple of years."

"Don't get all bent out of shape," Rachel said. "It's a short procedure. Tricky, but short. I should be back tomorrow night."

"Isn't there anyone else who can handle it?"

"Several people, actually. But the parents have been with me since we started. They asked me to do it. I agreed."

"And it's a one day trip?"

"If there are no complications. I don't anticipate any, but you never know. It's possible I might have to stay an extra day. Certainly not more. I have to get back for George's—"

"Right," Beth said. "Is there any way the operation can be put off?"

"That wouldn't be fair to the child."

Beth looked at Jack who had his eyes closed and appeared to have fallen asleep sitting up. His chin was resting in his hand.

Several seconds passed before Rachel said, "I apologized for hitting him and told him it wasn't his fault. I'm not sure he heard me."

"It might not make a difference if he did," Beth said. "He takes everything so personally. I'm sorry about Dr. Landry."

Rachel broke eye contact and looked out the window at the restaurant's patio. Candles fluttered in round glass holders on the tables. Between them were odd-looking portable outdoor heaters that resembled mini lampposts. Except for one couple who seemed immune to the temperature, the patio was empty. When the weather was warm, you couldn't move out there.

"I was wrong to have slapped him," Rachel said. "He's a good man. Tell him I'm sorry."

"Tell him yourself," Beth said. "You're the one who hit him."

"I was upset."

"You had every right to be," Beth said. "He nearly killed himself trying to get to you. Nobody could have stopped what happened."

"I get that . . . now," Rachel said. "Will was trying to defend me . . ."

"I know." She'd seen his body and the lamp he was holding when he rushed the killer. It was the desperate and courageous act of a brave man. The image just broke her heart. She looked at Jack and brushed the hair off his forehead.

"I'll tell him when I see him again," Rachel said.

"Any way I can talk you out of this trip?"

Rachel took a second to align her paper napkin with edge of the table. Dissatisfied, she made a few minute adjustments. Beth waited.

"In the last forty-eight hours, I've lost a husband, a friend, and learned there's a man out there who wants to kill me because I saw something in a parking garage. Now my medical practice is in danger of collapse. Stu's fighting to hold things together. Maybe he will. I don't know. What I do know is I can't give up anything else, like my self-respect, which I'd be doing if I ran off and hid someplace. Does that make any sense?"

"It does," Beth said. "How 'bout if we make a deal? Stay at our house tonight."

"Our?"

"Jack and I live together."

The surprise registered in Rachel's face.

Beth continued, "Along with the biggest German shepherd you've ever seen. She's awesome and totally protective. If you're not safe there, you won't be anywhere."

Rachel smiled and stared at her hands for a moment. "So you're the love of his life. I thought he was just being poetic." Glancing quickly to see if he was still asleep, she leaned closer and lowered her voice. Beth leaned in as well. "He wants to marry you."

A smile spread across Beth's face. She hunched her shoulders, and whispered back, "I know."

Chapter 32

Three Days to the Grand Jury

Mornings are a bad time for people who drink too much. The gargoyles from the night before tend to linger and reach out to their victims from the soft edges of sleep. Jack woke up with a headache and went straight to the kitchen to fix a cup of coffee and a bagel. When that was done, he took his breakfast out to the porch. A ground mist had formed, hovering just above the lawn. The cool air felt good. He swallowed two Tylenol, sat back on the glider, and closed his eyes. One of the gargoyles perched itself on the top rail, watching him through yellow eyes.

His belief that he was responsible for the deaths of Will Landry and Ed Mundas had retreated only marginally in the early dawn light. If he had only understood what the Sandman was planning sooner, both men might still be alive. Morris Shottner called that having irrational expectations. Maybe he was right. To Jack, they had never seemed irrational. Normal perhaps, but not irrational. Sometimes putting that kind of pressure on himself worked; sometimes it didn't. One day he'd have to find a balance between the two.

Marta sat beside him, content to be close. Every once in a while she'd look up at him, then back at the lawn. He wondered what those looks meant and what she was thinking. Vague recollections of the previous night came and went, but they were all a jumble. Beth was there, as was Rachel Lawrence. He just couldn't remember where "there" was, or how he'd gotten home, or getting into bed. Or why there was an unfamiliar suitcase in his living room with a name tag that said "R. Lawrence."

The guest room door was closed. Being a detective, he concluded Dr. Lawrence was now their houseguest. He didn't recall inviting her. Jack took a sip of coffee and felt the hot liquid moving through his body, warming him. It was a pleasant sensation. The gargoyle hopped off the porch and disappeared into the mist.

In the cherry trees at the back of his property, the birds were beginning to wake. A blue jay landed on the porch and looked at him. Like most birds, it was in a constant state of motion: its head moving in staccato fashion, wings fluttering, hopping. Marta watched it without visible enthusiasm. Jack broke off a small piece of bagel and tossed it onto the lawn. The bird flew down, grabbed it, and took off. Marta's look was reproachful.

They were still sitting there when Dan Pappas pulled into his driveway. The big detective got out. Marta trotted down the steps to greet him and stood on her hind legs while he rubbed her neck.

"Morning, Jack. You're up early."

"So are you."

Pappas bent down and put up with several kisses. "Thought I'd give you some advance warning. Carmine Donofrio called me at six AM wanting to know why Rachel Lawrence is running around loose."

"Loose?"

"His words, not mine."

"She's not loose. I imagine she's asleep in our guest room."

Pappas accepted two more kisses from Marta and said, "She likes my aftershave."

"She likes you," Jack said. "Coffee?"

"Stay where you are. I can manage."

That was fine because Jack had no intention of getting up. He was waiting for the Tylenol to kick in. Marta and Pappas disappeared inside and returned a minute later with Marta chewing a bone-shaped dog biscuit. "I had no choice," Pappas said, taking a seat. "She forced me."

Jack laughed, which only made his head hurt worse.

Pappas continued, "Donofrio was pretty hot under the collar. I thought I should be here when he arrives."

"He's arriving?"

"That was my impression," Pappas said, and took a sip of his coffee. "Where do you buy this stuff? It has a kinda—"

"Raspberry taste. Beth picks it up at Harry's Farmer's Market. They carry about a hundred different blends. That's her flavor of the week."

Pappas nodded and took another sip.

Jack summoned the energy to ask what Donofrio wanted.

"Ask him yourself." Pappas pointed to a black Crown Victoria that had just turned onto Jack's street. The car pulled into the driveway and parked behind the detective. Jack pushed himself up and came down the steps. Carmine Donofrio and a man shaped like a fireplug with short black hair that came to a point on his forehead got out of the car. Donofrio was already dressed in a suit and tie. Impressive for that hour of the morning. Everything about the way his companion carried himself indicated he was a cop. Donofrio said good morning and introduced Barry Newsome with the United States Marshal's Service.

"Barry," the deputy marshal said, offering his hand.

They shook.

"C'mon inside," Jack said. "I'll fix you some coffee."

"Your witness left police headquarters last night without permission."

"Actually, she's not my witness," Jack said. "I assume you're referring to Dr. Lawrence?"

"Don't jerk me around, Kale," Donofrio said. "You advised your switchboard she was with you."

"That's correct," Jack said. "Would you like to discuss it out here or come inside?"

"You'll admit this is a bit unusual?"

"I'll admit that."

"No offense," the marshal said. "But we need to see she's all right."

Without waiting for Jack's response, Newsome started for the steps. The moment he did Marta stood and growled low in her throat. Newsome stopped where he was.

"Hold your hand out and let her sniff you," Jack said.

"Really?" Newsome asked uncertainly.

"She tends to be protective."

The marshal did as instructed.

174

"How does she feel about lawyers?" Donofrio asked.

"Same as everybody," Jack said.

Pappas stifled a laugh.

Donofrio gave him a sour look and cautiously extended his hand to Marta. Her tail finally wagged. Jack led everyone into the den and told them to make themselves comfortable. Newsome and Donofrio declined the coffee.

"Helluva business downtown yesterday," Donofrio said. "It's a shame it didn't turn out better."

"Both witnesses would be dead if Jack hadn't figured out what the Sandman was up to," Pappas pointed out.

"It's possible. But if they were in a federal safehouse like I'd asked, both of them might be alive and we wouldn't have had to evacuate almost fourteen thousand people in the middle of the day. Any idea what that cost?"

"Not a clue," Pappas said, taking another sip of coffee.

"Have the model airplane guys we picked up talked?" Jack asked.

"About what, flying?" Donofrio said. "Because that's exactly what they were doing. We found no explosives and it's not against the law to fly them. We questioned them for five hours. It was a complete bust."

"Who's we?" Jack asked.

"My office and the ATF. After that, the Fulton County DA and I spoke at some length. Neither of us could think of anything to hold them. They were released early last night."

"So you think they were there just by coincidence?" Pappas said.

"Nobody thinks that," Donofrio said. "But you need criminal charges to hold people. The ATF thought it was best to cut them loose and see who they hook up with. They're following as we speak."

While Donofrio was talking, Beth came down the stairs. She took one look at the men assembled in her living room, nodded to everyone, and made her way into the kitchen.

"Not wise to speak to her before the first cup of coffee," Jack said.

"Wasn't that Detective Sturgis?" Donofrio asked.

"I believe so. Dan?"

Pappas leaned forward and looked into the kitchen. "No question about it."

"I'm sorry, I wasn't aware you lived together."

Jack smiled. Said nothing.

"You are the strangest group of people," Donofrio said. "Now, if it's not too much trouble, would you mind producing Dr. Lawrence?"

"She's in the shower," Beth said, coming back into the room.

"We'll wait," Donofrio said. He introduced Barry Newsome to her, then said, "Would someone mind telling me what a government witness was doing here last night?"

Beth informed him, "We figured Rachel was safer here than in her own home."

The U.S. Attorney nodded thoughtfully. "I guess I can't argue with that. My question is, why was she out in the first place? Look, I don't want to be an ass, but it's obvious things aren't working out. The facts pretty much speak for themselves."

"Facts rarely speak for themselves," Jack said. "It's the interpretation people put on them that gets us in trouble."

As they were talking, Rachel Lawrence came down. She was dressed in a navy-blue pant suit and her hair was still wet from the shower.

"Did I hear my name mentioned?"

Donofrio stood. "Dr. Lawrence, I'm glad to see you're all right. You went through a harrowing experience yesterday. I'm Carmine Donofrio with the United States Attorney's office. I believe you've spoken to Sandy Tatum who works with me."

"Ms. Tatum's the one who interviewed George and me, correct?"

"Yes, ma'am. She did."

"Coffee, Rachel?" Beth asked.

"Please. Black is fine."

Beth went back to the kitchen and returned with a large cup, which she handed to her.

Donofrio continued, "We were discussing you, Doctor. We'd like to take you someplace where you'll be safe. This is a terrible business we're dealing with."

"I was quite comfortable here," Rachel informed him.

"I'm sure you were. Obviously, this is a temporary arrangement. If I may be blunt, we're far better equipped to protect you. Now if you'll pack your things, we can be on our way and not bother these people anymore."

Rachel turned to Beth. "You agree with this?"

"First I'm hearing about it. I just woke up."

"What about you?" Rachel asked Jack.

"Same here. Mr. Donofrio has a point though. They are better equipped to protect you."

"There," Donofrio said. "Now if you'll just get your things—"

"Am I under arrest?"

"No, no, no, of course not," Donofrio said. "This is for your own good."

"I appreciate your concern. I believe I'll stay here for the time being."

"I'm afraid that's not possible," Donofrio said. "Please don't make me force the issue, Doctor."

The pleasant expression faded from Rachel's face slightly. "And how would you do that?"

"If I have to, I'll get a judge to place you in protective custody. I hope that won't be necessary."

"Meaning you'd have to file some kind of paper with the court."

"Yes. But that won't be a—"

"Thank you for your concern," Rachel said. "I'm sure we'll talk again. Now if you'll excuse me, I have some things to attend to before I leave."

"What do you mean, leave?" Donofrio said.

"I'm scheduled to do surgery in Houston later this afternoon. There's a very sick little girl there who needs me."

The attorney let out a breath. "I simply cannot allow that."

"You simply can't force me to stay. The last time I checked this is still the United States."

Donofrio turned to the deputy marshal and said, "Arrest her."

"For what?"

"I don't give a damn. I'll figure it out later."

Suddenly Newsome didn't look so well. He shook his head in resignation and turned to find himself staring at Dan Pappas, or to be more precise, the second button from the top of Dan Pappas's shirt.

Pappas looked down at him and smiled. "Don't do that, Barry."

"If you interfere with a U.S. Marshal in the performance of his duty, it'll mean the end of your career. What's more, I'll prosecute you myself," Donofrio said.

Newsome's face turned red. "I don't need you fighting my battles, numb-nuts. You produce a legitimate order, I'll serve it. But I'm not making something up." He turned back to Pappas and added, "And I ain't afraid of you."

Pappas frowned then turned to Beth and asked, "Where'd I go wrong?"

*

After Donofrio and the marshal left, Beth said to Rachel, "You told me the operation was in New York."

"Did I?"

"You did."

"With all the excitement, I guess I got confused."

"Is it really scheduled for this afternoon?"

"Absolutely. We need to get moving."

Pappas and Jack both caught the word "we" and looked to Beth for an explanation.

"Dwayne Stafford and I are going with her," Beth said.

"You are?"

"Mm-hm."

Jack considered that for a moment, then commented, "It's good to be in charge." He turned to Marta and asked, "You know anything about this?"

Marta looked the other way.

"What time is your flight?" Jack asked.

"Whenever we get there. The girl's family chartered a plane for us," Rachel said.

"And all three of you are going?"

"New York's a dangerous place, Jack. We'll be home tonight or tomorrow. You and Dan need to stay here and follow up on the Sandman. Rachel's probably safer there when you think about it. No one but the girl's family and the people in this room know we're going."

That made sense. Jack turned to Pappas for his opinion. The big detective lifted his shoulders.

Chapter 33

Wesley was furious. The detective in the condo hadn't so much as paused to ask his name. He fired without a second thought. Weren't the police supposed to give you a chance to surrender before they started shooting? Someone had issued a kill order. Probably that smartass Jackson Kale. Listening to the radio chatter going back and forth between the cops, he realized he'd been wrong. The behemoth who had tried to shoot him in the apartment wasn't Kale after all—just some stupid cowboy trying to make a name for himself. Jack Kale and his stupid hazel eyes were still out there. Hunting him.

More upsetting was that Elizabeth had come after him. Considering what he'd done for her on the mountain, it was just . . . well, ungrateful. He wished he could have been there when the drones made their appearance. People huddled together in the streets waiting for the explosion. Cops shouting orders. Traffic at a standstill. Spotters on roofs with binoculars relaying information to intrepid marksmen. The finale punctuated by a fusillade of bullets. How good it would have been to see their faces when they found they had just shot down two harmless model airplanes. Beautiful. *Oops, sorry about that, folks. Go back to your jobs now. Nothing to see here.* The great Jack Kale wasn't so great at all.

Not great, but smart enough to have guessed his intentions.

He repeated the old mantra about understanding not what your enemy can do, but what he's capable of. Kale was certainly capable of a great deal. Still, the mission hadn't been a total failure. The priest's voice whispered in his ear.

That's my boy. We're two-thirds of the way home. Are you on track for the last target?

Without a question, Father.

*

Leonard Steven Walpole, Lenny to his friends, had never been so nervous in his life. Before releasing him, the cops had yelled for five straight hours, cajoled, threatened, and basically raked him over the coals about his contact with the Sandman. Sandman? The only name Lenny knew was Rick. The same Rick who had rescued him from a park bench, bought him new clothes, got him a nice, clean room at the Clairmont Hotel, and paid him three thousand dollars to fly a model airplane.

"Nothing to it. Just open the laptop, touch the screen icon, and the program runs automatically," Rick had said.

"I won't be doing anything illegal, will I?"

"When was the last time anyone got in trouble for flying a model airplane in a public park?"

"Never, I suppose," Lenny said. "But I had a course in law school years ago on torts and nuisances. I was just wondering."

"Look, Lenny, if you're uncomfortable, I can find someone else. You can keep the room and your clothes."

"No, no, no. I want to help," Lenny said quickly. "Your movie sounds awesome. Will this really get you good publicity?"

"That's what we're hoping."

"When will *Drone Attack!* come out?"

"Around July fourth, we hope. It depends on the distributors. We still need to wrap up some postproduction shoots."

"I wish there was a part for me," Lenny said. "I always wanted to be an actor."

"If this works out, I'll talk to the assistant director about you."

"Would you, Rick? Would you really?"

"Hey, man, what are friends for?"

*

Lenny and Rick were sitting in the lobby of the Clairmont Hotel. At one time, the art deco structure had been a fashionable, trendy spot with dancing on the weekends and a six piece orchestra. Their rooftop

180

restaurant was called the Palm Court. The palms, if there ever were any, were long gone. Shortly before the start of the Korean War, the Palm Court had closed for renovations never to reopen again. Over the years, the Clairmont had been many things, from a nursing home to one- and two-room efficiency apartments for college students.

Plans to gut the hotel and convert it to luxury apartments came and went as the neighborhood around the Clairmont fell into decline. Eventually, the sad old building completed the circle back to a hotel—of sorts. Prostitutes now rented out rooms by the hour. Two different gangs formed a treaty and used the accommodations to house members who needed to be off the streets for a while. And druggies, like Lenny Walpole, stayed there whenever they had enough money, which, unfortunately, wasn't very often.

A large sign out front advertised free local phone service, but the only phones to be found were in the lobby office. Surprisingly, the electricity worked, as did a spotty form of steam heat whenever the owner purchased enough coal for the boiler. It was a blessing that Atlanta temperatures stayed mild most of the year.

To Lenny, who had once viewed his future with promise, but now only counted the days until his next fix, the Clairmont was paradise. Having a roof over his head and a bed to sleep in were luxuries. Things others took for granted, but were sorely missed once they were gone.

Lenny and Rick left the lobby and went to Lenny's room. "Are you sure no one followed you?" Rick asked.

"Real sure," Lenny said. "I changed trains twice like you told me and then walked from the Tenth Street Station to here. I never saw anyone the whole time."

"That's great, Lenny. Let me run a wand over you just to check. You can never be too sure."

"You really think another production company would try to follow me?"

"Cops provide security for them," Rick said. "They'd love to bug the room and get a jump on us. Believe me, I've seen it all."

Lenny stood while Rick ran the metal detector up and down his body. Nothing. He then had Lenny take off his shoes so he could check the heels. They were good too.

"You must be really smart," Lenny said when Rick finished. "There were thousands of people in the streets. Cops were looking up at the sky and there were even snipers on the rooftops with rifles."

What else would a sniper use? Rocks?

"Well, we're hoping our cameras picked up the realism. You ever read about Orson Welles's *War of the Worlds* broadcast?"

Lenny frowned. "I remember something about that. My grandpa told me he panicked the whole country. People thought the Martians had actually landed in New Jersey or someplace."

"Realism's everything. When the film comes out, they'll line up around the block to see it."

"Wow," Lenny said. "And I'll get credit?"

"Technical Advisor, Leonard Walpole," Rick said, handing Lenny an envelope with fifteen hundred dollars in it. "Payment as promised."

Lenny shook his head in disbelief. He was so happy he wanted to cry. "Rick . . . thank you for everything."

"My pleasure, buddy."

"What happens to that laptop you gave me?"

"Oh, that. I'll return it to the prop master tomorrow. Why?"

"I was just wondering if they'd miss it."

Wesley couldn't believe the little twerp was actually suggesting he steal it. He'd probably trade it for drugs the first chance he got.

"They watch these things pretty carefully, pal," Rick said.

"I understand. I was playing with it on the train and realized how long it's been since I owned one. They're so small and light now."

"Well . . . maybe I could tell them the cops kept it. Let me think about it."

"Would you really?"

Wesley smiled. "Sure thing. Tell me again what the cops talked to you about."

"Basically, they wanted to know where I lived and where I got the plane. They asked me a bunch of questions about what you looked like and where we met. I told the truth like you said I should, but I never mentioned a word about the movie. I swear."

"That's good."

"You were right about them giving me a lie detector test. That was a little scary, because I was so nervous. I hope it's all right if they keep the drone for a few days. The receipt's right there on the table."

Wesley shook his head and put an arm around the little man's shoulders. It was amazing the little drug addict could think at all. His brain was fried. Still, it was inevitable both men he'd hired to fly the models would be picked up and questioned. The most they could say was that they'd been hired by a movie company to help film a stunt. No one had gotten hurt and no laws were broken, so there was little the authorities could do. The evacuation of the buildings had embarrassed the city. They didn't want to compound it by being seen as picking on two innocent men to cover their blunder. Just beautiful.

"I have another one. C'mon, dinner is on the studio tonight."

Chapter 34

After Donofrio and the deputy marshal left, Beth told Rachel she needed twenty minutes to get dressed. Rachel also went upstairs saying she needed to finish putting on her makeup. The plan was to be gone by the time the assistant U.S. attorney returned with his order.

Pappas watched them disappear up the steps and asked, "Will it really be twenty minutes?"

"She thinks it will," Jack said. "And when she comes down she'll be convinced that it was. Fifty minutes is more the norm."

Pappas nodded. "Yeah, Monica's like that, too. Since we weren't invited to New York, you have any idea what to do next?"

"Several," Jack said indignantly.

"And?"

"They're still in the formative stages."

"I see."

"Out of curiosity, did we really let those model operators go?"

"We didn't. The ATF did. They swooped in and snatched them from us. Milner spoke to their tech people. They checked for explosive residue and had their fingerprints run. They're still looking at the airplane and the drone, but they didn't sound hopeful last night."

"Sounds like they're on top of it."

"Your girlfriend had a little to do with that. When you took a break, she ran with the ball."

"Polite way of putting it," Jack said.

"Everything copacetic now?"

"If I hadn't been so slow to react, Ed and Landry might—"

"Yeah, and if frogs had wings, they wouldn't bop along on their asses all day. The fact is, if *I* didn't hesitate, I could have taken the bastard out then and there. No one could have figured it out faster, Jack, so stop beating yourself up. We're always gonna be a step behind these guys unless we figure some way to see into the future. What is it you're always telling me about psychology?"

"That it's a bad predictor of future behavior."

"Right. I'm gonna head over to the lab. You give me a call later, okay?"

"Why?"

"When the ATF grabbed the drone guys from us, Beth arranged to have Nelda Latham check out their clothes and shoes. I'm curious to see what she came up with. That's one smart cookie, my friend. You taught her well."

"I know," Jack said, looking up at the ceiling.

"She let you in on the surprise yet?"

"What surprise?"

"Guess you'll find out soon enough, only don't say I told you. There's a reason she's going to New York and you're not. She figures you're better off here tracking down the Sandman."

"If I had some idea where to start."

"How about his name and who he is?"

Jack stared at Pappas for a moment. "All right, give."

The detective related what happened in the condo during his encounter with the Sandman and his supposedly checking Dwayne Stafford for a pulse.

"You picked up a latent print?"

"*She* picked up a latent."

Pappas took a folded piece of paper from his pocket and laid it on the end table, then stood, winked at Jack, and left the house.

*

Jack bounded up the steps two at a time and burst into their bedroom. Beth gasped. She'd been leaning over the dresser applying eyeliner using the dressing mirror. Except for a pair of lime-green bikini panties, she was completely naked.

"Whoa," Jack said under his breath, coming to a halt.

"Would you shut the door, please?"

Jack opened his mouth to speak and closed it again when Beth turned to face him.

"Was there something you wanted to say?"

Jack swallowed. "I forget."

"Perhaps you wanted to thank me for finding the Sandman's real name and where he's from," Beth prompted.

Jack nodded. His eyes pretty much remained focused on her breasts.

"Well," Beth said, drawing out the word.

Jack shook his head to clear it and held up one finger. "Don't move," he said and disappeared into their closet. He came out a moment later holding something behind his back and walked up to her.

"Would you like to go to New York as an engaged woman?"

"What?"

Opening the box, he showed her the diamond ring he'd bought yesterday.

"I'm standing here naked and you ask me to marry you?"

"Well . . . yeah. If you'll have me."

"And you think this is romantic? This is not romantic."

Jack looked at Marta, who raised her eyebrows. He took a breath and dropped down to one knee.

"Elizabeth Sturgis, I love you. I've been in love with you since the day we met. I can't imagine spending the rest of my life without you. I want you to be my wife. Would you *please* marry me?"

"No, you're a loser," she said, pushing his head away. "You can't even come up with the name of one dumb killer."

The look on Jack's face was simply too much. This was everything she wanted to hear. Beth dropped down to her knees and put her arms around him. "Of course I'll marry you."

They were still kissing when Marta tried to push her way between them.

Chapter 35

Dwayne Stafford stood on the tarmac at Charlie Brown Airport shaking his head. He was watching the pilot and copilot do a walk-around on the Lear jet. As a rule, he tried to avoid flying whenever possible. The plane looked sturdy enough and Doc Lawrence had told him she'd used the charter company before and was comfortable with their aircraft and maintenance program. There was no need to mention the last part. If the maintenance was so good, why were they out there checking up on the mechanic? One of them was staring at the wing and frowning. He knew what it meant when someone looked at something and frowned. Dwayne's stomach was already queasy. The pilot's double-checking things didn't help, nor did everyone telling him how safe flying was. None of these things raised his comfort level. It was also particularly disturbing to be flying out of an airport named after a cartoon character.

The day had started off badly and would probably get worse. Dwayne glanced at Beth and Rachel Lawrence. Neither seemed to have a care in the world. They were chatting happily with each other about Beth's ring, leaving him to watch for snipers and look at frowning pilots. Wonderful. It was about time Kale popped the question.

*

Jack spent the ride to his office thinking about the quantum change that had just taken place in his life. He was now engaged to the most beautiful, and at times frustrating, woman in the world. He shook his head and kept driving, thinking how much difference a few days could make in someone's life. When he and Katherine had gotten engaged, her parents had sent out announcements. He wondered whether it was right to do that again. At the very least, he should call his brother Stephen and his daughter to let them know the good news.

Todd Milner was on the phone at Jack's desk when he arrived. The agent appeared to be excited. Flashing Jack a thumbs up sign, he wrote "Scotland Yard" on a slip of paper and handed it to him. Jack took a seat in the guest chair.

"Inspector, the supervising agent just came in. In fact, I'm sitting at his desk. May I place you on speaker?" Milner waited for a response, then searched the base unit for a second before locating and pressing the right button. "Here we go. Mr. Bennett-Walsh, this is Jack Kale. Jack, Inspector Bennett-Walsh with Scotland Yard."

"It sounds like you have quite a problem there, Agent Kale. We've been interested in the Sandman for some time. How can we help?"

"Inspector, I was informed by Detective Pappas that Interpol forwarded a fingerprint to you that resulted in a match."

"Two prints, actually. The latent impression of the middle and ring fingers you sent us show a twelve point hit. They belong to a gentleman named Thomas Courtney, late of Dublin, Ireland."

"Late?"

"According to the authorities there, it's been some time since anyone has heard from Thom. Probably twenty-five years, I should say. I'm sending off our file once we hang up, but I'll be happy to provide some background if you wish."

"Please."

"Let me begin at the beginning, as they say. At eight years old, Thom Courtney became an orphan after his mother, father, and brother were killed in a motoring accident. If my addition is correct, this would make him thirty-six now.

"Following the accident, Thom and his sister Elizabeth, who also survived, went to live with his Uncle Sean and Aunt Lydia. Lydia was the sister of Pearl, Thom's mother. That relationship lasted eleven months."

"What happened?" Jack asked.

"One can only conjecture. I'm reading from the file my Irish counterparts put together on this man. The uncle was an ex-military man and given to strict discipline according to the neighbors. And by discipline, I mean physical reprimand. One of them noticed bruises on the boy's neck and shoulders and notified the authorities. You'll see in the report that Uncle Sean was a free one with his hands. That became worse when he was drinking which, unfortunately, was frequent. Police reports indicate they'd been out to the house on at least three occasions.

"Lydia, the wife, had been treated for a broken jaw and two broken ribs by a local doctor. As a result, her husband was incarcerated for a year. With his wife on the mend and him in jail, there was no one to care for Thom and Elizabeth, so they were placed in different foster homes where they stayed for several months. Ultimately, they were returned to the care of their uncle and aunt, as they were their only relatives. That decision was regrettable."

"Why?"

"Two weeks after Thom's return, there was a fire at the home. Aunt Lydia was not present when it happened. She was being treated for a ruptured spleen and a damaged kidney. Her condition was so advanced that she lacked the strength to recover and passed."

"What about the uncle and Thomas's sister?"

"Both burned to death in the house. The coroner noted the uncle's skull had been fractured. Local police concluded he must have fallen trying to escape the blaze. The sister fared no better, nor did a boyfriend who was with her at the time.

"Ultimately, Thom was transferred to a government home for indigents and orphans where things only got worse. He was almost ten years old at the time. One of the teachers, Father Michael Hardy, was not only a brutal man but a pedophile who preyed on his charges. The extent of his contact with Thom over a six-year period had to be both extensive and traumatic."

"Is Hardy still around?" Jack asked.

"I'll get to that in a moment. Eventually one of the boys worked up his courage and went to the local constable. Hardy was convicted and spent five years in a penitentiary. We do know that Hardy and Thom Courtney connected with each other sometime after Hardy's release from prison. This was at an Irish Republican Army demonstration they both attended in County Cork. Apparently, things got out of hand, the police were called in, and Courtney was arrested. That's where we obtained his fingerprints. The smart money is that it was the Father who introduced Thom to the IRA, or should I say a particular subgroup of it. Their methods were so heinous the IRA eventually distanced themselves from them. Father Hardy was well placed in that organization."

"Was?"

"He died seven years ago of congestive heart failure."

"About the time the Sandman got started," Todd Milner said.

"So it would seem," Inspector Bennett-Walsh said. "Prior to his disappearance, Thom Courtney was thought to be involved in the assassination of two members of Parliament who were opposed to Ireland's efforts to sever ties with Great Britain. That's how Scotland Yard became interested in him."

"He's a terrorist?"

"Perhaps at one time. Since Michael Hardy's death, he more or less adapts to whatever situation presents itself. I'm not sure he cares about anything but money. Let me amend that. I'm not sure he cares about anything but his mission. The money is a helpful bonus. But if asked, I'd say it's not the central driving force in his makeup."

Thinking back to the dead parrot at Mary Quinn's home, Jack decided to reserve judgment. It was now his opinion that the Sandman had arranged everything with the intention of shocking whoever came in, hoping it would hold them while the delay fuse burned down. But something didn't quite fit the inspector's theory, something in a study he once read. He realized with a start that Bennett-Walsh was still speaking.

"I'm sorry, Inspector. Would you repeat that last part, please?"

"I said, here's a tidbit from the file you may find interesting. In reviewing the National Health's records, a predecessor of mine made a note that a Thom C. Hardy was referred to a psychiatrist for treatment of a possible mental disorder. The address was given as Adams Close in County Cork, which is also Saint Ignatius's address. A cross-check of the orphanage records turned up no matching name. The age and gender of the patient, yes, but not the name. My colleague penned 'Thom Courtney' with a question mark next to Thom C. Hardy's name."

"Does the file indicate the nature of the disorder?"

"Indeed. Schizophrenia."

"Interesting," Jack said. "And the date or dates of treatment?"

Bennett-Walsh told him.

Jack did some quick math and noted that the first visit would have occurred just after Courtney's sixteenth birthday, which was when schizophrenia was thought to appear in males.

"If the medical file's accessible, I'd like to see it," Jack said.

"I'm afraid that would be a problem due to doctor-patient privilege. My predecessor simply looked up the National Health's coding number to determine the nature of the diagnosis."

"Understood. We have the same situation here."

"That's about it then. I don't envy you going up against this man. He's something of an automaton, if you know what I mean. Once he starts, he continues until the contract is complete. He doesn't allow for cancellation, nor does he leave any way to communicate with him from what we know, which is precious little."

"I read that in the file. Odd fellow."

Bennett-Walsh chuckled. "And I thought we English had a tendency toward understatement."

*

The plane climbed sharply and leveled off at thirty thousand feet to begin its trek to the northeast. Beth barely noticed. She was rehearsing names in her head . . . Elizabeth Kale, Elizabeth Sturgis-Kale, Elizabeth Kale-Sturgis. She didn't know about the hyphenated names. They always sounded pretentious. After a few minutes, she gave up and figured the right combination would come to her. For the last hour, she found herself using her left hand more than usual. Rachel had noticed the engagement ring immediately and chided her for coming on the trip.

"If a man asked me to marry him, I'd have consummated our relationship on the spot."

Beth laughed. "Is that what happened with George?"

"He popped the question at the top of the Empire State Building. Fortunately, our hotel wasn't far away. Those people had the slowest damn elevators. As soon as we got in the room, we tore each other's clothes off. Has Dwayne said anything?"

"He's a man," Beth said. "He asked if I brought a gun along."

"Tell me how it happened," Rachel said.

Beth lowered her voice. "I was putting on my makeup and was ninety-nine percent naked when he burst into our bedroom."

"Clever."

Beth slapped her on the thigh. "It wasn't planned. All I had on were panties."

"Also clever."

"Jack was so tongue-tied he couldn't get the words out."

"Details. I need details. What did he say exactly?"

"He asked if I wanted to go to New York as an engaged woman. I didn't think that was romantic, so he got down on his knees and asked formally."

"Oh, and you said yes."

"No, I told him he was a loser because he couldn't catch one stupid killer . . . then I said yes."

The women held their hands up and compared rings.

"What are y'all doing?" Dwayne asked.

"Beth was just telling me how she got engaged."

"Cool. Congratulations by the way."

Beth held out her ring for him to see.

"Sweet," Dwayne said. "Looks expensive."

Beth frowned. "It does. I hope it didn't . . ."

"Guess he can afford it," Dwayne said. "I heard he got a bunch of money from that TV movie he was in."

"Jack was in a movie?" Rachel asked.

"It was about him. He wasn't in it."

"Tell me!"

Beth began the story. Dwayne listened for a moment, lost interest, and looked out the window. He seemed to be gripping the sides of his seat tightly.

"Are you okay?" Rachel asked.

"I ain't a real big fan of flying."

"It's the safest form of transportation."

"No ma'am, it ain't. Walking's a whole lot safer."

"It's a long walk to Manhattan," Rachel said.

"I suppose," Dwayne said. "We couldn't let you head up there all by yourself. Beth knows her way around the city pretty good from when she used to live there. She was a big-time magazine editor."

"That's a heck of a career switch," Rachel said. "How come?"

Beth considered her response. "I suppose the easy answer is I wanted to do some good and I don't like predators."

"You even appeared in the magazine once or twice," Dwayne said. "Right?"

"Just for comparison purposes," Beth said. "Like our editor's wearing this dress or those shoes."

"Nancy Arnold told me it was lingerie," Dwayne said.

"Really?"

"Uh-huh."

"Nancy Arnold's an idiot. It was dresses and shoes."

"Damn, I'd have paid good money to find that issue."

Beth stuck her tongue out at him.

"Sounds like a fun job," Rachel said. "I'm terrible at writing. What about you, Dwayne? Why'd you become a cop?"

"Well, Ed and I had just graduated Georgia State and we wanted to take a year off and travel Europe. Ed figured we could support ourselves being male models for the art schools. He had a whole bunch of 'em mapped out in each country."

Beth caught the laugh Rachel managed to stifle. Fortunately, the engine noise covered it. The doctor succeeded in keeping a straight face.

Dwayne continued. "The modeling thing didn't work out so good, and after two months we were getting low on funds, so we came back. Anyway, Ed noticed an ad in the paper saying the Atlanta Police were looking for a few good men. We figured that meant us."

"Do you think there'll be any trouble in New York?" Rachel asked.

"I can't see how, but we're not taking any chances," Beth said. "Your trip was a spur of the moment decision. If the Sandman finds out about it at all, he'd have to figure out how we're traveling and when. The flying part's obvious, but not many people go private, which is really nice, by the way. I'm not terribly worried."

193

"And," Dwayne Stafford said, "if we have to stay over tonight, he won't know where we are, 'cause we don't even know where that'll be. I do have a question, ma'am."

Mentally, Rachel took a breath. She'd told Dwayne several times to call her by her first name, or doctor if that was too hard. What she got was "Miss Rachel" or, worse, "Doctor Rachel," which made her feel like a character in *Gone with the Wind*.

"Go ahead."

"You or your husband ever have any dealings with Sergei Borov?"

"I never heard his name until the investigators showed up at our home and started asking questions about what we saw in the garage."

"Strange," Dwayne said. "Seeing someone hand another person a suitcase don't seem like such a big deal to me."

"Which may be why Carmine Donofrio wants the Sandman taken alive. If he can tie Borov into the contract, that would make his case," Beth said.

"What contract?" Rachel asked.

"The one to kill you, Will, and your husband."

"Oh, that contract."

Chapter 36

Jack and Pappas had just gotten out of Pappas's cruiser in the crime lab parking lot when someone called out Jack's name. The detective was carrying a medium sized paper bag. They turned to see a large man, close in size to the detective, striding toward them.

"Can I help you?" Jack asked.

He probably weighed close to 275 pounds but was carrying it on a frame built for 225 pounds. His hair was a mixture of salt and pepper and his complexion was florid. Even his walk looked angry.

"You're Kale?"

"I am. This is Detective Dan Pappas. What can I do for you, Doctor?"

The question momentarily stopped what Stuart Patterson was about to say.

"There's a medical license plate on that car you were leaning against and a Johns Hopkins class ring on your finger," Jack explained. "I assume the two are related."

Patterson recovered and introduced himself, then said, "I'd like to know what's going on. I've lost two partners and nearly had another killed yesterday. You were supposed to protect them, goddammit."

"I know," Jack said, quietly. "Would you like to come inside?"

"Let's just talk right here. I've got an office full of people waiting on me."

"All right. First off, our condolences for the death of Willis Landry and, of course, Dr. George Lawrence. You have our deepest sympathies."

"Thank you. How about if we cut to the chase?" Patterson said.

"You have every right to be upset. We all are. Yesterday we lost a good man, a young Homicide detective, so you're not alone in this."

Patterson closed his eyes for a moment and gathered himself.

"Right. I heard about that. I'm sorry, too. This business has got us all crazy."

"I understand."

"Look, I don't mean to be a jerk, but I'm worried sick over Rachel. Is she safe?"

"Perfectly," Jack said.

"I've been trying to get in touch with her. She's not answering her phone."

"She's fine, Doctor. Or at least as fine as someone can be under these circumstances. She's up in New York to do an operation. I thought you'd be aware of that. Two of our detectives are with her."

Stuart Patterson shook his head as if to clear it, then said, "I probably should have asked our secretary where she was before storming over here."

"It's all right," Jack said. "The situation's somewhat strained. Rachel should be back tonight if all goes well."

"Somewhat strained. That's a helluva way to put it."

Pappas said, "We're dealing with a very determined assassin. I don't know how up to speed you are, but yesterday he faked an attack on our administration building to go after Dr. Landry and Dr. Lawrence at the safehouse. Unfortunately, we got there too late to help Landry. If it wasn't for Jack, he'd have gotten Rachel Lawrence, too."

"I didn't know that and I don't mean to come across as ungrateful. But it's hard to see this as a win, if you know what I mean. Will and George were both friends of mine."

"I understand," Pappas said. "We all feel like shit about what happened. I just want you to know we're doing everything in our power to stop this guy."

Two detectives who had just pulled into the lot exited their car. Hearing the tone of the voices, they slowed to a halt before going inside. Pappas motioned with his hand for them to continue.

"Look, I'm not pointing fingers," Patterson said. "Well, maybe I am. But it's obvious to me whatever you people are doing isn't working."

Jack and Pappas didn't respond.

Patterson continued to address Pappas. "I spoke with Steve Rollins last night. He said he knows you. Steve's in private business now and he's a top flight investigator. I hired him to help out."

Patterson handed the detective Rollins's business card. Pappas examined it for a moment then said, "I know his name, but I can't say I know him. Obviously, your heart's in the right place, but adding someone else to the mix at this point won't be helpful. In fact—"

"I respect you opinion. But this is a done deal, so I'd appreciate it if you'd cooperate with him."

"Dr. Patterson—"

"The mayor's a real good friend of mine and I imagine he'll be giving you a call later to confirm what I've said."

Pappas nodded and made no reply. Neither did Jack.

"I get you guys don't like someone looking over your shoulders. But Rachel Lawrence has been through hell and I'm going to do whatever I have to do to protect her. Tell me this. Are you anywhere close to nailing the killer?"

Jack thought about telling him they'd learned who the killer was and decided against it. He simply said, "No."

Patterson took a deep breath and looked around the lot for a moment. "Well, I appreciate your honesty. What about approaching Borov and putting a scare into him?"

"We don't think that would be helpful," Jack said.

"Goddammit, someone's got to do something."

"We intend to, Doctor."

Stuart Patterson held Jack's eye for a long moment. Nodded, then turned on his heel and walked back to his car. They watched him drive off.

"And the hits just keep on coming," Pappas muttered.

*

Once inside the crime lab, they found Nelda Latham and Ben Furman already at work. On Jack's advice, Pappas had sprung for that morning's bagels and coffee, thus ensuring their movement up the line of evidence waiting to be analyzed. Ben Furman was in the process of explaining what they found. He was dressed in jeans, a gray sweatshirt that said "Georgia Tech," and a pair of worn running shoes. As he always did when speaking to people, he shoved his horn-rimmed glasses up onto his forehead.

"The items in the first two trays were taken from Peter Shackelford, one of the drone operators. Not much interesting here except a trace of cocaine powder. Nelda located that in his pant cuffs. His shoes also have bits of grass and dirt, which you'd expect to find at Piedmont Park. I saw nothing out of the ordinary. The man's what he seems to be, a druggie with two arrests for possession who was hired to fly a model airplane."

"He's the one who walked past HQ?" Pappas asked.

"Correct. We checked the security cameras and it's definitely him. According to the beat cops, most nights Shackleford stays at the Salvation Army Center on Edgewood Avenue. During the days, he either panhandles or steals to support his habit."

"Naturally," Pappas said. "Easier than working."

"What about the other man?" Jack said.

"Leonard Steven Walpole," Ben Furman said, taking a bite of his bagel. "Love this walnut cream cheese. Good call, Dan."

"My pleasure."

Ben took a second to swallow, then went on. "Leonard's also a drug user, but on a more serious level than Peter. The polygraph examiner noted needle tracks on his arm and the back of his leg when he hooked him up to the machine. He was so fidgety they had to restart the test several times. Like our friend Peter, he was approached by a man wearing black jeans and a sweater and asked to operate the flying platform. Both men differ about the shoes he was wearing. Peter says brown work boots. Leonard was sure they were burgundy loafers."

Typical, Jack thought. Eyewitness identifications were notoriously unreliable, which was why, given a choice, he generally favored evidence. You might reach the wrong conclusion, but that would be your fault and not because someone had made a mistake or intentionally misled you.

Jack asked, "What did you find, absent their input?"

"Purple cashmere fibers, which would be consistent with what both said regarding the sweater's color. Nelda calls it eggplant."

Jack and Pappas both looked at Nelda, who repeated "Eggplant" through a mouthful of bagel.

"Eggplant it is," Jack said. "What else?"

"In addition to the fibers," Ben said. "The terra-cotta grains we've been seeing also make a reappearance, plus more of the marble dust."

"Now that is strange," Jack said. "I think we may need to talk to this man again."

"If we can find him," Pappas said. "The ATF geniuses lost the bastard."

Chapter 37

Jack had just left the lab when his cellphone went off. It was Inspector Bennett-Walsh.

"Agent Kale, I'm glad I caught you. Or would you prefer Doctor? I apologize for not being aware of your credentials."

"How about Jack?"

"Marvelous, I'm Ian. Now as to the reason for this call. After our conversation, I called Ireland and sent some chaps round to the Saint Ignatius Home where Thom Courtney lived. Of course, no one had seen him in years. Just to be thorough, two of our lads stopped at Courtney's old house outside of Dublin. Under the law, it passed to him as the sole surviving heir. We expected it would be something of a wreck, having been abandoned for so long, but that wasn't the case. It appears someone has been living there. Quite recently, I might add. The neighbors confirmed seeing a man on several occasions."

"How recently?"

"Four days ago, according to Mrs. Effie Callahan, who lives next door. We may well have found the Sandman's base of operations, Jack."

"Interesting," Jack said, doing some quick calculations in his head. Gabe Alonso had disappeared a week ago, which would make Courtney killing him difficult if he was in Ireland at the time. Possibly the partner had done it. Walpole? He voiced this to Bennett-Walsh, who had no answer.

"Their lab men went through the place and came away empty. Not even a single fingerprint."

"That's significant in itself."

"Are there any photos of Thomas Courtney available?"

"Our only one was sent to you along with our file as promised."

"Excellent. I've been out of the game for a while, but I assume you have facial recognition programs available over there."

"Indeed. They're not completely accurate, but they've proven quite useful in several cases. Would you like me to check and see if Courtney's been abroad recently?"

"Absolutely. An FBI agent connected with the case was killed a week ago. Given the date of his death and your Mrs. Callahan's statement about seeing someone at the house four days ago, we've got a pretty big hole here."

"It might not have been Courtney at all at the house."

"True, but assuming someone else just happened to be there by coincidence doesn't help us, particularly since your men found no evidence of fingerprints. There's no reason for that unless they were cleaning up after themselves."

Bennett-Walsh processed this for a moment then said, "Do you know, Jack, every so often this job is actually fun."

"Let's hope so."

"Do you still box?"

The question caught Jack by surprise, then he smiled. He shouldn't have been shocked Bennett-Walsh had checked him out. He made a mental note to do the same.

"Not for quite some time," Jack said. "My last match was in the Marines shortly before I mustered out."

"Win or lose?"

"It went the distance. I got a decision on points, not to mention a very sore jaw. You?"

"I did a bit of boxing at Leeds College and in the Royal Navy. I still belong to an athletic club near Wimbledon. Every now and then I'll step back in the ring to shake the rust off. If you ever make it over here, you can come as my guest."

"To box?"

"If you wish."

Jack thought for a few seconds, then asked, "What division?"

"Light heavyweight. You?"

201

"Hm, I might have to struggle to make weight," Jack said. "Would you settle for dinner and a hardy round of golf?"

"Good God, man. Golf?"

"The worst that can happen with golf is you wind up looking for your ball. You don't spend several days trying to remember where you live."

Bennett-Walsh laughed. "And I thought you Yanks were tough. Golf it is then. Loser buys dinner. I'll ring you back."

Chapter 38

Lenny Walpole and his new friend, a man he believed to be a movie special effects coordinator named Rick, had just finished an early breakfast in Virginia-Highlands and were walking back to the Clairmont Hotel. Lenny couldn't remember the last time he had pancakes and bacon. Years, probably. A sharp breeze was blowing down Ponce de Leon Avenue. Lenny pulled his jacket tighter and ran his fingers lovingly over the material, scarcely believing it was his. Rick had bought the jacket for him last night, along with a scarf, gloves, and a combination lock. Break-ins at the Clairmont tended to be a common occurrence. While most rooms had locks on the doors, they could be opened with a credit card or a sharp kick. For the most part, thieves were after the occupant's stash, though it wasn't unknown for clothing and electronics to disappear. Even eyeglasses weren't immune. Basically, anything that wasn't nailed down and could be sold, pawned, or traded for drugs was fair game.

Instead of putting safes in the rooms, the Clairmont's solution was to furnish metal foot lockers, which they rented out for a nominal fee. The lockers fit nicely in a closet. Residents were expected to furnish their own lock.

"I hope I don't forget the combination," Lenny said.

"Just write it on a piece of paper and stick it in your shoe," Wesley told him. "That's what we did in the army."

"I didn't know you were in the army, Rick."

"Four years. We had lockers just like you, except they went lengthways at the foot of our bunk. The locks were handy in case you got into it with someone."

It was obvious Lenny wasn't following, so Rick explained. "Locks and socks. Put a combination lock in your sock and swing it and it makes a hell of a weapon. It works fine at the end of a belt, too. Sometimes a sock can tear."

"I'd never have thought of that, Rick. Is that what you did?"

Wesley shrugged. "Once or twice."

"Wow. You could really hurt someone like that. Maybe even kill them."

"That's the point. I mean, you don't go looking for trouble, but you can't let someone push you around or get away with stealing your stuff. If they know they're in for a fight, they won't come back for seconds so quick."

"I'll remember that. It's just I'm not very brave."

"Everyone gets scared. How you deal with it is what counts. Anyone who says they're not afraid is a liar."

"You don't seem like anything could frighten you," Lenny said.

"I'm no different. There was one guy in our outfit, a big dumb kid named Kevin who had a mean streak a mile wide. I was the new guy. He started in with the jokes right away. I didn't react figuring he'd run out of steam. Of course, that didn't happen."

Wesley paused to let a gay couple walking hand in hand pass them. He watched them out of the corner of his eye, shook his head, and continued. "After the jokes, he started 'accidentally' bumping into me. When he couldn't get a rise, it only made him madder. One day in the chow line, he reaches over and takes the dessert off my tray. His mates thought that was hysterical . . . until I took the sock and lock I'd been carrying out of my back pocket and started pounding him. It took three NCOs to pull me off."

"What happened?" Lenny asked, wide eyed.

"We both went to the brig. Well . . . I went. He went to the infirmary first. They put him back together."

"And you never had trouble again?"

"No, he beat the shit out of me when we got out. I returned the favor with a shovel. Caught him full in the face coming out of the barracks. That cost me another sixty days in the hole. After that, we got along fine."

"Gee."

"I'll let you in on a secret. All the time I was hitting that dumb sonofabitch, I was scared to death. The bottom line is you don't control your fear, it'll control you."

"It'll control you," Lenny repeated. "I'll try to remember that, Rick. I'm so lucky to have met you."

Wesley liked the little man. Under other circumstances, he could see them hanging out together. Maybe exploring a new city, like Rio. It had been several years since he worked with a partner. It was nice to have someone to talk to, even if what was being said was pure bullshit. It was a shame he'd have to kill him.

"I feel that way too," Wesley said. "You've done a great job. We looked at yesterday's rushes and there are some really good shots. The director was impressed."

"What are rushes?"

"Daily raw footage. The editor and director use them to decide how the final scene will look." Wesley was pleased with himself for remembering that. He'd read it in a magazine several months ago.

"Did he say anything about the laptop?"

"The director? No. I told you that's the property manager's job."

"Right, sorry. It's hard to keep track of everyone. Did he mention it?"

"Haven't seen him. I'll try to cover for you, but if it becomes a problem, we'll have to return it. These people have so much money they'll probably write it off as missing in action and buy another."

Lenny asked, "Are they still expensive? They used to be, but that was a long time ago. I figured maybe the prices might have come down."

Wesley shrugged. "A couple hundred bucks, I guess." He could see the wheels turning in Lenny's mind trying to figure out how much cocaine or crack he could buy with it, or whatever it was he was addicted to. Totally disgusting.

"So are you ready for your performance today?"

"Sure," Lenny said. "It's kind of windy though, don't you think?"

Wesley checked the sky. It looked like the rain would hold off. All he needed was for Lenny to make a show if it for an hour or two.

There was no way the cops wouldn't be watching. In fact, he was counting on it. This time, they wouldn't be so quick to empty those buildings again. According to last night's news, the evacuation and mobilization of emergency services had cost the city more than half a million dollars. Nobody was looking to be embarrassed a second time. Beautiful. Father Mike was always right.

Wesley believed he heard his cellphone buzz. He excused himself and stepped into a doorway, explaining it was Brooks, their director, calling.

Can we trust this man, boy-o?

Of course not. He's a junkie. But we can control him. As long as he thinks there's a chance for drugs, he'll go along.

Carrot on a stick, you're sayin'?

Yes, Father.

You realize he's seen your face?

What difference will that make if he's dead?

What difference indeed?

*

At two o'clock that afternoon, Corporal Jim Fillet called Jack to say, "The fly boys are back."

Jack motioned for Milner to pick up the extension. They were at headquarters reviewing the files Bennett-Walsh had sent. Jack inquired if Fillet was alone and was told his partner, Charly Handler, and a third member of the Ghost Squad were also observing. Per Jack's instructions, they were concentrating not so much on the model planes but on whether Walpole and Shackleford had made contact with Thom Courtney. Photographs of the killer had been passed out to everyone on the Atlanta police force.

Jack also wanted to know where the men lived as they had promptly changed their residence after being released from questioning. According to the report, neither man claimed to know the other, which was probably true. The curious thing was why they were back at all. The Sandman—or Thom Courtney, now that he had a name—knew one of the witnesses was dead. He also knew they would move Rachel Lawrence since the safehouse had been breached and its location was now general knowledge.

Objectively, Jack was inclined to go with Carmine Donofrio's suggestion to place her in a federal safehouse, except he didn't trust the man. Donofrio knew his case against Borov was weak, which was why he was pushing so hard for a capture. Nothing wrong in that, provided a capture was feasible. But there was no way he was putting his people at risk. In the judicial system, deals were made all the time, only the thought of this one left his stomach feeling queasy, like when he used to reach for a cigarette first thing in the morning.

Shortly after Rachel and Beth left for the airport, he had received a visit at his home from Janet Newton and Sally Yellen, Atlanta's SAC, informing him the NSA and Homeland Security both wanted to interview Thomas Courtney. Borov's activities were drawing a lot of attention, not only on a domestic level, but on an international one.

Janet said, "Bottom line, the White House wants him shut down."

Deputy director or not, she was a cop, and like most cops, her eyes moved around Jack's living room taking in the details.

"Tell me about the deal Justice is offering," Jack said.

"Contact has been made with the IRA on the theory they can get in touch with Courtney. Beyond that, I'm not aware of any details."

"What about our British friends? Not to mention the French, German, Israeli, and Spanish authorities?"

"Possibly," Sally Yellen answered. "But that's not your worry. Whatever the final disposition is, it's way above our pay grade."

Jack wished Todd Milner had been present to hear that. It was his agent who'd been murdered.

"We have less than seventy-two hours to the grand jury," Janet said. "Can you protect the witness adequately?"

"I think so. She's with Detectives Stafford and Sturgis at the moment."

The deputy director's face was grim when she asked, "What about capturing the Sandman?"

"That, I'm less confident of, but we're trying."

Sally Yellen went on to tell him Donofrio was on the warpath and had actually called her at home last night. "He said you interfered with the deputy marshal."

"He's full of shit. Rachel Lawrence wasn't under arrest and she's not in witness protection," Jack said. "Therefore she had a right to come and go as she pleased. Someone gives me a legitimate order, I'll see it's executed. Frankly, I thought getting her out of town was a good idea."

The SAC had been feeding Marta dog treats from a dish. "She really likes these, huh?"

"Yeah, but she doesn't understand when they're gone," Jack said.

"Wh . . . what?" she said, with a panicked look on her face.

Janet told her, "He's kidding. Jack has a quirky sense of humor. Why did you name her Marta? That's so odd."

"Some idiot abandoned her as a pup on the elevated platform at the Dunwoody Station. I couldn't see leaving her there and I didn't know her name. I just said, 'C'mon, Marta girl . . .' and she followed me."

Janet shook her head and smiled. "But Mom, the puppy followed me home."

Jack smiled and said, "Something like that."

After more discussion, he promised to keep them updated. Sally Yellen, clearly not used to being around dogs, eased sideways out of her chair and quickly made her way to the door. Janet gave him a reproachful look and followed her out.

*

That afternoon, Jack was reviewing the meeting in his mind when Todd Milner's voice pulled him back to the present. They were in the Atlanta police department and the agent had been reading the Sandman's file Bennett-Walsh had sent.

"I'm sorry, what did you say?"

"This information on Courtney makes quite a story."

Milner glanced around to make sure no one was looking and lit a cigarette. Officially, the department was a nonsmoking area, a fact several detectives routinely ignored. At times, you could actually see a haze hanging in the air.

"It does," Jack agreed.

"You find it helpful?"

"To some extent. It's vogue for profilers to try to understand what makes a killer tick in the hope we'll uncover the key to their psyche and how to stop them before they kill again."

208

"I thought you'd be its biggest proponent."

"I'm not saying profiling isn't useful," Jack said. "It is. To me, it's only of passing interest to understand how a sociopath became one, unless they're so caught up in a pattern of behavior even they have no idea what's driving them. Unfortunately, there's a subclass that doesn't fit any mold. They're intelligent, manipulative, and sadly, enjoy what they do."

"Enjoy?"

"Like you and I enjoy doing our job. Knowing they grew up with a promiscuous mother or a drunken uncle or were victimized by a pedophile priest is all well and good. But if you speak to the crowd at the prison weight pile doing hard time, even they don't blame society as the reason they're behind bars."

"Interesting," Milner said.

"In one of the Batman flicks, Alfred, that's Bruce Wayne's butler, tells him, 'Some men just want to see the world burn.' We don't have to understand the Sandman; we just have to shut him down. And between you and me, at this point I don't care much how we do it."

Milner watched the ash form on his cigarette for several seconds, then nodded to himself and left.

Chapter 39

When the plane landed at a private airport twenty minutes outside Manhattan, Dwayne Stafford finally let out his breath. The pilot gave Rachel his cellphone number and told her he and the copilot would grab a bite to eat and stay close until they heard from her. It occurred to Beth that being a pilot had to be one of the best jobs in the world. Once you landed, that was it. No problems to take home with you. Nothing to worry about, just show up for the next flight. Awfully cool.

It had been a while since she'd been in New York and a variety of memories and emotions were competing for her attention. Some were happy; some were awkward. She wished Jack was there with her. It would be nice to show a country boy the city. They took the first taxi in line and left for the airport.

"Man, those are some huge smoke stacks," Dwayne Stafford said.

Beth came back to the moment. "That's Big Allis, one of the city's major power plants. A friend's father told me in 1965 there was a huge blackout in most of New England and part of Canada and Allis crashed. No streetlights, no electricity, nothing."

"You're kidding?" Dwayne said. "All of New England?"

Beth shrugged. "A lot of it. They fixed Allis the next day and things went back to normal . . . almost."

"Almost?"

"Nine months later the birth rate in New York took a sudden leap up."

Dwayne laughed. "Now you're pullin' my leg."

"Ask the doctor."

"It's true," Rachel said. "My mom was an obstetrician in Queens. She told me all about it."

"Hey, is that the United Nations?" Dwayne asked.

"Yep," the cabbie answered. "And that big building in the middle is the Empire State. You guys should check out the observation deck."

An awkward silence followed. On the flight up, Rachel had shared the story of how George proposed to her.

"I've been there," Rachel said quietly, then turned and stared down at the swirling gray waters of the East River.

*

Upon reaching NYU Langone Medical Center, they found their optimism about staying below the Sandman's radar was unjustified. Shortly after Rachel left to get changed and review the latest tests on her patient, Beth was approached by a slender black man in a suit. Her first thought was that he was there to serve them papers placing Rachel into a witness protection program. He showed her his credentials. His name was Raymond Price and he was with New York's FBI office. Beth placed his age around forty and his height about the same as Jack's.

"Detective Sturgis, I'm glad I caught up with you. Where's your partner?"

"Standing outside the doctors' changing room. What's up?"

"We have a problem. Shortly after you landed, Homeland Security got a hit on an individual matching Thomas Courtney's description at LaGuardia Airport."

"That's impossible."

"'Fraid it's not. The confidence factor's fairly high on the facial recognition scale. Sixty-five percent. Unfortunately, he was gone by the time the cops got in gear. It would have been higher but he never once looked up, meaning he pretty much knew where the cameras were. We were lucky to catch a head-on view of him from out of the remotes." Price took two digital photographs out of his briefcase and handed them to her. "One's for you and one's for your partner. I'm surprised your office hasn't alerted you."

211

"So am I," Beth said, pulling out her cellphone. "Goddammit," she muttered under her breath. She had shut it off at the airport and forgotten to turn it back on. There were two messages from Todd Milner saying, "Call me! Sandman in New York."

He inquired, "Is Doctor Lawrence in surgery?"

"Already, or about to go in."

"Can we stop her?"

"Not a chance," Beth said. "She has a sick kid on her hands. The U.S. Attorney tried and she told him to piss off. You'd have to haul her out of there in handcuffs."

"Well, that ain't gonna happen," Price said. "Which brings me to our second problem. A Mr. Carmine Donofrio called both his counterpart here in New York and our SAC to say he'll have paper on her early this afternoon. They want us to take her into custody."

"Damn," Beth said.

"However, Special Agent Todd Milner called me personally and asked if I would take my time serving her. He assured me he's speaking for the deputy director as well."

"Great," Beth said. "How much time can you give us?"

"Don't know. Obviously, I can't break into the operating room. That might endanger the child. So I'm wondering, in the spirit of interdepartmental cooperation, if you'd mind giving me a call when Dr. Lawrence is free?"

"That I can do," Beth said. "Do you know Todd?"

"I know *of* him. Never met the man. He worked out of the Phoenix office and just transferred to DC."

"What about Jack Kale?"

"Now Jack I do know. I was with him on a couple of cases."

"Really? You worked together?"

"Several times. I was surprised when he left the Bureau. Just before he got started on that Scarecrow case, we were assigned to a big kidnapping case in California involving four little girls. To this day, I have no idea how he figured out where those girls were buried. The bastard who snatched them had the kids in boxes with oxygen tanks to keep them alive."

"That's Jack," Beth said. "I've been trying to learn how he does it. Not sure I'm making much progress."

Price laughed to himself. "You're not the only one. I wouldn't let that laid-back attitude of his fool you. Push comes to shove, that boy can be tougher than a prison steak. Believe me. I've seen it firsthand."

"Sounds like you know him pretty well," Beth said.

"Better than most. We met in Afghanistan in the Marines, way back before we joined the Bureau. We were both assigned to CID as investigators, except neither of us knew our butts from a hole in the ground. Dr. Jack won himself a Silver Star over there."

"I read about that in his file," Beth said. "But there were no details and he never talks about it."

The agent nodded as if that was something he expected.

"Do you know what happened?" Beth asked.

"I do."

"Okay, give."

"Like I said, CID, right? For the first three months, everything we handled was strictly routine. Then one day out of the blue we receive information that a corporal in supply, a nineteen-year-old kid from Detroit, is selling ordinance to the Kurdish rebels. Can you imagine? One of our own guys. It was nuts.

"Anyway, the CO sends us to arrest him. So we grab two MPs and head out. According to the snitch, the transaction was going down in an alley on the outskirts of Kabul. It was good intel.

"The second they see us they all take off like a bunch of rats, except for the kid, who they shoot in the stomach thinking he set them up. Suddenly the alley lights up like the Fourth of July and all hell breaks loose. Five of their pals were waiting at the opposite end as lookouts. A grenade went off. Bullets started bouncing off the walls. People are screaming. It was a complete nut house.

"Jack took one in the leg, but managed to pull the kid into a storage room."

"Wow," Beth said.

"Yeah, wow. Unfortunately, the storage room was occupied by three of the rebels."

Beth's mouth opened. She'd seen the scar on Jack's leg but all he ever said was that he caught a stray bullet.

Price continued. "Jack and the prisoner were the only ones who came out of there alive."

It was Beth's turn to shake her head. At times, her fiancé reminded her of an iceberg. Only a small part of him was visible above the waterline.

She inquired, "Have you stayed in contact all these years?"

"Not as much as when we worked together, but we try to keep in touch. Just got a birthday e-mail from him the other day. Frankly, I'm glad he's back with us."

Beth's feelings on the subject were mixed, but she decided to say "Me too" and leave it at that.

Price said, "Sounds like you got a tough situation on your hands."

"More than tough."

Price nodded. "I only had a quick briefing from the ASAC. He informed him the deputy director is hands-on with this."

"I've met her. She told me we need him. Guess I wouldn't argue the point."

Agent Price seemed to find that humorous, prompting Beth to raise her eyebrows in question.

"Don't quote me on this, but back in the day, I always thought him and the DD had a little thing going, 'cept she wasn't DD then. She was our lead agent."

"Janet Newton?"

"The same."

The lobby temperature suddenly dropped by several degrees. Price took one look at Beth's face and asked, "I say something wrong, Ms. Sturgis?"

Beth held up her hand. "See this ring?"

"Lovely."

"Thank you. Jack Kale gave it to me this morning just after he asked me to marry him."

Ray Price stared at her and took a deep breath. "People sometimes ask me if black folks can blush. Now being an articulate and sophisticated individual, I've never found the need. Tell you what I'm gonna do, though. I'm gonna wander around and see if I can find me a doctor and have my foot surgically removed from my mouth."

Beth laughed. "If that's an apology, you're forgiven."

"It is. A very abject one. Congratulations to you both. What say I hang around and check the people going in and out?" The agent scanned the lobby. "This place is busier than Times Square."

"Appreciate it," Beth said. "Maybe you can speak with hospital security and see if there are any other ways into the operating room. I doubt it, but I'd like to cover all the bases."

Price handed her his business card. "That's my cell number on the bottom. Let's stay in touch every fifteen minutes or so."

"Sounds good," Beth said.

"Mind if I ask you something?"

"Go ahead."

"Milner told me the DD and U.S. Attorney want this dude alive."

"That's right."

"I get that he's the baddest motherfucker on the planet, but we're talking about a cop killer, right?"

Beth nodded. "One of the detectives he killed the other day was a friend of mine."

"So what's the deal here?"

"The U.S. Attorney's office is hoping to turn him. The real target is a Russian arms dealer named Sergei Borov, who they think hired him. My orders are to shoot first and ask questions later. If I can take him I will, but I'm not gonna push it."

Price held her eye for a long time. She didn't flinch or look away. He had no doubt this woman would make the right choice when the time came.

"Funny thing," he said. "Agent Todd Milner gave me the same advice. See you later, Detective."

Chapter 40

The operation lasted nearly five hours. Rachel emerged from it looking like she had just run the New York City Marathon. Nevertheless, she had a smile on her face.

"Success?" Beth asked.

"Awesome," Rachel said. "I'm really pleased with the result. I need fifteen minutes to speak with the parents."

"And then?"

"I'll shower up, change clothes, and we can head to the airport."

"You interested in a bite to eat, Doc?" Dwayne Stafford asked.

Rachel's eyes widened. "I'm so sorry. You've been waiting out here all this time. When I'm in surgery, I forget about everything but what I'm doing. Of course we'll eat first. I won't be long."

When she left, Beth and Dwayne resumed their discussion about whether to tell her the Sandman was in New York.

"What bothers me," Dwayne said, "is how he knew we'd be here. This trip wasn't exactly planned. Do you think someone in the doc's office is talking?"

"I don't know, but it makes sense. Maybe we should start running backgrounds on them."

They were speculating about who the leak might be when Beth came up with the answer. "The fire marshal."

"You lost me."

"The Sandman was posing as him, right?"

"It could have been his partner."

216

"Sure, but you said you had the man in sight the whole time he was there?"

"All the time he was in the office. The only time I didn't see him was when he went next door to the space they're expanding into. I figured it didn't matter because it's empty and my job was to protect the witnesses."

"No question," Beth said. "Dr. Patterson told us the marshal was checking to see if their wiring was up to code."

"Sure did."

"Isn't that something building inspectors do?"

Dwayne shrugged. "Maybe there's some overlap."

"Maybe," Beth agreed. "Only I don't think Courtney's talking to anyone—he's listening."

"You mean a wiretap?"

"I didn't see anything when I went in there, but I wasn't looking for that. They make pickup devices so small these days I might have missed it. Got to be the answer."

"Damn, I should have thought of that. Good thinkin'. I'd sure love to see ol' Jack's face when you tell him."

They were still undecided about how to handle the situation when Rachel returned from talking with her patient's mother and father. She told them to give her another twenty minutes to get ready. To be safe, Beth checked the locker room again before letting her go in. Apparently, the operation had a side benefit. Despite all she had been through, Rachel was carrying herself more erect and seemed less depressed. That would probably last until her thoughts turned to the funeral arrangements back in Atlanta. She had informed them that due to the number of people attending, the service would be held outdoors, which would make security a major problem.

*

Rachel was speaking on her cellphone when she came out of the locker room. "All right, I'll tell them."

"Something wrong?" Dwayne asked.

"That was our pilot. The mechanic checked the aircraft and told him one of the pressure seals on the doors needs to be replaced. It's a minor thing, but the part won't be here until tomorrow morning."

217

"Oh, boy," Beth said.

"We can go commercial," Rachel suggested.

Both detectives were against it. The Sandman's presence in New York had changed everything. The obvious priority was to protect Rachel and the FBI had far more resources and people. It was time to give in.

Rachel listened quietly and didn't comment. Beth's heart went out to her. This woman had suffered enough pain and aggravation to last a lifetime. At one point, she asked what Beth thought she should do. Beth told her.

"All right, call your agent. I'll check with the airlines just to be sure."

Ray Price already knew the operation was over. Beth was partway through dialing his number when she noticed him sitting across the lobby reading *Esquire*. She motioned him over, expecting to hear the decision had already been made, but he told her there was still no word from Carmine Donofrio.

"Must be having trouble finding a judge," Dwayne said. "Or I might be having trouble with my cellphone." He tapped the screen a few times and added, "Reception's a bitch in these hospitals."

Beth smiled. "So we're free to leave?"

"Until I hear otherwise. I take it you were calling me a minute ago?"

"We had a deal, right? Between you and me, we told her the Bureau can do a better job protecting her."

Price lifted his shoulders. "Frankly, I think it's the right decision. But if she says no, there's not much I can do."

Beth explained about the mechanical problem.

Price said, "As I see it, we can handle this a couple of ways. I can hang out with you guys and provide additional security. If the order comes through, I'll take it from there. Or I can meet you at the plane in the morning."

"We'd be happy for your company, Agent Price," Beth said. "Considering what we're dealing with, an extra pair of eyes would be welcome. This man scares the hell out of me."

"I'll let my office know."

Before he could call, Dwayne explained, "Ms. Sturgis figured out how the Sandman knew we'd be in New York. When he was up at Doc Lawrence's office posing as a fire marshal, he must have installed a listening device. Being a doctor, she needs to keep her staff informed of her whereabouts."

Price said, "I received a coded e-mail from a Detective Dan Pappas. Jack asked him to let me know he had your techs in Atlanta run a full electronic sweep of Dr. Lawrence's office and they found the bug earlier this morning."

Beth's mouth opened. "But I didn't even . . . never mind."

"Pappas said Kale's leaving it in place for some plan he is hatching. He didn't go into detail."

"He is so annoying," Beth said.

Price blinked. "This the same fella you plannin' to marry?"

"I'm thinking about it."

Price smiled.

Rachel returned to tell them, "I have good news and bad news."

"What's the bad?" Dwayne said.

"Even if we wanted to go commercial, we can't. All the flights to Atlanta are cancelled because of the weather. Apparently, there are storms up and down the east coast, so it looks like we're stuck here until tomorrow."

"What's the good news?"

"The family of the girl I operated on reserved rooms for us at the Plaza."

When she lived in New York, Beth had been to the Plaza several times and loved the place. It was sedate and elegant in an understated way. Staying there would be nice, but it presented a problem as far as protecting Rachel was concerned. There was no way they could leave her room unguarded, which meant she and Dwayne would be up all night in shifts. One glance at her partner was enough to tell her he had reached the same conclusion.

She let out a resigned breath, introduced Ray Price, and explained the situation.

Rachel said, "So you could take me into custody any minute?"

"I'm afraid so, ma'am. And to be honest, I don't think that's such a bad thing."

"But I don't have to go with you?"

"No, you don't. Look, nobody here wants to impose on you, Doctor. We know what you've been though. All of us are just trying to do our jobs and keep you out of harm's way."

Rachel shook her head. "He bugged my office?"

"Looks that way," Beth said. "I was just informed our techs found the listening device earlier today. Jack Kale wants to leave it in place for the time being."

"He's really quite smart to have figured that out."

Beth rolled her eyes at Dwayne. He shrugged.

"So no more communications with them until you clear it with us first, okay?" Beth said.

"I feel like I have a target on my back," Rachel said.

"And we're going to make sure nobody hits it. Agent Price has agreed to stay with us until word comes down about switching custody. Still interested in getting a bite to eat?"

"Absolutely. I'm starving."

Chapter 41

Beth was about to suggest a restaurant when she noticed a man in a tan raincoat standing in the shadows of a doorway across the street. This was the second time she'd seen him. Coincidence? She debated whether to mention it now and alarm the others. The fact was the Sandman did scare her. He seemed to be a step ahead of them at every turn. Dwayne Stafford solved her dilemma when he asked what she was looking at.

"That man across the street was here earlier. I think he's been watching the entrance. I didn't make anything of it the first time."

"What do you mean?"

She explained.

Stafford's face grew hard. "I think I should go over and have a talk with him."

"Maybe I should," Price said. "You're out of your jurisdiction."

Beth agreed. The agent was nearly at the front door when the hospital's fire alarm went off. She and Stafford immediately stepped in front of Rachel and drew their weapons. Slightly slower to react, Price did the same.

"We need to get Rachel out of here," Beth said. "*Now.*"

"You think Courtney will make a run at her in here?" Price asked.

"I'm not willing to take the risk. In Atlanta, he used drones for a diversion and then hit our safehouse. This could be another ploy."

"My SAC briefed me on that. He has to be working with someone. He couldn't pull the fire alarm if he's a hundred feet away."

They turned back to the man across the street only to find he was gone. People were exiting the building in droves. In the lobby, the alarms were so loud it made thinking difficult. All three of them were scanning the immediate vicinity for threats.

They had a problem. A big one. There was no way they could take Rachel into the street. Single assassin or multiple, being outside was far too risky. On the other hand, if the building really was on fire, staying inside wasn't an option. The firemen would be arriving soon and there'd be no choice but to leave. They needed to move.

"Price, did you bring a car?"

"Sure did."

"Drive it around to the doctors' entrance. Every hospital has one. Dwayne will bring Rachel down in five minutes. As soon as she's in, head to the Plaza Hotel. No stops. I'll meet you."

"And what will you be doing?"

"If that is the Sandman, I'll try to stop him or draw him off. If he finds out where Rachel's staying, we'll just have a repeat of this."

"Not smart, Detective. You need to wait for backup."

"We don't have the time."

"But—"

"Look, he basically walked through us in Atlanta. Maybe you'll have better luck. But I can't take that chance. If I corner him, I'll call and you can send in the cavalry. Get going."

"I really think I should be the one to brace him," Dwayne said.

"That's an order."

Price shook his head and headed for the stairs as the alarm continued to blare. People were still streaming out into the street. Senses alert, Beth holstered her weapon and followed them.

Chapter 42

The first responders had yet to make an appearance. The crowd filling the sidewalk was growing by the minute. Beth surveyed the street. No one looked suspicious nor was there any sign of a tan raincoat, which meant nothing. Switching coats wasn't hard. To make matters worse, traffic on Second Avenue was slowing down to see what the fuss was about, adding to the congestion. Sirens could be heard in the distance.

Ray Price's presence helped. The Sandman knew what she, Dwayne, and Rachel looked like. He didn't know Price or where he was taking Rachel.

Two blocks north, Beth caught a glimpse of a tan raincoat walking away from the commotion. Suddenly conscious she was very much alone, She started after him. If she could buy Dwayne and Price enough time, they could get away unseen.

Beth quickened her pace as a light rain began to fall. It would only mess up traffic further. A little less than a block ahead, the raincoat turned a corner. Fearing she would lose him, Beth started to jog. A one-person tail was incredibly hard to pull off without being seen, but there was no choice. She reached the corner in time to see the man walking west on Forty-Second Street. As she negotiated her way through a crowd of tourists gaping up at the buildings, she saw the tan raincoat disappear into Grand Central Terminal. Conscious there might be a partner lurking around she checked over her shoulder and spotted a tall man in a navy pea coat and black watch cap coming quickly up the street behind her. Her heart skipped a beat, but she kept going. Possibly their plan was to draw her out and come at her from both directions. Easy to eliminate the competition that way. She needed to call Price and let him know she was in pursuit, but there was no time to stop.

Acting on instinct, Beth accelerated into an all-out run and entered the Terminal. If it was the partner, she'd deal with him when he made an appearance. Grand Central was massive, and there was no telling which train the Sandman had jumped on. She took a chance and headed toward the 4/5/6—the most heavily used line in Manhattan. She went down the steps two at a time, bought a ticket, and headed for the platform one level below her, then came to a stop. The trains ran in both directions, uptown and downtown. She had no idea which way the Sandman had gone.

Fifty-fifty chance, if she'd even picked the right train line.

She chose the uptown line. Guessed wrong. She knew it the moment she reached the loading platform. At most, ten people were waiting for the train and none of them were wearing tan raincoats.

But she was in luck. On the opposite side of the tracks at the far end of the station, she spotted her quarry standing next to a trash can. He saw her as well, but didn't react.

Shit. A light at the end of the tunnel indicated the train was approaching. As she raced for the staircase, they made eye contact with each other. If he was concerned by her appearance, it didn't show. Once again, she checked over her shoulder. Still no one coming up behind her. Slowing as she crossed over, Beth found her phone and punched in Ray Price's number only to find there was no signal underground. Beneath her feet, the platform rumbled as the train pulled into the station. She gave up and ran for the southbound side of the tracks, hardly making it through the closing doors in time. The Sandman had been standing at the opposite end of the platform and would have boarded the first car.

At the next station, she stepped off the car and waited to see if Courtney would do the same. He didn't. She slipped back in and made her way to the next car. Her right hand remained close to the gun on her hip. Shoot first and ask questions later would result in disaster on a crowded train.

Thoughts of Ed Mundas and George Lawrence and all the innocents who had died as the cable car plummeted to earth flashed into her mind. It was the work of a heartless killer who had crawled out of the dark and settled in their midst. The closer she drew to the first car, the more her heart began to hammer. Taking a deep breath to calm herself, she continued to thread her way forward. Between the cars a damp, black ripple of a breeze passed over her skin. It was was sour and unsatisfying, drying the beads of sweat on her face. Despite a brief wave of panic that washed over her, she forced her feet to keep moving. Three cars to go. Still too far away to see if he was still on the train. Nevertheless, she could feel his presence. She tried placing herself inside the killer's head as Jack had taught her. What did he have in mind? How would he react when they came face to face? He could have dropped her off Stone Mountain and shot her at the safehouse, but he'd let her go both times. She wasn't complaining, but his actions made no sense.

The Sandman had come to New York to end Rachel Lawrence's life. No question about that. He was like some hideous, relentless machine from the movies. Yet knowing she was in the hospital, he hadn't made a run at her. Maybe things weren't going so well for him after all. Three times he'd tried, and three times he'd failed. Beth remembered looking up at his silhouette as she clung to the edge of the rock. The sound of his voice saying he was only doing a job had stayed with her.

Well, find another.

Chapter 43

She barely had time to squeeze through the doors when they reached the Fulton Street Station. The few remaining people on board filed out as the conductor announced the train was going out of service.

A peculiarity of New York's massive financial district is the mass exodus that takes place every day. Drop a bomb on Wall Street at noon and you'd wipe out three million people. Drop one at five thirty PM and you'll kill almost no one. In a few short blocks, Beth found herself walking through a ghost town of empty streets surrounded by skyscrapers.

She was positive the fire alarm had been a ruse to lure Rachel outside. But for some reason the killer had abandoned his plan. If this was his escape strategy, he'd picked the wrong place for it. They were seven blocks from Manhattan's southernmost tip. A few hundred yards ahead, she spotted a tan raincoat striding purposefully along, seemingly unconcerned she was following him. In minutes, they would run out of room. To the right was the newly rebuilt World Trade Center complex. Beyond that, New Jersey. Ahead, Battery Park and the mouth of New York's harbor. From there, you could press on to Brooklyn, provided you could swim. Beth drew her Beretta and continued down Broadway. Time to call for backup.

At Trinity Church, she took Ray Price's business card out and was starting to punch in his number when footfalls on the pavement stopped her. Spinning around, she leveled her gun at a deserted street. In the gutter, a candy wrapper tumbled along end over end. She'd been concentrating so hard on the Sandman and what he was up to, she'd forgotten about the partner.

For the first time, it dawned on her she might have been led into a trap. There had to be a reason the Sandman appeared so unconcerned. Certainly he knew she was there, because they'd seen each other.

How could I be so stupid?

To her left, the sound of another footfall reached her. Beth backed up to the church doors and tried them. Locked. What else did she expect at this hour? At the end of the street, the tan raincoat turned a corner. Worried and nervous now, she finished typing in Price's number. And reached his office.

"Federal Bureau of Investigation. May I help you?"

She cursed under her breath. She'd misread the card and had just called the general office number.

"This is Elizabeth Sturgis. I'm a detective with the Atlanta Police Department. I'm trying to reach Agent Ray Price. This is an emergency."

"Agent Price is out of the office, ma'am. What's the nature of your emergency?"

Beth explained the situation as quickly as possible. Movement caught her eye on a narrow side street intersecting Broadway.

I'm too exposed.

A moment later, a man named Otis Wheaton came on the line as Beth moved off the steps and hopped a small fence into the cemetery at the side of the church. The largest object there was Alexander Hamilton's mausoleum. At least that would afford her some protection. She relayed her story to the agent.

"I understand your situation, Detective Sturgis. Let me verify with Ray and we'll get someone down there to help you. I take it you're armed?"

"I am, but there are two of them and I'm in the middle."

"Got it. We're rolling. Just stay safe and wait for us."

"Step on it, would you? I think Courtney's heading for the Staten Island Ferry."

"Then it'll make picking him up easier. Just don't try any heroics. We'll be there as quick as we can."

After they disconnected, Beth checked the street again and saw nothing. It was possible she was imagining things and spooking herself as far as the partner was concerned. The agent's advice to keep safe had hit a sore spot. The memory of giving up Jack's name to the killer at Stone Mountain was still fresh in her memory, as was the feeling that she had committed a cowardly act. Jack had waved the episode away. She hadn't. Moreover, waiting wasn't her forte. She hadn't become a cop to hide behind monuments and let someone else do her job. Still, two on one wasn't smart . . . assuming there were really two of them. To make matters worse, believing they were in a low risk situation in New York, she hadn't worn body armor that day.

She glanced at the grave markers around her. They were the oldest in the city, some dating back to the 1600s before the country was founded. In a day or so, she'd be back in yet another cemetery for Ed Mundas's funeral and again for George Lawrence. The longer she waited, the more her anger grew. Convinced she was hiding from shadows, Beth stepped from behind her cover and back into the street. If Courtney really had brought his partner with him, he'd have to make a move before they reached the park. As she moved down Broadway, she used the ground floor windows on the buildings to check the street behind her. It was as empty as when she arrived.

The rain had turned into a blowing mist, reducing visibility. Wind coming off the harbor only made matters worse. Fearing that she would lose the Sandman, Beth began to run.

With its view of the Statue of Liberty and sails gliding across the water, Battery Park could be a pleasant place to spend an hour or two reading or strolling, but not on a day like this. There was no question in her mind now the Sandman was trying for the ferry.

She flinched when her phone buzzed. The screen said "Private Caller." Assuming it was Ray Price calling back, she answered.

"I'm not inclined to keep handing out second chances, Elizabeth."

The accent and voice were immediately familiar. The last time she heard it had been in the safehouse basement.

"There's no place for you to go, Courtney."

His hesitation in responding was enough to let her know she had rattled him.

"Very good, girl. You're a quick study. Always knew you would be."

What did that mean? Beth spotted him about seventy-five yards away standing by himself at the safety rail. She started toward him.

"Don't come any closer," Courtney said, holding up his hand.

"This place will be swarming with cops in about ten minutes. They have a green light to shoot on sight, but if you surrender now, I can promise you a fair trial."

Courtney laughed but didn't respond.

It was a long way for a shot using a handgun, particularly in those conditions. Plus he wasn't showing a weapon. Even if she could take one, the rules of engagement were stopping her. Too bad murderers didn't have to follow those rules. She started forward again, holding her gun low as the wind grew stronger. Beth wiped the mist from her face and ended the call. The killer stood there watching her. Once more, the phone buzzed in her free hand. This time the screen said Raymond Price.

"Where are you?" he said.

"At the entrance to Battery Park. Courtney's about sixty to seventy yards in front of me."

"Listen . . . do . . . attemp . . . yourself. We're . . ."

"Say again. You're breaking up." Beth rolled her eyes when the call dropped. What else was new? In the midst of all that concrete and steel, it wasn't surprising. Didn't matter if help arrived or not. She still had a job to do.

Near the horizon, dark clouds were lit by flashes of light. Closer in, she could hear the rumble of thunder. The harbor was gray and unsettled, filled with whitecaps.

The Sandman finally turned and started walking. He was definitely making for the Staten Island Ferry. It might be easier to pick him up on the boat, but she had a feeling he wouldn't surrender easily. Moreover, he'd take a number of people with him.

"Thomas Courtney! Stop or I'll shoot!"

Despite the rising wind and rain, the killer turned. He was holding something in his hand. Beth's foot chose that moment to slip out from under her on the wet grass. She hit the ground hard. Came up on one knee and brought her weapon to bear.

Factor the wind. Lead slightly because he's moving. Breathe.

There was still no weapon showing, but what was that in his hand? She couldn't take the chance. This man had killed Ed Mundas, Will Landry, all those people at Stone Mountain, not to mention shooting Dwayne Stafford point blank. The world was better off without him.

Her finger increased its pressure on the trigger.

A split second before she squeezed off the shot an arm closed around her chest.

Beth panicked. In her rush to stop Courtney, she'd taken her mind off the partner. *Fool!* That's why he hadn't fired. Desperate, she tried to break the grasp, but the man was too strong. The Sandman began walking back toward them. Fighting with all her strength, she twisted around and found herself looking into the face of Jack Kale.

"Jack! What?"

"It's all right. Let's see if we can convince Mr. Courtney to come along quietly."

Jack rose, keeping his eyes on the killer. He reached out and helped Beth to her feet. Behind him at the edge of the park were Todd Milner, Ray Price, and four FBI agents in blue windbreakers spread out in a semicircle. All of them had rifles trained on the Sandman. The killer stopped and surveyed them with a disturbing calm.

"How did you get here?" Beth asked.

"By plane, same as you, courtesy of our government. First things first, okay?"

Todd Milner called out, "Thomas Courtney, throw down your weapon, lace your fingers together, and put your hands behind your head then get down on your knees!"

Courtney remained where he was. Milner repeated his order as the agents began to advance. No more than forty yards separated them.

"This is your last warning. If you don't comply, we will open fire."

Beth too trained her gun on the Sandman. Like the others, she started forward. Once again, Courtney held his hand up for her to stop.

"Something's wrong," Jack said.

*

He could see the killer was holding a cellphone. He appeared to be talking to someone. Confused, Ray Price looked to Jack for a decision.

230

In Atlanta, there was no question Courtney was working with a part-ner. Maybe that's who he was talking to. Searching the area for a threat, he saw nothing.

Distracted by the conversation he was having, the killer glanced at them. More specifically, he glanced at Beth. Whatever he was argu-ing about and whoever it was with, the conversation was becoming more heated. Unfortunately, the wind made it impossible to hear what he was saying.

Courtney shook his head. Looked at Beth once again. Only this time his expression darkened. Something shifted behind his eyes. The sudden change reminded Jack of another killer he'd met a long time ago. Using hand signals, he motioned for the agents to hold their positions.

Could this man be reasoned with? Did he intend to fight or sur-render? The fact that he wasn't displaying a weapon didn't mean he was unarmed. Seconds ticked by. Jack looked from Todd Milner to Ray Price. Conscious of his orders from Janet Newton, he made his decision. He would try to convince the killer to surrender.

Out on the harbor, a solitary gull soared on the air currents under a threatening sky. Whipped by the wind, the rain was coming at them at an angle. As Jack started forward, Courtney's eyes moved off Beth and fixed on him. Two things changed: the phone conversation ended abruptly, and a faint smile appeared on Courtney's face.

"Down!" Jack screamed. "Down!"

Twin flashes of light accompanied by loud explosions ripped the air. The concussion lifted him off his feet, throwing him backward. He had the vague impression Ray Price was also down. Milner imme-diately dropped to one knee as he fired his weapon. The Sandman went crashing backward over the safety rail.

Jack shook his head trying to clear it. Got up. The sound around him suddenly seemed muted. Beth was still on the ground, but seemed to be all right. He looked to where the Sandman had been standing. The space was as empty as if no one had ever been there.

Chapter 44

After helping Beth to her feet, Jack ran to the railing and looked over, expecting to see a body floating below him. Water lapped against the rocks, but there was no sign of Thomas Courtney at all. Beth, Ray Price, and Todd Milner joined him. Price was bleeding from a gash on his forehead. They all stared over the edge in disbelief.

"Where the hell is he?" Milner asked. "I put at least four rounds in him."

Jack shook his head slowly and said, "I saw him go over. Have everyone who can stand spread out and start looking. I want to see his body."

Miraculously, apart from minor injuries, no one had been seriously hurt. The explosions were caused by a home-rigged bomb planted in a nearby trashcan and were mostly light and noise. Police and firefighters had already begun to arrive. Blue lights and sirens were closing in from all directions. New Yorkers, unfortunately, were all too familiar with the emergency scenario.

Along with the other agents, they scoured every inch of the shoreline. Milner seemed particularly upset. Courtney's disappearance was surreal. At one point, a street cop, seeing the FBI letters on Price's jacket, approached him and said their switchboard had lit up with calls about a terrorist attack.

"It's not," Price said. "You guys certainly got here fast enough."

"Not really. The first call came in about five minutes ago."

Frustrated, Jack slammed the safety rail with the flat of his hand. Courtney had planned his escape. What he couldn't understand was

232

how he'd survived four bullets to the chest. If the cop was correct, the first call had preceded the explosions by at least two minutes. His intent was obviously to create chaos. That was consistent if nothing else.

*

Aided by the police, a boat and divers went into the water and continued their search. Milner took charge running from one point of the park to the other to check on their progress. A tan raincoat was recovered floating in the harbor near the park's farthest point along with a bulletproof vest that showed multiple hits. A city-wide BOLO went out. Airports, bus terminals, and train stations were put on alert. Jack examined the bullets' spread pattern on the vest for a moment and frowned. He hadn't known the Bureau was using hollow-point bullets now. Hollow points were designed to maximize stopping power and tissue damage. He pushed the thought aside. It was more important to find the body, or how he'd escaped.

"No way that bastard's getting out of the metro area," Price said. "Everything'll be sewn up tighter than a drum."

Jack wasn't so sure about that. The man had vanished before their eyes.

"It's not possible," Beth said.

Milner looked grim. Price shook his head, as confused as everyone else there.

"What about Rachel?" Beth asked.

"At the hotel with two agents and a city cop we drafted. We're checking anyone who comes off the elevator. Detective Stafford's watching over things."

After two hours, the search was called off. The intention was to resume it in the morning, when the weather might be more cooperative. Todd Milner elected to stay downtown and join the cops when they started again. A chill rain continued to come down in the dark. They were all tired and soaked to the bone. Jack had lapsed into one of his silences. He separated from the others, walked to where the Coast Guard sailing ship *Eagle* was docked, and stared up at the masts. Beth watched him wondering what was going through his mind. She finally joined him and touched his shoulder to say they were leaving. At first she thought he hadn't heard her, but he came out of his trance and nodded.

On the ride back to the hotel, she asked him to explain why he was in New York.

"When we found the listening device at Dr. Lawrence's office, or I should say the office next door, I realized whenever Rachel let them know where to reach her, she was also letting Courtney know. It was concealed in the ceiling tiles."

"So why didn't you call and tell me that instead of scaring me to death?"

"Because I couldn't."

"That's ridiculous."

"It's not. There a reasonable chance Courtney's tapped into our cellphones."

"You need specialized equipment and the provider's cooperation."

"*Needed*. I was curious about what projects and weapons Sergei Borov was involved with, so I started checking. Eventually, that led me to the Department of Defense. Turns out Borov is in talks with them about licensing a new technology that makes accessing cellphone conversations quite easy if you have a computer, Wi-Fi, and the right software. Unfortunately, Borov's also in talks with a number of other governments and people we don't want to have this technology, like North Korea and ISIS. It explains why Donofrio and the White House have a full-court press on."

Beth still didn't look happy. "Jack, you could have found some way to get word to me. You managed to contact him," she said, pointing to Ray Price.

"After the fact, and I used a pay phone. You know how hard it is to find a pay phone in New York these days?"

The look he received could have frozen water. She was right to be upset, but the circumstances hadn't allowed him any latitude. Price chose to keep his attention on the road and stay silent.

She looked at the dark pea coat and watch cap he was wearing and asked, "That was you following me through the streets?"

"It was."

"And you lurking around the hospital."

"I wouldn't call it lurking, but yes, that was me."

"So why didn't you take Courtney out when you had the chance?"

"Because of his partner. He or she is a wild card we need to account for. Either of them could be the doer. We know he used one in Spain and at least two in Atlanta—"

"What do you mean, at least two?"

"Think about it. The safehouse location wasn't a matter of public record. I mean you can't just look it up in the phone book. It's unlikely the two men flying those models knew enough to supply that information. According the ATF interrogators, one's a wino and the other's a junkie. In other words, they're shills, or at least part shills."

"Which means someone in our department gave him the address . . . dammit."

"Exactly. That's why I'm not opposed to transferring Rachel to federal custody. It might plug the leak. If Courtney's still alive, and I have to assume he is, he's not going away. Wind him up, point him in the right direction, and he just keeps coming."

"You've stopped him three times now, Jack," Price pointed out.

"I've stopped nothing," Jack snapped. "At most, I've annoyed him."

"Still, he's got to be pretty pissed."

"Which is what concerns me."

Beth had gone quiet listening to the exchange. They were passing through Herald Square, which was teeming with people. Large red shopping bags were everywhere. Macy's had already decorated their windows for the holidays. Each year it seemed to happen a little earlier. It was one of her favorite seasons and the first Thanksgiving she would spend with Jack as an engaged couple. She'd called her folks from the airport in Atlanta to give them the news. They were delighted and immediately invited them to visit and spend the holiday. The conversation with her mother brought a smile to her face. She sounded like a young girl yelling for Beth's father to get on the line. Slowly the smile faded, replaced by another thought.

She said, "There's something strange going on with Thomas Courtney."

Jack twisted around in his seat to face her. Price made eye contact in the rearview mirror.

Beth continued, "This was the third time he could have killed me but didn't. When I was coming toward him, he held up his hand for me to stop. A few yards more and I would have been inside the bomb's blast zone."

"Why do you think he hesitated?" Price asked.

"I don't know."

"Maybe I do," Jack said. "Courtney's sister was named Elizabeth. She died in a fire at their home, possibly one Courtney himself set. I'm speculating of course, but it's possible he's experiencing some kind of transference where Beth is concerned."

"Meaning he associates Detective Sturgis with his dead sister?"

"Perhaps not on a conscious level," Jack said. "Transference is a mechanism that works below the surface in someone's mind. If that's the case, we should be grateful."

Beth said, "I think he knew I could have taken a shot at him, but I held off."

"Why?" Price asked.

"Green light or not, he wasn't showing a gun. Only that cell-phone. Who the hell was he talking to?"

"The unseen partner," Jack suggested.

"Tell you what," Price said. "If you find yourself in a life-or-death situation with him again, use his hesitation to your advantage and blow the bastard into next year."

Chapter 45

The water had been numbingly cold. It took Wesley almost thirty minutes to stop shaking. His chest was bruised and sore from where the bullets had hit him. Better sore than deceased. Thank God for body armor. He glanced at the dead officer staring up at him from the floor and continued to rub his arms and legs with a towel to restore some circulation to them.

Through the ship's cabin window he watched as police swarmed the ferry, assuming he would use it to escape to Staten Island. That was the original plan he decided on during the flight up. But a chance berthing of the brigantine *Eagle* changed that. It was in town for the holiday flotilla. Unfortunately, the hospital had been too well defended, and his time was too short. On top of everything else, Kale the magician had shown up and was actually stalking him. Amazing. Wesley rubbed his arms some more and shivered.

It was Sunday and the ship's complement was at a minimum. Thanks to the weather, everyone was below decks or away on shore leave. Only a skeleton crew remained.

A short distance from the *Eagle* were two more ferries. One went to the Statue of Liberty and one to Ellis Island. He decided on the latter. The museum was indoors and would give him a chance to think. This was the third time Kale had frustrated his efforts. It felt like the man was reading his mind. Too much to hope he'd take him out at Mary Quinn's house. Still, it was worth the try. Time to do something about him.

He picked up a tie and decided against it. Officer or not, it was the weekend and casual dress was the order of the day. Just another visitor to the great hall millions of immigrants had passed through. It was a fine, grand country. Light of the modern world. Wesley looked out the cabin window at the four minaret towers wondering if anyone from his hometown had been through there. It was odd, every year the memories of where he had grown up seemed to fade just a little more. He tried to recall the name of the street where his best friend had lived and couldn't. Only his visions of the orphanage remained clear. In his mind, his cellphone buzzed as he was putting on his white cap with the gold officer's braid.

Well, boy-o, that was close, wasn't it?

A little. It wasn't possible to attack the hospital directly. There were too many of them.

I'm given to wondering, Thom, are you goin' soft on me?

If you mean the girl, why complicate things? Killing for the sake of killing makes no sense.

Eliminate the competition, son. Eliminate the competition.

She's not competition.

Might you have feelings for her?

That's ridiculous, Father. We don't know each other.

Just askin', boy-o. Just askin'. To thine own self be true.

If she becomes an issue, I'll deal with her.

I know you will, son. Where do we go from here?

Jack Kale, Father. Jack Kale.

Wesley disconnected, found a raincoat and an umbrella in the officer's closet, pulled the cap low on his head, and left the cabin. On his way to the top deck, he actually had to return the salute of two cadets returning from shore leave. Their eyes focused on the gold lieutenant's insignia on his shoulder. Amazing, really. His hand relaxed its grip on the K-Bar knife in his coat as he passed them. Once outside, he opened the umbrella and walked briskly to the boarding line for the Ellis Island Ferry.

Chapter 46

Price dropped Jack and Beth at the Plaza and informed them of the additional security he had put in place. Three more agents had been brought in. All of them had been issued photographs of the Sandman. Another uniformed cop would come on duty at midnight and stay till nine AM.

Price looked around the lobby and shook his head. "Shame you have to stay in such poor accommodations. Don't give any thought to me driving back to my lonely little apartment in Kew Gardens."

"Sometimes you have to take one for the team," Beth said.

"Don't I know it. What time tomorrow will your plane be ready?"

"We're supposed to call. I hope it's late," Beth said, taking Jack's hand.

"Milner and I came in on the FBI's jet," Jack said. "We can just—" He broke off what he was about to say as Beth's fingernails dug into his palm. "Uh . . . stay here and get a good night's rest and start fresh in the morning."

Price looked from one to the other. "You sure you're not married yet?"

Beth smiled sweetly at him.

"Right. See you both around ten o'clock. Late enough?"

"Late enough," Beth said.

As soon as Ray Price had taken his leave, the expression on Jack's face changed. He took Beth by the elbow and said. "Come with me." She was so shocked by the sudden shift that she allowed him to lead her to the grand ballroom on the next floor. It was empty. As soon as they were inside, Jack shut the door and turned to her. "What you did earlier was not only reckless, it was dangerous."

"What are you talking about?"

"You know damn well what I'm talking about. This is the second time you went after Courtney alone."

"Jack, there wasn't time and I did call for backup."

"After the fact! Do you have a goddamn death wish?"

"What?"

"You heard me. It was a stupid rookie move. You simply cannot operate like a cowboy and go charging off after the bad guys. What's the matter with you?"

"Nothing, I—"

Jack knocked an old centerpiece off the nearest table and sent it flying across the room. "I won't have it! I'm halfway inclined to take you off the case."

They'd had arguments before, but she'd never seen him like this. Nor could she ever recall him raising his voice to her. The rookie reference rubbed the wrong way.

"Rookie? You're the one who's acting like a cowboy. You could have found some way to call me. I just told you I didn't have time—"

"Bullshit! I can't do what I do, worrying myself sick you might be killed. He led us into another trap. Thank God he's half nuts or he'd have blown you up when you got too close."

"You don't know that."

"I sure as hell do. And you do, too. I want you to promise this won't happen again."

Beth took a breath to calm herself and looked around the ballroom. He had a point. She could have called for backup several times in the first few blocks to say she was in pursuit. But she was angry about what happened at Stone Mountain and still embarrassed by it. Nailing Courtney would have gone a long way to curing the problem. But she didn't want to admit that right now. She'd gotten mad first and now he was angry at her.

Jack took her by the shoulders and turned her around. "Beth, I want you to look me in the eye and tell me you won't do that again."

"Which one?"

It broke the tension. Jack was struggling to be stern and not really succeeding. She could always make him laugh.

"Promise me," he repeated.

"I promise," Beth said in a small voice. "I'll try not to do it again. But you're not getting the ring back."

Jack closed his eyes and shook his head. "As long as I get you back."

*

True to his word, Ray Price had security already in place in the hotel. Rachel's room was just down the hall from Beth and Jack's. Dwayne Stafford was directly across the hall from her. Even so, he agreed to check every four hours and make sure everyone was awake and on their toes. In addition to the FBI, two uniformed cops were on duty at each end of the corridor. All the officers were instructed not to discuss who was in the room and Rachel agreed not to tell her office or mention the location they were staying in on her cellphone. So far, so good.

Satisfied that everything was under control, they said goodnight and headed for their rooms.

When they entered theirs, Beth looked around, nodded her approval, then rang for the valet to have her clothes cleaned and pressed. She informed Jack she was taking a bath.

"You won't have anything to wear . . . except that bathrobe," Jack said, as Beth pulled two matching robes out of the closet. "I knew that. I was just testing you."

Beth giggled, kissed him, and left her clothes in a pile on the floor.

Jack waited until the water was running before he picked up the phone and ordered room service: a hamburger and fries for himself and a Caesar salad with grilled chicken strips for Beth along with a side of edamame. He then called the concierge and asked him to find a flower shop who'd deliver a dozen red roses. In all the excitement, there hadn't been time to celebrate their engagement. Figuring the Bureau accountant would go nuts if he put any of those charges on his expense account, he gave them his credit card.

After hanging up, he located a mini-bottle of scotch in the mini-fridge, found an Andrea Bocelli selection on the music channel, and sat down to relax. Outside large raindrops bounced off the window-pane turning Fifth Avenue and its never ending stream of lights into a moving impressionist rendition. Below him, people passed each other like anonymous ships in the night on an ocean of concrete.

Try as he might to think about other things—pleasant things, like Beth and the opulent room they were in with its lovely black marble fireplace—his mind returned to the Coast Guard yacht. Had the police searched it thoroughly? What about the adjacent ferries?

The Sandman wasn't a sorcerer and hadn't suspended the laws of physics, so disappearing into thin air was out. There were only so many places he could hide. The man's vanishing act confounded him.

Slowly, he reviewed what he knew about ships, their soaring masts, myriad lines, and the shapes of the hulls. Without realizing it, his heart began to beat harder. A moment later, his vision blurred and his breath went short.

*

Beth found him on the floor trying to reach for the bottle of pills on the dresser. She'd seen his panic attacks several times, and they were frightening because they had the appearance of a heart attack. She ran to the dresser and opened the bottle, shaking out a single pill. Jack had a tendency to gulp down two or three at a time in an effort to relieve the crushing pressure in his chest, something he'd been battling against at his NA meetings. A small bottle of scotch lay on the floor, its contents drained out. Beth hurriedly filled a drinking glass with water and helped him sit up.

Two months earlier, without telling him, she'd gone to his doctor and asked how to handle the attacks. Without getting into the specifics of his illness, Morris Shottner explained the general mechanics to her. They both hoped after their battle with the serial killer earlier that year, the attacks would decrease and eventually disappear. Apparently their optimism was premature.

Beth was still holding him twenty minutes later wishing she knew how to fight the demons that tore at his mind. Slowly, the pill began to take effect.

Jack blew out a breath and shook his head. "Whew, that was a good one." He seemed unable to meet her eyes.

Beth pushed his hair off his forehead. "All right now?"

"I think so," he said, getting to his feet.

"Don't you have any idea what causes them?"

That was always the question, and one he'd obviously never found an answer to. It wasn't something he liked to talk about because the attacks were an embarrassment to him. Beth was waiting for an explanation. He took a breath and told her about the painting in Connie Belasco's house and about his dream of being on the ship that appeared in it with her. He left out that, occasionally, Beth would take her place. He didn't know what that meant.

"You think seeing that big ship at Battery Park had something to do with it?"

"I don't know. The easiest answer is yes, but when I looked at the brig, I remembered Connie's painting and had no reaction to it. Then this hits out of the blue. You sure you want to marry me?"

Beth shrugged. "I guess so."

"Gee, thanks."

She smiled and kissed him. He'd said "out of the blue," but she'd seen him staring at the ship, transfixed. How could that brilliant mind of his miss something so obvious? Her thoughts were interrupted by the arrival of room service. The episode began to fade.

When they sat down to eat, Beth frowned at the hamburger and fries Jack had ordered for himself.

"We're at the Plaza Hotel and you order a burger and fries?"

"I like them."

Then her eyes happened to fall on the bill, saw it was seventy-three dollars, excluding the roses, and nearly had a panic attack of her own. She shook her head.

"You should really try eating healthy, honey."

"This is healthy, a nice mixture of yellow and brown," Jack said. "Very balanced."

"Try this," she said, passing him an edamame pod. "You might like it."

He remembered someone saying the same thing about his first marriage. He chewed the pod without enthusiasm. It had no taste. Beth seemed encouraged.

"And you should try more salads. I want you to live a long time."

"It'll seem like a long time if I have to eat this stuff."

Beth responded with a look. He raised his hands in surrender and promised to expand his food selections in the future.

"Good," she said, taking a fry off his plate. "Do you really think Courtney associates me with his sister?"

"It's probable. He didn't hesitate to kill Ed Mundas or shoot Dwayne or anyone else for that matter. Obviously, there's something special about you. I, of course, know that, but it's good to keep it in mind. Like Ray Price said, that knowledge might save your life."

Beth nodded thoughtfully, then asked if Jack had told his daughter they were engaged. Her ability to switch to a different subject on a dime never ceased to amuse him.

"Not yet," he said, checking his watch. "She should be home now. How about if I give her a call?"

Morgan answered on the second ring and responded to the big news in typical teenager fashion, saying, "Oh, cool." She then asked to speak with Beth who had a more animated and prolonged conversation with her. Part of which included an invitation to meet Beth's family over the holidays.

Jack wasn't certain when he lost control of the situation, or if he ever had control in the first place. His worries about how his daughter would take the news evaporated. Judging from Beth's end of the conversation, she was clearly excited.

While they were talking, he walked to the window and looked out. They were high enough to see the South Street Seaport and Maiden Lane in the distance. Another sailing ship was tied up there, now functioning as a museum. He wondered if it might be the one in Connie's painting. She'd died because he had let his guard down with Howard Pell. He shook his head. He should have been there to protect her. Images of her body mutilated almost beyond recognition forced their way up from the farthest corners of his mind. Images he could never forget.

The rain continued to beat against the window and trees in Central Park. In the street, he could see people hunched over, holding newspapers and briefcases above their heads as they walked. Rachel Lawrence had done nothing to merit the hand she'd been dealt. Despite the pain she was in, she had acquitted herself nobly in his opinion. He swore a silent oath: the Sandman would not have her.

Thus far, the contest between them had been deadly, and one that he was determined to end. There were enough two-legged monsters walking the earth. By increments, Jack was beginning to understand the engine that drove Thom Courtney. More important, he perceived in it a weakness he could exploit. They'd failed at the safehouse, or more accurately, he had failed. That wouldn't happen again. He picked up the hotel telephone and placed a call to the FBI's equipment and tech center. When that was done, he placed another call to their field office in Phoenix.

The conversation with his daughter ended with Beth sending a video of their room and her ring over her cellphone. When he asked what they had been talking about for so long, she replied, "Boys."

"Oh, you mean that Josh kid she mentioned the other day?"

"He's history."

"How? They haven't had time to make history."

Beth shrugged. "Morgan's excited about a new boy she met on their class trip, or maybe it was two boys. I forget because she was going so fast."

"I see. How did her trip go?"

"Fine. Mostly she wanted to talk about your ex and her new boyfriend. The guy sounds like a jerk."

"Really?"

"She asked again if we'd talked more about her moving back to Atlanta."

"I'd be delighted, but how would you feel?"

Beth was quiet for a moment. "If that's what she really wants and she's thought it through, tell her as soon as the wedding's over she can start packing."

*

Later, when they were in bed, Beth folded herself around him, throwing one leg on top of his and one arm across Jack's chest. Both were exhausted and sleep was coming quickly. So many thoughts were bouncing around in her head: getting married, starting a new family, keeping Rachel safe, and Jack's outburst earlier. She conceded he had a point but something else was bothering her. Well, not bothering exactly. It was more like an unanswered question.

"Did you love her?"

Jack's eyes opened. She was referring to Connie Belasco.

"No," he said, shaking his head.

"It's all right if you did."

"I know. But I didn't. Connie was a sweet kid who I was supposed to show the ropes to. Instead, I let Howard Pell turn her into a freak. I should have killed the bastard when I had the chance."

"You didn't *let* him do anything. Pell acted on his own. He never asked for your permission, Jack."

She felt him nod in the darkness and knew her words had no effect. Of course he wanted to protect her, and she loved him for it. But his senses of remorse and guilt were so deeply ingrained, it would take a miracle to make him see what was so apparent to everyone else. It hurt her to hear him talk that way. She'd give her right arm to find some way to loose the gargoyle's talons affixed to his neck and free him from the pain he was in.

Beth held him tighter, as if by doing so she could shield him from the nightmare that usually followed one of his attacks. Waiting in the dark, she was ready to fight the demons. Eventually his breathing became regular and she felt his body relax. Beth closed her eyes and went to sleep.

Chapter 47

Two Days to the Grand Jury

In the morning, she awoke to sunlight streaming through the window, a robin's-egg sky, and the sight of a dozen red roses in a green vase on the dresser. But no Jack. The light was off in the bathroom and the room was deserted. The sun had already burned the shadows away. He'd obviously gotten up early and stepped out. Thankfully, the expected nightmare had failed to make an appearance. She was about to get up and check her phone when she heard someone at the door. It opened and her new fiancé came in holding two paper bags.

"Good morning. I have cappuccino, a latte, and bagels. Lady's choice."

Beth held her arms open for him. "The hotel didn't mind you bringing that in?"

"There are two schools of thought on that. The receptionist seemed disdainful, but the bellman gave me a thumbs up. Eighteen dollars versus sixty-eight for room service."

"My hero," Beth said. "Put the difference toward our honeymoon."

Jack blinked. Things were certainly moving along quickly. They hadn't been engaged forty-eight hours and she was already thinking honeymoon. Not unreasonable. It simply took some getting used to. Beth Sturgis took some getting used to. In their second meeting, she had virtually snatched him from the front of his house to help with a case. He smiled. That association had grown into something special. As far as he was concerned, they could stay in this room for the next month. They just needed the Sandman to cooperate.

Their hug might have developed into something even more pleasant but for a knock on the door causing Beth to duck under the covers. It was the hotel valet returning her clothes. Jack signed the bill and tipped him. If they didn't get out of there soon, they wouldn't be able to afford a honeymoon.

Once the valet was gone, Beth tossed the covers aside and began getting dressed. Jack moved to a chair by the window and picked up a magazine. Distracted, he spent more time surreptitiously watching her than reading. He loved the way she moved and the curves on her body. She'd gotten as far as her undergarments and was in the process of putting some lotion on her legs when she noticed his interest.

"What are you looking at?"

"Checking for concealed weapons, ma'am."

Beth giggled. "Down, boy. Ray Price will be here in a little while."

"I was being subtle about it."

"Extremely."

The cap on the lotion bottle chose that moment to slip through her fingers and onto the floor. Beth bent from the waist to pick it up.

"Uh . . . I'm going for a walk," Jack said. His voice suddenly sounded slightly hoarse.

She was still smiling as the door closed.

*

Rachel rang their room to tell them the plane would be ready at two o'clock. She informed Beth she had also told Dwayne Stafford. Beth used the hotel phone to update Ray Price. He told her he had spoken with the hotel management, who agreed to move all other guests off the end of the floor where their rooms were located. That would help a great deal because it meant less people coming and going.

When Jack returned from his walk, she passed on the news that they were stuck for a few more hours, and that Ray Price and Dwayne seemed to have the security situation under control.

"Wonderful," he said, slipping his arms around her waist. "Perhaps we can put the time to good use and . . . ah, discuss police procedure."

"Honey, I just got dressed."

Jack's shoulders slumped.

"I'll make it up to you back in Atlanta. Promise," Beth said.

"Sure, give 'em a ring and it's all over," Jack muttered.

"Don't pout. Take me for a walk."

"But I just went . . . never mind. Ready when you are, dear."

Their stroll up Fifth Avenue was a welcome respite from the case. Stores had holiday displays in their windows and people on the crowded sidewalk seemed to share in the sense the holidays were upon them. Beth slipped an arm through his and squeezed.

Coming to New York always took some getting used to. The city had an energy unlike anyplace he'd ever visited. There was so much culture in its museums, libraries, galleries, theatres, and concerts he always had a vague sense of guilt just walking the streets and sightseeing. It felt like he should enroll in an adult education course and learn a new language, or study postmodernist art, or learn to make his own pasta. The city had a way of stimulating some hidden brain cells that governed self-improvement as soon as he crossed its rivers.

Beth seemed quite at home and began a running commentary on its attractions, pointing out Rockefeller Center, the statue of Atlas holding up the world, Tiffany's, Saint Patrick's Cathedral, Saks Fifth Avenue, and the Forty-Second-Street library before they turned back.

"Despite all the craziness of the last three days, I'm really happy," she said.

Jack smiled at her. "Me, too."

When they initially passed Saint Thomas Church a few blocks south of the hotel, she slowed and came to a halt. Sitting on a thin wool blanket against the wall was a blind man and his dog. Alongside him was a little tin bucket passersby occasionally tossed coins into. Beth took five dollars from her purse and made her own contribution. Tempted to follow suit, Jack sensed what she was doing was somehow personal and stayed where he was.

"That was nice of you," he commented as they continued walking.

After a half-block with no conversation, Beth said, "Being blind is terrible. Some people adapt better than others, but the truth is you're frightened all the time."

It was a strange thing to say. Jack looked at her and waited.

Another block went by before she spoke again. "When I was fourteen, I was blind for nearly two months."

The revelation took him completely by surprise. "Was it an accident?"

"Depends on how you define an accident. I came home from school one day and found my sister hanging from the ceiling in our bedroom."

"Jesus," Jack said. Dan Pappas had told him the bones of this shortly after they first met on the last case. The information had been passed along by Beth's original partner. She had never seen fit to share the details, possibly because they didn't know each other well enough at the time. He figured she was entitled to her privacy and kept Pappas's confidence.

Beth's eyes seemed to dull over as if she was no longer standing on the street with him, but observing a distant memory replaying in her mind. "Cindy was two years younger than me and I knew she'd been having problems at school with a group of girls. Eventually they convinced a few boys to join in and started putting things on the Internet, really mean things. Kids can be terribly cruel if they want to."

Jack said nothing.

"I went to them and told them to stop, which only made matters worse. My little sister was a quiet girl who had always been a little overweight, and that made her an easy target. She tried dieting and exercising. Nothing seemed to work. Later we found she'd been taking pills and purging. At night, I'd hear her crying. The poor kid was just miserable. I tried talking to her, but what do fourteen-year-olds know?

"I've seen some pretty bad things since I joined Homicide." Beth shook her head. "There's been nothing to compare with that, for me at least. When I saw her hanging there, I started to scream. A neighbor and his wife heard me and came running. They called my father and mother, who put me to bed. The next morning I woke up and couldn't see." Beth shrugged.

"Traumatic blindness," Jack said quietly. It was an old outdated term but it applied.

"You once asked me why I react so strongly to bullies. I should have stopped those little bastards from turning my sister's life into a living hell. We make quite a pair, don't we, Kale?"

Jack stopped and took her face in his hands. "Quite a pair. But there's no one I'd rather have than you."

"Still want to marry me?"

Jack smiled and lifted his shoulders. "I guess."

Beth punched him in the arm as they crossed to the opposite side of Fifth Avenue. On the way back, she slowed at the church once more. The blind man and his dog were gone. Jack remained quiet, assuming she was immersed in past events—something he seemed doomed to do himself. She stood there staring at the old church.

He was searching his mind to come up with what he hoped would be a comforting remark when Beth surprised him by asking what the church entrance was made of.

Jack studied it for a moment. "Brownstone and . . . *terra-cotta*."

"Probably have marble inside, huh? I wonder if any churches in Atlanta are built the same?"

Another piece of the puzzle dropped into place.

*

At noon, Ray Price picked them up at the hotel accompanied by two SUVs filled with FBI agents. He informed them Milner had caught a commercial flight back to Atlanta earlier that morning to resume surveillance on Borov. The bad news was, there had been no sign of Thomas Courtney since Battery Park. Just when Jack thought things couldn't get any worse, Price added that the commander of the *Eagle* had been discovered late the previous evening with his throat cut. With the exception of two cadets who reported seeing someone they thought was the commander leaving the ship, there were no witnesses. That had been an hour after the explosions. Neither cadet had been able to offer a description. Not surprising. It seemed clear the man they saw was the Sandman.

Jack asked Price to have his tech team go over the cabin thoroughly. The agent said he had already called them and briefed Janet Newton. The next part of his message came as no surprise. The deputy director wanted to meet with him when he returned. After some discussion, they decided to keep the latest news from Rachel Lawrence, as it would only upset her further. Good-byes were said and they boarded the plane.

Encouraged by Beth's deduction, Jack made a mental list of the churches he knew that contained marble and terra-cotta on the flight back to Atlanta. There had to be dozens. But at least it was a starting point. There was a good chance the Sandman was using one as a hideout.

On arrival at Charlie Brown Airport, two federal marshals met the plane and took Rachel into custody. There were now less than thirty-six hours until the grand jury met. Dwayne Stafford volunteered to stay with her.

One of the marshals handed Jack a package received from Quantico that morning. It contained six cellphones capable of scrambling their calls and encrypting their texts and e-mails. Supposedly, they were immune from Sergei Borov's software. He hoped that was true, because they might be betting their lives on them.

Chapter 48

When they were in the car leaving the airport, Beth asked what Jack was hoping to find in the commander's room.

"They call it a cabin."

"What do you expect to find in the cabin?"

"Something that's not supposed to be there."

"I understand that, Jack. It's obvious Courtney killed him. Is there something specific you have in mind, or do you just want me to guess and see if I come close?"

"More of those reddish grains. I'd like to compare them to what showed up at Gabe Alonso's house and in his car."

"That would just confirm Courtney killed them both."

"Or not."

His answer was cryptic and Beth didn't quite get what he was talking about, but another thought occurred to her. "If we capture Courtney and convince him to talk, it would tie Borov to the murders, obstruction of justice, and conspiracy. That's what Donofrio's aiming for. Nobody will even remember the money laundering charge."

Jack leaned over and kissed her on the cheek. "I have great taste in fiancées."

*

After dropping her off at the station, Jack proceeded to the local FBI office in Century Center. When Price told him Janet Newton wanted to meet, he assumed it would involve a conference call with her and Todd Milner. He was surprised to find them both there. The gravity of the situation was highlighted by her having flown in from Washington, DC. She had appropriated the SAC's office, as Sally Yellen was out of town.

Janet, dressed in a black suit and a white silk blouse, began by saying, "Todd's already explained what happened in New York. Thank God we didn't lose anybody."

"Except for a Coast Guard commander," Jack said.

"You know what I mean. So far we've had no luck pinning Courtney down, Jack. I need a clear idea how you intend to proceed."

"Fair enough. Before we left, I asked Ray Price to expand the search to include private charter flights coming out of the New York area. If the Sandman's going to make another run at Rachel Lawrence, he'll have to do it soon, because he's almost out of time. The problem is we have a number of airports to cover and a lot of territory. Borov also has access to his own aircraft."

"Speaking of that," Milner said, "I've had the FAA pull the flight plans for his two jets. Interestingly, one of them was in New York the same day we were. Borov was here in Atlanta, but that doesn't mean Courtney didn't catch a ride."

"Excellent," Jack said. "Motive and opportunity never hurt."

"But are we any closer to nailing the son of a bitch?" Janet asked.

"Maybe. We know his name and a fair amount of background on him, such as where he's from and what his early life was like. It's also clear he's working with someone."

The deputy director beat a rhythm on the desk with her pen for several seconds, then told him that really didn't answer her question. She continued, "The White House and the Senate Intelligence Committee are all asking for daily reports. Is there *anything* we can give them?"

Jack noted the use of "we" rather than "I." Janet had always been one of the good guys and a team player, but it was clear she was on the hot seat.

"I've told you where we are," Jack said. "That's an honest assessment."

"Can you stop him?"

"Yes."

"Just like that?"

"I'll stop him. Capture is another matter, but I will stop him."

The deputy director sat back and considered Jack Kale. She'd known him for years, and he was not given to boasting or unrealistic speculation, neither was he an egocentric individual. If he said he would stop the killer, he was stating what he perceived as fact. His confidence was reassuring, but the White House and Senate committee were interested in results. If that didn't happen, it would be her head on the chopping block.

She said, "You were in visual contact with Courtney outside the hospital."

"Correct."

"Yet you chose not to take him there."

"I did. He was scoping out the entrance and lobby. More important, he was waiting."

"For what?"

"Exactly what took place. Someone pulled the fire alarm. When that happened, people began to evacuate the building. He's used variations of that technique several times now in Spain, Israel, Germany, and here. He was waiting for the crowd to make his move. Fortunately, Beth Sturgis had the presence of mind to have Ray Price take Dr. Lawrence out through the doctors' entrance rather than risk the street. I don't think he was counting on Price and two detectives being there."

Todd Milner commented, "I don't either. That was a good call on both your parts."

"Maybe," Janet said.

"Our orders are to take the Sandman alive. If Courtney didn't trip the alarm, someone else had to," Milner said. "Jack and Beth did the right thing."

Janet nodded, then said, "Price told me you want to set another trap for him. You think it'll work this time?"

Jack outlined what he had in mind.

When he was finished, Milner said, "That's putting the cops or agents at risk."

Jack agreed it would. "We know Rachel Lawrence's phones are compromised, but Courtney doesn't know we've discovered that yet. If he believes he's privy to our thinking, that should give us an edge."

"Let's try it," the deputy director said. "Did you receive the secure phones?"

"They were passed out when we landed in Atlanta. I see Todd already has his."

"If Borov's technology falls into the wrong hands, it could be disastrous for the country. When will you put your plan into action, Jack?" Janet Newton said.

"No later than tomorrow morning."

Janet stood, indicating the meeting was at an end. Todd Milner said good-bye and left to resume his surveillance on Sergei Borov. According to the wiretap, they were picking up bits and pieces of conversations that indicated Borov was in the final stages of negotiations with Hamas and al-Qaeda representatives. The situation was precarious.

Janet was quiet as she walked Jack to the elevator. When they reached the doors, she said, "I understand congratulations are in order."

"Thank you."

"Beth seems like a good person."

"She is."

The deputy director brushed some lint from Jack's shoulder, then said, "I hope you'll both be happy."

"Thanks, Janet."

She searched his face for a moment and then nodded and walked back inside.

Chapter 49

Thirty minutes later, Jack was in Dr. Morris Shottner's office talking about his latest panic attack and the recent changes in his life. The aroma of tobacco from Shottner's pipe filled the room. Not politically correct, but not unpleasant. It was a clear fall day with the temperature close to forty-five degrees. A sparrow was sitting on the windowsill watching them.

There's a man running around trying to k²l people, and I'm looking at sparrows.

Jack realized Shottner was waiting for an answer. The psychologist was in his late sixties and possessed intelligent features. His hair was mostly white with a sprinkling of brown thrown in. That day, he was dressed in charcoal gray slacks and a pale-yellow shirt with a tiny polo player logo on the pocket.

"I'm sorry, would you repeat the question?"

"I asked if you can recall what you were feeling when you saw the Sandman in New York."

"You mean at Battery Park?"

"No, the first time. You said you spotted him outside the hospital. Tell me what went through your mind."

Jack considered his response for a moment. "Initially, I remember a wave of fear."

"Normal, considering you were in the presence of a killer. I might have the same feeling if a shark swam by a boat I was in."

"It wasn't so much that I was afraid for myself. I knew he was there to kill Rachel Lawrence and anyone else who got in his way."

"Like Beth."

"And Dwayne Stafford and Ray Price."

"Yet you elected not to confront him."

Why does everyone keep asking about that?

"My orders are to take him alive if possible. Plus, he wasn't showing a weapon. I couldn't start shooting on a crowded New York street. And there was the issue of his partner."

"But you could have stopped a known killer," Shottner pointed out.

"And the partner might still have succeeded in carrying out their mission. Half a victory won't do in this case. Win the battle, lose the war."

"Very sensible. What about this man scared you? I know that seems like an obvious question, but think about it for a moment."

Jack glanced out the window. A second, more vibrantly colored bird had joined the first.

"My first thought was that he would hurt Beth, which might not make complete sense because he saved her life at Stone Mountain and again at the safehouse. Unfortunately, you can't count on a reaction like that to remain consistent. Courtney's experiencing some type of transference with his dead sister. According to the file, she was in the auto accident that killed his parents."

"She survived?"

"Right. He and the sister entered into foster care together. She was six years older."

"What happened to her?" Shottner asked.

"The sister, her boyfriend, and an abusive uncle all burned to death in their home. Courtney disappeared after that."

Shottner's pipe had gone out. He took a moment to relight it using a long wooden kitchen match, which he placed in an ashtray with a cork knob at the center when he was through.

Jack said, "I thought we were going to talk about my panic attack."

"We are. But first I wanted to discuss why this man scared you."

"I see."

"Since you didn't answer my earlier question, let me ask this. Was there any time to enlist help?"

"Not really. I was watching him hoping I'd spot the partner when the hospital alarm went off. Once Beth went after him, I used a pay phone to call a fellow agent and followed them to the subway and then the park."

"Thinking to protect her?"

"Of course. And capture the Sandman."

"But you didn't."

"No, he beat me again."

"He beat you? That's an odd choice of words. Why do you put it that way?"

"I don't know. That's just what came to mind."

Shottner sat back in his chair and waited.

"You think I was afraid of losing to him?"

"I don't recall saying anything. Seeing the ship and having it remind you of your dead partner's painting is a very simplistic answer. If this, then that. But I wonder whether the source of your panic attack might have deeper roots. What do you think?"

"That's what I'm here to find out, Moe."

"Of course. How did your daughter react to the news you're getting married again?"

"She seemed pleased and wants to come visit for the holidays. Beth's already making plans to introduce her to her family."

"Also good," Morris Shottner said. "Your fiancée seems to be quite organized and moving things along quickly."

"Sometimes too quickly," Jack said.

"Oh?"

"I don't mean with respect to the marriage. That's fine. Beth's unquestionably bright and like a sponge when it comes to learning. But she has a tendency to throw herself into a situation without thinking of the consequences. I suppose that comes from having a competitive streak and wanting to prove herself. Unnecessary, because she has already—several times. Connie was the same way."

"You think a competitive streak is a bad thing?"

The question seemed to annoy Jack. He said, "It can get you killed."

"Oh?"

"She went after the killer twice on her own without waiting for backup. That was not only wrong and against procedure; it was stupid. Connie was the same way. In a life-or-death situation, particularly one where others might be at risk, you need to look before you leap."

"Sensible," Shottner said. "Did you discuss this with her?"

"Yeah, she promised to be more careful in the future."

Instead of feeling better when he left the session, Jack felt more unsettled than when he went in. The doctor's questions had started him thinking along several lines. Losing to a superior opponent was always a possibility, but one he acknowledged only in an academic sense. It was simply unacceptable. Just as Beth's going after the Sandman alone was unacceptable. Courageous, yes, but reckless. Thomas Courtney was an accomplished killer and nearly prescient in the plans he made.

The more he thought, the more the word *prescient* kept going round and round in his mind.

It was the same when he got behind the wheel of his car. Prescience was a product of science fiction, not real life. He had yet to meet a criminal who could see into the future. The simple explanation therefore was that Courtney was getting help from someone. Prescient, no. Well informed, yes.

He dropped off the evidence he'd collected during his flight up at the crime lab, then called Beth and asked her to meet him at the library.

Chapter 50

Rachel Lawrence hated the safehouse. Being there made her feel like a prisoner. It wasn't that the house was unpleasant. It simply wasn't home, the place where she and George had spent their lives together. The place they talked about raising a family. If she couldn't have children of her own, adoption would have been fine, or foster children. George would have been such a good father. He was much more patient than she was and seemed so excited by the prospect when they had discussed it. He went on and on about what he would do if they had a son, and about not letting any daughter of his date until she was at least thirty (he knew what men were like). George could always make her smile. Good Lord, how she missed him. Rachel finished her drink and went downstairs to fix another.

The three marshals sharing the house with her and Dwayne Stafford were solicitous and gave her all the space they could. They explained all about the bulletproof glass, closed-circuit TV—except in the bathrooms of course—and the sensors in the lawn. They explained about everything except how to make the hurting stop.

The euphoria she felt after the operation had now faded. At best, it was a temporary bandage. Alone in her room at night, the realization that half of her life had been destroyed and she was once again alone in the world came flooding back. Not gradually. Not in pieces. But all at once with the violence of an avalanche.

Rachel found Dwayne Stafford in the living room starring out the window. He was still fighting his own loss and wasn't quick enough to wipe moisture from his eyes. Rachel pretended not to notice. He was a big, sweet boy, awkward and distraught over the death of the friend he'd grown up with. She remembered their conversation on the plane. Male models. It brought a smile to her face, which faded almost immediately. Rachel poured another gin and tonic and sat down across from Dwayne.

"Hi, Doc. Speak with your office?"

"Stu Patterson's holding down the fort as best he can. The poor guy's been working to nine every night. He wanted to visit, but I told him that wasn't possible."

"Dr. Patterson seems like a good sort. Hope his wife doesn't mind him being gone so much."

"Oh, he's not married. Stu has a whole stable of women he sees. George used to call them the flavor of the month."

"No kidding."

"He takes a different one with him to Las Vegas each time he goes on one of his monthly junkets."

Dwayne laughed. "Sounds exciting. Personally, I'm not much for gambling. Maybe a dollar lottery ticket now and then."

"Me too. I actually dated him before I met George. Stu was my hematology teacher in med school. What about you? Anyone special in your life?"

"Melissa Sue Townsend. Been sweet on her since the seventh grade."

"And does she feel the same way?"

"Oh, yes, ma'am. Melissa Sue was the hottest girl in middle school. They retired her cheerleading sweater when she graduated."

This time Rachel did laugh. "Are you planning to make an honest woman of her?"

"Sure am. Been saving up for a ring for about a year now."

Rachel held up her glass in a toast and asked Dwayne if he cared to join her.

"No, ma'am, but you go right ahead."

She took a sip she didn't taste and put the glass down and looked out the window at the dormant lawn. Except for a thirty-yard buffer of woods that separated the properties on both sides, the rest of the trees had been removed. The house sat on a small rise with the nearest neighbors about an acre apart. Directly behind them was a reservoir making it difficult for anyone to approach the home unseen.

"Do you have a picture of Melissa Sue?"

"I sure do," the young detective said, taking out his wallet. The photo was taken on a beach somewhere. Melissa was blonde with a kind open face. "She's the one on the right," Dwayne said.

"I never would have guessed. You like to joke, don't you?"

Dwayne shrugged. "It helps to keep me from thinking about other things. A little while ago, I spoke to Ed's daddy. They're gonna hold his funeral the day after tomorrow to give folks a chance to come in from out of town. If the marshals don't have a cow, I'd appreciate it if you'd join us."

"I'd be honored, Dwayne," Rachel said. "We're holding George's service the morning I testify. Why don't you bring your young lady?"

Dwayne Stafford shook his head. "If those ain't the two damnedest dates I ever heard of. If Melissa still wants to marry me after that, I'll know I have a keeper."

"Back to back funerals," Rachel said. "Who'da thunk it?"

*

Lenny Walpole was having dinner at Mary Mac's Tea Room with his friend Rick. Mary Mac's had been an Atlanta staple for as long as he could remember. Except for the metal napkin holders, the tables were all bare. The cooking was unabashedly Southern, featuring black-eyed peas, collard greens, mashed potatoes, and chicken. If you didn't opt for a Coca-Cola with your meal, the beverage of choice was either coffee or sweet iced tea.

On the chair next to Lenny was the laptop computer. Since Rick had returned it to him that morning, he hadn't let it out of his sight.

"How was your trip to New York?"

"Hectic," Wesley said. "We were scouting locations for the cut-in scenes after we wrap up here."

"Cut-in scenes?"

"Crowd shots and such. It's easier up there because they have so many people."

"Did the director say anything about me?"

"He sure did. You're being given credit as technical advisor. The pay isn't much, just union scale. It was the best I could do."

"That's still great," Lenny said. "So I only have to fly the model two more times?"

"Assuming the shots come out. We'll be using a telephoto lens, which makes the perspective tricky."

"Wow," Lenny said. "Will you be going up to New York for the crowd shots?"

"Absolutely."

"I was there once in high school. It's huge, and all those people . . ." Lenny shook his head. "Rick, I can't tell you how much this has all meant to me. I was checking online, and there's a methadone clinic I can get into. I'd like to get myself clean."

"Brilliant," Wesley said.

"Do you think afterward we could maybe hang out together?"

"I don't see why not."

Lenny seemed pleased by his answer. Rick was a gift from heaven. Maybe his luck was finally changing.

"So the shooting will be finished in two days?"

Wesley took a sip of his Coke, then said, "Day after tomorrow at the latest."

"Tell me about the new location."

"It's a park, like Piedmont. A lot smaller, of course, and on the other side of a reservoir."

*

Save for two figures hunched over a table studying the location of the city's churches, the reference section of the Atlanta Public Library was empty. Jack's original estimate of dozens of churches was high. Not quite that many, but close. Beth compiled a list as they went. Many of the buildings Jack was familiar with, having grown up in Atlanta. He was able to eliminate a fair number because the construction was either different or they didn't have the requisite terra-cotta and marble combination.

Earlier, Beth had shared her observations about the church in New York with Dan Pappas, who agreed she might be onto something. Thom Courtney was probably hiding in either a church or a government building, which explained the marble and terra-cotta trace evidence they'd collected. Her partner was concentrating his efforts on the latter.

According to an architect they spoke with, terra-cotta had been commonly used in buildings at one time, but was now difficult to obtain and presented too many problems because of its lack of durability and failure to meet code. The majority of its uses, he said, were confined to accents around windows and entrances.

Beth's cellphone buzzed.

"Detective Sturgis? This is Armand Tucker with the City Inspector's Office. I just received your message."

"Thanks for returning the call, Mr. Tucker. I'm in the midst of an investigation and could use your help. We're looking for a building here, like an abandoned church or a school, that we think a suspect might be holed up in."

"Holed up?"

"Hiding from the police, sir."

"I see. A suspect in what may I ask?"

"Seven murders."

The statement caught Tucker by surprise. "My goodness. Unfortunately there are a great many of those."

"So I'm finding out. This might help narrow it down. The one we're searching for probably has terra-cotta and marble as part of its entrance. Possibly the flooring, too. I was hoping you might point us in the right direction."

"Nothing comes to mind off the top of my head. Let me check with my colleagues. How quickly do you need this?"

"Ten minutes ago," Beth said. "We think the killer's planning to strike again quite soon."

She explained the situation to Jack once the call ended.

"I have six possibilities," he said. "We can divide the list in half. We'll take three and Pappas and Childers can take the rest. If your friend calls back, we'll add that to whatever he comes up with."

"How about drafting Todd Milner?"

"He's stuck on surveillance with Borov. Apparently something big's about to go down in terms of a deal."

*

Beth made the calls while they were driving. The first location was a bust, a school in Cabbage Town that was in the process of being torn down. Only half of it was still standing and the roof was completely gone.

The second location was the former residence of an Atlanta law school on Martin Luther King Drive, abandoned years earlier when the school moved to new headquarters. The old brown brick building was still there—barely. Its front doors had been replaced by warped plywood. Above the doorway was a chipped terra-cotta arch.

Jack studied it for a minute, then looked down at a layer of dust covering the steps and went around to the back entrance. Like the front door, it too had been boarded up. The only way in was via an unstable-looking metal staircase. The iron safety rail was pitted with rust and moved when he grabbed it. He had the feeling one good tug would probably pull it away from its moorings. At the bottom of the landing were wine bottles, crushed soda cans, hamburger wrappings, cereal boxes, and orange juice containers, a favorite of junkies. Jack could see one of the plywood boards had been moved aside to allow someone access. He told Beth to stay where she was, drew his gun, and climbed the steps. She didn't argue. At the top, he squeezed his way in and was back in less than ten minutes.

"Empty."

"What about all these food items?"

"Ancient history. Even the junkies have moved on."

"What was it like inside?"

"The rats seemed happy enough."

A shudder went up her spine. They headed for the car.

On the way to the third location, Dan Pappas called to say he and Childers had found nothing yet and would touch base when they finished.

*

The Rutherford B. Hayes Elementary School had been destroyed by fire and closed several years earlier. Not much was left but a shell. Nevertheless, they went through what they could, negotiating their way across debris and piles of leaves that had accumulated around the entrance. Jack didn't look happy. "Maybe Childers and Pappas'll have better luck," he said, kicking a can out of the way.

Beth was about to answer when her cellphone went off.

"Ms. Sturgis, this is Armand Tucker again. I'm afraid we didn't come up with much. I have ten buildings that may be of some help and one possibility."

"Let's hear them. I'll put you on speaker so my partner can listen."

As it turned out, Jack had already identified eight of the locations. She wasn't surprised. As a native Atlantan, his knowledge of the city was extensive. Then again, his knowledge of everything was extensive.

"One of our inspectors was in the field close to number nine, so I asked him to have a look around. It's an old power company building that's been abandoned for years."

Beth's antennae went up. "You sent someone there knowing we're looking for a murderer? This man has killed seven people."

"Oh, Bernie was very careful. He used to be in the Marines."

What the hell does that mean?

"Bernie," Beth said.

"Bernie Rapkin."

"I see. Has he checked in, Mr. Tucker?"

"Just a moment ago. That's why I'm calling. He told me the place was locked up tighter than a drum. You'd have to scale a big fence topped with barbwire. They also have a security company who checks once a day to make sure kids don't get in."

Beth exhaled. "All right, that doesn't sound good. Tell me about the possibility."

"Well, it's been quite a while since I've seen it. At one time, the building housed a small Pentecostal church. They were located a few blocks from the King Center. When the church moved, it sold the property to a slumlord. I don't know how many times we cited that man for code violations. First, he tried to run a nursing home and billed Medicare right and left. When that didn't work out, he rented it to a lady photographer. She may still be there for all I know. It's just an oversize house, really. But I remember all kinds of terra-cotta inside along with a marble cistern the church left behind."

Beth and Jack looked at each other.

"May I have the address, please?"

Chapter 51

It took twenty minutes to make their way through Atlanta's traffic. The neighborhood was a mixture of small, single-family homes trying to hold the line against the encroaching warehouses and factories that surrounded them on three sides. I-75 bordered the fourth. Most of the houses were clapboard. None had garages. A traffic pole with a sign indicating the street's name lay on the sidewalk, snapped off at its base.

Dogs prowled the empty lots and alleys, malnourished, ribs showing, and crouching low as they reverted back to a time before the coming of men. What little color existed came from graffiti on the walls of defunct businesses. Everything else was the color of the dogs. A few houses had porches with empty flower baskets hanging from under aluminum awnings. For the most part, the neighborhood felt empty.

The home they were looking for was nearly at the end of the block. Jack pulled up to the side of the house into what was once a gravel parking lot capable of holding twenty cars. It was now filled with large ruts and potholes. A white twelve-year-old Dodge Charger was parked against the side by the rear entrance. Its windshield had a spider crack.

They went to the front and knocked. In the manner of most gothic style churches, the double doors were peaked in the middle. No one responded. Jack knocked again. Same result.

"The photographer's car is here," Beth said. "I also noticed a light on when we pulled up."

"Let's try the back door."

After several seconds without a response, they peered through a window. Beth suddenly let out a yelp and jumped backward, startling Jack as a white cat leaped onto the inside ledge.

"Sorry," she muttered.

"Don't be. I'd have done the same."

She doubted that. Through the window, the cat meowed at them.

"We should call for a search warrant," Beth said.

Jack shook his head slowly and moved to the door.

"Jack, we can lose the case. It won't take that long to—"

"Look at the cat's paws."

Beth did and saw they were covered in irregular brown stains.

"Oh Christ," she said, drawing her weapon.

Jack tried the door and found it unlocked. Slowly, he pushed it open but didn't enter. Beth understood why a second later as the smell of death nearly made her gag. After several months in Homicide, she thought she'd become used to it. Hadn't happened. She placed a hand over her mouth and stepped back, reaching for her phone as the white cat darted past her legs.

"This is Detective Sturgis. I'm at 4205 Ivy Way reporting a possible homicide. I need backup and the medical examiner."

Her attention returned to Jack, who also had his gun out. For the most part, he was immobile as he studied the scene. They were looking at a kitchen filled with appliances a shade of green Beth hadn't seen since she was a child. Beyond the kitchen was an open area swarming with black flies.

"God," she said.

No matter how many times she steeled herself, the sight of those robbed of their lives was jarring. The smell was ubiquitous. Unconsciously, she put a hand on Jack's shoulder, as though the connection to him would somehow strengthen her.

Jack said, "We go in from opposite sides of the room. At the door, I'll move left, you right. Once the house is cleared, we'll need your evidence kit."

Beth nodded.

"Ready?"

The woman's body lay in what was serving as her living room. At one time, it had probably been the church's assembly hall, judging from the stained glass window and marble cistern at the side of the room. Her throat had been cut and her eyes were open. Blood had pooled around her head, leaving her skin a chalky white color. She was tall, slender, and the expression on her face seemed one of surprise rather than pain. Beth stared at the body for a moment. The position looked posed.

She pulled her eyes away and continued to the next room, sweeping her gun in both directions. Jack called out "clear" from the bedroom and moved to the staircase. Beth expected they would find nothing. There's a certain feel to empty homes and this one had it. The crackle of a police radio outside indicated the first uniforms had arrived. She backed out and went to meet them.

"I need this area sealed off. Then let's start knocking on doors. I want to know who this woman was and if anyone saw anything."

"Her name's Nancy Rosen," one of the uniforms said.

They turned to look at him.

"She works as a dancer at Plato's on Cheshire Bridge Road."

"I thought she was a photographer," Beth said.

"Part-time. I do security there three nights a week. She has a son in some special school for disabled kids out in Villa Rica. Man, I hate this."

"I'm sorry," Beth said. "You okay to be here, or do you want me to call someone else?"

The name on his uniform shirt read "G. Henderson."

"I'm fine," Henderson said. "You mind if I see her?"

"Let me get you an extra pair of shoe covers."

Jack would probably fuss at her for letting anyone in without a full Tyvek suit, but she didn't have the heart to keep him out. She brought another set for his partner.

Henderson entered the kitchen and made his way to the living room. He stood there staring at Nancy Rosen for a full minute and then reached down to straighten her skirt.

Beth put a hand on his arm to stop him. "Not till I finish, okay?" she said quietly.

Henderson nodded and left the house. His partner shook his head and followed. At the far corner of the room, Jack flipped the lights on. To his right on the wall were a series of unframed black-and-white photographs, each dry-mounted on display. One showed an old-style fedora, forlorn and sitting by itself on a park bench. Behind it, the trees were barren. Another was a photo of an empty playground. Beth studied them and looked back at the woman whose name appeared in the lower right corner of each picture. There had been life in this room once, and conversation, and maybe laughter. A sense of what had happened began to press down on her, not unlike the way she felt when looking at the skeletons at the museum several days ago.

"They feel like winter," she said, staring at the photographs.

Her statement pulled Jack out of his reverie. He nodded his agreement then shifted away from them, focusing his attention to a platform and a set of three steps at the front of the room. The steps were made of red terra-cotta. Behind them were two columns of the same substance. The pulpit was marble.

Beth began the task of collecting evidence. Working in the kitchen, Jack mirrored her efforts. He noticed two gray plastic slivers on the table and brushed them together with one of his business cards. There was no reason for their presence, which made them significant. An hour ticked by as they gathered bag after bag of samples. At one point, he got down on his stomach and used a pair of tweezers to pick up several tiny bits of a white substance. He sniffed them, nodding to himself as if their presence confirmed a conclusion he'd already reached. A video recording of the scene was made, chain-of-custody cards were filled out, and plastic bags were sealed. That Thomas Courtney had taken yet another innocent life seemed clear now.

"I don't understand why he killed her," Beth said. "You told me he's not a sadist."

"Janet Newton and the British investigator I spoke with agree he's an opportunist. That's not a bad description. Courtney needed a base to construct his bombs. Two at Stone Mountain and one at Mary Quinn's house, probably two in New York. Ben Furman'll confirm it, but I suspect some of what I recovered in the kitchen will turn out to be RDX, the same material he used at the first location. The woman was killed because keeping her alive was inconvenient."

"Bastard."

"He is that."

"What about New York? He couldn't get a bomb on a commercial airline."

"I agree. That's where our friend Sergei Borov may come in. Borov owns two jets. When you fly private, security is almost nonexistent. He probably used his contacts to get the bomb materials to Courtney or his partner."

Beth looked back at Nancy Rosen and realized Jack's earlier comment about the Sandman not caring who he killed or what he had to do to reach his goal was true. When you came right down to it, people of Courtney's ilk were no different from a disease ravaging humanity's collective body. Whatever redeeming qualities he might once have possessed paled in comparison to the acts he performed. Indifferent to everything but his wants, the Sandman had killed a mother struggling to support a disabled child for no reason. Where did that leave the boy now?

Her job was simple: cauterize the disease.

Chapter 52

One Day to the Grand Jury

The following morning Beth left Jack at the crime lab to analyze his evidence with Ben and Nelda. She was convinced a weakness in Courtney's plan lay in the two men he employed to fly the drones. The feds were positive they were dupes, but she had adopted Jack's theory that there was a reason for everything the Sandman did. And those reasons usually defied an obvious explanation.

At eight o'clock the previous evening, Dan Pappas had called to let her know the body of Peter Shackleford had been recovered from a dumpster in Sandy Springs. At first, the name meant nothing to her until Jack identified him as one of the two drone operators. There was no way she could write this off to coincidence. If Leonard Walpole wasn't dead already, he soon would be.

*

According to T. J. Cameron, a Narcotics detective, Eddie Marks controlled a good portion of the drug traffic in Atlanta along with its prostitutes, protection rackets, and a loan sharking operation. He also had a tenuous truce in place with the Russian mob. An area of Atlanta had been carved out for them. Marks's operation, Cameron said, was larger and better organized and could have wiped them out, but he'd taken the position avoiding an ongoing bloodbath was preferable to giving up a little control. In return, the Russians paid him a handsome royalty for the privilege.

As Beth drove to meet him, she reasoned that Marks probably bore no great love for the Russians, of which Sergei Borov was one. Cameron agreed and told her Borov was widely thought to be their primary source when it came to supplying weapons, a fact that she felt could be used to her advantage.

Janel's was named after Eddie Marks's daughter and had gone through several phases as a restaurant before settling into its present incarnation on Peachtree Road. Outside, the architecture was modern, upscale, and matched an interior filled with black leather booths, white tablecloths, granite floors, and a long, mirrored bar that ran the length of the establishment. The name "Janel" appeared across the entrance in glittering silver letters. Their food was distinctly Cajun. T. J. Cameron had arranged the meeting.

Marks was in his early fifties and dressed in a burgundy suit with a yellow silk shirt. His receding hair was sprinkled with gray at the temples. He was heavyset with a neck that appeared soft but wasn't. When Beth came in, he was sitting at a table near the back of the restaurant having breakfast. He saw her but displayed no reaction to her presence. Marks fit Cameron's description. She started for his table, but only got a few steps before a tall black man stepped in front of her.

"Hep you, Miss?"

Beth showed her badge and said she was there to speak with Eddie Marks.

"Whatchu want to talk to the boss about?"

"That's between Mr. Marks and me. Step aside, please."

"You real polite. I like that in a woman," he said, looking her up and down. "Why a fine looking girl like you become a police officer?"

"Because I love being around big, strong men. Now move aside."

The bodyguard was about two inches taller than her and at least fifty pounds heavier. Around his neck was a heavy gold chain. He was dressed completely in black. The aftershave he was wearing hung in the air like a cloud, reaching her from three feet away. He remained standing in front of Beth until Marks said, "Willis."

The smile never left Willis's face, though he did step aside. Marks watched Beth come down the aisle and motioned for her to sit when she reached his table.

"Thank you for seeing me, Mr. Marks."

"Get you something to eat, Detective?"

"A cup of coffee'd be nice and maybe a Danish if you have one. I skipped breakfast earlier."

"Most important meal of the day." Marks raised his hand to a waitress who was standing near the kitchen doors. "Would you bring Detective Sturgis a cup of coffee and one of them pastries we got in this morning?"

"Anything else?" she asked.

"No, thank you," Beth said.

The waitress left.

"I used to have a Danish every morning. The kind with cherry in them. But the doctor told me I need to watch my cholesterol."

Beth glanced at the plate of bacon and eggs in front of him and said, "That won't help."

"I'm starting small and working my way up. What can I do for you today?"

"I'm looking for a junkie named Leonard Walpole. From what I'm told, he used to panhandle around Little Five Points. Sometimes he sleeps at the Salvation Army Shelter in East Point."

"Always glad to be involved with helping our police. Why do you want this man?"

"Do you remember that fuss we had downtown the other day?"

Marks nodded. A ray of sunlight streaming through the window caught his diamond tie pin. He laced his hands together and rested them on the table. Like the diamond, his fingernails were smooth and polished.

"Walpole was one of two men operating the model aircraft," Beth said.

"Y'all looked pretty foolish rushing people out of those buildings."

"Better than not getting them out if we guessed wrong."

Marks considered that for a moment then asked, "Y'all plan to give this man a ticket for disturbing the peace?"

"It's a bit more complicated," Beth said. "We think Walpole's a shill for a button man named Thomas Courtney, who was hired by Sergei Borov."

At the mention of Borov's name, Marks's eyebrows lifted slightly. Beyond that, his reaction was silence.

"Courtney's target is a doctor named Rachel Lawrence, who's supposed to testify in front of a grand jury the day after tomorrow."

"Like I said, I have a deep commitment to lending a hand to the cops when I can, but I'm wondering how this is my problem."

"Involved or committed?" Beth asked.

"Say what?"

"A moment ago, you said involved. Now you say committed."

"What's the difference?"

"You're eating bacon and eggs. The chicken was involved. The pig is committed."

Eddie Marks stared at Beth for a moment before he started chuckling. "Good one, Detective. You got a mouth on you, I'll say that."

"Gets me in trouble sometimes."

Marks leaned back. "No way."

"I'm afraid so. Didn't mean any offense by my remark."

"Didn't take any."

"So, will you help?"

"Here's my problem. My business thrives 'cause I don't give people up. The folks I deal with know I protect them regardless of the heat. That means not broadcasting their names around."

"There's a good chance if Courtney succeeds, Sergei Borov will become stronger than ever. I don't think that's in your best interest."

"No, it isn't," Marks agreed. "It's not like I'm in contact with any street junkies, but say I knew someone who was. It wouldn't do for this person's name to be mentioned around the police station, if you get my meaning."

"Anything you say will stay between us."

Marks considered Beth for a long moment. "T. J. Cameron says your word is good."

"I like to think so."

He nodded. "You and the Georgia Tech professor were the ones who caught that crazy man a few months ago. The one who killed all them people at Underground Atlanta."

Beth nodded but didn't reply.

Marks took a moment to arrange his knife and fork on the table. "One of them was a nineteen-year-old girl named Rochelle. She was in the, ah . . . business, if you know what I mean. I got a daughter who's eighteen. Rochelle reminded me of her. She was sweet and well mannered, but the girl never had any luck. Daddy left when she was eight years old and her mama ran off with some no-account. I set her up in school and gave her a little money. But she went back to doing what came easy." Marks shrugged. "Some folks you can save; some you can't."

"You're a good man, Eddie."

"No, I'm not. In about an hour, if you was to be at the Central City Fountain, there might be a man there that can help you. Large fella named Ramone."

"I owe you one," Beth said.

Marks smiled. "Yes, you do, Detective."

The waitress arrived with Beth's coffee and Danish. They ate in silence for a few minutes before she commented on how attractive the restaurant was.

"Town needs a place where people of color can get dressed up and enjoy good ol' fashioned cookin' without being embarrassed ordering it." He pointed to Beth's engagement ring. "Next time you come back, bring your significant whatever with you."

Beth thanked him and stood. She was nearly at the front door when Willis stepped in front of her again. The man had a mean, arrogant face.

"Got everything you need, missy?"

"And more. If you'll excuse me," Beth said and waited for him to move.

Willis's eyes roamed up and down her body with a look that was hardly less than obvious. "Them high heels sure do lift you up, don't they?"

Beth said nothing.

Willis brought his face inches from hers. "Why'nt you sit and rest for a bit. Maybe we can get acquainted."

"Maybe another time."

"Got to be hard walking around in them shoes. Don't they hurt?"

"I don't know. What do you think?" Beth said, bringing her heel down on his instep.

Willis gasped and let out a curse and drew his arm back to hit her. The blow never arrived, because he found himself staring at a 9 mm Beretta pointing directly between his eyes.

Marks observed the exchange as he brought a forkful of eggs up to his mouth.

Chapter 53

A charcoal gray Mercedes with incongruous chrome wheels pulled up to the Central City Park and stopped behind Beth's unmarked cruiser. A large black man weighing close to three hundred pounds exited the backseat. He spotted Beth standing by the fountain and began walking toward her but stopped and looked up at the park's only statue, a bronze sculpture of a woman with arms above her head. She was holding a strange looking bird by its legs. The bird's wings were fully extended, suggesting it was about to take flight. Frowning, Ramone stared at the sculpture. Beth joined him.

"Why that woman holding a goose?" Ramone asked.

"That's not a goose," Beth said.

"It's not?"

"It's a phoenix. A bird from mythology."

"Mythology?"

"That's right."

"Them Greek stories?"

"Originally."

Ramone frowned and looked back at the bird. "Mythology mean it don't exist, right?"

"I suppose so," Beth said.

"Then how they know what it look like if it don't exist?" Ramone asked.

Beth shrugged. "I guess the sculptor used his imagination."

"Yeah?"

"When the phoenix dies, its body burns up, then it rises from its own ashes."

Ramone looked at Beth not understanding.

"The phoenix is Atlanta's symbol," she explained.

"A bird?"

"A city rising from ruin after the Civil War. General Sherman burnt Atlanta to the ground and we came back again."

Ramone turned back to the bronze work and commented, "Musta cost a lot."

"All the drug dealers in town chipped in," Beth said.

"For real?"

"No, I made that up."

"Yeah," Eddie said. "You pretty funny. You lookin' for Squeaky, right?"

"Leonard Walpole."

"One and the same. I haven't seen him in a few days. He come into a little money and got himself some new clothes and a computer. Looked like the man's doin' okay now."

"Where did you see him?"

"Cross the street from the Clairmont."

"That hotel on Ponce de Leon?"

"Uh-huh."

"You just ran into him?"

Ramone avoided answering her question directly, but suggested his meeting with Lenny might have involved a business transaction. She decided not to press for details and asked if Walpole was staying at the Clairmont.

"Could be. I don't run credit checks on my clients. It's pretty much a cash business."

"You do a lot of business with him?"

"Lenny been a steady customer over the years. It's a shame, 'cause he come from a good family up in Dunwoody. At one time, he was gonna be a lawyer."

The surprise must have shown on Beth's face.

Ramone shrugged. "Shit happens."

"That's what you call it?"

"I try not to make moral judgments."

Beth's eyes met his. Ramone's ghetto-speak had dropped away with the last statement, leading her to conclude he might not be as clueless as he appeared. She asked if Walpole was alone.

"Appeared to be. He . . ."

Ramone held the rest of his comment as a passing police cruiser slowed and flicked its siren once, indicating they wanted the driver to move his car.

"We appear to be impeding traffic," Ramone said.

"Half the fun of being a cop," Beth said. She showed her badge and motioned for the cops to move on.

"Lenny mentioned something about getting into a methadone clinic. Tell you the truth, I might lose a customer, but I wouldn't mind seeing that. Hope this helps."

"It does," Beth said. "Have a nice day."

They separated and started for their respective vehicles. Beth had nearly reached hers when Ramone asked, "Think I should lose some weight?"

Beth smiled. "You're perfect as is."

"That's what I think."

*

Beth had never been in the Clairmont Hotel and would have been just as happy to have kept it that way. As soon as she entered the lobby, she became conscious of an odor that fell somewhere between sour and stale. She approached the desk clerk and asked which room Leonard Walpole was in.

"Number 635. Your partner already went up."

"My partner? How long ago was that?"

"Maybe two minutes," the clerk said, pointing to the elevator.

Her first thought was that he was referring to Jack or Dan Pappas. Jack had a habit of developing strategy on the fly. But if he was operating on his own again without telling her, they were in for a fight. She had no way of knowing at the moment. Nor could she call. If one of them had tracked Leonard Walpole down, the last thing they needed was a cellphone going off at the wrong time.

She took the elevator up to the seventh floor, then used the stairs to come back down and nearly collided with Special Agent Todd

Milner. He was as startled to see her as she was to see him. Milner put a finger to his lips and pointed to the stairwell.

"Didn't expect to see you here," he whispered.

"Likewise."

"I was just about to call for backup. Walpole's inside. At least I think he is."

Beth nodded. "How'd you figure out he's here?"

Milner explained that he'd spoken with the ATF agent who initially picked up Walpole and Shackelford and was curious to see where they'd go after being released. Once Walpole checked out of the Salvation Army shelter, he followed him. His supervisor decided it was a dry hole and told him to drop the surveillance. "I think there's more to this guy," Milner said.

"We can discuss that later," Beth said. "How do you want to handle it?"

"There's two of us. I say we brace him."

"Let's go."

They moved into the hallway and went to opposite sides of the door. Inside the room, music was playing. Milner's knock was loud enough to wake the dead. The music stopped. "Federal Bureau of Investigation, Mr. Walpole. We need to speak with you."

A moment later, a nervous Leonard Walpole cracked the door open and peeked out. Beth and Milner showed him their badges.

Milner asked, "Are you alone, sir?"

"Ye . . . yes."

"Would you mind if we come in for a moment? We have a few follow-up questions."

"But I already spoke with you people. I haven't done anything wrong."

"Of course not. We won't take up much of your time," Milner said.

"Are you arresting me?"

"No, sir. Not at the moment," Milner said, leaving open the possibility that might change. "We just have a couple of questions."

"I know my rights," Lenny said.

"Sure you do," Beth said. "And we know ours. We can talk here or you can take a ride with us. We're hoping you'll cooperate, that is if you have nothing to hide."

"I don't," Lenny said, opening the door. "See? No one's here but me."

Milner took that as an invitation and stepped past him. Beth followed him in. The little man tried to act indignant but couldn't pull it off. "What is it you want?"

"Just to talk," Milner told him. "You like this place better than the shelter?"

"It's all right."

"Yeah, looks great. Probably costs a penny or two staying here."

"Some."

"So where'd you come into all the newfound wealth, Mr. Walpole?" Milner asked. "You told the ATF agents you were unemployed."

"I do odd jobs here and there."

"Odd jobs?"

"Yes, sir."

Beth was content to let Milner go on. He was doing a good job. Leonard Walpole probably weighed no more than 145 pounds and was barely five foot seven. For all the bravado he was trying to display, he was unable to meet their eyes for more than a second or two. After listening to him for several minutes, she was ready to conclude the ATF had been right. The guy's brain was fried. Oddly, despite the room being cool, Lenny had broken out in a sweat. He kept glancing at the foot locker at the front of his bed.

Probably where he keeps his stash.

She said, "Mr. Walpole, let me cut to the chase. We're not here to hassle you and we don't care about whatever's in there. We also don't care about the money you have or how you got it. But we are interested in the man who gave it to you."

"I earned it," Lenny said. "Really, I did. And I found a wallet with some cash in it."

Milner commented, "Of course, and it didn't occur to you to return it to its owner, right?"

"I guess not."

"In other words, you threw the wallet away and kept the money."

Lenny looked down at his feet and said nothing.

"Finders keepers, huh?" Milner said, trying to prompt him in responding.

Still no answer.

"Let's say we believe you. There's no crime in finding money. The thing is, if you received it from who I think you did, we're dealing with a whole 'nother problem."

"What do you mean?"

"Conspiracy, harboring a fugitive, accessory to murder, to name a few."

"Murder! I haven't hurt anybody. I wouldn't do that. I don't know what you're talking about."

Milner looked disgusted with the answer and turned to Beth.

The unspoken message was clear. He wanted her to take over.

"Lenny," Beth said, sitting on the bed next to him. "You seem like a good person and I believe you. But you need to level with us. I'm going to show you a picture and I want you to tell me if you've seen this man before. If you tell the truth, I promise nothing bad will happen to you."

"I know what you're doing," Lenny said. "This is good cop, bad cop."

"It's more like good cop, truthful cop."

Beth took the photo of Thom Courtney out of her purse and showed it to Lenny. By rights, she should have used a line-up, but she wasn't hoping for that kind of identification. She already knew who was behind the killings.

The reaction was immediate. Lenny's eyes widened and he leaned forward, his jaw dropping.

"You know this man, don't you?"

"I, I . . ."

She and Milner exchanged glances.

"What's his name, Lenny?"

"Rick."

"Rick what?" Milner asked.

"He told me once, but I don't remember. I just call him Rick. He's my friend."

"Man, you picked one helluva friend," Milner said.

"He's the one who asked you to fly the model airplane, wasn't he?" Beth said.

Lenny was becoming agitated, wringing his hands and rocking back and forth on the bed. "It was for the movie. The stunts."

"What movie?" Milner said. "What are you talking about?"

"'*Drone Attack!*' Rick's company is shooting it here. I'm one of the technical advisors. You've got it all wrong. Rick is a good person. He'd never hurt anyone."

Beth exhaled and looked out the window. Across the street was a triple-X-rated video rental store. Next to that was a liquor shop. She hated what they were doing to him. *How the hell do people get into situatÑns like this?*

For the next twenty minutes, they talked to Lenny and explained who Thom Courtney was and why they were after him. Adamant, he shook his head and refused to accept it. Not surprising, because the fantasy Courtney had spun of promised wealth and helping him find a way out of the gutter to a normal life was like throwing a life preserver to a drowning man. There was an old saying that went, "A man convinced against his will is of the same opinion still." It applied here. Lenny Walpole simply could not believe the man he thought was his friend and savior was anything other than noble and kind. There had to be some mistake.

"Lenny," Beth said. "When the ATF agents were questioning you, there was another man present. He was flying one of the drones for the stunts. Do you remember him?"

"Sure, we spoke a little. He didn't do anything wrong either."

Beth thought for a moment. He was in denial, but then a lot of people were and they weren't going to get anywhere unless reality grabbed him by the neck and shook him. It wouldn't be fun, but she had an idea.

"Come with me," she said.

Chapter 54

Atlanta's City Morgue always creeped Beth out. The smell of antiseptic and bleach reminded her of visits to the doctor that generally ended with her getting a shot. On top of that, they kept the temperature so cold her hands went numb after fifteen minutes. Milner knew exactly what she had in mind and nodded his approval as they drove there. Lenny hadn't said a word. He simply stared out the window. Tears streamed down his face. Seeing his crestfallen expression only made her feel worse. Having a dream snatched away from you was a tough thing to take. She didn't like herself much at the moment.

Peter Shackleford's body had not undergone an autopsy yet. The cause of death listed in the report was fairly obvious. A technician led them to the refrigerated locker, opened the door to one of the units, and slid Peter Shackleford out. The slash across his throat was like some hideous smile. His skin was colorless and his mouth was open, revealing the pain he must have felt as his life spilled away. The two days he spent in a dumpster hadn't helped. Lenny took one look at him and began to hyperventilate. A second later, he threw up.

The technician looked at the floor, then said to Beth, "Thank you. This makes my day."

Outside in the hallway Milner sat Lenny down on a bench and Beth went to get him a soft drink. The little man appeared as miserable as she had ever seen someone look.

Beth knelt in front of him. "I'm sorry, Lenny. I know that wasn't easy. The man we're after isn't shooting a movie. He's a murderer, plain and simple. We really need your help because he's going to kill again."

"More importantly," Todd Milner said, "you've seen his face, so there's a good chance you'll be next on his agenda. Let us help you, man. When was the last time you saw him?"

"We had dinner last night."

"Where?"

"Olympus."

Milner looked to Beth to see if she knew the restaurant.

She informed him, "It's a Greek diner on Roswell Road."

"I was going to get myself clean," Lenny said.

Beth and Milner exchanged glances. The agent shook his head and turned away. Jack had explained sociopaths to her. Whether they operated on a small scale, stealing money from their parents or shoplifting or hurting defenseless animals, or on a larger scale like the Sandman, who killed without regard to the consequences or cost, narcissism lay at the core. Their checkbooks were always balanced, but with the currency of others. All the explanations about how hard his youth was and how devastating the loss of his parents were interesting, but in the end, it was Thomas Courtney's actions that defined him. He was the embodiment of everything vile and wrong with a tiny segment of society the rest of them could do without.

Chapter 55

On the way back from the morgue, Beth called Jack and told him they had picked up Leonard Walpole. She gave him a rundown of what he told them about Rick and the movie. He said he would meet them in the conference room of the Atlanta PD.

"Mr. Walpole, I'm Jack Kale with the FBI. I appreciate you coming here. Can you describe your friend Rick to me?"

"He's a little shorter than you and in his early thirties, I guess, with light brown hair."

"Any scars or tattoos?"

"I don't think so, but I really wasn't looking."

"Detective Sturgis tells me you and Rick had dinner on Roswell Road last night. Is that the last time you saw him?"

"No, it was at the hotel."

"Really? Is Rick staying there, too?" Jack asked.

"I'm not sure where he and the crew are staying. Probably at one of those big hotels downtown. I don't understand all this about Rick. He's a totally decent guy."

Jack was continually astounded at the ability of some people to deny reality. Lenny had just been to the morgue and had seen the man who was flying models with him with a cut throat, and here he was defending the probable murderer.

"I'm sure he is," Jack said. "I'm just a little confused. You say you didn't get the drone at the restaurant."

"Right."

"And you were with Rick the entire time."

"Until he dropped me off at the Clairmont with his car," Lenny explained.

"So where did he get a new drone? The police still have the other two, and they're not something you can buy in a store."

A line of sweat had broken out on Lenny's forehead and he had begun to rock back and forth in his seat.

"You're trying to confuse me."

"I'm really not," Jack said. "Actually, I'm trying to help you. The last thing you want to do is lie right now. Concentrate a little harder."

Several seconds passed. The only sound in the room came from air passing through the vents high up on the walls.

"I don't want to get anyone in trouble," Lenny said.

"And you won't," Beth told him. "We're trying to save lives here. Yours as well. Just go slow and tell us what happened. I promise everything will be all right."

Lenny looked from one to the other. They waited.

"After Rick dropped me off, Brooks came by and brought me the drone."

"Brooks?" Jack said.

"He's our director."

"I see. Was this the first time you met him?"

"Uh-huh."

A little tick of excitement started in the pit of Jack's stomach. He was talking about the partner.

Jack, Beth, and Todd all exchanged glances.

"Okay, so Brooks came to your room. Is that correct?"

"Well, he met me in the staircase. It's right next to my room."

"I understand," Jack said. "You're doing great. Tell me what he looked like."

"I'm not sure. He was wearing a hat and dark glasses and only stayed a few seconds."

"Was he the same height as Rick?" Todd asked.

"Maybe a little taller."

Todd turned to Jack and asked if he wanted a computer sketch artist. Jack nodded. The agent stepped out of the room to make the call. While they were waiting, Jack asked Beth to get her evidence kit and go over Lenny's clothes with the sticky roller. It took a few minutes to complete the task.

"Did Brooks say anything or touch you?" Jack asked.

"Touch me?"

"Like to shake your hand."

"No, he just gave me the drone and said, 'Here you go, man. I gotta run. Do a good job for us.'"

"Was there anything distinctive about his speech, like an accent or something like that?"

"Uh uh."

They spoke for a while longer, but there wasn't much more to be gained.

"Mr. Walpole, I'd like to thank you for your help and ask if you can stay with us for another hour or so. We'll make you as comfortable as possible and get you something to eat if you like."

"I don't have much of an appetite right now," Lenny said.

"Understandable. One last thing. May I borrow your shoes for a few minutes?"

*

Todd Milner met them outside and told them the bureau sketch artist would be there within the next three hours. He had tried the APD artist but learned she was out on a call. That was fine. Jack explained they were taking the samples Beth had collected to the lab for analysis.

"You worried he'll run away?" Todd asked, pointing at the shoes Jack was holding.

Jack smiled. "Not really. When he and Shackleford were picked up the first time, the report mentioned Lenny was wearing running shoes. These are leather and look new. I'd like our techs to give them the once-over."

"Sounds good. See you in a bit."

*

At the lab, they found Dan Pappas waiting to pick up a report Ben Furman was working on. Jack handed Nelda the shoes and asked her to examine them while Beth brought Pappas up to speed on Lenny Walpole's revelations.

Nelda put on a pair of magnifying glasses and went to work.

"We have one or two of the terra-cotta grains and a couple of new ones I haven't seen before. They're white."

Ben Furman stopped what he was doing and went over to join her. After several seconds, he whispered something in her ear. She responded by whispering back in his, then announced the white grains were coral stone commonly found along the coast of Florida.

"Maybe he's been to the beach," Pappas said.

"The man's a junkie who, until recently, was living under a bridge. What are the odds on that?" Jack said.

Nelda informed them, "These are Trek Striders. The company uses a proprietary rubber compound on a one piece heel and sole design. The rubber acts like a magnet."

"Any chance of a mistake?" Jack asked.

Nelda stared at him as if he had lost his mind.

"Forgive me," Jack said contritely.

She sniffed and tucked a strand of brown hair behind one ear and smoothed her skirt.

"Either he picked up the grains by being in direct contact with coral stone, or someone brought them up here and transferred them to him."

After some speculation, they concluded that Lenny probably lacked the means to travel. According to his sheet, he had a spotty employment history and a vagrancy charge pending for the last three months.

"Okay," Pappas said. "I'm officially fascinated. What good does knowing this do us?"

"Gabe Alonso," Jack said.

"The murdered FBI agent?"

"Correct. Ben, do you have the forensic report from Alonso's car here?"

Furman went to his computer and punched a few keys. A moment later, the FBI's analysis appeared on the screen. Jack, Beth, and Pappas read it over his shoulder.

"There," Jack said, pointing. Gabe Alonso had been staking out Borov's factory in Duluth, an Atlanta suburb.

"It says the vehicle was thoroughly examined for any sign of foul play and nothing was found," Pappas said.

"At the bottom, under 'Trace Items,'" Jack said.

Pappas looked and pulled his head back in surprise, "Sonofabitch. 'Several white grains of what appears to be coral stone residue were noted.' Was Alonso in Florida?"

"I don't know," Jack said. "My focus hasn't been on him at all. I remember reading that Borov has a warehouse there. Whatever he produces here travels by rail or truck and is eventually off-loaded for shipping overseas through Port Everglades in Fort Lauderdale."

"I'll ask Milner about Alonso's travel record. Beth, would you check with Lenny and see if he's been there recently? Maybe he couldn't afford it, but someone else could have paid for him."

"Like Rick or his friend, Brooks," Beth said. "I'll ask him when we get back."

"I'm not getting the whole coral stone thing," Pappas said.

Jack informed him, "You see a lot of it around South Florida, particularly in the older homes in Miami and up into Palm Beach. Before it was banned, an architect named Addison Mizner used to incorporate it into his designs. It's probably harder than cement and a lot more attractive."

Incredulous, Pappas stared at Jack. "You just know this shit?"

"I read a lot. I also had a case down there ten years ago."

"Ten years?"

"Might be eleven."

"Jesus, Kale."

Jack shrugged and then went quiet for a moment. Another piece of the puzzle had just dropped into place. An important one. It was entirely possible Walpole was an innocent dupe. The ATF agents were convinced of it and they were no amateurs. The glaring fact was those grains had come from south Florida, and if Courtney had been in Ireland at the time the senator's aide had been murdered, that left the partner.

Jack left to speak with Milner while Beth agreed to call the FBI's travel desk to see if Gabe Alonso had been to Florida shortly before his death.

Chapter 56

On exiting the conference room, they found Carmine Donofrio in a heated discussion with Jack, or to be more accurate, Jack was listening while the U.S. Attorney talked. Donofrio's assistant, another U.S. Attorney, was hovering close by, as were Todd Milner and Dan Pappas.

"Kale, the grand jury meets in less than thirty-four hours and you're no closer to catching the Sandman than you were three days ago."

Jack said nothing.

"You can see I was right for wanting to put her in federal custody. After that fiasco in New York, there's no way I'm allowing her to attend a funeral."

"Seriously? You're not going to let a wife attend her husband's funeral? I don't think you can stop her, Donofrio."

"I can ask the judge to modify his order."

"Get real."

"The marshals will back me on this."

"And I'll overrule them. We're not having this discussion."

"It's irresponsible. You told me yourself security arrangements would be difficult."

"I told you they'd be a nightmare and they will. This is a matter of basic human decency. I understand your case is important, but not at the expense of Rachel's soul. We'll make sure she's safe."

"You've lost your fucking mind."

"Watch your language, there's a woman in the room."

294

Donofrio finally noticed Beth and Milner standing there. "I apologize. I'm telling all of you now, if we lose this witness, I'll do everything in my power to prosecute each of you."

Milner leaned closer and whispered in Beth's ear. "I'm terrified. Hold me."

Donofrio continued to rant. Jack continued to listen. Ultimately, the attorney turned to Beth and asked if she agreed with Jack's decision.

"I do. Rachel's being a witness doesn't mean she has to put her life on hold."

"That's exactly what it means until I decide to release her. She's an important link to Borov."

"Todd Milner and I picked up one of the drone operators a little while ago," Beth said. "Maybe you should hear what he has to say about a man named Rick, who's making a movie here in Atlanta."

"What are you talking about?"

She began a capsule summary of what Lenny had told her. The U.S. Attorney folded his arms and leaned back against the edge of a desk to listen.

Pappas said, "So he plans to make a run at the feds' safehouse?"

"Looks that way," Beth said. "He'll use the park across from the reservoir."

Jack inquired where the drone was.

"It was delivered to Stan Kaufman on the way in."

He nodded his approval. Kaufman was the Atlanta bomb squad's chief technician.

Donofrio said, "I want to interview this man. Where is he?"

"Conference room three. Down the hall on the right," Beth said.

The two attorneys left.

"Fun and games, kids," Milner said. "I'd love to stay and listen, but I have to get back on surveillance. Borov's set to meet with a recruiter for ISIS."

"Who is he?" Pappas asked.

"He is a woman."

The detective shook his head. "There are times I feel like I'm working in a nut house."

"Good work on finding Lenny, Todd," Jack said.

"Actually, Ms. Sturgis and I finished in a dead heat at the witness's door." Milner flashed a smile at Beth and left the room.

"Congratulations to you too, Detective. Let's join Mr. Donofrio."

*

Beth didn't think it was possible for anyone to look more beaten down than Leonard Walpole. He was leaning back in his seat trying to put some distance between himself and Donofrio. The attorney bore in, firing off question after question. Lenny remained adamant about never having met or even hearing Sergei Borov's name. Either Donofrio didn't believe him or he thought he could browbeat him into changing his story. It was plain the little man was terrified, not so much at what he'd gotten himself into, but because he'd come to realize he was now the target of someone who intended to kill him once he had no further use for him. When threats and cajoling didn't work, Donofrio changed tactics.

"Mr. Walpole, we may be able to help each other. I understand your reluctance to testify. A minute ago, you admitted to accepting money from Thomas Courtney because you want to get into a methadone clinic. That's an admirable goal. It's also an expensive one, as I'm sure you know. What about if we were to help?"

"Who's we?"

"Your government. My office has access to certain funds for people who cooperate with us."

"What good will that do me if I'm dead?"

"Have you ever heard of witness protection?"

"Uh-huh."

"We can set you up with a new identity and place to live, a nice place. We might even furnish enough for you to go into that rehab program you're talking about."

"How much?"

Donofrio shrugged. "I'd have to look into the costs, but—"

"It's nine thousand dollars," Lenny said.

Donofrio turned to Pappas and asked, "How much can your department kick in?"

"I don't know. We have a budget, but the final decision's up to the bosses."

"Check on it, okay?"

"Sure."

"Now this is what I want to do," Donofrio said, returning to Lenny. "I want to call in a court reporter and have your statement taken down."

"Can I speak to a lawyer first?" Lenny asked.

"What for? You told us you have nothing to hide."

"I don't. I just think it's . . . it's a . . . a good idea," Lenny stammered.

Beth and Jack remained off to one side listening to the exchange. What little resistance Lenny had was crumbling quicker than the Iraqi army. The second attorney followed his boss's lead and moved in close. Donofrio continued the press. They reminded Beth of two grade school bullies trying to steal someone's lunch money.

"Mr. Walpole, maybe you don't understand the situation you're in. Regardless of what anyone has told you or promised you, I make the decision whether to prosecute. No one else. Right now, I could put you away for a very long time. You've already admitted to being an accessory to a felony. How long do you think someone like you will last in a maximum security prison? You'll be locked down twenty-four hours a day in an underground facility. The only visits you'll ever receive will be over a closed circuit television. They won't even give you a book to read for the first year. As far as seeing the sun again, forget about it. Some people are strong enough to survive that experience. I'm told others go insane."

Tears started to fill Lenny Walpole's eyes. Beth was disgusted at what she was hearing. Donofrio leaned over him; his aide followed suit.

"Listen to me you little maggot, this is a one-time offer. Either you take it—"

"That's enough," Beth said.

"Stay out of this," Donofrio snapped.

She responded by interposing herself between Lenny and the U.S. Attorney. "I said that's enough. First of all, this man came here voluntarily. That means I'm responsible for him. If he says he wants to speak to a lawyer, he's goddamn well going to get one. Both of you back away right now."

The attorney opened his mouth to reply. Beth cut him off.

"I mean it, Donofrio. Back off."

The second attorney reached for Beth's shoulder, only to find his hand suddenly twisted back toward himself and turned outward by Jack.

"Hi there," Jack said to him.

The man's face went red as he tried to break free. Jack responded by increasing the pressure, which sent the aide down to one knee.

"Let him go this instant," Donofrio said. "You're assaulting an officer of the court."

Jack shrugged and released his grip. The aide went over sideways.

"In the hall," Donofrio said and left the room.

Jack and the others followed.

"What the hell's the matter with you people? That man was about to cave."

"That's not the way to do it," Beth said.

Donofrio took a breath and let it out as his assistant joined him, rubbing his wrist.

"All right, maybe I came on too strong, but we're nearly out of time. So far, the best you've been able to manage is keeping half the witnesses you were assigned to protect alive. I don't call that a raving success. We need to bring this to a head."

"How?" Beth asked.

"I have an idea."

Chapter 57

The U.S. Attorney felt he could ensnare the Sandman by concealing officers around the park and safehouse who'd be ready to pounce once they established his location. He was convinced Courtney intended to attack the safehouse directly or use the drone to cause another evacuation. This would give him another chance for a shot at Rachel Lawrence. As a precaution, Donofrio wanted marksmen available to shoot the drone down if it started across the reservoir.

Pappas and Beth both thought the logic was sound and looked to Jack for his opinion. To their surprise, he disagreed. Frustrated, Donofrio threw up his hands and told them he was going over their heads.

"You have that right," Jack said.

The attorneys marched off down the hall.

Pappas told him, "The guy has a point, Jack. We're out of time."

"We are, but this isn't the way. His plan is flawed."

"How so?" Beth asked.

"His thinking is one dimensional. The Sandman will certainly make a move, but it won't be something as obvious as faking a second drone attack. A feint is consistent with what he's done before, but he won't employ the same strategy a second time. A variation, perhaps, but not the same tactic. It also doesn't take his partner into account."

"Assuming there is one," Pappas said. "We're not even sure he exists."

"Oh, he exists. One person couldn't have pulled off what Courtney's been able to accomplish without help."

"I'm not saying you're wrong, but is it possible we're chasing a ghost?" Pappas asked.

"Anything's possible, Dan. We're not. Which is why Beth is leaving for Arizona in two hours."

Startled, Beth and Pappas looked at each other then back at him.

*

It didn't take long for the events Jack had foreseen to unfold. Politics was a great catalyst. Janet Newton and Carmine Donofrio both had careers riding on the outcome. The telephone call Jack expected from the deputy director came in shortly after Beth had left for the Charlie Brown Airport on the west side of the city. She was clearly not happy about being sent out of town, but in Jack's view, there was no choice. He wanted her as far away from Thom Courtney as possible. The hold on Courtney's sanity was tenuous at best and apt to give way at any moment. He had spared her three times. A fourth wasn't likely. Worse, he could decide she needed to share the same fate as Courtney's sister. There was little question in his mind Courtney had killed her boyfriend and his uncle before setting fire to his house. Promise or no promise, Jack didn't need Beth charging after the killer again.

Janet Newton said, "I've been on the phone with Atlanta's SAC for the last thirty minutes. We were discussing Donofrio's plan. I think it's worth pursuing."

"I don't."

"Tell me why."

"I agree the Sandman will try for Dr. Lawrence, but what he's planning is far more complex than what Donofrio has in mind."

"I'm listening."

"In each of his previous assassinations, Courtney set up a diversion to distract authorities away from the target. The complexity varied from case to case, but it always matched the circumstances. This is too obvious and too simplistic."

"He doesn't know we have Walpole or that he's cooperating with us."

"Donofrio presumes he'll strike the safehouse and forgets George Lawrence's funeral is an opportunity too. There's also some evidence I've been looking into that—"

"Jack, the grand jury convenes at two o'clock tomorrow afternoon. That gives us just over twenty-four hours. Donofrio says Walpole is supposed to fly the drone at nine AM."

"Correct."

"I also received an e-mail from Todd Milner about the techs finding an explosive in the drone's body. To me, that indicates he's planning to come at the safehouse."

"I received the same message."

"So it makes sense."

"Smoke and mirrors. The amount is too small. It's basically a glorified fire cracker. We're jumping the gun. There's a better way to do—"

"Even so, the explosive makes a pretty strong argument for a distraction," Janet said.

"Only if you happen to be holding the drone."

There was silence on the line.

"All right, Milner says he's on the fence, so I guess it's up to me to make the call. I want you to set up the sting using Walpole. When he makes contact with Courtney, we'll triangulate on his cellphone signal. We'll also put marksmen in place to shoot it down if it starts across the water. Afterward, Walpole will go into federal custody for his own protection, since he's now a witness."

"You're the boss, Janet."

"Can you get behind this, or do you want me to shift to Todd Milner?"

"Todd's a very competent agent and apparently you work well together."

"This is a first for the both of us. My first month as deputy regional director and I get this crap dumped on my head. Do you want to continue?"

"I'll do my best," Jack said. "Todd mentioned Borov is about to meet with an ISIS representative. Stopping that may be more important in the overall scheme."

They went on to discuss how Jack intended to handle the security arrangements for George Lawrence's funeral in the event Donofrio's plan didn't succeed. He could tell his old friend was nervous and under pressure.

She said, "Between you and me, I'd stop the funeral if I could, but there's no judge in the world who'll keep a wife from attending her husband's memorial service."

"I agree."

"Can you keep her safe?"

"We can and we will."

Janet Newton was silent for so long he thought she had broken the connection. She finally spoke. "Jack, I'm sorry to pull rank this way. You know how much I think of you. Unfortunately we're out of options. We're . . . I take that back, I'm under a microscope. Stop this bastard for me."

Jack was about to respond when he realized she had hung up this time.

Chapter 58

Six Hours to the Grand Jury

Wesley answered the phone on the second ring. It was eight o'clock in the morning and Lenny was calling.

"I'm so glad I got you," Lenny said. "The police picked me up yesterday."

"For what?"

"More questions."

"The same officers?" Wesley asked.

"Those were ATF agents. This was a lady detective and an FBI agent."

"Describe them."

"The woman's tall, slender, and really pretty. The man's about six feet and blond, maybe sandy-haired."

Wesley's hands tightened at his description of Elizabeth. He'd given her every chance, but she was still with other men. Men, with their pawing hands and filthy minds. What did Father Mike say? Once the devil grabs hold of your soul, you'll pay a dear price to get it back. Fire might cleanse and burn the stain away, but some part always remains. How? How? How could she continue this after all he'd done for her? Betrayal had to be the worst sin of all.

"Rick, are you there?"

"What? Sure. I was just thinking."

"I have to tell you something else. Please don't be mad."

"I won't. Go ahead."

"They told me your real name is Thomas Courtney and you're a contract killer. They said you killed the other man who was flying the airplane. They really scared me."

Wesley laughed. "A contract killer? That's a good one."

"They even showed me a photo of you. At least I think it was you. It looked like you were younger then."

"There are a lot of photos of me on the Internet," Wesley said. "Remember, I told you the competition was awfully cut-throat and they'd try to screw the picture up if they could."

"I remember."

"Let me ask you this, who provides security for the equipment we use?"

"The cops, I guess," Lenny said.

"Well, it's the same for the other company. They want to get their film in the can first. If they stop us even by a few weeks, they win."

"I never thought of it that way," Lenny said.

"There you go. Was that fellow Jack Kale there when they questioned you?"

"I met him, but he didn't say much."

"Okay. Where are you now?" Wesley asked.

"At the park."

"Is anyone else with you?"

"There are a couple people around, but no one's paying much attention to me."

Wesley adjusted the lens of his scope and scanned the area. It took only a moment to spot the blond agent and three marksmen in camouflage hiding in the bushes and in the trees. Two U.S. Marshals were "casually" hanging out by the safehouse, smoking cigarettes, their weapons carefully concealed behind the trees.

What a joke.

Kale was the one he wanted. Cut off the head, Father Mike said, and the body dies. He was furious with Lenny for betraying him. He could see the little man on the phone. A moment ago, he'd been talking to the FBI agent. All alone, was he? Liar! That Wesley had even thought they could be friends made him sick.

He looked harder at the house. There she was, passing by the window, Elizabeth, the ultimate traitor. He was about to show them how safe that house was.

"Rick?"

"Yes, Lenny?"

"I thought you hung up. Are you angry?"

"Not at all. You did right by telling me. Just crank up the drone and let her fly. I'll pick you up for dinner tonight. Studio's treat."

*

Jack studied the drone on the ground, six arms each with an engine in a starburst pattern. The oval control unit at the center looked like a spider's body. The previous evening Stan Kaufman had removed the RDX rendering the machine harmless. The switch Courtney used was clever. It contained a mercury trigger that would immediately activate if the wrong wire was clipped. Its GPS capability could put it within ten feet of its target.

One by one, Lenny Walpole started the engines and then moved to his precious laptop to initiate the flight sequence.

*

Fifteen hundred yards away Wesley watched the craft lift into the air and hover above the ground like something out of Star Wars. The three agents kept themselves well in the background. Having used his cellphone, he knew he only had a few minutes before they closed in on him. Even if they managed to fix his position, he'd be long gone by the time they arrived. Still enough time to do what he had to.

I told you, boy-o; the man was not to be trusted.

You did, Father.

I'm sorry he turned out to be a disappointment. I'd have spared you that if I could.

It's all right.

Ah, but I know there's some pain involved.

I'll get over it. Elizabeth is the one that hurts the most. Once a harlot, always a harlot, I suppose.

Now, now. Judge not, lest ye shall be judged yourself.

I understand.

About time to put an end to this, wouldn't you say, son?

Yes . . . about time.

Wesley took one final look at Lenny as his finger moved to the button on his cellphone, the one that would send the signal. He had no room in his life for liars and Judases. Closing his eyes, he took a breath and pressed the button.

The explosion was muffled. More muffled than it should have been. He grabbed his spotting scope and saw Lenny crouched behind one of the unmarked cruisers. Impossible!

The drone was still hovering in the air twenty feet above the agents' heads. Kale was no longer watching it. He was scanning the trees looking for him. He could see those eyes searching.

Time to take our leave, boy-o. They're onto us.

I don't understand.

Figured out the plan, son. That Kale's a smart one. Out of here now.

I can still take a shot. Elizabeth has to pay.

There'll be other opportunities. He who fights and runs away lives to fight another day. Move it. Move it.

*

Todd Milner turned to Jack Kale. When the RDX exploded inside the bomb-proof container, destroying Lenny's laptop, the little man's shoulders slumped. He looked terrified and totally defeated.

"How did you know?" Milner asked.

"What we recovered at the photographer's house showed bits of C-6, but there were also traces of high impact gray plastic, the same color as Walpole's computer. When we checked the screws under a microscope, it was obvious they'd been removed. In addition, the case had some pry marks indicating it had been opened. Because Courtney gave Lenny the laptop, I assumed that's where the main explosive was hidden. It was clever because there was nothing when the ATF examined it. The fact that it was there now meant he planned to force Lenny out and cover his tracks."

"So he was just trying to kill Walpole?"

"You said it yourself. Lenny knows what he looks like, just as Peter Shackelford did. If he could take us out in the process, so much the better for him."

"It looks like the funeral's in play now."

"I think we have to assume it is."

"Solid stuff, buddy," Milner said, squeezing Jack's shoulder. "By the way, where is Beth now? I haven't seen her around this morning."

"Running down some leads. A police officer who looks like her volunteered to walk past the window hoping it would give our guys some time to pin Courtney down."

"Bright," Milner said. "I take it Dr. Lawrence isn't here either."

"No, she's home getting dressed. She left at five AM."

*

The name of the game was cover your ass. Carmine Donofrio, who'd been monitoring the situation, was livid. He was convinced the FBI had responded too slowly to establish a fix on the killer's cellphone, allowing him to slip through their fingers again. At the press conference, Sally Yellen, Atlanta's SAC, implied the U.S. Marshals had been remiss. When interviewed, the Marshal Service declined official comment other than to state their men were on alert and in position at all times, but did not see any threats in the form of snipers. Wayne Ruckhouser, vice chairman of the Senate oversight subcommittee, concluded the matter had been improperly handled from the outset and urged Janet Newton to change the lead investigator.

*

Todd Milner reluctantly agreed to take over and indicated he would personally stay with Rachel Lawrence at the safehouse until after her grand jury appearance. Jack received the news of his dismissal in an e-mail from the deputy director.

He had just pulled into the church parking lot where George Lawrence's funeral was to be held. There were so many cars, he was forced to park in the last row. Dr. Lawrence had been a popular and well-liked man.

Working in combination with the APD, Milner had erected a temporary tent-like enclosure around the front entrance that extended all the way to the parking lot. It allowed the limousine carrying Rachel and her family to pull up and unload, taking away any chance for a sniper to get a clear shot at her. Jack nodded his approval and wondered what sort of arrangements Milner would have in place at the cemetery.

The church was huge. He had seen it a number of times rising majestically on a hill alongside I-75, but had never been inside. Calling it a cathedral wouldn't have been out of place. On the rooftop were two marshals armed with rifles. A line of mourners, there to pay their respects, had formed and were waiting to pass through a metal detector, which Milner had also installed. Even so, he doubted the church could hold everyone. Jack took his place at the end. After a minute, he saw the rumpled form of Dan Pappas striding across the lawn toward him. The big detective motioned for Jack to join him.

"Never saw you in a suit before," Pappas said.

"That's what you got me out of line to tell me?"

"About an hour ago the uniforms pulled a man's body out of the Chattahoochee."

"And?"

"He had no hands and no face."

"Unusual," Jack said.

"*Unusual?*"

"Sounds familiar, doesn't it? Do we know how long he'd been in the water?"

"A few hours, according to the ME. The body was just letting go of rigor."

"Interesting," Jack said.

"Anyone ever tell you you have an amazing capacity for the understatement? Interesting? That's the best you can come up with?"

"You have a better word?"

"No. That's why I'm here," Pappas said.

"I'm not on the case anymore, Dan. I was fired, or hadn't you heard?"

"I did and it's bullshit. They're looking for a scapegoat."

Jack smiled. "I know. Describe the body for me."

"Five foot nine and around a hundred seventy-five pounds, brown hair, gray-blue eyes. Pretty good shape, except for the no hands and no face part."

"Cause of death?"

"Two bullets to the head at close range. The ME said stippling and powder burns were visible."

"Were his teeth intact?"

Pappas pulled the report out of his pocket and glanced through it. "Looks that way. Getting an ID will take time, and we'd need comparison records. You think this is related?"

"Hard to believe it isn't considering its similarity to the fire marshal's condition. We need to make sure though."

"How can we do that? The guy's ID-proof."

"Maybe not," Jack said. "I saw Richard Sklar going inside a minute ago. He used to teach at Emory's dental school, if I remember correctly. Let's ask him to take a look at the body. Was the vic dressed?"

"Yeah. The clothes are on the way to the crime lab. Nelda said she'll look at them later."

Jack checked his watch. "Maybe you can convince her to do it right away."

Chapter 59

Three Hours to the Grand Jury

Beth Sturgis stood across from a one-story ranch house at the end of a street, studying it. About a week's worth of newspapers had accumulated at the front door, and the mailbox was filled to capacity. She was used to Jack coming up with unusual ideas, but flying her halfway across the country on a hunch was crazy. Then again, as she had learned, his hunches were never purely guesswork. She was still annoyed. This was a crucial time in the investigation, and she needed to be in Atlanta, not Phoenix. Pappas had called to let her know Jack had been fired. It made her blood boil.

The more she thought about the Sandman, the angrier she became. He might be an opportunist as Janet Newton said, but so was an anaconda slowly squeezing the life out of its prey. She pushed these thoughts away and returned her attention to the house.

The lawn was in what locals called a natural state, as was the backyard. Save for a few cactuses and bushes she couldn't name, it looked like an extension of the desert. The house was modest, tan in color, and reminiscent of adobe. The roof was composed of red barrel tiles.

Beth crossed the street, checked to make sure no one was watching, and went to work on the door lock with a set of picks she'd inherited from her last partner, Leonard Cass. Dan Pappas taught her how to use them and was surprised at how quickly she picked up the technique. It took under two minutes to gain entry.

Once inside, she checked the air. Stale. Apparently, no one had opened a window for a long time. Beth moved into the kitchen and looked in the sink where several dishes had been left unwashed. The refrigerator contained a milk carton two weeks out of date and a peach that had turned into a science experiment. From there, she checked the other rooms, trying to place herself in the frame of mind Jack so often adopted when he viewed a possible crime scene. Everything was important. Everything told a story. Even the little details.

The more she looked, the more the house began to disturb her. Some of what she was seeing made no sense. In the living room and bedroom, the dresser and shelves had once held framed photographs, all of which were now empty. The pictures had been removed and the frames tossed to the floor. Her heart rate began to speed up. Maybe Jack's hunch wasn't so odd after all. She could feel something was wrong but had yet to identify what that was.

A search of the garage revealed nothing. The attic was the same: hot, dusty, with no air moving. Boxes had been neatly stacked along the walls. Like the rest of the home, it contained nothing suspicious—no bodies, no bloodstains. Judging from the clothes in the closet, it looked like the owner had left in a hurry. The bathroom contained a razor and toothbrush. Her impression was that the owner had stepped out for lunch and would be back any minute, which she knew wasn't the case.

Beth returned to the living room and sat down trying to make sense of what she'd seen. Nothing came to her. She pulled out her cellphone and looked at the message Jack had left while she was in the air, shook her head, and dialed a number. Eddie Marks answered on the second ring.

"Eddie, this is Beth Sturgis. I'm calling from Phoenix. You mind if I ask you a couple more questions?"

"Phoenix? Sounds like you're across the street."

"I'm sitting here looking at the desert and a bunch of cactuses."

He laughed to himself and asked what she needed.

"I know you're in the loan business. I'd like to run a few names by you and see if any of them ring a bell."

"This have to do with that situation we discussed?"

"It might. I'm not completely sure myself."

There was a pause.

"Same agreement on confidentiality?"

"Same."

Marks sighed. "Go ahead."

Beth read the names off her list and was surprised by his answer. She thanked him and disconnected, then called Dwayne Stafford and told him to start preparing a subpoena. When that was done, her attention shifted back to the house and why Jack had sent her.

Through the sliding glass door that led to a patio and a backyard was a three foot stucco wall. Beyond that, the desert's broad expanse lay waiting to take back the land once men were gone.

Movement a hundred yards from where she sat caught her eye. It was just two coyotes scavenging for food. She watched them. After a while, they were joined by a third, who cautiously approached the first two and pawed the ground. In the distance, a series of purple peaks rose up like jagged fingers lit by flashes of dry lightning. Above them, the sky had assumed a crimson cast. Moments later, a fourth coyote joined the group and, like the newcomer, began digging away at the brittle landscape. Slowly, it began to dawn on her what was wrong. She stood and drew her gun.

*

Two Hours to the Grand Jury

At least two hundred people filled the chapel. Dan Pappas approached Dr. Richard Sklar and spoke with him. The dentist leaned over to his wife and whispered something in her ear, then he and Pappas left the church together.

Sunlight streaming through a large stained glass window created a rainbow on the floor as the minister addressed the congregation. The death of George Lawrence and the others at Stone Mountain was something outside their scope of reference. You could see it in their faces. Evil was an abstract concept spoken about in sermons, but they were at a loss on how to deal with it now that the serpent had entered their midst. These were men and woman of ordinary sensibilities, decent, and content to live good lives with their families. The events they saw in movies and on television were removed and unreal. Far different from the stark reality of a friend lying in his casket at the foot of the altar.

No hands. No face.

Thankfully, the service was brief. Jack barely realized it was over. He'd been preoccupied and sorting facts. People were filing past the casket speaking a word or two to Rachel Lawrence. A few feet away, dressed in a dark suit, was Todd Milner, alert and scanning the crowd for any sign of a threat. It was the same with the two marshals posted at the back of the church, and those posted by each of the four side exits.

Every case Jack had reviewed indicated they were dealing with a slight of hand artist. What happened at the safehouse and in New York were good examples. The real blow was yet to come. But how, and from where?

Rather than pay his respects, Jack left the church and drove to the crime lab. An attractive young female officer with dark hair was standing behind Nelda Latham watching her separate a number of tiny particles in a metal dish with a slender probe. Nelda introduced Marina Brady and explained why she was there.

"Marina and her partner fished the floater out of the river. I've been examining the clothes she brought me."

Nelda paused and looked at Jack's empty hands. She sighed. "Guess the honeymoon's over."

"I apologize. I was at a funeral and didn't have time to stop for bagels. I'll make it up to you."

"That's what they all say."

"I was an eagle scout."

"The last eagle scout I dated got me pregnant."

Jack smiled. "How's Oscar doing?" he asked, referring to her husband.

"Still the same. If anyone told me marriage was picking one person to annoy for the rest of your life, I might have given it more thought."

"Send him my regards."

"I will. A little bird told me you finally popped the question to Beth."

Jack considered asking who the bird was and promptly discarded the idea. Knowing the police department, the bird was probably a flock by now. Instead, he confirmed the rumor. He'd probably read about it in the newspaper tomorrow. He inquired if she had found anything interesting.

"There's not much to go on. The vic wasn't in the river long, but it did a good job and removed almost anything useful."

"Almost?"

"Am I not the queen of forensics? I was just separating what appears to be some tobacco shreds from the cuff of his pant leg."

A tuning fork struck in the back of Jack's memory. Early in the case, Beth had found some grains of tobacco at Stone Mountain.

"Is there enough for a comparison?"

"Maybe. Beth's evidence kit shattered when it hit the ground, but our Boy Scouts finally managed to find a few of the plastic bags she collected," Nelda said, pointing at a second tray.

Jack and the officer leaned over and looked at the tray. There were three miniscule shreds present.

"You can tell if there's a match just from those?" she asked.

"Well, they look bigger under a microscope," Nelda said.

"Did this belong to the victim?" Jack asked, picking up a white oxford shirt from another tray.

"It did. If you'll notice the label's been removed, which means I can't trace it back to the manufacturer."

"What's this?" Jack asked, pointing to an irregular shaped spot on the side of the shirt.

"A stain."

Jack sniffed it. "Smells like garlic . . . vinegar, and something else." He offered the shirt to Officer Brady and she sniffed it as well.

"Lemon."

Jack went to the white board and wrote down all three. Returned. Picked the shirt back up and tried sniffing again. Annoyed, he shook his head, and brought it up to his tongue.

"Gross," commented Marina Brady.

"Dill, I'm sure of it."

"So he's a sloppy eater," Nelda said. "What good does that do us?"

"I'm curious. Is there enough to burn?"

Putting a sample through a gas chromatograph-mass spectrometer would provide a breakdown of the chemical components, but it would also destroy whatever was in there in the process.

Nelda examined the shirt closer, then removed a pair of scissors from a drawer under the table and cut a patch out. She ran the sample. While the spectrometer was working, Jack added "dill" to the board.

Once the analysis was complete, Nelda studied her computer screen and announced, "All right, I'm seeing sodium and chloride and what looks like . . . yogurt. We also have olive oil."

"The sodium and chloride are salt," Jack said.

"What's this?" the officer asked, tapping the screen.

"Some type of lactose product. Sour cream, maybe," Nelda said.

Everything went up on the board. They all stared at it. Jack's cellphone rang. It was Pappas.

"I'm here at the ME's office. Dr. Sklar doesn't have much to report except the fillings are old and the type commonly used overseas. Any progress on your end?"

"Possibly. We're about to compare a tobacco sample with what Beth found at Stone Mountain. I'll call you back."

Jack disconnected and turned to the women and asked, "Ideas? Speculation?"

Several seconds passed and no one ventured any guesses. Nelda began looking at the tobacco samples using the electron microscope.

Jack stared at the board and folded his arms across his chest. He was frustrated because the answers were there but just out of his grasp.

Nelda abruptly stopped what she was doing and raised her head. "Tzatziki sauce," she said, pulling him out of his reverie.

They both turned to her.

"What sauce?" Jack asked.

"Tzatziki sauce. My maiden name is Skoros. We're Greek. You use it to dip pita bread in. I should have recognized it right away."

Jack and Marina Brady looked at each other as he felt his mouth go dry. He knew who the man in the river was. Suddenly, his head felt like it was filled with helium. He suspected, but never believed it was possible. Without warning, images began colliding in his mind. Their urgency grew in relation to the pressure building in his chest. In moments, the pain spread down his arms.

Neither Nelda Latham nor Marina Brady immediately grasped what was happening. Jack tried to speak, but the air in his lungs was gone. His eyes fell on the wall clock. The minute hand ticked forward a notch. Twenty minutes remained until Rachel Lawrence and Todd Milner left for the grand jury.

Somewhere at the end of a distant tunnel, he heard Nelda's voice shouting, "Call nine-one-one! He's having a heart attack!"

Jack was conscious of both women trying to lower him to the ground. The clock ticked off another minute. His arms felt like lead weights had been attached to them. It took nearly all his strength to reach for the bottle of Ativan in his pocket. Nelda finally recognized what he was doing and helped him open it. The officer ran to the sink, filled a cup with water, and brought it back, supporting his head as he downed the pill.

Another minute ticked by, and then another.

Nelda Latham's voice was faint, exhorting him to breathe. Jack's eyes fluttered.

Gradually, the world around him began to alter. He was lying on a cold granite floor. The wall clock ticked off another minute. Five more passed before he was able to sit up.

"Don't move," Nelda said. "The ambulance will be here any moment."

Jack shook his head. "Help me up."

"Absolutely not. You stay where you are. Let the medics check you out first."

"I'll be all right. Call Dan Pappas."

"*What?*"

"I know who the Sandman is, Nelda."

Jack reached for his cellphone. Dropped it.

"Listen to me. My uncle had a heart attack. I've seen them before."

"Call him," Jack said, glancing at the clock. "We don't have much time. I'll be in the car. Tell Dan I need SWAT at the safehouse right now."

"You're insane. I'm not letting you—"

"It wasn't a heart attack. Trust me."

By the time she found Pappas's number in Jack's call log and punched it in, Jack had struggled to his feet assisted by Officer Brady. Nelda held the phone out for him.

"What the hell, buddy? Nelda said you just had a heart attack."

"Panic attack," Jack said, lurching toward the door. "They can look alike. Where are you?"

"On my way to the North Precinct. Listen, are you sure—"

"Positive. The floater's Thom Courtney."

Jack reached his car and was struggling to put the key in the door. "Say again."

"Thomas Courtney's dead. He's not the Sandman. Have you heard from Beth yet?"

"Negative. Maybe you should let the docs check you out like Nelda says. You're not making any sense."

Jack finally managed to open the lock. Got in. Started the engine.

"Greek food. Hair and eye color are the same as Courtney's photo, so's his height from the British police report, plus the tobacco's a close match. Everything is misdirection. The Sandman's going for Rachel. How far away are you?"

"Wait a minute. Greek food?"

"Walpole told us he and his friend had Greek food last night. How far away are you?"

"Thirty minutes."

"Shit. I'm en route now."

"Let's call Milner and—"

"Absolutely not!"

"Why?"

Before Jack could answer, his phone beeped, showing Beth was trying to call in. He told Pappas to hold.

"Beth—"

"Todd Milner is dead. At least the real one is. I'm here with the Phoenix cops. We just took his body out of the ground. A detective who knows him made a positive ID."

Jack jammed the accelerator pedal to the floor and began flashing his lights as he cut across three lanes of traffic. "I'm ten minutes from the safehouse. No time to talk. Pappas is on the other line. I need you to call Glen Sheeley."

Jack broke the call and returned to Pappas. "Dan, listen, Milner's the Sandman. I don't have time to get into details. That was Beth. She's calling Sheeley. Get there as fast as you can."

*

Beth phoned the Atlanta switchboard and asked to be connected to the SWAT commander. She reached Lieutenant Carl Garvey, Sheeley's second in command.

"Sheeley's in the field right now, Detective. What's up?"

"I need an emergency response team at the federal safehouse right now. The man posing as Agent Milner is a fake. He's the killer, and he's going for the witnesses."

"Say that again."

"I'm telling you he's not Milner. He's the Sandman."

Garvey hesitated. "Look, the feds assumed jurisdiction this morning. We're off the case. I'll put a call in to—"

"Did you just hear me? I said the Sandman's about to kill the witnesses."

"I heard you. But it's out of our hands. The order came down from the commissioner's office. The feds want to run with the ball. There's not much we can do. I'll be happy to call them if you—"

Beth wanted to scream at him.

"Jack Kale's on his way right now. So is Dan Pappas. Dwayne Stafford's already on site. Their lives are in danger. Officers needing assistance override everything."

"Goddammit," Garvey said under his breath. "You sure about this?"

"Positive. I'm looking at the real Milner's body."

Chapter 60

One Hour to the Grand Jury

As soon as Dan Pappas broke the connection, he reached under the seat, slapped a magnetic blue light on the dashboard, and swung a U-turn on Roswell Road, cutting off a delivery truck. One wheel of his cruiser jumped the curb and took out a trash can. Angry drivers in both directions began sounding their horns at him as he raced back toward the highway.

Milner the Sandman? He was definitely living in a nut house.

Even with no traffic, the trip would take him twenty minutes. He said a silent prayer he'd be in time.

*

Dwayne Stafford stared at Beth's text message in disbelief and read it again.

M²ner is the Sandman. Get Rachel and Walpole out of there!! Calling SWAT. Jack and Pappas en route. Move now!!

It took another moment to recover from the shock. He immediately started looking around the room for a weapon. Saw nothing. His own gun had been locked away in a safe by the marshals when they arrived. Dwayne gave up and stepped into the hallway. The house was unnaturally quiet. By rights, he should have heard conversations in progress or at least people moving around. Suddenly it felt like his mouth was filled with cotton. The first priority was getting Rachel and Lenny Walpole to safety. Accomplishing that would be another matter. The bedroom Rachel was using was directly across from his. Walpole's was at the opposite end of the house.

He paused and listened again. Directly above him was the command center with all its electronic gadgets the marshals used to monitor the house and surrounding property. Two of them should have been on duty up there, another one on the lower level, and one out walking the grounds.

A second before his hand closed on the door knob something stopped him, the sound of a heavy thud coming from the floor above, as if a body had hit the ground. His heart began to beat harder. With a quick tap, he opened the door and went in.

Rachel was lying on her side on the bed, propped up on one elbow. She was already dressed for her grand jury appearance and waiting for the marshals to let her know when they had to leave.

"Dwayne, what—"

The detective put his finger over his lips and moved to her side.

"Miss Rachel, don't say anything. We're in trouble. I need to get you out of here."

"What's happening?" Rachel whispered, swinging her feet to the floor.

"Todd Milner's the Sandman."

"That's impossible."

"I wish it were. Beth Sturgis just sent me a text message saying he is. Our SWAT team's on the way now. Trust me. She ain't the kind to joke about something like this and we don't have time to discuss it. You think you can climb out that window over there?"

"I grew up with three brothers," Rachel said, slipping her shoes on. "I can climb anything."

"Great. Soon as you're outside make for that house next door. It's just the other end of those trees at the bottom of the hill."

"What about you?"

"I need to find Mr. Walpole. With any luck, there's still a marshal—"

The rest of what he was about to say was interrupted by a sound he recognized. Someone had just fired a silenced weapon on the second floor.

"Oh, Lordy," he said to himself. "This ain't good."

Both of them froze and listened to footsteps going down the back staircase. It was followed by a door closing. Dwayne told Rachel to stay where she was. He darted into the hallway and checked the safe, praying it was open. No luck there either. Returning to the bedroom, he motioned her over to the window and carefully slid it open.

"Look," she said, pointing.

At the rear corner of the property, close to where the trees began, one of the marshals was lying on the ground. Standing above him, Todd Milner was in the process of pulling the man's windbreaker off. The trick Thom Courtney had used at the safehouse when he disguised himself as a SWAT officer flashed into Dwayne's mind.

That ain't gonna work again, fella.

"Change of plans," he said. "Let's use the front door. He'll be coming around back. If we time it correctly, you'll be down the hill in a second."

Leonard Walpole was reading a book in the living room. The moment he saw them he started to complain about something, but stopped when he noticed the detective's expression.

He stood up. "Wh . . . what's wrong?"

"I need to get you out of here, sir. The killer's on his way. There ain't no time to explain, so just follow me."

At the front door, Dwayne told them, "When I give you the signal, you both hightail it over to the neighbor's house. Don't look back. Don't stop. When you get there, lock yourselves in. Our people should be here any minute."

"What will you be doing?" Rachel asked.

"Gonna see if I can find me a weapon and have a word with the Sandman."

"No, Dwayne—"

"There's no time to discuss this, ma'am," he said, moving to the living room window.

The Sandman was halfway up the hill and he was carrying the marshal's rifle. Dwayne held his hand up to them. He just needed to wait a few seconds longer.

"Go!"

After Rachel and Lenny were out the door, he ran into the kitchen hoping to find a knife. What he found was one of the U.S. Marshals lying dead on the floor with a gaping wound where his right eye should have been. The man's service weapon was next to him, but the clip was missing.

Cursing under his breath, he began checking for a backup. Almost every law enforcement officer he knew carried one. It was in an ankle holster: a five-shot .38-caliber revolver with a two-and-a-half-inch barrel.

He was in the process of checking the cylinders when Todd Milner's face appeared in the kitchen door. His momentary surprise showed. Dwayne fired off two shots, destroying a glass pane. Both missed. The detective turned and ran for the front door. He needed to buy some time. Certain he hadn't hit the Sandman, he only had three shots left. Two bullets crashed into the wooden doorframe behind him as he left the house. The Sandman would follow, but he'd have to do so cautiously knowing he was armed.

Oddly, he didn't. Whatever the killer was planning wouldn't be obvious. Dwayne raced for the second marshal. Patted him down and found his backup weapon, a 9 mm semiautomatic with eight shots in the magazine. Better still.

There was still no sign of the Sandman. Maybe he had decided to run rather than risking a firefight with a police officer. When he turned toward the trees to make sure Rachel and Walpole were safely away, his heart stopped. Instead of going to the neighbor's house, they were waiting for him.

No!

He was waving at them to get back when a puff of dirt kicked up inches from his ankle, followed by the sound of a rifle's report. Instead of following him, the Sandman had gone around the house. He shifted the barrel away from the detective and was now sighting in on the witnesses. Frantic, Dwayne fired two more shots and started running, yelling for Rachel and Walpole to run as well.

*

Jack Kale dodged between cars on I-75, the speedometer edging over one hundred miles per hour. A rickety flatbed in front of him refused to move. Jack swung his car onto the shoulder and passed, destroying the paint on his BMW and a good portion of the side panel when he scraped the highway's retaining wall. He fought to keep the car under control. Two miles ahead lay the Moores Mill Road exit. He was traveling too fast to answer the telephone when it rang. His hands gripped the steering wheel so tightly his knuckles showed white. He jerked the steering wheel hard over and slid back into the traffic again. The exit was now less than a mile away.

His car shot up the exit ramp, fishtailing as he took the corner on two wheels. His BMW looked like it had been through a demolition derby. Jack cursed and righted the vehicle.

The moment he turned onto the street where the safehouse was located the sound of gunshots reached him. Some part of his mind registered they were different in character, one small arms, the other some type of rifle. Without bothering to slow down he drove straight across the lawn toward the house, skidding to a halt and throwing the door open. If the sensors picked him up, so much the better.

At the base of the hill, he spotted Dwayne Stafford trying to herd the witnesses to the safety of the trees. Directly above the detective's head a branch exploded. Rachel Lawrence and Lenny Walpole both flinched. Stafford returned the fire, but was too far away to do any good. Jack knew at once the situation was hopeless. There was insufficient cover and Milner had a rifle. He thought rapidly. After being removed from the case, it was pretty much over as far as he was concerned. It also meant he hadn't brought a weapon to the funeral. As another shot rang out, Stafford's body twisted abruptly and he went down. Jack felt his heart stop.

In the next second, something happened that would stay with him for the rest of his life. Incredibly, Dwayne Stafford regained his feet, turned, and began charging up the hill firing his guns with either hand.

Jack broke into a run as the Sandman calmly took aim. Another shot exploded from the rifle. Stafford staggered, twisted sideways, and nearly went down, but righted himself, and kept coming, screaming as he fired. At that moment, he was the most dangerous thing in the world, a man who no longer had any regard for his own safety. The Sandman forgot about him, swung his rifle around, and took aim at Rachel Lawrence. After three more steps, Dwayne Stafford collapsed face down on the ground and didn't move again.

The next shot went over Rachel's head as Jack came flying around the corner of the house and smashed headlong into the bogus FBI agent. Both men went down, recovered, and got to their feet. The killer hadn't lost his rifle but recognized there wasn't enough space or time for him to aim it. Instead, he swung it like a club, catching Jack on the shoulder.

Jack stepped in and threw the overhand right he'd been saving since his Golden Glove days, connecting with the side of the Sandman's head. Ducked under a left, and hit him again. The killer was stunned. A leg lashed out and caught the side of Jack's knee almost dropping him. The Sandman went for his gun again. Using the side of the hill to gain momentum Jack hit him with an open field tackle his high school coach would have been proud of.

They both rolled partway down the rise in a tangle with the killer coming out on top. At the last moment, Jack saw the knife. He managed to block it. His opponent responded by pressing down with all his weight, forcing the knife's point nearer and nearer to Jack's chest. Jack's hand came into contact with a rock lying next to him. Grabbed it and swung, knocking the imposter off his stomach. Both men scrambled to their feet. The Sandman's face was covered in blood. Despite his injuries, he still had the knife.

The best Jack could do was partially deflect the next thrust at his stomach. Pain tore through his insides. A lung collapsed, and as the killer drew back for another stab, Jack stepped in and swung his elbow at the side of the Sandman's head. Bone connected with bone. A second blow to the opposite of his head hurt him badly and he went down. Jack got on top of him and hit him three more times. He was about to land another punch when he realized he was hitting an unconscious man. He looked down to see his shirt covered in blood. That pause was a mistake.

The moment he let his guard down a searing pain blossomed in his thigh. The Sandman had been acting. Before he could withdraw the blade for another thrust, Jack reached forward, grabbed the opposite sides of his collar, and brought the edge of his forearm across the killer's throat. Pinning him in place, he pressed down with all his weight, shutting off the carotid artery and blood flow to the Sandman's brain. Seconds later, Milner's mouth opened and his tongue started to loll. He finally went silent. This time he stayed that way. Maybe he was dead, maybe he wasn't. Jack didn't care.

"You lose," he said, rolling off him. The knife was still embedded in his thigh.

It was becoming harder to think. He knew the adrenalin that had been sustaining him was about to disappear. In moments, he would lose consciousness. He started crawling toward Dwayne Stafford. Dialed 9-1-1. His hands were shaking badly.

"This is Jack Kale," he gasped. "Officer down. I need assistance and an ambulance."

"Sir, what's your location?"

"Stafford's dying. We need . . . medical . . ."

The young man's face was white as a sheet. No way to tell if he was dead or alive. Two yards from the detective, Jack's strength gave out. His arms collapsed. He rolled over onto his back and looked up at the clouds. His breathing was labored and shallow. Through the haze, he could see an old sailing ship pulling slowly away from the shore into the open sea, water slapping against its sides, its intricate lines reminiscent of a spider's web. His fingers moved over the deck's polished teakwood as Constance Belasco walked toward him, her hand outstretched, face serene and at peace. Eyes kind. Jack reached for her. The colorless ocean merged with a white sky at the horizon. At its center was an area of darkness growing ever larger as they sailed on. It was time.

Letting the rise and fall of the ship take him, his head fell back onto the deck. Like a clock winding down his heart slowed . . . and slowed, and eventually came to a stop. The objects around him faded and became indistinct until there was nothing left but the dark.

Chapter 61

Rachel Lawrence used CPR and managed to get Jack's heart started again. She rode with him to the hospital and, assisted by another surgeon, she performed the surgery that saved his life. By her estimate, he had been dead for nearly a minute.

When he awoke in the recovery room, Jack managed to croak out a question.

"The witnesses . . . Dwayne . . . out of danger?"

Rachel moved to the side of his bed and laid a hand on his shoulder.

"Dwayne didn't make it, Jack. I was too late to save him. I'm so sorry."

Jack shut his eyes and said a silent prayer for the young man before the drugs took hold and he lapsed back into unconsciousness.

For the next three days, indistinct images came and went: Dan Pappas's scared face looking down at him, Noah Ritson and Beth standing by the bed. It was like being in the audience in a theater and watching a play about his life.

At the end of the fourth day, he regained consciousness. Beth, with the blessing of the department, had been there nearly the entire time going home only to feed Marta. She told him Dwayne Stafford had been laid to rest near his childhood friend, Ed Mundas. Nearly the entire Atlanta Police Force and most of the local FBI agents had attended the funerals. In the last week, Atlanta had lost five officers. The city was in shock.

She also told him she had met Dwayne's fiancée, Melissa Sue, who sent her best wishes for a speedy recovery. In view of the circumstances, Rachel's testimony before the grand jury had been postponed until the following month. By his ninth day in the hospital, Jack was restless, irritable, and ready to leave.

*

Shortly before checking out of the hospital, he received a visit from Janet Newton, who advised him Carmine Donofrio was in negotiations with the Sandman's attorney. The man who had been posing as Todd Milner was found still unconscious when first responders reached the safehouse, and he was safely taken into custody without further incident. Janet didn't know what the Sandman and his attorney were bargaining for. The deputy director let on that the powers that be weren't particularly happy with her and were hinting at a possible reassignment to the Bureau's field office in Omaha, Nebraska.

By far the most interesting news was that no one had been able to establish the Sandman's real identity. Both DNA and fingerprints had turned up nothing. The man seemed to have dropped out of the sky. She further informed him that governments in five countries were pressuring the Justice Department to return him to them so he could stand trial. For lack of a better name, he was being referred to as Prisoner John Doe.

"I have a question," Janet Newton said. "How did you know he'd taken Milner's place?"

"A few things never made sense, and I began to suspect Milner after the confrontation with Courtney in New York. From the beginning, it was obvious Courtney had help. Not only did he know about the APD's safehouse, he managed to transport two bombs to New York on extremely short notice. A private jet was the only way to accomplish that. When I checked the available charter services, the only flight that morning besides Beth's was ours, so someone on our plane had to have brought the explosives. Security at private airports is incredibly lax. It's virtually nonexistent when the FBI is involved. I mean, who checks a federal agent's suitcase? Most importantly, only a limited number of people knew Rachel Lawrence would be in New York that day to perform surgery. Our imposter was one of them.

"I have no idea what to call him now, but when I saw Milner about to shoot Thomas Courtney in Battery Park, it threw me. I examined the vest myself and noted there were four bullet marks, but they were spread out, which meant hollow points. More misdirection."

"We don't use hollow points in our assault weapons."

"Exactly."

"Then there was more misleading evidence we found. I'd already begun to suspect Milner wasn't on the level after the explosions, so I decided to test my theory. Using Scotch tape, I checked under his seat when he went to the restroom during the flight back. I found what looked like more of those coral grains. Just one or two, but they were enough to ask Ben Furman to confirm it. Our impostor said he'd never been to South Florida. It was the same with Gabe Alonso. I looked at his travel records and they were clean. Remember, the coral grains were found in Alonso's car. If he didn't track them back, it meant someone else had."

Janet folded her arms across her chest and leaned against the side of his bed.

Jack continued. "The clincher was Lenny Walpole's shoes. Either he got them from Thom Courtney or his partner. But according to Scotland Yard, Courtney wasn't in the country when Alonso was killed. That left one person, the partner."

"Which left you with Todd Milner because he was the last one to see Gabe Alonso alive when he went to New York to check on him," Janet said.

"Bingo," Jack said.

The director shook her head. "That wasn't much to go on."

"Evidence doesn't lie. The only time we get in trouble is when we misinterpret it. Sherlock Holmes once said, 'When you eliminate all other theories, whatever's left, no matter how improbable the answer, has got to be the solution.' I began doing just that, until I decided to check Milner's shoes, or whatever his real name is. That was the smoking gun, for me at least. It's also why I sent Beth to Arizona. You told me the real Todd Milner had recently transferred from there. I couldn't believe anyone would be audacious enough to impersonate a federal agent. Obviously, I was wrong."

Janet Newton shook her head.

"Courtney also didn't know Beth Sturgis was going to Stone Mountain the day she nearly slid over the edge. But 'Todd' did, because she told him. Kind of a stretch to think the killer decided to go back to the scene of the crime and hang around. That works In the movies, not real life. Milner passed the information along."

"I'm sorry I didn't have more faith in you."

"You were under a lot of pressure. What about my request?"

"May I ask why you want to speak with the prisoner?"

"Let's say I'm curious."

"That I can believe, but I'll need more. Donofrio doesn't like you."

"Hard to imagine," Jack said. "If you must know, the Sandman sent me a note through his lawyer saying he'd like to meet."

The surprise on the deputy director's face was apparent. Jack reached into a drawer in the little side table next to his hospital bed and handed it to her. The writing was neat and precise.

Congratulations Jack,

The first round is yours. I guess it had to happen sooner or later. If you have a moment, drop by and say hello. There's much we have to chat about. My best to your future bride.

The Sandman

The deputy director shook her head. "That's one sick puppy. Are you sure about this? I mean, with your health and all?"

"I'll be fine," Jack said. "Can you arrange it?"

"When do you want to see him?"

Jack told her.

The deputy director looked out the window and didn't speak for a time. "How could I have let all this happen?"

"You didn't. It was planned a long time ago. Months to a year, probably. You've been on the job, what? Less than thirty days? Basically, you inherited a mess. You couldn't possibly know everyone working under you in that time. No one in your position could. Like I said, his plan was not only audacious; it was genius. He was just biding his time to get the witnesses alone."

"You think he tortured Gabe Alonso to obtain the passwords and contacts he needed to infiltrate us?"

"I'm sure of it. Alonso's body bears that out. Nobody could have foreseen what happened."

"You did," Janet said.

"I figured it out. There's a difference. All the planning originated with 'Todd' or whatever his real name is."

Behind Jack's head was a monitor showing a continuous readout of his vital signs. Next to the bed was a metal stand with a bag of wheat-colored liquid and a tube that ran into his forearm. Janet Newton watched one drop make its way along the tube, then leaned down and kissed him on the forehead.

"I'll let you know when the arrangements are made."

Maybe in another time and in another life things might have turned out differently between them. When she left the room, the scent of her perfume remained.

Chapter 62

The Sandman was waiting when Jack entered the room. One eye was still bandaged, and one side of his face was purple. It was hard to tell which of them looked worse. Prisoner John Doe was sitting in a chair, his arms loosely shackled to a belt that ran around his waist.

"Good of you to come, Jack. How's the leg?"

"Hurts. How's your face?"

"Hurts."

"And your side?"

"Same."

"I'm glad the knife didn't do more damage. We had a hell of a time, didn't we?"

"Is that what you call it?"

"For lack of a better expression. You enjoyed yourself, though, didn't you? You felt alive when the game was on. Am I right?"

"You wanted to see me?" Jack said.

"As much as you wanted to see me. I felt I . . . owed it to you. We're very much alike."

Jack's eyebrows rose.

"Come on, Jack. You know it's true. I wanted to give you the opportunity to ask your questions. In return, I have a few of my own. Call it a quid pro quo."

"Fair enough."

"Right now you're trying to place where my accent is from. Mid-Atlantic. California. Someplace in the midwest, perhaps."

"Am I?"

"Of course you are. But a little mystery in any relationship is a good thing."

"Have you been in the business long?"

"About fourteen years. You?"

"Close to the same," Jack said. "What about Leonard Walpole?"

"Not my idea," the Sandman said, "but exactly what he appears to be, a harmless druggie. Basically, a puppy who wants to please."

"And he really believed Thom Courtney's story about making a movie?"

The Sandman turned his palms up. "From what I could see, Lenny is inclined to believe anyone offering a helping hand."

"Which you made sure was held out to him."

"Of course."

"And you're telling me this now because . . ."

"I'm not a monster, Jack. Sooner or later people will start looking for retribution. It's human nature. When that happens, the innocents tend to get run over. It would be a shame if Lenny goes to jail."

Jack nodded and looked around the conference room. Beside the two chairs and table they were sitting at, the only other object there was a small camera in the upper corner near the ceiling. The Sandman followed his gaze and asked if they were being filmed.

"Not to my knowledge. I asked the marshals to make sure it was off."

"And I have your word as a gentleman on that?"

"You do. Where did you find Thom Courtney?"

"Ah, dear old, confused Thom. I was wondering when you'd get around to him. If you must know, I found him in France after placing an ad in a magazine. *Soldier of Fortune*, I think it was."

"He answered it?"

"Complete with a resume. Very impressive. My turn. Thom was not particularly recognizable when he went into the river, so how did you identify him?"

"From a stain on his shirt and the general description we had. Also, the fillings in his teeth are mostly used in Europe."

The killer laughed to himself and said, "A shirt stain. Really?"

"Tzatziki sauce. Walpole told you that he and his friend Rick had Greek food the night before."

"Marvelous."

While the Sandman was processing that information, Jack realized his questions weren't based on idle curiosity. He was compiling a checklist to avoid future mistakes.

"You said Courtney was confused. About what?"

"Reality. Schizophrenia, I think you people call it. He had whole conversations on his cellphone with a dead priest named Father Michael."

Jack thought back to the episode at Battery Park when the agents were approaching him. Courtney had been talking on his cellphone.

"Knowing he was wearing body armor, you were the one who opened fire. But you were using hollow point bullets, which wouldn't penetrate the vest."

The killer's smile was self-effacing. "You're quite good at this, Jack. Have you ever considered switching teams?"

"Not really. Is it profitable?"

"Oh, very. After expenses, I'll still net a hundred thousand dollars."

"Expenses?"

"Mr. Courtney? Fifty thousand dollars went to him."

"I see. I suppose Borov can afford it."

The Sandman frowned. "That last question was beneath you."

Jack shrugged. "It was more of a comment. You obviously took a great deal of time putting this together. Objectively, I'd have to say the planning was meticulous. Brilliant even."

The Sandman inclined his head at the compliment, then said, "Six months isn't that great an investment."

"But sufficient to recover from plastic surgery," Jack said.

"As you say, these things take time."

Both men regarded each other for several seconds. It felt much longer. Move—countermove. They were already past the midgame.

"Does your lawyer think he'll be able to work a deal with the government regarding Borov?"

"Actually, it's a she. And she's quite intelligent. I imagine I'll be inconvenienced for several months. But the prosecution is looking at the larger picture. Fortunately for me, they already have a scenario in place in their heads as to what the truth is. They want Borov so badly I imagine they'll be quite receptive to our offer of cooperation. Negotiations are still ongoing. Perhaps when I'm free, you and I can sit down over a quiet dinner and explore an extended partnership."

Something the Sandman said struck a chord in Jack's mind, but he chose not to comment just then.

"Your record with partners isn't encouraging," Jack pointed out.

"Any successful partnership is based on mutual respect. When I say we're much alike, I'm not merely flattering you. Kindred spirits tend to attract one another."

Jack started to reply, but the Sandman held up a hand. "Everyone thinks your panic attacks grow out of what happened to your partner. Janet Newton shared a little bit about them with me. She was discreet, of course, but I learned enough and it fascinated me, so I began to study you. Certainly a simple explanation is possible. But if you'll forgive my speculation, I'd say your fear goes far deeper."

Jack nodded slightly acknowledging he heard the comment, but neither agreeing nor disagreeing with it.

"Here's the way I see it," said the Sandman. "You've never met a problem you couldn't solve or an opponent you haven't prevailed against and the possibility that either might happen one day terrifies you. Consider that some people define you, just as the right partner can complete you."

The door opened before Jack could respond.

"Time's up, Dr. Kale," the deputy marshal said.

Jack stood.

"Come see me again," the Sandman said. "Believe it or not, I enjoy your company. I think we're going to spend a lot of time together."

334

Chapter 63

Beth was waiting for him in the car. The temperature had dropped and a sharp breeze was blowing piles of yellow and red leaves along the street, occasionally tossing them around and up into the air in circles. Some businesses had placed carved pumpkins and Christmas trees in their windows. Women who worked at the federal building and the Fulton County Justice Center wore gloves and light coats on their way to lunch. Beth had put on a white turtleneck sweater and a black pair of pants. She smiled as Jack got in and asked how the meeting went.

"Fine. He'd like to partner with me as soon as he gets out."

Beth blinked. "You really think he will?"

"It's hard to say. Group psychology is funny. Everyone is so eager to nail Sergei Borov, they probably don't see what's going on in front of their faces. The Sandman's manipulating them."

"It's like you told your class the first time we met?"

Jack frowned and tried to recall what he had said.

"You have very little chance of finding out the truth if you know in advance what the truth ought to be," Beth prompted.

"Did I say that?"

"Mm-hm."

"Well, I must be a clever fellow."

"Brilliant," Beth said. "Are you going to take him up on his offer?"

Jack leaned over and kissed her on the cheek. "I already have a partner."

Beth smiled and handed him a manila envelope that had been resting on the back seat. "Dan Pappas picked it up from the bank yesterday afternoon."

Jack opened the package, removed the records, and studied them for a minute. Two of the pages had paper clips attached. He slid his finger down the columns until he found the transfers he was looking for, nodding slowly.

"Let's go," he said.

*

Dr. Stuart Patterson flicked on the light to his office and was startled to see four people waiting for him.

"Jesus, Rachel, you scared the crap out of me. What are you doing in here?"

"Waiting for you, Stuart. Tell me why."

"What are you talking about?"

"Why did you do it?"

Patterson looked from one person to the other, then at Dan Pappas, standing next to the door. He said nothing.

"Key man insurance," Beth explained. "With your partners dead, two and half million dollars would go to the medical practice, of which you would have been the sole officer and stockholder. It was all about money, wasn't it, Doctor?"

"You're crazy," Patterson said. "I want all of you out of here now."

Rachel shook her head as though she couldn't process what she was hearing. The expression on Patterson's face was enough to tell her Jack had guessed right.

"Why didn't you come to us?" Rachel asked. "We'd have helped you."

"You're accusing me of hiring an assassin? That's ridiculous. Where's your proof?"

Beth tapped the package in her lap. "You're in debt up to your eyebrows. Particularly with the people in Las Vegas. Six months ago, you managed to pull enough cash together to wire $150,000 to a numbered account in the Cayman Islands. That account belongs to the Sandman. We contacted the Cayman government and they've agreed to cooperate. The bank sent us their records yesterday. Considering that Rachel, George, and Will only saw Borov's transfer four weeks ago, he couldn't have been the one to hire the hit man since he wasn't in the picture when the Sandman was hired. And finally, as the medical practice's managing partner, you took it on yourself to increase your company's insurance policy a month before the cable car event took place."

"Bullshit."

"No," Beth said. "For the last year, you've been borrowing money from a loan shark named Eddie Marks to pay off your casino markers, which are a matter of public record under Nevada and New Jersey state law. You're also spending about fifteen thousand dollars a month to maintain your lifestyle. Those, and your monthly trips to Las Vegas and Atlantic City, are the marks of a degenerate gambler, Doctor."

"You're not hanging this on me," Patterson said. "You people are just looking for a scapegoat."

Beth removed yet another paper from the envelope and read through it for several seconds, shaking her head.

"Hard to see you as a scapegoat. The Sandman signed an affidavit acknowledging you're his client and that he received the hundred and fifty thousand dollars from you. Months later when you found out your partners had to testify in front of the grand jury, you saw an opportunity to deflect suspicion away from you and took advantage of it. Convenient, but it didn't work."

Patterson was silent for a moment, then without warning he turned and bolted for the door. He got as far as Detective Dan Pappas, who spun him into the wall face-first and snapped a pair of handcuffs on him. When he was through, the detective read him his rights. Beth nodded for Pappas to take him away.

Jack sat there observing the exchange. Once they were gone, Rachel asked to see the Sandman's affidavit.

"This?" Beth asked, holding up the paper. "It's my Christmas shopping list."

Rachel's mouth opened. "You made it up?"

Beth's eyebrows lifted and she pointed at Jack with her chin.

Chapter 64

Beth and Jack walked hand in hand along the street, browsing the shop windows. For the first time anyone could remember, Atlanta was experiencing a November snowfall. Large flakes the size of dimes were coming down and sticking to the pavement. Cars were driving with their lights on. Windshield wipers were going. No one seemed to mind. It was part of the season and shared adversity made everyone friends.

Earlier that morning she informed him she'd accepted her parents' invitation to spend Thanksgiving with them and had called his mother to invite her as well. Morgan would be there, too, as would Jack's brother, Stephen, who was flying in from London. He liked her mom and dad and thought his family would too.

Combining families. A tradition that had been going on for millennia, probably longer. His mind turned to the three skeletons at the Carlos Museum who had passed from this earth fifty thousand years ago. He thought then of George Lawrence, Will Landry, Dwayne Stafford, and Ed Mundas and hoped all their souls were at peace. Rachel was a strong woman who would heal and go on. Of that he was certain.

A few days earlier, she had sent them a holiday greeting card of a horse-drawn sleigh pulling up to a house. Yellow light streamed from the living room window onto the snow and smoke came from the chimney. The inside was blank. All it said was "Thank you" followed by her name.

"You're welcome," Jack whispered.

Now that the case was over, he decided the FBI was not the place for him any longer. He turned in his resignation. His teaching position at Georgia Tech also didn't seem quite right. Time would tell where he'd end up.

At the mall, workers were putting up a large Christmas tree on top of Macy's department store. In a few weeks, the lights would come on and a different feel would be in the air. Children would stare open mouthed at the sight and the memory would stay with them over the years to come. He remembered looking at just such a tree when he was a boy and eating hot chestnuts his father had bought from a street vendor. The world he'd grown up in was not a dangerous place, or if it was, he hadn't known it. Certainly it was less complicated.

At an art gallery, they paused a few moments to look at a John Stobart painting of an old sailing vessel, then resumed their stroll. The sidewalk was sparsely crowded and filled with people like himself— not demons, not gargoyles, and not killers stalking the innocent. It was a fine time to be with family and friends. A time to sit in front of a fire and watch the University of Georgia or Georgia Tech play in a bowl game. It was a time to be on dry land with someone you loved and not in the bow of a ship on a stormy sea. He felt at peace with himself for the first time in a long while.

After another block, Jack paused to brush some snow off Beth's hair and kissed her.

"What was that for?" she asked, looking up at him.

He shrugged. "Nothing."

She took a contented breath, smiled, and slipped an arm around his waist, holding him tighter. And together they continued up Peachtree Road as the snow came down.

Acknowledgments

I would like to acknowledge the advice and wisdom imparted to me by my agent, Jane Dystel, and all the fine people at Dystel Goderich Literary Management. Any new author, though I suppose I can no longer claim to be new as this is my second book, should be willing to walk across hot coals for such a dedicated team.

Also, a large nod of thanks to Matt Martz for all his help and encouragement and to editors, Natasha Simons and Heather Boak, who contributed greatly to the book and offered suggestions and insight that opened my eyes and pushed me to see things in ways I couldn't. Crooked Lane Books is a wonderful company that has brought my two stories to life and offered support in every possible way.

A special note of thanks goes to my publicist Dana Kaye with Kaye Publicity and Julia Borcherts who worked tirelessly to bring the books to the public's attention, and to the amazing Sarah Poppe, who was always there to help.

As always, none of this would have been possible without the contributions of my dearest friend, Jane Mashburn. God got it right when he made her. And my thanks to Gary Peel, who acted as my first reader and offered his advice and encouragement. My appreciation also goes out to the many readers who have taken the time to write and share their thoughts with me. You may believe I listened to every one of them.